Misjudge *Day*

Richard Milne

By the same author:

Bojo's Woe Show book 1: A Cabinet of Horrors (Kindle/Print-on-demand)

Bojo's Woe Show book 2: A Plague of Idiots (Kindle/Print-on-demand)

Rhododendron (Reaktion Books)

Follow me on Twitter: @milneorchid.

For Nenya, who makes it all worthwhile.

Misjudgement Day

Prologue

"Have you managed to look any further?"

"You always ask this and the answer, as always, is no. You will point the gun, but I cannot predict the answer."

The first speaker began to pace around the darkened room. The only source of light was an eerie blue glow from a stone nestling among a jumble of wires, some of them connecting the seated second man to a now blank display screen.

"I had hoped, now that the beginning is so close, and we have almost everything in place," said the standing man.

"That we might predict Satan's mind? No, I don't think we could ever do that. You are having last minute nerves? It would only be natural."

"I just don't like uncertainties," said the pacing man, as he nearly tripped over a wire.

"There is no indication that anyone knows of our plans – except *him*, of course," offered the seated man.

"That's good. But even so…" the pacer's voice trailed off.

"If you're worrying about me, then don't. I have no regrets."

There was an awkward pause. Each man felt relieved that it was too dark to see the expression of the other.

"It's not the answer that worries me," said the pacing man. "It is that you cannot predict what will follow, whether that answer is yes *or* no."

"Could you really do it? Unleash the fury of a billion souls? Throw open the door to Armageddon? End the world?"

"You know I could," said the pacer. "And you haven't given me a proper answer."

"I can only tell you what I said before," said the other. "The involvement of a psychic sensitive can confuse the predictor. It took extraordinary effort to ensure that she fulfills her role in our plan. And there is something associated with the Devil Fenwick that I cannot see clearly. Something that I don't think exists yet. I wish it had been possible to use a different one."

"Yet the woman sensitive will die, and Fenwick will be buried under thirty feet of concrete! We are sure of these things! The two other sensitives work for us! How can any of them interfere with the culmination? Where is this uncertainty coming from? You must look harder!"

"I am doing all I can," said the seated man, his voice suddenly weary.

"I know you are," the standing man replied, his voice softer now.

"Now do you think you could get on with changing the light bulb?"

Chapter One

"FOUL, WORTHLESS CREATURES!!!! WHY HAVE YOU VIOLATED MY CHAMBERS?" Flames roared around the huge body of Satan Beelzebub III as he spoke.

"I-i-i-i-it's an emergency Cabal m-m-meeting, my Lord," said Horsley. Like everyone in the room, he was bright red and possessed of horns and a tail. They ranged from four to eight feet tall, and Horsley was the smallest, and hence the most junior.

"He knows that, you useless idiot!" snapped Aldershot, smacking the back of Horsley's head with his tail. "That's his traditional greeting. Now tell him what you found. Now!!"

"M-m-m-me?"

"Yes, Horsley, you!" yelled Aldershot. He was tall and thin with a cropped moustache, and was standing bolt upright. "Sit up straight, you useless cassock," he added. "You're a disgrace!"

The terrified junior Devil tried for a moment to compose himself. "We found Fenwick, sir!" he blurted. "In Room Zero!"

"Found?" said Satan, cocking his head to the side. "I wasn't aware he'd been mislaid. What was he doing in there?"

"H-h-he was lying on the floor going 'mmm-mmm-mmm'," said Horsley.

"You mean he was bound and gagged?" asked Woking, the Ruler of English Hell. Other than the eight-foot Satan, he was the largest and most senior Devil in the room. He had a broad face with a triangular beard that reached his ears, and an even broader belly.

"Y-y-yes, sir," said Horsley. "The human souls appear to ... errr ... they've been using him as furniture, sirs!"

"Furniture?" asked Woking.

"Futons, mainly," quivered Horsley.

"Thank Lucifer we found out quickly," said Woking, stroking his red beard.

"If you call 23 years 'quickly', then yes, thank Lucifer," said Horsley.

"Twenty-three YEARS??" boomed Satan. "Aldershot?! You have mislaid an underling for more than two decades!? Explain!!"

Aldershot's mouth hung open, his pointed teeth glinting in the firelight. "Fenwick is a proven incompetent – Sir!" he proclaimed. "Not fit for service – Sir!"

"And you did NOTHING? All this time??" roared the Lord of Hell.

"We assumed he'd got lost – Sir!" barked Aldershot. "For the ongoing glory of Hell, a year without Fenwick is a year without reportable accidents – Sir! Hell is better off without him – Sir!"

"But it WAS a reportable incident," countered Woking.

"He was being used as furniture!" roared Satan. "By condemned souls who should have had none. For twenty-three YEARS!!"

"L-like I said, incompetent!" said Aldershot. "Sir!" he added quickly. He remained rigidly upright, but his tail was swishing around behind him like that of a frustrated cat. "He's a blessed liability – Sir!!"

"And your responsibility, Aldershot," said Woking.

"I should dispel you, Aldershot, and promote someone who can keep better track of his underlings!" boomed Satan.

"Th-that isn't fair – S-sir! I had no way of knowing he was there, and the last record we have of him shows him on a surface mission!" He struggled to compose himself. "What happens within the torment rooms is Camberley's responsibility – Sir!!!!"

Satan's fearsome gaze shifted towards Camberley, sitting opposite Aldershot. Camberley was round-faced with a hunched back, which made him look like he was cringing, even on the rare occasions when he wasn't. He spoke quickly: "while that is technically correct sir it is also true that my remit only covers the practical upkeep and the human souls contained therein sir and consequently there is no provision within my duties for incompetent Devils going in and getting themselves tied up sir it wasn't my fault sir!"

"I wonder where they got the rope?" pondered Woking. "Room zero is supposed to contain nothing at all."

"Why was Fenwick in there, Aldershot?" demanded Satan.

"He should never have been in there – Sir!" declared Aldershot. "But Fenwick's presence there is incidental – Sir!! The main issue is that the wrong souls were in the room – Sir!!!" He glared meaningfully at Camberley.

"*I* shall decide what the main issue is," hissed Satan. "And who is to blame," he added. Still, his burning red eyes moved round to fix on Camberley, again.

Camberley admitted, "there had been an exchange of souls between room zero the empty room and Room 5705 the nightclub room sir all the souls from the nightclub room were in room zero and all the souls from Room Zero were in the nightclub room sir I don't know how it happened but I'm sure it's Fenwick's fault sir please don't dispel me!"

For a moment, no-one spoke. Condensed Devil sweat dripped from the stalactites above the table, and ran down the sulphur-coated walls.

"Tell me the purpose of Room Zero, Camberley," said Satan quietly.

"It is for souls who crave constant distraction, sir. Young airheads who in life could not go out without music in their ears and a phone to their mouth. Instead they get nothing! They must endure their own thoughts!"

"Now tell me the purpose of Room 5705?" asked Satan with a deadly soft voice. The others in the room watched Camberley, with the air of zebras who knew that the lions had chosen someone else for their dinner.

"It is for old gits and miserable sods who hate the young and long for peace, quiet and tranquillity, sir. So they serve their sentence in an eternal nightclub, sir," cringed Camberley.

"And now," said Satan, his voice rising, "tell me again where these two groups of souls have been for the past 23 years?"

"W-well as I said the souls who like noise and music were all in the nightclub while all the ones who crave tranquillity have been in the very quiet room zero enjoying the silence and sometimes the furniture sir I'm sorry sir it's all Fenwick's fault please don't dispel me!!"

"Gabriel's wings!!" bellowed Satan. "What a disaster!"

The others all winced at the profanity.

"My Lord, before you dispel one of these two," said Woking, indicating Camberley and Aldershot, "or maybe both, we should establish the full facts. How did these souls get between the two rooms?"

"A hole in the wall, sirs," said Horsley.

"Impossible!" said Camberley. "Hell's walls are indestructible, unless…"

"Unless someone had a Devil Knife," said Woking. "They cut through anything. Was such a knife found, Horsley?"

"No, sir. But the wall had been cut into thin strips. That's what Fenwick was tied up with."

"If an enemy had a Devil Knife, he could have killed Fenwick outright," pondered Aldershot, with a look of profound disappointment. "Faster and more efficient – Sir!"

"You forget, we are all aspects of our Great Lord Satan," replied Camberley, with a sycophantic smile. "The death would have been felt."

"What does Fenwick have to say about this?" asked Woking.

"Nothing so far, sir" said Camberley.

"Why not?" demanded Woking.

"Because no-one has untied him yet."

"Mmm-hmm-bbllhh-hhmmbllhhhm-hmmmphhh!" said a voice from the far corner of the room.

"Would it not be wise to hear his account of events?" said Woking.

"Mmm-hmm-bHHHMMMM-bllhhmmhhmm!" said Fenwick urgently.

"Well, there was concern that he might have lost his mind, whatever there was of it," said Camberley. "Last time a Devil was tied up for that long, he went mad, causing … "

"So untie him under controlled conditions!" said Woking. "I want to hear from him what happened!"

"And then, Fenwick, I will decide your punishment!" boomed Satan. "Now all of you, begone from me!!!"

"He means, the meeting's over," whispered Woking to the still cowering Horsley.

*****

"Suzy McCabe's going to let you do THAT?"

"Yep."

"All weekend?"

"That's what she said," said Michael. He was sitting with Roger in a quiet corner of the bar in the Stoke University Student Union Bar. Michael had short neat hair and a smart shirt, whereas Roger as always sported precisely messed up hair, and a t-shirt advertising a band only he had heard of.

"This is Suzy 'Piss off, you're not rich enough' McCabe we're talking about?" asked Roger.

"She'd booked a dirty weekend away with some posh git, but he's got mumps."

"Mumps?"

"Mumps. Making a comeback, apparently. So she needed a stand-in, and I, Michael Price, am rising to the occasion."

"I can see that," said Roger, leaning back on his chair. "It's very romantic."

"Bollocks to that! I haven't had a shag since Fresher's week."

"Hence your desperation to get out of this weekend trip."

"I'll owe you big time if I do. Have you got anywhere?"

"I managed to get two people to drop out by offering a full refund, and exaggerating the weather forecast."

"Not that it needed much exaggeration," said Michael. "It looks horrendous."

"So that leaves five committee and two other blokes who certainly want to go. With seven I can make a case for cancellation. But if even one more signs up, there'll be no chance of persuading them. Are you sure you can't just make an excuse and drop out, again?"

Michael sighed and shook his head. "I'm president. Plus there's no other driver for the minibus. If I drop out for the second time in a row, Helen will no-confidence me, and she'll probably win! I still don't know how I won the election in the first place."

"Does it matter?" asked Roger. "I mean, I'd much rather you than her, but do you really need it?"

"CV, Roger. Plus I got two dates out of saying I'm the Pres, even if it is president of the Wacky Walkers club. I'm not dropping out. If we can't get the trip cancelled, I'm using Project Strawberry."

"Oh God, Michael, not that again."

"It'll work, and no-one will accuse me of shirking my responsibilities!"

"Let's just hope we can get it cancelled, okay?"

*****

"I declare this committee meeting of the Stoke University Wacky Walkers open."

"Hang on, Mycroft, the President isn't here yet," said Dylan, the transport secretary, playing with his forelocks. "Nor's the Treasurer, or the Social Secretary."

"That is irrelevant," said Mycroft, club secretary. He wore an immaculate tweed waistcoat over a checked yellow shirt, and had pale brown frizzy hair. "The scheduled start time has come and gone, a point in time specifically selected to permit ample opportunity for all persons to arrive from their preceding activities. The president knows this, and in his absence the vice president is empowered to act in his stead."

"Again," added Dylan, quietly.

"Okay, let's just get on with it," said Helen Black, the vice president, a small girl with short dark hair. She and the two boys were seated in a small dark room in the basement of the Student Union building, surrounded by piles of folding tables. Three more chairs stood empty. "So we need to talk about the weekend – "

"The first item on the agenda is the last meeting's minutes," said Mycroft.

"Approved," chorused Helen and Dylan wearily.

"...and matters arising."

Helen sighed, and was halfway through asking Mycroft to list these matters, when the door swung open and Michael and Roger walked in. "What have you two been conspiring about?" asked Helen.

"Helen, will you leave off with the conspiracy thing?" Michael took his seat.

"I will, when you tell me where all the postal votes in the election came from," replied Helen icily.

"From people who thought I'd do the best job, madam VICE president."

"Fifteen people. None of whom, by your own admission, you have actually met."

"Yes, so they clearly voted based on objective opinions," said Michael, his face set in what he thought was a Prime Ministerial expression.

"They haven't been to a single event between them! Mycroft checked!"

Now Michael looked angry. "Mycroft? Why?"

"The vice president persuaded me that the possibility of foul play was sufficient to warrant further investigation."

"Now see here," said Michael, struggling to keep from shouting. "I had no contact with any of those people. I didn't ask any of them to vote for me, I didn't tell anyone else to ..."

"You're missing the point," Helen cut in sharply. "I'm not accusing *you*. I'm saying, what if someone outside the club had decided to interfere?"

If she'd thought this would placate him, she was wrong. "So now you're saying ... what? That the Orienteering Club are out to destroy us, by hacking our elections? Or maybe you think it was Vladimir Putin? And that somehow, I'm their unwitting agent of destruction?"

"I'm just saying that it's odd, that fifteen people with no connection to the club, no stake in it, all suddenly decided to vote in this election. Mycroft, how many postal votes were there in the last ten AGMs?"

"Last year, none. The year before, none ..."

"In total!"

"Three, over the ten years. Two of which were Richard Hames, who was a regular member, but often had rehearsals on Thursday nights."

"Then suddenly, fifteen," said Helen, her arms folded.

Michael folded his arms as well. "Mycroft, do you have any actual evidence for any of this, anything that would invalidate the election result."

"No," replied Mycroft.

"Then I suggest that we let the matter rest." Michael's eyes challenged Helen to respond, but she did not. "Mycroft, strike everything from the minutes until this point," said Michael.

"Done," said Mycroft. "The first item on the agenda is to approve the last meeting's minutes."

***

Five minutes later, they finally got to the subject of the weekend trip. "How many do we have signed up, Mycroft?"

"All committee members except Roger," said Mycroft, "plus two others."

"Is that all?" said Helen, in shock. "I thought there were more."

"We had some drop-outs," said Roger.

"Michael, you said you had a plan to recruit people."

"I did. It seems it didn't work."

Mycroft said, "As I stated in my report, which I assume you all read before the meeting, I did as instructed, and composed a precisely worded statement informing the membership that unless at least one further member joined the Arrochar trip, it would be financially unviable and that cancellation would therefore become inevitable," said Mycroft. "It was sent at eight o five GMT yesterday."

"I can't think why no-one responded," said Dylan, nibbling at his fingers.

Helen was looking at Michael curiously. He didn't meet her eye. "Perhaps if we'd knocked on a few doors," she said. "Can we really not absorb the loss?"

Roger the treasurer spoke for the first time. "It would jeopardise all of our remaining events this year. But if we cancel today we can recover all but the deposits."

"And the weather's looking terrible, both days of the weekend," said Michael. "Therefore, I move that –"

The door to the room flew open. "Bernie to the rescue!!!" The improbably named Bernard Wilkinson, club social secretary, danced into the room, spinning twice on his heels as he made for the empty seat beside Dylan. Today he was clad in bright red trousers and a lurid green shirt to match the current shade of his hair. "How's it hanging, cats? Feeling a bit of a negative vibe here, oooh, I am *so* gonna fix that! Bernie saves the day!! Cinderella *shall* go to the ball!"

Michael could feel the disappointment brewing in the area most affected, inside his underpants. "What are you blathering on about, Bernie?"

"Cashflow, darlings. Turning loss into profit! Bums on seats!"

"You mean you've found extra people to come on the trip?" asked Helen.

Bernie pushed his finger into the corner of his mouth, pretending to think. "In a way, Darls, in a way. I've got the most spec-TAC-ular plan, you'll want to have its babies! The Megadance Festival is in Glasgow this weekend." He looked at all the blank faces in the room, shrugged, and went on. "Oh come on! The Megadance!

All the Dance Socs who are anybody just *have* to be there. Only our little FolkSoc foursome have a bit of a getting-there problem. Can't afford the train, but then, who can? So I get to thinking, why don't we drive them up and drop them off? Aren't I brilliant?"

"And they'll be paying for the transport?" asked Helen.

"Well it was either that or sexual favours, Darl, but you girls can be *so* touchy about that." He made ready to duck, but Helen was too busy watching Michael to respond. "So yes, good hard cash, duckies," concluded Bernie.

Dylan said: "twenty pounds for each of them would make up for the two who dropped out."

"They're saying sixty between them," said Bernie, "and not a penny more!"

"I can't agree to this without meeting them," said Michael. "And we have to tell the minibus hire people one way or another tonight!"

"Calm yourself, Mikester. Old Bernie's got it in hand." He threw open the door. "Bring on the Dancing Girls!!"

Through the door strode four young ladies. The atmosphere in the room changed completely as it filled with things never normally associated with Wacky Walkers events: make-up, heeled shoes, perfume, jewellery, and skirts. Michael said nothing, hoping the mutual awkwardness would scupper the deal.

"Oh, where are my manners?" said Bernie. "Ooh, if Mumsie could see me now there'd be stern words, I tell you. Stern words. Michael, Helen, Mycroft, Roger and Dylan ... I present to you Lucy, Janelle, Lysandra and Natalia."

"So, you're the Pres, huh?" grunted Lucy to Michael, in a gritty voice utterly at odds with her colourful, feminine outfit. She had a round face and brown curly hair.

"Uh, yes," he replied, feeling that events were out of his control.

"Sixty pounds, there and back. To the door, mind. I'm not having my girls getting soaked trying to find the bloody place. And you pick us up four thirty Sunday. Pronto."

"Now hold on a minute," said Michael.

Mycroft spoke up. "Owing to the vagaries of hillwalking, including such possibilities as minor injuries reducing the speed of a group, which must progress at the rate of its slowest member, we cannot guarantee to you a precise pick-up time. Furthermore traffic problems introduce an additional confounding variable. Therefore you would be advised to find some hostelry in which to await our arrival, which we shall endeavour to expedite as close as possible to your allotted time."

Lucy shrugged and nodded. Bernie rubbed his hands with glee. Helen declared, "I say we do it," and Dylan readily agreed.

Defeated, Michael accepted the plan and shook Lucy's hand. Then a thought struck him. "Do any of you girls drive minibuses?"

The front three girls shook their heads, but the one at the back, Natalia, raised a hand. "I nearly drive one time for Russian Society. They say is okay because I have license and drive big tractor in home. Then trip is cancel."

Michael asked, "but you've driven in this country before?"

"I drive in Mother Russia many time."

"Good, well, it's always nice to have a spare driver in case one of us breaks a leg or something. Just for safety. I'll put you on the insurance." Michael was already forming a new plan to save his dirty weekend, as he eagerly took down Natalia's details. The meeting went on, with all of them quite unaware of the tiny camera in a dark corner of the room.

In another city, a short man in a suit nodded his head, and clicked off the screen. "Exactly as we'd planned," he said.
"Of course," said the figure beside him. "How could it not be?"

Chapter Two

"Do you think I'm a bad man?" The question came out of nowhere. Lydia looked back at Theo, with a look of stunned astonishment.

"What??" she replied.

"Am I ... well ... evil?"

"You're serious?"

"Of course I am! I mean, look at me! Look at what I do! Selling weapons to dictators who aren't quite brutal enough to get on the news. But that's not even the greatest pleasure of my job. Firing people. I mean, I really love firing people! Sometimes I do it just to see the look on their faces, or scare the rest of them. And cheating on my wife. A lot. With women half my age."

"I know the last bit. I mean, you're standing right here with your cock inside one now."

"And you're not even the only one! And then my daughter. My God, I paid her three thousand pounds to set up a dirty weekend with some nerd from the student rambling club!"

"And she did it?"

"Yeah, she did it. Set it up, I mean. She doesn't need to actually turn up."

"Won't the bloke come after her?"

"Won't be an issue. The Broker promised it."

Lydia sighed. She was used to the sudden personality changes men underwent at the moment of ejaculation, but even so this was a bit extreme. "Theo ... where's all this coming from? I've got Geography in twenty minutes and I haven't finished the marking!"

"I'm dying," he said, and pulled himself out of her. Surprised, she scrabbled for a tissue. Meanwhile he sat on a dusty table, naked from the waist down, with his wet, deflating manhood hanging despondently between his legs.

Lydia Margate composed herself. She felt it again now, that annoying fluttering in her heart, such a lovely feeling, but no good could come of it. She pushed it aside and concentrated on searching for her knickers, finding them among the cricket bats. "Are you sure?" she asked him, in what she hoped was a gentle voice.

"Doctor says six months. Cancer. Good old fashioned dead-in-a-year cancer. My mum and uncle both had cancer and got better. Every fucker I know that's had it got better. But not me. I'm 47, for God's sake!"

"Then I guess I'd better free up a few more periods for you. Enjoy you while I can."

"Is that all you can say?" he spluttered.

"What do you want me to say?! I'm not your bloody keeper! I'm your casual shag. You wanna fucking whinge, go see your wife!" She yanked her knickers up, under her skirt.

"You know what he said? My oh-so-compassionate doctor?"

"What did he say?"

"'You should have come sooner.' How in Hell's that supposed to help? He's making it my fault, that he can't make me better. How can it be my fault?"

Lydia felt a cold shiver down her spine. Seven months ago – yes, they'd been at it that long – he'd had a spate of feeling sick at odd times. He'd cancelled a few morning assignations. Thrown up during another. At a critical moment, too. She'd had to bribe a kid to take the blame for the chunder down her front. Luckily no-one had asked how it got into her bra. He'd joked that it was morning sickness, that she'd made him pregnant. She'd assumed he was seeing a doctor. Evidently not. But it had hardly been her business to tell him to, had it? It would have broken the rules, anyway. Rules he was breaking, now.

"You'll get a second opinion?" she asked carefully.

"Already got two. And if those results are true … I'm fucked. Utterly, totally fucked."

He looked down sadly at his penis, and she followed his gaze, watching a little drip fall from it. Lydia felt as though it was a part of his life force falling away, never to be regained. She leant with her back to the wall, in the exact spot where he'd pinned her and ripped her knickers off, ten minutes earlier. He hadn't felt like a dying man then.

"Do you believe in the afterlife?" he asked.

"What?" Her eyes widened, the flicker of sympathy vanishing. "I spent half my life getting shot of that crap. You have no idea what I went through! So, no, no I don't. This is all we get, so make the most of it. I'm sorry you're dying, really I am, but I've got nothing to offer you but, well … this."

He looked up at her, puppy-eyed. Her lips pursed, and she almost withdrew that offer, as well. If he didn't buck up soon, she certainly would.

"But this is a faith school!" he pleaded.

She threw her head back and laughed. "Theo McCabe, how stupid are you? McCabe Incorporated calls itself an ethical arms business! Doesn't make it so!"

He nodded, taking the point. "The Broker says there's an afterlife. And he's never wrong."

"Everyone's wrong about something. And how can you trust a man you've never met?"

"He predicted the lottery numbers last week."

"You're lying. No way."

"Not the winning six numbers. He told me some numbers that would scoop twenty thousand, and they did."

"Okay, so he's Derren Brown. Doesn't give him a hotline to the Almighty. There IS no Almighty."

"And he knows I'm dying. The text came an hour after I left the hospital."

"So he plays golf with the consultant? Big deal. Look, you want my advice? You should make the most of the time you've got left, instead of hero-worshipping some – "

His phone made a gonging sound. He snatched it from his trousers.

"The Broker!" he said, looking in awe at the message. "He wants to meet!"

She shrugged, and stalked from the room.

∗∗∗∗∗

"HOW DARE YOU BRING THIS INSUFFERABLE INSECT BEFORE ME, YOU HIDEOUS FAILURES?"

"W-well you asked for hi – ow!" said Horsley, as a tail slapped his face. In the centre of the cave, the surface of Satan's giant stone table had changed. Previously smooth, it had now erupted forth a thousand stalagmites, each one impossibly sharp at the tip. They moved, slowly rocking from side to side or probing upwards, searching for flesh to prick. On the table, still bound but not gagged, lay Fenwick, his face a silent mask of exquisite pain. Aldershot's cruel eyes bore into him, enjoying his torment.

"Fenwick has given his account, such as it is," said Woking. "He remembers inspecting a series of rooms; we have Devils checking all of those, now. But he has no memory of entering the zero room, nor how he ended up there."

"Oh, well, then we needn't trouble you any longer, Fenwick" said Satan, his voice nonchalant and soft. Familiar with this particular tone, Woking, Aldershot and Camberley shrunk back cautiously. "After all, why would anyone remember being overpowered by human souls *who are compelled to obey our every command*!!!"

"I-I-I can't explain it, Lord!" pleaded Fenwick.

"This cannot go unpunished, hopeless one…"

Aldershot, Woking noticed, was looking improperly gleeful. He was trying to hide it, but his tail was sticking right up in the air. Woking raised a disapproving eyebrow and said:

"There may be others to share the blame as well, sir."

"Indeed," agreed Satan "what shall your punishment be, Aldershot?"

Aldershot's tail hit the floor with a slap. "I live only to serve – Sir! With this incompetent dispelled, my performance will improve – Sir!!"

Satan stared at Aldershot thoughtfully, then returned his attention to Fenwick. "Failure of this kind requires severe punishment," he said. "Although he's had twenty-three years of humiliation already…"

"It's not his first offence!" cut in Aldershot. "He once unleashed chaos throughout Hell! Sir!"

"Chaos?" Boomed Satan. "When?"

"I believe he's referring to the *Pteres infurians* incident, under Beelzebub II," said Woking. "Before your ascension, my Lord. You were Celestial Liaison back then. Fenwick accidentally released a few of Gomshall's creatures."

"A few?" countered Aldershot. "There were thousands." Several of the Devils in the room were now absent-mindedly scratching their heads or batting things away from their heads.

"I wish to know more," boomed Satan. "GOMSHALL!!!"

There was a flash, and a shocked figure appeared, surrounded by sulphurous smoke. A jar fell from its hand and smashed.

"You idiot!" the figure shouted. "You made me drop th ... oh. Um, sorry, Lord. Didn't know where I was."

Satan's eyes narrowed. "You will explain to us how the – *what in Heaven?!?*" A large spider had jumped onto his face and was stabbing him with poison-tipped needles on the ends of its legs. Within moments, everyone in the room was fighting off similar arachnids, as a seemingly endless supply of them sprung forth from the broken jar.

"ENOUGH!" roared Satan, and from his raised arms erupted pillars of fire that in moments filled the room. When the fire receded, charred husks of spiders fell to the ground, shortly followed by Woking, who'd taken refuge from the spiders on the ceiling.

"Took me weeks to make those," muttered Gomshall, sorrowfully.

"Too bad!!!" roared Satan. "I wish to know about the – "

"You ..." screamed Gomshall, suddenly wild-eyed, and jumping to his feet. "It was you!! I've waited centuries for this!" He hopped onto his chair, then onto Fenwick's back, driving him further onto the stalagmites. Fenwick howled with pain. Gomshall began leaping in the air, each time coming down harder on Fenwick.

Satan cocked his head to the side. "Remind me," he said. "Did I give you permission to supplant my role as master of torture within my domain?"

Gomshall paused, balancing on Fenwick's back. "Please, Lord! The *Pteres infurians* were my greatest creation! Creatures of such perfect torment, as have never been seen before or since! Any fool can inflict pain, but these could irritate a soul to the point of insanity in mere hours! And he released them! All of them! Opened the door to my room without knocking. There was a clearly written sign! And yyeee-aaAAAARRRGHHHH!!"

The last utterance was prompted by Fenwick, who'd rocked suddenly to one side, causing Gomshall to topple backwards and impale his own bottom on the spikes.

"Well you should have made the writing bigger!" retorted Fenwick.

"You should have been dispelled for that," sneered Aldershot. "Beelzebub II was too merciful."

"Why wasn't he?" asked Satan Beelzebub III.

"Fenwick found an ... ahh ... unconventional solution to the problem, my Lord," explained Woking. "He released them all into the Mortal World!"

"Breaking just about every rule in the book – Sir!" shouted Aldershot.

"Including, I recall, several put in place by the *Others*," added Woking.

"Ohhh," said Satan, his face forming almost a smile as an ancient memory began to reform. "So *that's* how it happened. We had a visit from Gabriel, did we not?"

"Several, my Lord," agreed Woking.

"They tried to make us recapture them; we refused of course," boomed Satan happily. "In the end, they tried to catch them themselves! Fifty Angels, swooping over the Fens with giant nets, every night for a month! How many did they catch, Woking?"

"Three, Lord, though I suspect they rounded it up. Out of fifty thousand."

"They might have done better," sniffed Gomshall, "if you hadn't waited sixty years before telling them of the escape."

"What would be the fun in that?" boomed Satan. "Now, Gomshall, don't be sad. According to Gabriel, your *Pteres infurians* have tormented human beings ever since. A fine legacy for your work. What do they call them again, up there?"

"Horseflies, Lord," said Gomshall, sulkily. "Shows a woeful lack of imagination, if you ask me."

"This changes nothing! Sir! Fenwick's a liability – Sir!" barked Aldershot, "An example must be made – Sir!!!"

"NO!" boomed Satan. "Then and now, that incident reminds the Others that they cannot and will not control us! Gabriel demanded Fenwick's head. Demanded! He did not get it then, and he shall not now. Instead we shall put him where Heaven can see him. Fenwick, you shall be assigned to soul harvesting duty as of tomorrow. Even you can't make a hash of that!"

"Yes, Lord," said Fenwick, careful to conceal his relief.

"And Aldershot," continued Satan. "I did consider a month of continuous torture for you, but your dedication to duty impresses me. So I shall instead expand your duties to include oversight of some of the surface team. Specifically, him!" he indicated Fenwick. Aldershot's tail hit the floor with a slap, again.

"Now go!" declared Satan. The assembled Devils bowed, and made for the door as fast as they dared. It was not quick enough. "Oh hang on," added Satan. "Have we forgotten something?"

The Devils glanced nervously at one another and the still bound Fenwick, fearing a trap. Silence reigned.

"Oh yes!" boomed Satan. "Someone needs to look after Fenwick, help him recover from his ordeal, give him the care that's due to him, before he resumes duties tomorrow evening. Gomshall, perhaps you? You can use my cave if you like, it has excellent facilities. Remember, I need him untied and still just about alive by tomorrow evening. Gomshall's eyes blazed with sadistic pleasure, and the others filed out, leaving Fenwick to his fate.

*****

"You haven't told me the rest of your plan and I haven't asked, but ... will I be the first? The first living soul to pass through the veil?" Kane Winkle, a tall man in a colourful suit, felt a frisson of excitement.

"No," said the Broker, a short man in a grey suit and sunglasses. "I can tell you some of it now, if you want. In fact, some students will be travelling to the Abysmal Plain tonight."

"Students?"

"There's only one person on Earth powerful enough to pierce the veil, and even she could only do it if she's not aware of what's happening. The barriers between our world and the next are almost absolute."

"Almost," smiled Kane.

"Almost," agreed the Broker.

"And this is the thing that's going to weaken the barriers, and allow us through?"

"That's right. We have to knock over the dominoes in exactly the right order, if we want them to fall. Each one bigger than the last."

"And the biggest domino is?"

"Satan, of course."

Chapter Three

Helen did her best to look cheerful as her companions assembled outside the student union. Other than the sheeting rain, the only sounds to be heard were Bernie's rendition of *Club Tropicana*, and Mycroft lecturing the four dancers about Union rules concerning joint events between societies. One of the new walking club members was a thin, bespectacled young man in a battered coat, who'd given his name as Martin, then fallen silent. The other hadn't spoken at all, but he was unmistakeable with jet black skin, perfect in its smoothness, and a gentle face. He looked like he'd been dressed by his grandmother, in a big-collared pale shirt and a chunky jumper, the nerdy outfit somehow utterly at odds with his skin tone. Helen wondered what his story was, but there was no way of knowing, since she'd never yet heard him speak. He'd signed his name as Denny on the sheet.

When Michael arrived with the minibus, everyone rushed to board, desperate to avoid getting any wetter, or having to sit next to Mycroft. Janelle and Lysandra gasped with disdainful amazement when they learned that the side and back doors of the minibus didn't open, meaning they had to join members of the Wacky Walkers in climbing their way backwards from the front passenger seats.

"You'd better stay in the front, Natalia," said Michael. "I can show you the controls on the bus."

Natalia slotted in beside him and watched intently as he showed her the controls, one by one, while he looked at her legs with similar concentration. It reminded him of how he would be spending the weekend. "And which one is choke?" she asked.

"There's no choke."

"Then how it start?"

"It starts without choke."

"I no understand."

Michael started and restarted the bus three times. "See? No need for choke."

Natalia gave a worried nod. Helen slipped into the third seat at the front. "You guys going to be dancing as soon as you arrive?"

"Just fun dance tonight. We have big demonstration dance tomorrow. Much practise. Every day."

Michael felt a twinge of guilt. But these girls wouldn't be going anywhere without his club, he reminded himself. He looked again at Natalia's legs, and fingered the strawberry in his pocket. With the passengers all loaded up and the spaces between seats packed with rucksacks, he pulled the bus to the car park exit. There, he found the way blocked by two arguing cyclists and their prone, entangled bicycles.

"Get out the fucking way!" Michael yelled. The two cyclists both stopped and looked at him with curious expressions, then resumed their argument. "I don't care whose fucking fault it was," shouted Michael, "but if you don't shift arse this minute I will personally flatten your fucking bikes!"

"I no think that will be good for minibus," said Natalia.

Then, quite suddenly, one of the cyclists glanced at his watch, and they both picked up their bikes and walked away. "Arseholes!" yelled Michael as he pulled the bus, at last, onto the road. The windscreen wipers were already going at full speed, and an oily smell filled the bus as the heating system gasped out tepid air from the dashboard. A few minutes passed, and then Michael rubbed his head and gave a little groan.

"You OK?" said Helen.

"Had a headache all day," he lied. "It's nothing."

"Many people die with meningitis," said Natalia. "Always first say is only headache."

Michael smiled. This girl was a godsend! Behind him Mycroft was earnestly describing to Lysandra some recent changes to traffic regulations, while Bernie was attempting to start a singsong.

"'Ere, stick this on," grunted Lucy from behind him, handing forward a CD.

Helen tried, but the minibus sound system proved to be utterly dead. She handed the *Frozen* soundtrack back to Lucy. "Waste of fuckin' time bringin' it," muttered Lucy.

Ten minutes later, Michael surreptitiously pulled a strawberry from his pocket and slipped it into his mouth. Most people would regard a strawberry allergy as an annoyance, but Michael believed that from adversity came opportunity. Soon after that, as they made their way out of the city, the disquiet in his body began to build outwards from his stomach.

⁎⁎⁎⁎⁎

The two cyclists arrived at the door of their flat. "How the hell did he know that minibus would come at exactly that moment?" asked one.

"Dunno," said the other. "Easiest hundred quid I've ever earned though."

"But why would anyone want us to hold up a minibus for exactly two minutes and forty-one seconds?" pondered the first.

⁎⁎⁎⁎⁎

"WHY MUST I AGAIN ENDURE YOUR EXECRABLE PRESENCE, YOU SUPPURATING SORES?"

Satan looked even more furious than usual; a third visit from the same underlings could not be a good sign.

"There was … ah …, a complication that Camberley omitted to tell you about, my Lord," said Woking carefully.

"It wasn't my fault sir I was going to tell you once we'd finished with Fenwick sir but you ended the meeting before I had the chance so I couldn't sir there was one human soul that we couldn't find in either room sir please don't dispel me!"

"What Camberley means, my Lord, is that one of the souls who should have been in the Zero Room was in neither that room nor the Disco Room – "

"SAINTED INCOMPETENCE!" roared Satan.

"... however, this soul has now been located, my Lord," completed Woking.

"Where?" asked Aldershot.

"Room X10101," said Camberley.

"In a single-soul room?" bellowed Satan. "How is that possible?"

Camberley replied, "we do not yet know sir but there was a second hole in that wall going from X10101 to the zero room sir it had been crudely concealed so we didn't see it at first sir please don't dispel me!"

"Bring the human in! I wish to question it!" boomed Satan.

"Sir, I don't thi – ouch!" said Horsley, his voice cut off by a sharp stab from Woking's tail. "I mean, yes sir straight away sir." Horsley scuttled out, and returned moments later with a naked human in tow.

"Shouldn't there be a small tail at the front?" enquired Satan.

"This one is a female, my Lord," explained Woking. "They don't have them. Humans, as I understand it, can be either – "

"I do know SOMETHING about human life!" roared Satan. "There are ..." he paused for a moment, thinking " ... three kinds of human, and you need one of each to make a new one. I remember, now. A male, a female, and one of the small ones, whatever they're called."

"Children, I believe," said Woking.

"Ah yes. We don't get many of those down here," said Satan.

"No," agreed Woking.

"Human!" boomed Satan. "Tell us how you came to be in the room where you were found!"

"Biddle-oo-doo, biddle-oo-doo, biddle-oo-doo-deeeee" said the woman.

"Is that French?" said Satan.

"No," said Woking. "I'm afraid she hasn't said anything else since we found her."

"Biddle-oo-doo, biddle-oo-doo, biddle-oo-doo-deeeee" said the woman, again, in a tunefully insistent fashion.

"A similar noise was coming from the torment machine she was strapped into," said Camberley.

"Is that supposed to happen?" asked Satan.

"No," said Camberley. "The machine in X10101 is extraordinarily sophisticated."

"Biddle-oo-doo, biddle-oo-doo, biddle-oo-doo-deeeee" said the woman.

"Not any more, it would seem," said Woking. "Is there evidence of damage to the machine?"

"We are checking that now" said Camberley. "A primitive human communication device was inserted into the machine, we think in place of another component. It kept making the same noise."

"Biddle-oo-doo, biddle-oo-doo, biddle-oo-doo-deeeee" said the woman.

"A piece had been removed?" asked Woking.

"Like I said, we are checking," said Camberley.

"But the main thing is, the missing soul was found – Sir!" barked Aldershot.

"Absolutely," said Camberley.

"Good," said Satan. "Then all we need to do is speak to the soul that room X10101 was built for, and then we can bring this disastrous episode to an end, yes?" He regarded his underlings with gimlet eyes.

"Ah," said Camberley.

"Hm," said Woking.

Satan's eyes glowed red, and sulphurous steam rose from his back as he rose slowly to his feet. This time he spoke slowly. "Am I to take it that we are now missing a different soul, one guilty of more serious sins?"

"Yyyyyyes," said Camberley, cautiously.

"How serious?" roared Satan.

"Responsible for over three thousand deaths, my Lord," said Woking, cringing.

"And he is LOOSE?" bellowed Satan. "Camberley?"

"We have not yet checked all possible rooms but he is not in any room adjoining his own room or the other two rooms where souls were misplaced sir so technically yes he could be anywhere sir please don't dispel me and really it's Aldershot's fault because someone should be checking X rooms regularly and nobody noticed the soul in there wasn't the right one!"

"He has a point, actually," said Woking. "Aldershot, the room should have been checked, at least once a year."

"It was checked!" shouted Aldershot. "Sir!" he added, quickly. "It was checked! Fenwick was in charge of it – Sir! Then Bagshot..."

"Fenwick's own account bears that out, my Lord, what there is of it," said Woking. "Going into Room X10101 is the last thing he remembers, until he woke up in a different room, bound and gagged."

"And then this imbecile Bagshot checked the room every year for two decades, and didn't even notice that the prisoner had changed sex?" roared Satan. "I would speak with him alone!!" He clapped his hands, and everyone else vanished from the room, except Camberley, who looked alarmed to still be there.

"Meanwhile, Camberley, I have two words for you, about this lost soul. Come closer," said Satan softly. A quaking Camberley shuffled towards him as slowly as he could. "Closer," said Satan. When Camberley was close enough, Satan bent down so that their noses almost touched. "FIND HIM!!!!!" he roared.

In a chamber some way above, Woking and the others appeared. Woking watched them all scurry away, as if dispersing quickly could spare them further wrath. Yet Woking himself felt anything but relief. Satan ruled by fear and intimidation, as was proper, but Woking had risen to and held his job using the unfashionable art of thinking. Someone had obtained a Devil knife, and not even Fenwick could have accidentally removed one from a stone safe in Satan's cave before unwittingly giving it to a soul who was strapped into a torture machine. No-one could have done that. Not by accident, at least.

*****

In the middle of the minibus, Dylan was assessing his options. Lucy scared him. If by some miracle he got a date with her, he'd probably spend it hiding under the table. She was meant for one far bolder than he.

Natalia, he thought, was much more shaggable. Round face, big soulful eyes, and well supplied in the breast department. However, he'd noticed the way that Martin, one of the two new recruits, had been gazing at her since he'd taken the seat behind her. As if divine light radiated from the back of her head. Although he suspected that Martin might be even more inept with girls than he was, Dylan did not want to intercede, having experienced for himself that kind of hopelessly intense longing.

Janelle had long pale brown hair that a more critical eye than Dylan's might have called lank. From Dylan's simpler perspective, she had nice eyes, nice lips and a pulse. However she also had a silver crucifix hanging on a chain around her neck, which would probably mean too much church and too little sex. There was a certain solemnity about her, too.

This left Lysandra. She was tall and thin, with a skin tone that suggested mixed ancestry, and her jet black curly hair reached her shoulder. Face pretty, but in an unusual way; she looked frighteningly intelligent. But she'd do. Yes, she'd definitely do. It helped a lot that she was squashed in beside him, and trying to extract herself from being talked at by Mycroft. Even so, it took five minutes for Dylan to think of something to say:

"Hello."

"Hello," she said back.

"I'm Dylan."

"Lysandra."

"That's an unusual name."

"It's Greek, I think. My mum's into ancient history."

"It is indeed of Greek origin," said Mycroft. "Lysandra was a Macedonian queen, married to Alexander the fifth. The name means '*one who brings freedom*'. Although in her case, '*one who repeatedly marries powerful cousins*' would have been more apt."

"Thank you for that," said Lysandra.

"I think it's a nice name," said Dylan.

"Thanks. That's a really sweet thing to say."

"Dylan, on the other hand, comes from the Welsh for 'intensive flow'," said Mycroft.

*****

The minibus now moved onto a slip road, and a sign announced that they were joining the M6. "We go on motorway?" asked Natalia, worriedly.

"Of course," said Helen. "Otherwise it would take all night."

"You no say we go on motorway. I never drive on motorway. In home always little roads."

"Well, don't worry," said Helen. "You won't have to drive unless it's an emergency."

"Quite," said Michael, as his skin started to get hotter. He tried not to think about what Natalia had just said.

Fifteen miles further on, Michael was clearly unwell. The traffic was heavy and made slower by the sheeting rain, so they hadn't got as far as he'd expected. It was another ten miles to the services. He was beginning to shiver. That had never happened before. Then a voluminous fart erupted from beneath him, forcing Helen to wind down her window and get splattered with rain. Natalia held her nose and looked at him. "I think you are ill. You must stop driving."

"I'm fine," he croaked.

"Traffic regulations state..." began Mycroft.

"Shut up!" said Helen. "Michael, I think you need to pull over. You're shaking."

"I'm fine. I can make it to the services, then we'll see," he said.

As he spoke there was a rumbling sound as the bus strayed onto the hard shoulder.

"I'm not asking, I'm telling. Stop the bus right now," shouted Helen, and she reached over to hit the hazard lights. Michael, his head starting to spin, had no choice but to obey. He didn't understand it. His last reaction, two years ago, had been nothing like this. There'd been an impressive rash and a temperature, but nothing more, and it had been gone inside three hours. But those had been cooked strawberries, he suddenly realised. He managed to stop the bus, and another resounding fart issued forth. Some of the others piled out of the bus onto the verge, like Helen preferring the rain to the smell. Mycroft dutifully placed the red triangle exactly 45 metres behind the bus (he paced them out). Meanwhile Lysandra, who was a medical student, examined Michael and pronounced herself stumped. Helen and Lucy had a quick conference and agreed to call an ambulance and have it meet them at the services.

***

"I can't tell the difference! I can never tell!! I try! Please, Lord, have mercy on your pathetic servant!"

Satan regarded the quivering figure prostrating itself before him. Bagshot was one of the shortest Devils in Hell, and managed to combine the face of a fat teenager with the hair of a fifty-year-old bank manager, complete with bald patch. "It is not difficult!" Satan declared.

"Yes it is!! It really is!!" wailed Bagshot. "Females have bumps on the front, but sometimes they're really small, and sometimes the men have floppy bits there, too. Females wear make-up, but not always, and sometimes men do too! The hair is no help, because some men have it long as well!"

"Simply remove the clothes and check for the tail at the front!" bellowed Satan, recalling the conversation from earlier. "It is foolproof!!"

"Y-y-yes Lord. B-but if we did that with all of them ... w-we already have terrible backlogs, sir. I-i-it used to be that you could tell from the clothes, but that doesn't work anymore, either! The males even wear skirts sometimes, but only where it's cold and wet!"

"Yes, I've never understood that either," pondered Satan, then a memory struck him. "Hang on," he roared. "I know where I've heard your name before! Room 393! You put a toilet into a room full of souls who were supposed to spend eternity needing one!"

Bagshot felt a sudden brief surge of relief. "N-no sir, that was Fenwick! Aldershot told him to create some raw sewage for another room, so he ..."

"Ahhh, then ... Room 807! That one *was* you, wasn't it??"

"W-w-w-well, I did make a minor error with that room once, yes," quailed Bagshot. "He was wearing a tartan skirt and had a ponytail, so I assumed..."

"You put a male into a room that is specifically – SPECIFICALLY – designed for sexually frustrated old females to take their misery out on each other for eternity!! Those females were smiling when the mistake was discovered! SMILING!!!" Sulphurous flames erupted not only from Satan's back, but also all of the walls.

"W-w-well, the man himself wasn't," pleaded Bagshot. "A-a-and it did give us an idea for a new room!"

"And now, NOW," bellowed Satan, "a soul has been walking free for two decades because YOU never checked that the X10101 prisoner was the right sex, never mind the right person!"

"I couldn't ... I didn't ..."

"I should dispel you right now!!" roared the Lord of Hell.

Bagshot sobbed as Satan pointed a burning arm towards him.

"However, we are a bit short-staffed," added Satan, lowering the arm. "Tell me, pathetic one, which Devil do you despise most? Other than yourself?"

"Mickleham!" said Bagshot immediately.

"You are assigned to work as his junior, on soul greeting duty, until I say different. Begone!!"

Bagshot fled from the room.

Alone, Satan shook his head as his rage subsided. Over countless centuries, the best and the brightest of Hell's Devils had, one by one, challenged for the top job. He, of course, had succeeded, but all those who failed had been summarily slain, as was proper. The trouble was, it had applied a sort of negative selection to the denizens of Hell, leaving behind the dull, the cowardly and the incompetent. It hadn't mattered, so long as nothing important had gone wrong. He sighed, and turned towards the great mirror set into the wall. It had the power to show him possible futures, and he usually avoided it because an older, even more tired version of himself would stare back. Yet this time, an unfamiliar face looked out from it. A human face, which as he watched sprouted great red horns from its head. Then it met his eye, in a way no human soul ever had, and laughed.

For the first time in many millennia, Satan Beelzebub III felt a shiver of fear.

Chapter Four

The room was long and white, with rows of white seats, about half of them occupied by Devils. Each seat faced a screen. From time to time, one of the Devils vanished. Into the room marched Aldershot, and behind him Fenwick, who was aping his superior by wildly swinging his arms as he walked.

Fenwick eyed the seats longingly, for he hadn't sat down for 23 years. Been sat on, mainly.

"Pay attention, you useless cassock!" barked Aldershot, spinning around to face him. "The Devils of Hell have two sacred duties! To give torment to the damned, and to harvest their souls! Harvesting has been the same for millennia! Only a total idiot would need to have it explained to them!"

"Yes," said Fenwick.

"So listen carefully! When a human being dies, a portal forms close by, by which they must journey to the afterlife! If that human is adjudged to be significantly evil, one of us is automatically summoned to the portal at the same time, officially to force compliance, but mainly to scare seven kinds of Heaven out of them!"

"Yes, Sir!" barked Fenwick.

Aldershot paused, unsure if Fenwick was mocking him, then went on. "By the modern accord, condemned souls are compelled to descend, so you need do nothing – nothing, you understand, except stand there and look terrifying! If you can't do the terrifying part, just stand there!"

"I'll do my best – Sir!" said Fenwick.

"Now, this happens countless times every year and nothing ever goes wrong. But this is you so I'm going to spell it out!"

"Spell it out – Sir!" barked Fenwick.

"It is only through such portals that we may travel to or from the mortal world! And even then, only under tightly controlled conditions! You must not walk out of the portal area!"

"I know that! Sir!" shouted Fenwick.

"You must return immediately after the dead soul has passed over!"

"I *know*," insisted Fenwick, his tail now swishing furiously.

"Otherwise you may become visible, and stranded in the mortal world. Again."

"There were exceptional circumstances last time," said Fenwick. "There was a psychic sensitive present, and ..."

"Fenwick, you can render any normal situation exceptional by your mere presence!" yelled Aldershot. "And that reminds me – you're banned from hospitals!"

"What? I can't control which death I'm summoned to, and, y'know, people die in hospitals. A lot. Dunno why they go there, really."

"If you are summoned to a Hospital, then do your duty and return! But if – or when – you next get stranded, you are to stay away from hospitals! Am I clear?"

"Yes, Sir!

"I do not want to be explaining another fifty unscheduled deaths to the Wimples!"

"I was trying to get home!" snarled Fenwick.

"You caused the biggest diplomatic incident since the War! Heaven almost invaded again! You are also barred from killing under any circumstances! Am I clear? Now sit! You must watch the Mortal Flashback and the Tolling Of Deeds. When it ends, you'll be summoned. Dismissed!" Aldershot turned and headed for the door. Fenwick made a crucifix sign with his fingers and thrust them at Aldershot's receding figure. Then he turned his attention to the screen.

****

Barry Walton's life was flashing before his eyes. He felt himself hanging in the middle of some kind of theatre, above all the empty seats, while scenes from his life unfolded in front of him on a giant screen. Barry found the whole thing strangely unconcerning, although the little red guy in the bottom right corner taking notes had been a bit of a surprise. At one point, when a nine-year-old Barry added dog shit to the lunch box of a much larger boy who'd been bullying him, the little red man grinned at him and gave him a few theatrical claps. Barry also saw his own father, now long dead, hitting both him and his mother. Again the little red man caught his eye, this time pointing first to his father, and then downwards, in a gesture that Barry instinctively understood. Perhaps he'd be meeting his father again very soon.

As time moved forward, he saw himself turning into his father: drinking, slapping girlfriends, starting fights. Occasionally, when his opponents fought back, the little red man would swing his fists in encouragement. With every strike, and every cruel word Barry uttered, the little red man typed, and a red column on the right side of the screen grew a little bit higher. Then he saw himself suddenly in a hospital, by the bedside of the mother who'd run out on him when he was eleven, taking his baby sister with her. She told him she was dying. Barry watched his former self telling her that he forgave her, even though he'd known he couldn't. He'd wondered then if she believed him, and seeing it again now, he wondered still. She smiled anyway. A little blue man with wings appeared in the bottom left corner of his screen, looking surprised to be there. After a moment searching his pocket, he drew out a device like the one the red man had, hit a few buttons, and a blue column appeared. It was totally dwarfed by the red one. The watching Barry looked on miserably. Was that really the first good thing he had done in his life?

Barry realised, now, the cruel irony of it: how that one good thing would lead to his end. He'd come to see his mother almost every day after that, missing only the days when he had to sign on. The little blue column crept up slowly. After a week, he'd gone in and found his mother not alone. A little boy had been with her, and a young woman. Emmie, Barry's sister. The sister he'd once promised to protect, before his father's fists had showed him that he couldn't. That day with Emmie and the boy had also been the very last time he'd seen his mother; he hadn't known it then, and because he'd been overcome with shock at seeing his sister, he'd barely even said goodbye to his mother. The watching Barry wanted to cry, but he couldn't.

Next he saw himself with his sister, standing together at their mother's funeral, promising to look after each other, as the little boy wept between them. For Barry, it had turned out, this meant picking fights with whatever man his sister was going out with at the time, because Barry could see in them the things he hated in himself. Some he sent packing, others dared him to hit them in front of Emmie. When he wasn't battling them, he was having shouting matches with Emmie over whether he should be minding his own business. Had his whole life been one big argument? Even the red and blue men were arguing now, each trying to claim these crude attempts at chivalry for their own column. Watching them, Barry felt himself smiling for what he knew might be the last ever time. Let them squabble, he didn't care. What else did he ever have to offer his sister? Then the screen showed the time when he'd got wind of someone bullying little Austin, his nephew. Barry had tracked the boy down, and made sure he wouldn't be hurting Austin again anytime soon. That went firmly into the red column.

When Austin's eighth birthday approached, Barry had been able to afford nothing more than a few tatty toys from a charity shop. Then, coming home from the pub, he'd seen a magnificent kid's bike, sitting by the front gate of a big garden. *'What kind of mum lets kids leave valuable things where they could get nicked?'* he'd thought. *'One who can afford to replace them, that's who.'* The red column grew again. Austin had loved his new bike. But two weeks later the original owners had somehow found out, and claimed their bike back. Barry then saw himself sitting in his dusty mess of a flat, hearing his sister scream abuse at him down the phone. When at last she'd gone silent, he'd muttered that he would make it right.

He'd found the same model for sale in a shop. So expensive. He'd accepted a loan from Sonny Money. Paid for the bike with the wad of cash. Saw Austin's delighted face when he got his bike again, accepted a hug from his sister. The red man clicked his fingers, reviving the blue man, who'd apparently fallen asleep. The blue column rose again, but still it was so far behind.

A month of trying and failing to get money. Sonny Money's toothy grin as he gave his ultimatum, mentioning how sweet he thought little Austin was. Acting like some Vegas crimelord, as if his many visible fillings were gold, not crumbling grey amalgam. Barry had borrowed the gun from Mad Gordie, thought about using it on Sonny, but he knew the guy had friends. He'd opted for robbery instead. The final act.

Barry watched himself walk into that corner shop. Saw how his hand shook like crazy as he pointed the gun at the shop assistant. Heard himself telling the man he had nothing to lose, and the man readily believed him. Then that terrifying voice from behind him:

"Barry Walton!"

The screen showed it all in slow motion, just like a movie. Barry saw himself spin round, heart pounding, eyes locking with the fearful visage of Mister Howarth, his English teacher from long ago. Greyer hair, but those same piercing eyes. Muscles clenched all over Barry's body. Including his trigger finger. Mister Howarth's chest exploded into a mass of blood. For a moment he stood still, as if ready to prove school rumours that Howarth really was a Lord of the Undead. Then Howarth spoke, in a whisper. You knew it was big trouble when Mister Howarth spoke softly. "You stupid, little, … uuuhhhhh." Then he fell to the ground stone dead. Barry turned round to the shop assistant, but the man had disappeared off somewhere.

"I didn't mean to!" Barry cried, to anyone who could hear him. "That man scares the hell out of me, always has! I didn't mean to!!" Then he turned and fled. The little red man pulled a lever, and the blue one fell through a trapdoor. The red man waved him goodbye, as the red column swelled to fill half of the screen, and started flashing.

Barry was running; sirens were wailing. He saw a man getting out of a car, grabbed him and threw him over, took the keys and drove off. The red man cheered. Barry's new car screeched through the city, gunning red lights, flattening a fox. The red man was now eating popcorn, sitting back and enjoying the ride. No need to take notes anymore. Barry made it onto the motorway. Rain was sheeting down, and Barry loved that. Again the watching Barry experienced that strange mixture of despair and elation he'd felt at the time, as he'd screamed through the traffic, faster and faster. Despair, because he knew that within minutes – hours at the most, he'd be dead or locked up. Elation, because that meant that nothing mattered. He was finally free. He reached the motorway with the police close behind him, but they couldn't get ahead without causing an accident themselves. Hah! Advantage Barry. But all those idiots in the fast lane doing only 80 were blocking his way. He cut through the middle lane into the slow lane, slammed his foot down even harder, zoomed past the middle lane slowcoaches. Then one of them switched lanes suddenly, right in front of him. An ugly yellow minibus. There was nowhere to go except the verge, but he lost control, thundering through the grass up the embankment, until the front wheel hit something and the car took off, spinning. The concrete of a motorway bridge rushed to greet him.

Down in Hell, the video of Barry's life ended, and the watching Fenwick disappeared.

*****

Back in the corner shop, William Howarth blinked as the recording of his own life came to an end. The memory of it faded fast, like a dream. He was pleasantly surprised to see an Angel appear inside the shop, along with a shining blue stairway, and a strangely familiar guitar chord.

"Does that music play for everyone?"

"Only Led Zep fans," smiled the Angel.

"I wasn't sure where I'd go, you know. I spent most of my life terrifying children."

"Perhaps they needed it," replied the Angel.

"Could I ask that … could I hang on a few minutes? Only I was supposed to meet my daughter here, and I haven't seen her in three years. Would be nice to see her, one last time."

The Angel looked puzzled. "Your daughter is still in Australia."

"But she called … it was a local number," said Howarth.

"Wasn't her," said the Angel. "It was someone pretending."

"But why?" asked Howarth, looking down at his own dead body. "Why would someone do that?"

"That's not my concern," said the Angel. "Nor yours, anymore."

*****

Natalia was bundled into the driving seat, and Michael into the back, after which everyone had to wait for Mycroft to retrieve the red warning triangle. Lucy jumped into the front passenger seat with Helen.

"How you make it start?" asked Natalia.

"Just pretend I'm holding the choke," said Helen. "See, I'm pulling it now."

The engine roared into life, and the bus lurched as the engine fought the handbrake. Natalia searched on her right side for a handbrake to disengage, while Helen eventually did it for her. The bus jumped forward, and a horn blared out as a car shot past in the next lane.

"I can go in lane now? Is okay?" asked Natalia. The minibus puttered along the hard shoulder at walking speed. More cars whizzed past. A rumbling sound as the bus strayed towards the slow lane. More angry horns. Natalia tried to change gear and stalled.

"Maybe I should drive," said Helen. "I've not passed yet but this is an emergency!"

"I regret to inform you that if you did, I would be forced to effect a citizen's arrest," said Mycroft.

"Try it," snarled Lucy, "and I'll effect this handbrake right up your – "

"Indicate right!" shouted Helen, as Natalia restarted the engine. "Now watch in the mirror!" A few moments passed. Helen craned round to see in the mirror herself. "Yes pull out now!" The bus lumbered into the slow lane. For a minute or so they tootled along at ten miles per hour. Then a mass of traffic began passing them in the middle lane, and a pair of headlights appeared close behind them. The hooting started again.

"I have to go faster?" asked Natalia.

"A little faster, yes," said Helen. To her surprise, Natalia now seemed to have grasped how to change gears and accelerate. Gradually their speed picked up, until miraculously they were zooming along at the same speed as everyone else. Natalia sat hunched forward, her eyes locked on the road ahead, her right leg jiggling under her skirt. They were coming up fast upon a lorry in the slow lane.

"And now I am taking-over, yes?" she said joyfully, and pulled the bus into the middle lane without waiting for an answer. Helen winced as tyres screeched behind them. Yet more angry horns.

"S-services!" said Michael from behind them. Helen saw the big blue sign as they moved in front of the lorry. But there was another lorry ahead of it.

"I should go there?" asked Natalia, pointing at the exit looming ahead.

"Slow down a bit," said Helen. "NOT LIKE THAT" she shrieked, as Natalia pushed down hard on the brake, forcing everyone forward in their seats. The lorries moved ahead once more, but there were cars behind them now.

"Now I move big arrow lever?" said Natalia, meaning the left-indicator.

Helen thought fast. "No, stay in this lane! We'll have to get the next services." The exit flew by. Behind her, a shivering Michael thought miserably of his car, sitting in the services car park, where he'd left it earlier that day, before hitching back. The service station had an on-site first aider, and his plan had been to be left with him while Natalia drove everyone else on to Glasgow. Michael would have then driven back to collect Suzy as soon as he felt well enough. And he'd planned it so well!

"Call the ambulance again," said Helen.

"No signal," said Lucy.

Helen noticed some flashing lights far behind them. "Dammit, that must be the ambulance coming already. Natalia, when you can, please move into the left lane and stay there. Once we get a signal we can pull over."

Natalia glanced to the left and turned the wheel.

"No wait!" screamed Lucy.

From nowhere, a car had caught up with them in the slow lane, doing well over 100. It swerved as the bus lurched into that lane, then the speeding car was searing up the sloping verge ahead of them, still at a ridiculous speed. For a moment Helen thought it would reach the top and take flight. Instead, it suddenly started to roll, tumbling as it rocketed forwards, but there was a bridge ahead –

The explosion shook the minibus, flames shooting out from the wrecked car ahead of them. Natalia seemed to have frozen, and they were heading straight for it.

*****

Helen grabbed the minibus steering wheel and forced them first into the middle lane, then to the fast lane, while other vehicles braked hard and dropped behind them. The fire and smoke from the crashed car came closer and closer, then in a moment it whipped past.

"Bad thing happening," said Natalia.

"Well we just pretty much killed someone, so yeah, you could say," snarled Lucy.

"Visions come back. Very bad. Babushka have them many times. I, also. See people who are gone. Very bad!"

"Natalia, please, you're in shock. Just pull us over to the slow lane, we need to stop the bus!"

"I should leave this road?"

"We need to stop," said Helen. "Pull over!"

"But there is car!" Natalia complained.

Lucy glanced at the empty slow lane. "There's nothing! Pull over."

Natalia decided she must have failed to understand how mirrors worked. Maybe the reflection she saw was her own vehicle? If she didn't pull over now she'd miss another turning. The exit was clearly marked ahead, and there was even a man standing there, beckoning with his arms, grinning. Perhaps he was with the ambulance? Natalia pulled the bus across into the slow lane and indicated left for the exit. The white car in the wing mirror veered onto the verge, its brakes screeching. Natalia steered towards the exit, but now the man was running into the road, waving his arms like crazy, looking horrified. His face, in fact all of him, was a bright shade of red. Natalia tried to steer around him, but the wheel had locked. She waved back at the man, "Go way go way go way!!!" But the man didn't move.

There were three bumps – front bumper, front wheels and back wheels. Everyone felt them.

"What the fuck was that?" said Lucy

Natalia watched the prone figure in the rear view mirror recede. She said nothing.

"Where did the motorway go?" asked Helen. "Where are we?"

The road they were on had only one lane, and it was going steadily downhill.

Chapter Five

Barry woke up. He had the feeling that something important had happened, but whatever it was fell away as he tried to recall it. He remembered coming off the road; somehow he'd missed the bridge support, though judging by the commotion behind him, someone else hadn't. A cop, maybe. Let it be a cop, he thought. He was still in the car, and the engine was running. The motorway was almost empty, blocked he supposed by the accident behind him. He shrugged and started driving. There was just one vehicle ahead, a minibus. Big, yellow and battered. The bastard that had cut him up! He decided that at the very least, a gesture of response would be appropriate. He began steadily catching it up. Then he noticed an extra exit on the motorway, far ahead. It wasn't signposted at all, but he could just see a figure there, waving at him. *Forget the yellow bastard*, he thought. *Just get off the motorway before the cops work out that I'm still alive.* He crossed to the slow lane and begun indicating. As the turning approached, the yellow bus suddenly slowed down, and he found himself almost level with it. Then they did it again! Lurched over into his lane, without warning. He hit the brakes hard, ploughing the front of the car into the thick grass of the verge. This time he didn't flip over, just stopped. Ahead of him, he saw the man by the junction suddenly panic, run into the road, desperately trying to stop the yellow bus from taking the turning. The bus didn't even slow down, it just ran straight over him, then trundled off down the turning, out of sight.

Barry felt a strange urge to help the poor man, or at least hold his hand before he carked it. For a moment, a thought of a strange blue column flashed through his mind, but he had no idea what it meant. He forced open the car door, tumbled out across the grass and ran forward to find the stricken man. But the turning must have been further ahead than he'd thought, because he walked for ages and couldn't even see it. Eventually he gave up and turned around, then as he headed back his attention was caught by a flock of yellow birds, pecking at something in the grass. As he came closer, the birds vanished and a moaning sound came from the spot where they'd been.

A battered, bloodied Fenwick stood up, swayed, and tumbled forward. "Living souls ... in Hell ... disaster ... Heaven and Salvation!" stuttered Fenwick. "Everything ends if they go through the gates ... gotta tell ..." then he collapsed into Barry's arms.

Barry felt the ground shake then, just a little. So did everyone else in the world. Not knowing why, he bundled Fenwick carefully into the car, managed to start it again, and drove off in the hope of finding a hospital. The earth shook a couple more times as he did so.

Kane Winkle was, among other things, a failed comedian. The last few times he'd got up before an audience, he'd been booed off without ever hitting his stride. Yet this audience, the Broker had assured him, would be an easy one as long as he kept to the script. He'd walked into the room to find a sea of fifty bland, inexpressive faces; mostly male, often bespectacled. Chairs were laid out in five rows of ten, and all were occupied; except that a few of the audience had decided their seats weren't precisely in line with the others, and were on their feet trying to align the chairs properly. One went all the way along a line of ten, adjusting each chair's position in turn as its occupant obligingly stood for him. This calmed Kane a little – there'd be no heckling from this lot.

"Ladies and gentlemen, thank you for coming. I know we have been a little secretive about our purpose here, but trust me, you will not be disappointed.

"First, let me tell you about just one of the remarkable people who I have the pleasure of addressing today. Gareth Rawle. His colleagues call him 'The Wanderer', wanna know why? Because he walks the streets every day, doing his job, not just office hours but evenings and weekends, too. Rain or shine! He passes hundreds of dwellings every day, and if you've started building a loft extension or conservatory without the correct documentation, or maybe a new porch or a lean-to greenhouse, Gareth's gonna know. Even little things – taking out a door, knocking through a wall – if Gareth sees sawdust on your drive, workmen going in, or a skip, you'll be rumbled. Cos our Gareth knows every house that has a building warrant, and every house that doesn't! Then once he's inside, well, you'd damned well better have followed the rules to the letter. There are some of his colleagues who might look the other way if a fire door closes that little bit too gently, or a velux window is a quarter inch too big. Not Gareth!

"Gary deserves a medal, yes a medal, for helping to stop the cancer of illegal home improvements from destroying our country. Outside this room, Gareth would be exceptional. But here, he's just one of fifty Housing Heroes! I could heap the same praise on each and every one of you – you are the best, the very best our councils have to offer. The best at maintaining order in the chaos of home ownership. We are the thin grey line!"

Winkle paused, expecting applause, but had to make do with stern but meaningful nodding. "But I've not brought you here for trinkets, I've brought you for something far greater. Duty!! Because, you have dealt with illegal houses, illegal extensions, but tonight we face something worse!" He paused for effect, while his audience struggled to work out what could possibly be worse. Then he told them: "an illegal town!"

This time there were a few gasps and hands put up to faces. Winkle clicked a button, and a silent video began playing behind him, showing the town whose birth he described. "It began with a patch of unremarkable land on the boundary of three local authorities. A corrupt company called Red Demon Homes acquired the land, and through bribery, trickery and altered records, they convinced each authority that the land belonged to another. Then they went right ahead and built the whole town in just a few years, *without any kind of planning permission*."

The audience now looked both horrified and raptly attentive at the same time, like a room full of priests at a sex show. "By the time anyone cottoned on, it was too late. The town was there, and the authorities have chosen to accept it, rather than admit their own failings. Worse still, they've emptied the local tenement blocks of old ladies and ran schemes to help them buy homes in this new town, in an attempt to claim the moral high ground, lining the pockets of the rule-breakers!"

"Shame!" called one bold man in the audience.

"So they think – they *believe*, these cowboy developers, that they've got away with it. But they reckoned without one thing. Us!!"

"Yes!!" cheered a man in the audience, standing up. When he saw no-one else doing likewise, he sheepishly sat down again. Then he had to stand up once more, because he'd moved his chair slightly, and the man beside him wasn't having that.

"You see," said Kane, building to a crescendo, "Red Demon Homes set up a phantom local authority to contain this new town, and that shall be their undoing! I have transferred you all, for forty-eight hours, to the temporarily established New Town local authority. That authority ceases to exist on Monday, so we must move fast. We'll hit them like a wrecking ball, find fault with every single property. We'll stick it to them with history's biggest correction bill, bankrupt the bastards, and teach them respect for the rules! Who's with me?"

He was greeted by a demure show of fifty raised hands.

*****

Two red figures hung in the air, high above the Abysmal Plain. One was long and thin and handsome, the other was Bagshot. The tall one looped the loop a couple of times, making engine noises and sticking his tail out like a tailfin. "Wheeeeeeee!!!"

"Do you have to?" said Bagshot.

"I don't have to, I just can," said Mickleham happily, through his usual cruel smile.

"It's making me dizzy."

Mickleham stopped, and drifted close to his colleague. "Oh I'm sorry," he mocked. "I forgot poor Baggie is scared of heights."

"Don't call me that! Why do we have to be so high up?" moaned Bagshot.

"For show, you idiot!" grinned Mickleham. "Oh come on, this is the best job in Hell!"

"I was happy where I was. I like the back room jobs."

"Oh, and you were SO good at them," said Mickleham. "No-one else would have thought to stick a male into a room full of sex-starved old females!"

"And I haven't forgotten what you did to me afterwards!" whined Bagshot. "Thirteen years mincing around room 219 in makeup and a tutu. Thirteen years!!"

"I did you a favour – you'd have been dispelled otherwise. Even Satan himself laughed when he saw you! Anyway, you looked great in that outfit. All the guys in the video room thought so, too!"

"You sainted messiah!!! You said you'd wiped it!" Bagshot took a swipe at Mickleham with his fist, but Mickleham easily dodged out of his way.

"Have to catch me first, Baggie-boy!" cackled Mickleham, swooping around Bagshot in giddying circles. Bagshot tried and tried to catch him, eventually giving up, spent.

"Ooh ooh, here he comes!" said Mickleham, pointing to a speck in the distance below them. "Have you done a vehicle before?"

"No, last time I did this there weren't any," said Bagshot, glumly.

"It's the moment when they realise," said Mickleham, baring his teeth in savage delight. "That's what makes this the best job in Hell. We're the ones who see it, when it dawns on them where they are."

"Really?" said Bagshot, uncertainly.

"Yeah," said Mickleham. "You never got that reaction?"

"Well, one of them cried, but another just said, 'I thought you'd be taller'."

Mickleham cackled. "It's not about height, Baggie-boy, it's attitude!" He touched a control on the studded leather collar around his neck, then stuck out his arms in a cross shape as flames erupted all around his body. His eyes turned jet black. "Now," he said in a matter-of-fact voice, "With vehicles, what you do depends on what they do. We need to appear just after they see the Gates of Hell. Sometimes they just keep driving, in which case we just wave and hope they cack themselves, then onto the next one. But once in a while there's a strong one, who'll stop or turn round; then we swoop through the windscreen and grab them. The car's only a figment of their mind, see? It'll vanish. We pull them straight out and put them in a burning cage on a prison truck. Scares the life out of the buggers, not that they have any. Okay, light up."

Bagshot had been worried about this. He screwed up his face, and gingerly touched a control on the collar he'd been made to put on. A massive jet of flame erupted from his rear end. Mickleham sighed. "Guess they're not idiot-proof after all." He fiddled with Bagshot's collar, and the flames spread around Bagshot's body. "Now, we look the part," he said. "Ready?"

"I s'pose."

Below them the yellow vehicle continued down the lonely road.

*****

"Looks like thunder ahead," said Helen. She wasn't sure how much time had passed since they'd turned off the motorway. There had been no place to pull over. At least it wasn't raining now. But the massive black cloud ahead promised more.

"Big fucker," agreed Lucy, gazing at the cloud.

Natalia watched two orange lights dancing around in front of the cloud. Looking down, she saw a distant pair of massive red gates hoving into view. "Is service ahead! I find service!" she said happily.

"Can't see nuffin," said Lucy.

"Are you sure?" asked Helen.

Natalia looked again. Pillars of flame erupted from behind the distant gates, and on either side, burning walls hundreds of metres high stretched out of sight in each direction. Feeling uneasy, she looked up. The two orange lights had detached themselves from the cloud and were searing through the air towards them.

"This no good place," said Natalia. "I turn round." The gears screeched and clunked as the bus shuddered forward and backwards, during a gradual thirteen point turn.

"For God's sake, Tash, let Helen drive," snarled Lucy. "What if someone comes up behind us? This is a one way road!"

"I no care! Is fire ahead! You no see?"

Lucy couldn't. Ahead she saw nothing but a white haze, with the black cloud hanging above it. "Helen, back me up," she said.

"Natalia, this road goes nowhere but back to the motorway, and I think she's right, it's one way."

Natalia didn't respond, simply wrenched the wheel around and turned the lumbering bus back onto the road, heading away from the gates.

*****

The two approaching fireballs pulled up. "Look, they're turning!" said Mickleham. "Great! That means we get to grab him out!"

"They?" said Bagshot uncertainly. "I thought it was only one soul?"

"Didn't you see the extra faces? It's part of the illusion. You die in a car, you imagine the car coming with you," said Mickleham. "Sometimes they'll imagine passengers too. Come on, we need to get ahead so we can swoop down on him dramatically!"

Natalia had her foot to the floor, but the bus was only doing fifty, struggling as it was up a seemingly unending hill. Something about her new-found determination had silenced Helen and Lucy, and they were instead trying to shut Mycroft up about regulations for single lane roads. The orange lights had reappeared in front of them, closer this time. For a moment they held still, then they were plunging towards them at terrifying speed. They were going to hit. At the last moment Natalia tried to dodge with the bus, but there was no time to –

CRASSSHHH!!!

The centre of the windscreen exploded inwards, leaving a hole the size of a football and showering Lucy and Helen in fragments of glass. "Whatthefu-" screamed Lucy, then the bus shuddered again as something else hit it, but neither Helen nor Lucy saw what it was.

Natalia did. She'd seen Mickleham's head crash through the windscreen, seen Bagshot attempt to slow up at the last moment, just enough for his face to smack into the screen in front of her without breaking it. She expected him to slide off but he didn't. "Get off! Get out of way! Why you red men keep jumping in my way? Get off!!" She craned her head sideways to try and see the road beyond him.

"C-can't," said a dazed Bagshot. The flames had briefly melted the metal of the minibus, and now he was welded to its front. "I'm stuck! M-Mickleham! Wake up!"

Both he and Natalia looked across to Mickleham's lolling head, which had acquired a flock of bright yellow birds circling and tweeting around it. One by one the birds started pecking at his face, first gently, then harder. Mickleham barely twitched. Helen and Lucy acted like the head and birds weren't there, staring instead at Natalia.

Bagshot screwed up his face. Another sainted foul-up, he thought! Yet this one surely wasn't his fault. Mickleham had said the vehicle would be imaginary. He'd said it would vanish at their touch. Bagshot had just followed. Still, with Mickleham out of it, Bagshot could save the day and leave Mickleham to cop all the blame.

Bagshot darkened his eyes. "Barry Walton, I command you to turn your vehicle around," he said in his deepest most booming voice.

"I no Barry Walton," said Natalia. "I am Natalia Petrovna Vokzalnova, I am woman from Russia. Who is Barry Walton?"

"You won't fool me that way, Barry," growled Bagshot. "Not again! I know a man when I see one!"

"You are crazy red man," said Natalia. "What are these then?" She indicated her ample breasts with her free hand.

"Some men have flobbly bits there too! You can't trick me again!"

"You see my face?" she said angrily. "Do I look like man to you?" She hit the windscreen wiper control, and the wipers leapt up and twatted Bagshot in the face.

"Ow!! I don't know, I can never tell!"

"Get off my screen," she snarled, hitting the wiper control again. "Get off now!"

Bagshot yelped in pain again. He needed to get back in control, and there was only one way to be sure. "You give me no choice! I command you to remove all vestments from your lower parts!"

"WHAT?" she screamed indignantly, correctly guessing what he meant. She hit the wiper button again and then, in a flash of inspiration, the screen-washers too. A jet of soapy water hit Bagshot square in the eye. He wailed with pain.

Half-blinded, Bagshot nonetheless persevered. "I command you! Remove all items of clothing from your body below the waist! You cannot refuse!"

"Perverty red man!" she squirted him again with the screen washers. "You want see fanny, you go on computer like everyone else! Mamushka warn me England have men like you! She tell me no go! Get off my bus! GET OFF!!" She hit the washers again and again, eventually getting a jet into Bagshot's other eye.

"Y-you weren't driving, were you?" said Mickleham, who'd finally been forced back into consciousness by persistent pecking of his nose. Unlike Bagshot, he knew a woman when he saw one, even in this dazed state. "When you came off the motorway the first time?"

The yellow birds, their work done, vanished. Natalia looked across at the battered red head sticking through her windscreen, noticing the one broken horn. "Him behind me, he was drive, but stupid. Try to drive when sick. But you are more sick! Crashing into me like crazy man. Go away and take perverty man with you!" She hit the washer button again for good measure.

Lucy had seen enough. Natalia seemed to be ranting at thin air. "She's lost it, Helen. Grab the wheel!" When Helen did nothing, Lucy lunged across her, but her head hit something invisible and hard, and she flopped down onto Helen's lap.

Helen saw, for an instant, an angry red face yelling something that sounded like "aarrghh!" before pulling itself out through the windscreen. Then it blurred again.

Mickleham instinctively drew both hands up to his eye, where Lucy's inadvertent headbutt had landed. Natalia hit the brakes, and Mickleham pitched backwards onto the road, smashing his head even harder into the asphalt. The yellow birds, annoyed at being called on again so soon, began pecking him again with increased vigour, as Natalia managed to swerve the bus around him. Then she drove on, renewing her efforts to detach Bagshot from the windscreen via washer jets and wipers. After a minute the tormented Devil managed to wrench one arm free, then rapidly found himself helplessly peeling off, crashing down hard onto the road, after which the front wheel of the bus went right over his head.

The minibus roared away, leaving behind it a bloodied mess attended by pecking yellow birds.

Chapter Six

The injured man in Barry Walton's car was clearly very religious. He was screaming out the names of various angels, and appeared to have a particular affinity for the Sainted Archangel Gabriel. Barry had noticed the red skin and tail of course, but some block in his mind had prevented him from seeing this as in any way unusual.

Barry was determined to save him. A voice in the back of his mind was saying something about balance. Once more he was gunning the car along the motorway at top speed, but now it was in the other direction, heading for the hospital where his mother had died. At one point the other vehicles had slowed to a crawl, apparently all gawping at some dramatic accident in the other carriageway, but Barry simply zoomed past along the hard shoulder. He didn't care if the Police caught him, because if they did he'd just let them get Fenwick to the hospital. He'd have done his part, saved a life to atone for the one he'd taken.

Fenwick was in agony. His injuries would have killed a mortal man several times over. His torso was half as thick and twice as wide as it should be, with tyre marks running across it. Barry's hopelessly inept attempts at first aid would have killed him a few more times, were he capable of a normal death. Eventually, Barry had somehow managed to get the screaming Fenwick into the back of his car, where he'd folded down the back seats to let Fenwick lie down, albeit on a hard, uneven surface. Then he'd accelerated off, throwing Fenwick onto his side and causing yet more grievous injuries.

Now, at least, Fenwick had acquired a position where he didn't get shifted whenever the car swerved. He felt the shooting pains within him as his body calmly knitted itself back together. With it came a clearer understanding of what had happened. He knew it to be impossible, but the evidence of it was imprinted across his chest. He had to use the emergency contact protocol. Dipping his finger in the blood still trickling from his mouth, he drew a pentagram on his chest. Nothing happened. Perhaps he was doing it wrong. He drew two more on parts of the car. Still not a flicker. Did the blessed thing *ever* work?

Living souls were heading for Hell. If they passed through the gates … Fenwick shuddered in horror at the disaster it would cause. He had to warn Hell! The mortal veil would be weakened, at least, which would make it easier for him to get through. There was only one way. He fought back the pain as he stretched forward and picked up the discarded gun from under the passenger seat. Then he levered himself upright, managing not to cry out as incomplete bones ground against each other. In a strained voice, in between coughs, he asked Barry,

"Are you a good man?"

"I am not," said Barry immediately. "I killed my English teacher today."

"That'll do," said Fenwick, and he aimed the gun at Barry's head and pulled the trigger. Or rather, tried to, for the trigger was jammed.

"Why do you ask?" said Barry.

Fenwick checked the safety catch and tried again. Still nothing. Yet Fenwick could smell death on the gun. What was wrong with the stupid thing? He gripped the barrel with his other hand, to see if it was bent somehow.

BANG!

"AAAArrrrrgggghhhhhhhh!!!!!"

Ten minutes passed before Fenwick had two hands again. By then he'd noticed the horrible burns on the side of Barry's face, and worked out what they meant.

"Have you ever wet the bed?" asked Fenwick.

"Every night till I was thirteen," Barry answered immediately. "And a few times since then, when I was pissed."

That confirms it, thought Fenwick. "You're dead, which means you have to answer my questions truthfully, and obey my every command."

"Oh," said Barry. Finally all the strange things about Fenwick that he'd been ignoring made sense to him.

"And I couldn't shoot you before, because I thought you were alive," Fenwick said to himself.

"You wanted to shoot me?"

Fenwick ignored this. "Who is the most evil person you know?"

"Sonny Money," replied Barry, without thinking.

"Take me to him," said Fenwick, his eyes flashing black.

To his surprise, Barry found himself automatically turning the car, once more, away from the hospital and back towards the town where he'd died.

*****

Martin Gryce was ridiculously thin. At school the other boys had played a game where they took it in turns to pick Martin up and invent a use for him. The caretaker had never found out why the fallen leaves of autumn were frequently raked very clumsily into a nice pile, by someone other than himself. Nor could he understand why inept attempts were sometimes made at mopping the floor of the boys' toilets. Martin had played along in the hope that the boys concerned would become his friends, and on one memorable occasion they had indeed beaten to a pulp a bully who had been picking on him. But he gradually learned to accept that they saw him as more of a pet than a friend. Still he hadn't resisted their games.

He'd come to University in the hope that some magical transformation would befall him. He would find the love of his life, some beautiful girl whom he would rescue from her loneliness, while at the same he'd find some male friends. Neither had happened. He'd joined the Science Fiction society, but its members were merely people who sat in the same room as him, watching DVDs. His presence was also accepted at chess club, but the clique of older students there didn't talk to him, while the younger members just didn't talk. The only word anyone ever said to him was "checkmate". He rarely said it back.

Somewhere he'd read that walking clubs were a good place to make friends, so he'd jumped in with both feet, signing up for a weekend away with people he'd never met. He'd turned up at the student union car park at the appointed time, watching disappointedly as several attractive women had walked past and not joined them. Then *she* had appeared. Martin had barely registered her three female companions. And unlike Michael, he had barely paid attention to Natalia's legs, nor her breasts. He'd simply got lost in her big, puppy-like eyes. When the time had come to board the bus, he'd done so in a doddery haze, oblivious of somebody muttering that the club had picked up yet another weirdo. Martin had quietly sat down as close to the front as he could, and spent the journey staring at the back of Natalia's head. When she'd taken the wheel he'd made a half-hearted attempt to get in the front with her, to lend her strength through the irrepressible love now coursing through his veins. But Lucy had elbowed him aside and he, unsurprised, had resumed his vigil on his original seat, and begun desperately to think of a way to join Natalia at the Megadance Festival.

His love for Natalia only intensified after the strange attack that had come through the windscreen. He'd assumed it a trick of the light, because at first there'd seemed to be no-one there; only later had he started to see glimpses of red faces. Yet Natalia had seen them clearly. As she fought them off, she became in his mind a Valkyrie, cutting through her enemies while he stood at her side being somehow useful. Soon after, she'd unexpectedly taken the bus off the road, and driven it off across the grass, much to the distress of the other girls in the front. Yet she'd somehow found a road again and they'd grudgingly fallen silent. Was there anything this perfect beauty couldn't do?

Martin's heart had sunk when the Glasgow dance venue had suddenly hoved into view. He hadn't expected it so soon, as they'd been in open country just moments before. Similar thoughts had passed through both Lucy and Helen's minds, but they'd quickly flickered out. Remarkably, beyond the hall, the road wound up a lone hill, on which the gothic looking building of the Youth Hostel was just visible through the rain. They were much closer together than he'd expected!

"I leave you out here then take walkers to Hostel, yes? Then come back?" said Natalia. Martin thrilled to the sound of her voice.

"Great plan," said Lucy.

"What about him?" said Helen, gesturing behind her to the hapless form of Michael.

"He's your problem," said Lucy. "Stick 'im in a taxi to A&E, I would."

For a moment, just a moment, Helen wondered what on earth she was doing. They'd continued on to Glasgow despite having a sick man on board, and a head-shaped hole in their windscreen. Plus there'd been an accident, hadn't there? No-one else – not even Mycroft – had suggested they should pull over, seek a garage, or even try to get home, after the windscreen had smashed. Her memories were hazy, like a dream. Was she dreaming now? Yet one thought dominated all others: the journey had to be completed. Then she noticed a white taxi waiting right outside the dance hall, and the doubts evaporated. "Look, there's one there," she said.

Natalia pulled the bus to a stop, and her three colleagues disembarked, dragging Michael with them. Helen went over to the cab driver, noting with approval that it was a woman, and gave her twenty pounds to get Michael to the nearest hospital. With Michael bundled into the cab, Helen hopped back into the bus and Natalia drove them on. Soon they were ascending the hill, and rain began to lash the windows.

"You are all crazy people," said Natalia. "You are paying to do this? You should come and watch dancing instead."

Helen, her mouth clenched shut, shook her head. For some reason the road stopped half a mile from the hostel, blocked by a gate, with a forest track beyond. They would have to walk the rest of the way through the sheeting rain. Everyone had a waterproof coat, but no-one had waterproof covers for their big packs. Their luggage would be soaked. Dylan had held everyone up by insisting on putting on about eight layers of clothing under his waterproof, saying that this was the only way to stop his clothes getting wet. This gave Martin the time he needed to build his courage. Then he announced:

"I've forgotten my waterproofs!"

There was a chorus of 'you bloody idiot!' from just about everyone. Helen bore down on him, livid with fury. In fact, Martin was sure there actually was steam coming off her. "You can sleep on the bloody bus, you moron! Honestly?! How many times do we have to tell people! I wash my hands of you. If you're still on the bus on Sunday we'll take you home, but I don't want to see you before that!"

Martin remained rooted to the spot in the rain, shocked by the venom in Helen's voice. Then Bernie sauntered up to him. "Packed the Armani by mistake, have we? Don't sweat, Duckie, we've all done it!" Then he pulled his face so close Martin could smell the aftershave even through the rain. "Go get her, tiger," Bernie whispered.

Bemused, Martin meekly got onto the front seat of the bus. Natalia barely seemed to register him. Helen slammed the bus doors as if trying to flush him from her life. He and Natalia watched the walkers disappear into driving rain. Then she turned the bus around. She was getting the hang of this driving thing now.

"I don't care what the others say," said Martin, finding a courage that had been long hidden. "I think you're a brilliant driver!"

"They no say anything," said Natalia, looking straight ahead.

"Do you think I could come in and watch your dance?" he asked, his voice wobbling all over the place.

"You like the dancing, yes?"

"L-love it," he said.

"And you tell the big lie about waterproof coat, yes?"

"You're very clever," he replied.

"And you are the only one of them who has the brain. They all get the bad colds and flus now I am sure. I am happy you will watch the dance."

In Martin's heart, a chorus of angels began to sing. He was shaking so much he didn't notice that the ground below the bus was suddenly doing the same. No-one in Hell had ever been as happy as he was, at that moment. Cracks began snaking away across the grass into the distance.

*****

"Where the hell have you been?" said a furious older woman as Lucy, Janelle and Lysandra hurried inside. "You've missed your slot!"

"For what?" asked Lucy.

"The demonstration dance!"

"It was tomorrow!"

"Tonight, idiot!" growled the woman. "Didn't you get the message?"

Lucy gulped.

"We've managed to work around it but you're on very thin ice," snarled the woman. "You're on in four minutes. You'd better be bloody good." Her eyes flashed with venom.

"That's barely time to warm up!" said Janelle.

"We'll do it behind stage," said Lucy. "Come on!"

"Where's your fourth one?" snarled the angry woman. "Or did you lose her as well?"

"We had a medical emergency," replied Lucy. "She'll be here, just send her to the stage."

"Just remember, you're only here because you promised a spectacular and complex demonstration dance routine. I expect you to deliver."

*****

Michael found himself alone in the back of the cab. The driver looked round at him. "Geez, I thought I was going to be stuck in that cottage all on my own," said Suzy McCabe. Michael gasped with astonished delight, then was thrown back into his seat as she gunned the engine and sped away.

Even driving at what felt like twice the speed limit, Michael was amazed how fast Suzy got him to the cottage. His rash hadn't abated, and he'd had to discretely roll down the windows to release his ongoing strawberry-induced flatulence, but Suzy didn't appear to have noticed. He hoped he'd be able to hold it in at least until he'd got her into bed. Once there, he could try to waft it away from her nose with the duvet.

"You seem tense," she said seductively, as she held the door open for him to get out. Her long blonde hair was piled up under a cap on her head, and she was wearing some sort of chauffeur's tunic on her top half. Only one button was done up, and beneath it was a white dress with a skirt so short that there really wasn't much point in it being there. She took him by the hand and led him inside.

"You've got a rash," she said. "Drink this." He downed the small bottle of sweet pink liquid she'd given him.

"I have an idea," she murmured. "Let's get that top off you and lie you down." Within a minute he was stretched out face down on the bed, finally able to forget his condition as her hands rubbed his shoulders. He drifted into a haze of pleasure as she slipped leather straps round each of his wrists, and quickly tied them tightly to the bedposts.

"Hey!" he said, but she ignored him, doing the same to both his ankles.

She cocked her head to one side, pursing her lips at him. "I thought you liked the experimental stuff," she said, sounding hurt. "You did say to bring some ties just in case." She stroked the front of her inadequate skirt gently.

"Yes, but ..." he'd imagined things the other way round. "I can't take my pants off! And I'm the wrong way up!" he said helplessly.

"Not for what I have in mind," she said huskily, leaning forward and blindfolding him with black silk. "Wait here." He lay there alone for ten minutes, occasionally shouting her name. Eventually she returned.

"Now," she said. "For the strawberry allergy rash, I know just the thing. Stinging nettles! My aunt absolutely swears by them."

He began to protest furiously, but this was cut short when she calmly tied a gag into his mouth. "Sshhh, save your energy," she said. Then pinpricks of itchy pain began to appear all over his back as she carefully began placing nettles onto it. "Himalayan nettles," she purred. "Ten times the potency of normal ones." Indeed, every sting from them felt like a wasp sting. He moaned and shuddered with pain. "Don't move," she advised. "Not a muscle. If you do, more of it will touch you. The dose should be just right." She slipped his blindfold off, allowing him to crane round and see what she was doing. She was piling more nettles on top of the others! "You'll need to stay very still," she told him. "One move and the whole lot will come cascading down all around you."

"Uhhm-mghhh-mghhh!" he said.

"Now," she told, him, bringing her face close to his. "I'm going to go next door and pleasure myself. I brought a whole box of tricks, should keep me going all night. So I'll probably have a long lie-in. That means I'll come and look in on you, tomorrow afternoon. The nettles will probably have wilted by then, so I'll get you some new ones."

"Muugggggggghhhhh!" he said. But she ignored him, throwing her tunic onto the ground. She walked slowly from the room, waggling her barely skirted bottom at him.

"Oh yes, almost forgot, that pink stuff I gave you was a powerful laxative. I like my men to have willpower. If your pants are still pristine by tomorrow afternoon, then I might be tempted to untie you. If not, well you can't expect me to touch you, can you? I'd have to up and leave. And no-one else has booked this cottage till the spring, so you really would be a little bit stuck. Good luck!"

Michael let out a long, muffled wail and he felt the pressure already beginning to build at his rear end. Suzy clicked off the light and closed the door.

*****

"Well, this is a problem," said Helen. After walking for ten minutes, they were stood at a five-way junction in the dirt track that led from the car park, surrounded by thick pine forest.

"Logically, there should be a signpost informing us which track leads to the hostel," declared Mycroft, through the sheeting rain.

"Logically, based on the available visual evidence, there isn't," replied Dylan.

"So which way do we go?" asked Helen.

"I fear this might be a question for Messrs Eeny, Meeny, Miny and Mo," said Bernie.

Half an hour later they were hopelessly lost, and feeling colder and colder as the intensifying rain gradually penetrated their clothing.

Chapter Seven

"I see your belly has grown some more, Woking." Byfleet, Overseer of English Hell, leaned back in his chair and grinned. As always, he had seven lit cigarettes in his mouth, and the room reeked of stale tobacco.

Woking tried to keep his voice level. "It does not grow. It cannot grow. You know that."

"And yet, it does." Byfleet rose from his seat, showing off his perfectly muscled body, rippling chest and pancake-flat belly. He was also lantern-jawed and absurdly handsome, despite the perpetual smoking. "Our height can change as we climb the ranks, so why not our girth, in response, perhaps, to indolence or over-indulgence?"

Fury rose within Woking, but still he fought it back. "Indolence? Indolence? I work non-stop to ensure the smooth running of this place while you – you – sit here doing nothing except wait for your little spies to come here and seek out some minor error that you can go running to Him to report!"

"It is a thankless job, but someone has to do it," agreed Byfleet cheerfully. "But a visit from you is rare indeed, I can only assume you've made some blunder so terrible that you feel compelled to convey it to me yourself."

Woking thought about lifting up the huge oak desk that stood between them and using it to slam Byfleet into the far wall of his office (stacked with books, like a human's – what was wrong with a proper cave?). Then, while Byfleet was stunned, Woking could pierce his neck with his fingers, and rip the head clean off. But Woking just stood, unmoving.

"Yes?" prompted Byfleet.

Woking abandoned his happy fantasy, and instead conveyed tersely everything that he'd learned about the prisoner escape.

When Byfleet had finally finished laughing, he asked, "are you going to resign, or wait for Him to fire you?"

"You want my job?" said Woking? "Perhaps we should ask the Lord to swap our responsibilities? Give you all the hard work, while I do the snooping and tale-telling? "

"I think I'll pass," said Byfleet casually. He belched forth a thick cloud of tobacco smoke.

"You misunderstand your position, Byfleet. He escaped not only from Hell, but out of the world of the dead. And he may have taken a piece of Devil technology with him."

"WHAT?" Seven cigarettes tumbled to the floor.

"On an incident of this magnitude, the Overseer bears equal blame with the Administrator. Otherwise, what is the point of you?"

Byfleet scrabbled to pick up his lit cigarettes from among the mass of dog-ends on the floor. "What do we know?" he asked, cautiously.

"That he somehow passed from the Abysmal Plain back into the Mortal World, something that you once assured me was no longer possible. The Failsafe Protocol, wasn't it? You set it up, back when you did actual work. You told me that, as soon as a dead soul tries to pass into the Mortal World, then bang! Every portal seals up, and remains sealed for hours, until a senior devil unlocks them."

"Well, we had to, ahhh, relax it a bit after the Hat Incident," Byfleet admitted.

"Remind me," said Woking.

Byfleet sighed. "It was 1607, and we'd had the protocol in place for 82 years with nothing going wrong, but then this man who'd just died and walked through a portal, suddenly realised that he'd forgotten his hat, so he nipped back to get it."

Woking roared with laughter. "And he set off the failsafe! I remember now! The Others were furious!! All those dead souls who couldn't pass over. A lot of them wandered off before we managed to reset things. Some of them are still hiding in old mansions and rickety houses, aren't they? How did you not get dispelled for all that?"

"I was deemed too valuable," sneered Byfleet.

"Yeah, right," scoffed Woking. "Poured the blame onto some underling, I'll bet. So you modified the failsafe, I assume?"

"We were all for getting rid of it, but the Others wanted a defence against mass escapes. You know how they're always so skittish about dead souls invading the world of the living."

"Satan does like to remind them," smirked Woking.

"So it's been greatly relaxed. The barriers don't shut down unless fifty or more souls try to exit in rapid succession."

"Which couldn't possibly happen, so it's basically useless," concluded Woking.

"Yes. The Others told us we ought to be perfectly capable of stopping one or two souls sneaking out, and if not, well, they'd be happy to send a team to take over!"

"Sanctimonious Wimples!" said Woking. "So one soul could have slipped back into the mortal world, undetected?"

"Or two, three, or even ten or twenty! You are sure it's just the one escape, are you?"

"Yes," lied Woking.

"You don't sound very sure," Byfleet's smug grin had returned now, with interest.

Black smoke started hissing out of Woking's ears and back. "Perhaps you would like to assist with the ongoing room check, if it concerns you so?"

"If your team is really so inadequate, I could ask Satan to find you reinforcements," said Byfleet.

"I'd prefer if you checked our defences," said Woking.

"Defences?" said Byfleet, surprised.

"You've felt the earthquakes, haven't you?"

"You know why they're happening?"

"No, and that worries me. It can't be coincidence. I think the escaped soul might want revenge."

"On us? How ridiculous! Based on what evidence?"

"None yet … just a feeling."

"Oh, a *feeling*," mocked Byfleet, dropping a spent butt from his mouth. "Well then, we'd best summon the armies of all the other Hells immediately!"

Woking scowled.

Byfleet casually conjured a new lit cigarette between his fingers, and added it to his mouth. "If you do have cause for concern, double up on surface duty, that's standard procedure," he said, rising to his feet. "But otherwise, while I do enjoy hearing about your blunders, I don't see how else this concerns me." Woking stood with clenched fists for a moment, then strode from the room.

Outside the office, Woking found Aldershot. "You here for me, or him?" Woking growled.

"You, Sir! I was told you'd be here, Sir!" barked Aldershot. Woking could not tell if he was lying. But he did guess, correctly, that Byfleet was now eavesdropping from the inside of his door.

Byfleet could not hear what Aldershot said next, because it came out in a quiet mumble. But he had no trouble at all hearing Woking's reply:

"WHAT DO YOU MEAN, YOU'VE LOST HIM AGAIN!?!?"

*****

Natalia reached the back of the stage with twenty seconds to spare, and Martin trailing mutely behind. "Everyone ready?" said Lucy. They'd just seen an impossibly complex Scottish country dance on the stage: twelve women interweaving and twirling with metronomic precision. Lucy's heart filled with terror: even on their best day ever, they could never follow that.

"I no warm up," said Natalia.

"I know and I'm sorry," said Lucy. "Just do your best, okay? I'll make it up to you. Anyone any questions?"

"Uh, yeah," said Janelle. "Can you remind me how it starts?"

The announcer was calling them forward onto the stage. They obeyed. "Oh come on, you gotta remember," hissed Lucy. "We practiced the fucker every day last week!"

"Yeah, it's just the first step … it's totally gone. Must be the stress. What is it?"

"Lys, fill her in, for God's sake!"

"Actually, Lu, I kinda forgot it too."

"'Talia? Please?" said Lucy helplessly.

"I just follow. You say that okay. You say need fourth person, you say I just follow and it okay."

"Lu, quit messing and just tell us how it starts!"

"I can't bloody remember it either," snapped Lucy.

"Then what the fuck do we do?"

"Someone name a dance – any dance!"

"La Macarena?" said Natalia.

"I mean a bloody folk dance," growled Lucy. The band played an opening chord.

The four girls looked helplessly at each other. Even their everyday barn dance routines refused to be recalled.

Then the music started proper, and the four of them stuck out their arms, and did the Macarena to it in perfect time.

*****

"There it is!! The h-hostel!! We've f-f-f-found it!!" declared Helen, as a gothic looking building hoved into view in a clearing ahead of them.

"Two f-f-f-fuckin' hours, it's taken," said Dylan.

"When I meet the warden there will be stern words," said Bernie, who for once wasn't smiling. "Stern words!"

"Those t-tracks were like a m-maze," stuttered Dylan.

"Indeed there were similarities," said Mycroft. "Repeated branching, irrational bending and lots of dead ends, all separated by impenetrable barriers of a vegetable nature. Moreover none of the tracks bar the correct one served any clear purpose. However, a few simple signposts would have shortened our walk to just ten minutes."

"L-lets just get inside and dry off," said Helen.

The main door was locked. They banged on it for several minutes before working their way round the building, looking for lights, movement, and signs that the building was inhabited. They found none.

"Whadda we do?" wailed Dylan.

"I feel obliged to remind everyone that the minibus is spending the night in Glasgow, and therefore we lack the option of retreat," contributed Mycroft.

"Yes, thanks for that," said Helen. "Look, the rest of you shelter in this porch while I keep looking. Mycroft, try and get a signal and call the hostel association."

"The chance of success is exceedingly small. I have been checking for signal periodically in anticipation of such a request, and there has been none."

"Then check some more! Climb on the fucking roof if you have to! Give me strength!" she stalked off for another circuit of the building. Dylan, Bernie and the still silent Denny hunkered down in the porch, trying to protect themselves from the wind with their rucksacks. They watched Mycroft make a systematic sweep of the yard, with his mobile held high, before he moved out of sight. Ten minutes later, all three felt chilled to the core, but then the door swung open behind them.

"What is this?" came a deep voice from the dark corridor.

"We-w-we-we-we're …" said Dylan, through chattering teeth.

"G-g-g-guests," said Bernie.

"Do you know the time?" said the very tall man from the corridor.

The three sodden boys tried and failed to locate their watches from under their clothing.

"I'll tell you shall I? A quarter to midnight. Is this, I enquire, an appropriate time to be arriving at a hostel?"

Dylan tried to explain that they'd been outside for the last twenty minutes at least, trying to get in. Bernie wanted to say that they'd been lost for two hours before that, because there weren't any signs, but neither got past a few stuttering words.

"No excuse? Why am I not surprised? Well I've locked the bedrooms. The only room still open is the drying room. You can sleep in there.

"W-w-warm?" said Dylan.

Dragging the sodden rucksacks, they followed the man to a door. "In there," he grunted. "I've locked the toilets, so you'll have to hang on till morning. You're lucky I let you in at all."

"Uhh, th-there's two more outside."

The warden's expression darkened ever further. "And why, pray tell, did they not come in with you when they had the chance?"

"Th-they were looking for a way in."

"Well they can keep looking. I'm not opening that door again. They can sleep in the coal shed. Now get in there before I kick you out as well!"

Too weak and cold to argue, they stumbled into the drying room. A wall of damp steam hit them. The room was warm, yes, but not very. It was just about big enough for three people to lie down in, not that they'd want to, given the layer of grimy water on the floor. The top half of the room was completely filled by perhaps a hundred sodden items of walking gear, most of them dripping, and all of them stinking. The boys had to crouch, push them aside, or squeeze between them. The air was so moist they could actually see droplets in the air.

Dylan heard the click as the landlord locked the door. He tried the handle, just to be sure. "Oh Helen, I hope you're OK out there," he whispered to himself.

Miserably they forced off their clinging damp clothes, and searched in vain for a free space to hang them.

"No point anyway," said Dylan. "Nothing's gonna dry in this."

"We can't sleep in here!" said Bernie, indicating the centimetre deep puddle on the floor.

"Urghh, there's a nappy" said Denny. The other two looked round in puzzlement, before they realised who'd spoken.

"Machine washable nappies are the vogue, darling," said Bernie, making a heroic effort at levity.

"Maybe, but this one hasn't been," replied Denny.

"If you find any clean ones, let me know," said Bernie. "There's no toilet in here, so we might be needing them."

*****

Mycroft and Helen stared at the empty porch. "Maybe they got in?" she suggested.

"Then why would they abandon their colleagues in such a way?" replied Mycroft.

50

Helen banged on the door. "They took our stuff in, they must be intending to come back." She continued banging for fifteen minutes before she felt too cold to continue. "I th-think they're in t-t-trouble," she said through chattering teeth.

"Notwithstanding that you may be correct, I believe our own predicament is more immediate," said Mycroft, who'd been running on the spot to keep warm.

"S-s-suggestions?" stammered Helen.

"Our only asset is shared body warmth," said Mycroft. "I suggest we retire to the coalshed in the yard, remove our clothes, and embrace one another in a non-sexual fashion."

"C-coalshed," said Helen, and she staggered across to it, Mycroft striding calmly alongside her. "B-b-burn coal," she said, but the wind was blowing in exactly the wrong direction, and the coal was all sodden.

"We can pile up the coal at the entrance, make a shelter inside," said Mycroft. Helen could barely think now, so she nodded. They scrambled in under the corrugated roof and began shoving the coal out from under them, gradually piling it up under the entrance, until finally they had a sort of cave where at last they had respite from the wind. Helen felt marginally warmer for the work, but desperately tired. "Now we need to share body heat," said Mycroft, calmly stripping off his clothes.

Helen paused, miserably wondering if she'd live till the morning. Half-naked in a coal shed with Mycroft. Was that what it would say on her tombstone? Still, her fevered mind supposed, she'd slept with exactly one man and one woman during her short life, so perhaps one Mycroft would complete the set. And he did somehow seem to have kept himself warm. *It's the only chance you've got, girl*, an inner voice told her. She sighed and fought her way out of her sopping wet clothes. But even as she clung to Mycroft for his meagre body warmth, she felt the outside temperature start to plummet. On the few coal chunks that caught the light, she watched ice crystals forming with unnerving speed.

Dylan, Bernie and Denny had piled up all the wet clothing on one side of the room, and were sitting on it. The legion of hangers above them were now empty, save for three soiled nappies and a used condom that they'd thought were best left where they were. The three boys sat on top of the pile, in their underpants, watching drops of sweaty water form on the ceiling and plunge one by one into the lake on the floor. The lake was now four centimetres deep.

"Where's the water coming from?" said Dylan.

"Condensation, baby" said Bernie.

"No, no, he's right," said Denny. "If you filled the whole room with water vapour and condensed the lot, it wouldn't be as much water as there is on the floor now. It's being pumped in from somewhere."

Yet there was no pump. No vents of any kind letting air in or out. Just a tightly shut door and a lukewarm radiator. The stinking, muggy air was getting thicker. So thick, in fact, that it was starting to rain. Drops of liquid that could have come straight from a wrestler's armpit began to patter onto their heads. Half an hour later the water was more than a foot deep, and they were struggling to breathe.

*****

"How many is that, now?" asked Lucy.

"Twenty-six," said Lysandra.

"Why we no go?" asked Natalia.

"Yes, we should leave," agreed Martin.

"We can't leave," said Lucy. "We've already arrived late AND done the most embarrassing demonstration dance in human history. I don't want the hat-trick! Plus we don't know where we're staying – they booked it."

On stage was the grumpy old dance teacher woman who had met them when they arrived. She was tall and wiry, with very sharp looking nails. "Now, the award for the cleanest shoes worn by a demonstration dance team," said the woman on the stage. The nominations are…"

"I no care," said Natalia. "Is most boring thing ever."

"Yes," said Martin. "It is."

The woman called out the names of every visiting society except theirs, as she had done for every set of nominations.

"There'll be a polka dance at the end," said Lucy casually. "It's a simple couples dance that any fucker can do." Martin's face lit up, and his heart started beating faster again. He didn't notice a new set of tremors from the floor below.

"What's with all these little earthquakes?" said Janelle nervously.

"We should stay to the end," said Martin cautiously.

A group of seven women and one man trooped onto stage to collect the award for cleanest shoes. "Their shoes aren't even that clean," muttered Lysandra.

"And finally," said the woman on stage. She paused, shaking her head theatrically. "We've never done this before, and I suspect we never will again. However … it is with great regret that I must introduce the award, if you can call it that, for the worst dance of the evening. There is only one nomination."

"Oh no," said Lucy, burying her head in her hands.

"I told you we should have gone," said Natalia.

"And you were right," said Martin.

"They were late. They were unprepared. They did a dance other than the one that was on the program. Worse, it was not a recognised folk dance. They have brought shame on our organisation, and that cannot go unpunished. Please bring to the stage, the Stoke University Folk Dance Society."

Suddenly surrounded by burly men and women, Lucy and her group had no choice but to walk onto the stage.

"You are not among the accused," the old woman said to Martin.

"I stand with my ship-mates," he replied, boldly. "I mean, my minibus-mates."

"Then you shall bear witness. Stoke Folk Dance Society, I find you guilty of a series of unforgiveable crimes against folk dancing. There can only be one sentence. Bring out the scaffolds."

Five mouths fell open in horror. "But it wasn't THAT bad?" said Lucy, desperately. "We – we were trying to do something post-modern."

"Post-modern?" Said the woman. "Don't make it worse for yourselves."

The curtain behind the stage drew back to reveal a four-person scaffold. The four girls were roughly grabbed, and their hands tied behind their backs. Tartan-patterned shoe bags were then pulled over their heads. Strong hands gripped Martin as he tried to prevent it.

"Hang them," said the woman.

Chapter Eight

Sonny Money was dead. Either that, or he was very soon going to be. He wasn't sure which, but he also didn't think it mattered much either way. He was tightly gagged and taped to a chair in his own flat; he had no idea how Barry Walton had found it. Of all the little creeps he'd dealt with in his time, he'd never have believed that Barry would be the one to come back at him. Perhaps that was why he'd fallen for that sucker-punch.

There were two captors, and he couldn't work out which one was more terrifying. Barry was walking and talking like Barry, seemingly oblivious to the hideous physical injuries he was carrying. The other was bright red, with horns and a tail. It felt horribly like a bad trip, but very real as well.

"Now let's go through it once more," said the red one. "After the moment of death, a portal will open. It'll be larger than usual and last longer, because the veil has been weakened. That helps us. He'll get out of the chair, believing himself to have escaped somehow. He'll try to get to the lift."

"Lift's out of order," said Barry. They'd had to ascend five flights of stairs.

"I know, but it won't be for him. Understand? But you have to delay him, make sure I get there first. Otherwise the portal could vanish!"

"H-how? He's tougher than me, and you said he'll be the same as me afterwards."

"He'll be confused. He can no more harm you than you can harm him. Wrestle him, or talk to him. Tell him the lift is going to take him to Hell. It'll be true!"

"Will there be another Devil in the lift?"

"Usually one would be called," agreed Fenwick, pausing to recall the exact rules, "but because I'm here, that won't happen. It'll be empty. Probably on fire, though. They're usually on fire."

"So you and he ... go down to Hell."

"Yes."

"Wh-what about me? Should I come with you?"

"Technically, yes. But since you've helped me, I'm willing to let you run loose for a while if you want."

"Not sure I do," said Barry sadly. In the few hours he'd spent with Fenwick, he'd felt a strange sort of peace. Fenwick had taught him how to be seen, and to interact with the physical world, something that other ghosts took centuries to master, if they ever did. Once this was done, Barry had spent most of the time hitting, threatening and generally terrifying a series of people who had swiftly led him to Sonny Money. He felt no guilt though, for this at least, because he'd simply been following orders that he'd been compelled to obey. He found himself wishing that someone had been pulling his strings like this for the rest of his life, as well; it'd take away some of the remorse that was tormenting him. Perhaps only Hell could do that, he thought.

"Whatever," said Fenwick. "Guess we're ready as we'll ever be. Shoot him."

Barry waited emotionlessly for his arm to pick up the pistol and put it to Sonny's head. It didn't. He looked down at it in surprise.

"Go on, shoot him," repeated Fenwick.

Again, no response. "Is that an order?" Barry asked, gently.

"Umm, no," said Fenwick. "More of a suggestion."

"I assumed you were just going to order me, like you did everything else."

"Well … this guy is your arch enemy, not mine. I've got nothing against him. You're the one whose life he ruined. You should be the one to kill him."

"It wasn't really him," said Barry. "Don't get me wrong, he's a heartless bastard alright, but it was my stupid fault it all happened. I knew what he was when I borrowed money from him."

"This is ridiculous!" said Fenwick. "This man is scum! You killed a good man today, a teacher! This is your only chance to make amends!"

"No," said Barry.

"NO?!!" yelled Fenwick, his eyes blazing red.

"No," said Barry.

"And why, in the name of Gabriel and Every Sainted Angel, not?"

Barry turned to Fenwick, and raised a wobbling arm to point at him. "Hello?!? B-because you're a red Devil with horns and a tail. Tempting me to do terrible things. Why on earth do you think? I'm not falling for it! I killed one man by accident, but no, that's not enough for you, you want me to damn myself completely by killing another in cold blood. Well I won't! If it's so important to you, order me to do it, like you did everything else! Go on!"

"But then it would be me killing him, not you," screamed Fenwick.

"And the problem with that is?" yelled Barry.

"Not allowed," mumbled Fenwick, sheepishly.

"Not allowed?" repeated Barry.

"The bastards have taken away my license to kill."

"Why would they do that?" asked Barry, smirking.

"There was … an incident. It wasn't my fault. Look, just shoot the guy, please!! I've got to get back! If those living souls pass through into Hell, the whole place will implode! It'll be an apocalypse!"

"Don't be ridiculous," said Barry.

"It's true!!"

"So you're not allowed to kill, but it's fine to manipulate some other poor sod into doing it for you?"

"Yup."

"Then we've got a problem, because I'm not doing it," said Barry.

"All of creation's in danger!" pleaded Fenwick.

"Bullshit," said Barry.

"Do you know how much torment I can cause you?" hissed Fenwick, his eyes narrowing.

"At least it's torment that's due to me."

Dammit, thought Fenwick, *why did I have to get a contrite one?* He changed tack, bringing his face close to Sonny's instead. "You. You're going to kill Barry's sister and her kid if you get out of here alive, aren't you? Nod if you agree."

Sonny shook his head vigorously. If by some miracle he got out of this, he was going to run off and live in a monastery somewhere.

Fenwick howled with frustration. "I'm not kidding. There really are living souls heading for Hell. You saw them, that minibus."

"Yes, it killed me!!"

"And now one of two things will happen. Either they cross into Hell still alive, and undo all creation, or the Abysmal Plain will feed off their nightmares and destroy them. Helping me will save lives!"

Barry sighed. "Even if that's all true, I can't just shoot this man. There has to be another way. You have to *find* another way. What about the hospital? People die there every day – some of them must be headed your way!"

"Again, not allowed," mumbled Fenwick.

"You're useless!"

"That's what Satan said, too," agreed Fenwick, sadly.

"Where else do people die? How bad do they have to be?" asked Barry.

"Anyone who isn't a total do-gooder would do, I suppose. Most of you are 'grey' souls – somewhere in the middle. You get a sign and a door and a stairway down to Hell, where you serve your time and then go on to Heaven."

"What? That's not right!" said Barry.

"No, it's just not what they *tell* you. People can't wash away all their sins with a couple of Hail Marys and expect a free pass up to Heaven! Every sin has to be paid for, in Hell! Unless the balance is way into the blue."

"So I get to reach Heaven, in the end?" Barry wore a pleading expression, as he felt the sudden torment of hope.

"Not you, I'm afraid. You're too far in the red."

Barry sagged, accepting his fate once more. "So you picked out Sonny Money here because you thought I might shoot him, but in fact any old bugger who's done a few sins would get you back to Hell?"

"The staircase would be slower, but yes."

"Mmmm!" said Sonny, suddenly.

"Got something to tell us?" asked Fenwick. "Something useful?"

Sonny nodded. Fenwick ripped the tape off his mouth as roughly as he could, enjoying the resultant yelp. Sonny spoke rapidly: "Informant, Peter Bellman, they're going to off him tonight! Grassed on Redmond's mob! He lives on Craven Terrace! Number six I think!"

"Do the Redmond Mob normally tell you their business?" asked Fenwick.

"They offered me to join the hit!"

"What do you think, Barry?" asked Fenwick. "Telling the truth?"

"I believe him, let's go!" said Barry.

"If you're lying, you'll regret it," said Fenwick, slapping the tape back on Sonny's mouth. Then they ran from the room.

*****

Martin watched in horror as four kilted men tried to get nooses over the struggling girls' heads. "WAIT!" he shouted. "Let me take Natalia's place!"

"Prepare a fifth sc-" began the old woman, but she was cut off by a massive rumble as the floor shook wildly. The four hooded girls fell to the floor, and the kilted men toppled backwards off the stage. Cracks appeared in the ceiling above, and showers of white dust fell from them. The massed people on the dance floor began screaming in fear.

Something clicked in Martin's mind. "Yes!" he called. "I will die a thousand deaths before I let you hurt Natalia!!"

Another tremor shook the stage. The thugs who'd been holding him fled the stage and joined the throng trying to squeeze through the exit doors. But the old woman rounded on him, her eyes burning with hatred. "What have you done?" she snarled.

Martin ignored her, scrambling to untie Natalia's hands. He couldn't find the knot. "She's the most beautiful woman I've ever seen!" he declared. A third tremor followed, the strongest yet. A zigzag crack appeared in the stage. The old woman drew a ski-dubh knife from her sock, and bore down on Martin.

"You'll have to fight her," said Natalia, who'd also caught on. "Fight her for me!"

The fourth tremor threw the woman to the ground. Martin found his feet. "One chance," he said to her. "Leave now."

The old woman cracked a grin. "Get ready to die, boy." Her teeth were sharply pointed, like those of a crocodile.

"Are those false teeth?" Martin asked.

"All mine," she replied. Her flesh was redder than it had been, he was sure, and there was a strange bulge around the back of her dress, over the bottom. He made a grab for her knife-hand, trying to wrestle it from her. Yet she was impossibly strong. She pushed the knife towards his chest, and even with both hands he couldn't hold it back. Closer it inched, closer. He caught a whiff of stinking sulphur on her breath.

At the back of the stage, Lysandra had managed to grab Lucy's hood with her bound hands, and pull it off. Lucy made it into a kneeling position, and returned the favour, before getting unsteadily to her feet. "Get Natalia's hood," she whispered.

Martin lay on the stage with the old woman on top of him, the knife now almost touching his flesh. "I'll do your girlfriend next" she whispered. Yet even so close to death, Martin's heart leapt at her choice of words, bringing another tremor, distracting the woman just enough for him to push the knife back an inch. Then it was moving towards him again and –

"Take that, bitch!"

Lucy's foot connected hard with the old woman's face. Martin pushed his stunned assailant off him, and turned to see Lucy spinning helplessly on one foot and crashing to the floor, shouting "Ow, my fucking foot!" as she went. Martin staggered to his feet, and the old woman did likewise.

"Ooh, she's got some spunk," said the woman. "That almost hurt."

Martin saw that there was hardly a mark on the old woman. Impossible. She was grinning again. Her teeth had got sharper, her skin redder. A ripping sound came from behind her. Martin wondered how he could possibly beat her, but he was willing to die trying. She put the knife in her mouth, began sharpening it on her teeth.

"Martin, look up!" said Natalia. He obeyed. A huge concrete beam was hanging perilously above where he was standing.

"Come on you evil bitch," he said. "Let's finish this." He backed away carefully, drawing her under the beam, and himself out from under it. The old woman swished her knife at him, the blade glinting as it sliced through the air.

"Come to granny," she purred.

"Natalia, you're wonderful!" cried Martin. A slight tremor.

"Martin, I love you!" she called back. A deafening rumble began, by far the strongest yet, and the ground moved so violently that both he and the woman lost their footing. The building vibrated and wobbled, and an almighty crack came from above. The old woman crouched, raising her knife again. Her eyes blazed red and two horns erupted through her hair. Then five tonnes of concrete fell on her and smashed her through the stage.

"Or maybe just friend," called Natalia. The rumbling abruptly stopped.

"Can you get her knife?" gasped Lucy, wincing from the pain in her foot.

Martin, feeling dazed, confused and a little bit devastated, stumbled over to the huge hole in the stage. Luck was with them: a red hand was sticking out from under the slab of concrete, and a knife was in it. He scrambled down and took it. The red fingers flexed as he did so; Martin yelped. Something was moving in the rubble too, moving like a snake. Something red with a pointed end. He scrambled from the hole as fast as he could. "She's still alive!"

"So cut us free and let's get out of here!" said Lucy.

*****

"The afterlife is real, and I have proof," the second text message had said. It had correctly predicted the major headlines from the following evening and morning, including some that no amount of inside knowledge could have helped with, like the fatal accident on the M6 involving a killer on the run from police. He'd even known the man's name. Yet the last line had surprised Theo most of all: an invite to a meeting. The Broker was about to reveal himself.

Since the cancer diagnosis had been confirmed, he had been feeling unwell. He realised now that he'd been unwell for a long time, but had simply denied it, and managed to feel well in his head. That pretence had been shattered, and nothing much mattered now – not image, not sex, not even money. Nothing but the Broker and his claim to know what waited for Theo on the other side. Because, surely, that was what the texts really meant.

The receptionist in the foyer of the large building directed him up. There was no company listed for the floor he was sent to; no names at all. Just the number 18. Before the lift doors could close, another man joined him. He was about Theo's age, and wrapped in a tobacco-soaked leather jacket. The man had loose, scruffy hair and two scars on his face. He too pressed 18, and they rode up together. The doors opened and the other man sauntered out, walking with shambling confidence. Theo almost asked him outright if he was the Broker, but instead merely followed. It was no challenge finding the way: the lift opened out into a single corridor, with firmly shut doors along it, but an open one at its end. He followed the man through.

He walked into what looked like a board meeting. The room contained a huge, long table, with a dozen men already seated at its sides, and several more seats empty. At the near end of the table were glasses of champagne; he took one. At its head, the far end from him, stood a short, dull looking man in his fifties. "Come in both of you, please take a seat and a drink. Our final guests will be with us shortly."

It took ten minutes for the last few to arrive. No-one spoke. Theo recognised some of his fellow attendees: one was a disgraced politician, and a few others were millionaires. Of the rest, some looked and dressed like businessmen, but others had a much rougher air about them, like the man from the lift. Yet they acted a lot less out of place here than Theo felt. He'd expected a one-on-one meeting.

One of the older businessmen coughed, projecting a large luminous glob of mucus across the table, landing just short of the leather-jacketed man. "Don't worry," croaked the businessman. "It's nothing you can catch."

"Fortunately, I did," said the short man, walking over and peeling up some clingfilm that covered an area a foot across, into the centre of which the glob had landed. He balled it up carefully and dropped it into a bin, leaving behind a spotlessly clean table. One by one the astonished guests began running their fingers over the table, searching for more clingfilm. There was none.

When the last guest had taken his seat, and the short man cleared his throat. "Thank you, Sir Herbert, for that unexpected demonstration. Well, I expected it of course. But then, I can tell the future, as you have all seen. You all know me as the Broker. Everyone in this room has benefitted from my advice to the tune of at least a million pounds over the past ten years. However money, nice as it is, is not really very much use anymore. Not to dying men, at least, which all of you are."

Theo saw many different reactions in the room. A few showed horror, as if they hadn't known; others did a double-take, indicating perhaps that they'd known, but thought no-one else did. Yet half the room, like him, gave no reaction.

"From a few months to five years. Some of you don't even know it yet. One person here has a trained assassin on his tail, a man who doesn't miss. I could stop him, of course, if I chose to, but I'm offering something better. To all of you."

"Let's start at the beginning. When most human beings die, our consciousness, or soul if you prefer, travels first to a place called the Abysmal Plain. This has existed for as long as we have, perhaps far longer. When the first humans died it was empty and featureless. But it responds to conscious thought, and when a few living humans found a way to go there, they inadvertently constructed an afterlife that conformed to their beliefs. Devils and Angels were called into being, and later Heaven and Hell. These beings are compelled to pass judgement, and to treat our dead souls accordingly, because that is what those first visitors believed that they would do."

"You're saying Man created God?" said one man. "How can you possibly know all this? How do I know you're not a cheap showman?"

"Not God, that's a whole other issue," said the Broker. "As for your accusation, I believe I've earned the right to be heard out. After that, you'll be quite free to shuffle off. Now where was I? Oh yes. Human travellers to the afterlife created Heaven and Hell, and the denizens of both, which gradually organised themselves into the forms that exist today. Hell has become an extremely complex operation, because over a hundred thousand human souls die every day, and most of them go first to Hell."

"First?" said one businessman.

"Oh yes. About three fifths of humans live lives that are judged to be 'grey' – somewhere in the middle – they do some good things, some bad. Heaven and Hell fought a war over what happens to them! But now it's been agreed, they serve time in Hell for the bad things they've done, then go on up to Heaven to be rewarded for the good ones. Only if you've been overwhelmingly good, do you get to skip Hell. And for those who've mostly been bad, it's a long time in Hell, and no Heaven."

"You're serious? It's supposed to be one or the other!"

"Says who?" asked the Broker. "You're just parroting one religion. In reality, the deeds of our lives are weighed up objectively, by one representative of each side, a bit like our adversarial court system. The dead man gets no plea, no appeal. Every action, every word is totted up. Any consequence that a person knew, expected or even suspected for his actions, is included. So if you dump a barrel of toxic waste into a lake and it ruptures a hundred years later, killing a child, you would pay the same penalty as if you had dropped it straight onto a child's head today.

"Which is not good news for many of us here," he continued. "There are men in this room who have killed with their bare hands – don't worry, they're friends. My point is, that's just one death on their card, albeit one they get full credit for. Yet a business decision that helps cause a hundred deaths, maybe a thousand? Even if responsibility is equally shared among ten men who may never meet each other. Well, the credit gets shared equally, too. Ten deaths each, maybe a hundred. And some of us are making decisions like that every week. If you work in arms, in chemicals, in oil. If you cut corners on safety to boost your profits. They even get you for obstructing action on climate change!"

"That is a legitimate viewpoint," bristled newspaper proprietor Duncan McGregor. "And now I know that you are talking nonsense."

"Let me say to you this," declared the Broker. "All of us here are damned. We are going to Hell when we die, and there's not a thing any of you can do to prevent it. But there may be something *I* can do. However, first of all there's a little tradition that needs to be followed." He picked up a stuffed white cat from the chair in front of him, and started to stroke it. "Anyone who does not believe in me, will be free to exit at this point. To exit this life, I mean. Because, the first man who attempts to leave this room will be dead before he reaches the door."

The Broker drank in all the horrified looks, and tickled the ear of his inanimate cat.

Chapter Nine

Fenwick and Barry parked the car a block away from Peter Bellman's house. Fenwick was dressed in one of Sonny Money's tracksuits, his tail duct-taped to his back. With a baseball cap and shades, he just about passed for human in the yellow glow of the streetlights.

"We mustn't spook the hitmen," said Fenwick. "If they see us outside, they'll think we're cops and abort. Make yourself invisible, and follow them in. Your job is to intercept Peter when he dies, give me time to reach the portal. I'll wait outside, out of sight, until I hear gunshots. Assuming he is a 'grey' soul, the white sign and stairway will probably form in his garden, but it could be in his bedroom. But if he's a badass, there'll be a fiery portal to Hell of some sort, but no Devil if I'm close by. Same thing – delay him. Now we walk the rest, find me a hiding spot, and wait for the action"

As they walked, they passed a white van that had been there from before they'd arrived. Its occupants were neither policemen nor Redmond mob hitmen, but they watched Barry and Fenwick keenly, nonetheless.

*****

Searing pains in his tongue forced Bagshot awake. He snapped shut his mouth, beheading the two yellow birds that had been biting into his tongue. The two severed heads tweeted angrily at him as he spat them out, then all the birds vanished. Alone, Bagshot staggered to his feet, trying to ignore the burning pain as the parts of him injured by the tyres knitted themselves back together. He tried to work out what had just happened.

The soul who'd been driving could not be Barry Walton, because a dead soul would have been compelled by his voice. Therefore, the driver had to be a construct, a figment of Walton's imagination, but those constructs created at the point of death were exceptionally weak, and this one had not been. The minibus, too, had been solid. Bagshot felt a wave of dread. Humans who died with psychedelic drugs in their veins were a major problem for Devils, for they could conjure far more powerful constructs. Once – Bagshot shuddered to remember it – a dead soul who'd died from an LSD overdose had attacked the Gates of Hell with an army of giant polka-dotted flying rhinoceroses. It had taken weeks to clear up the mess. Now, souls weren't allowed to pass over until the drugs cleared from their system, but Bagshot reasoned that with Fenwick on harvesting duty, he'd probably forgotten. The only other possibility was live souls on the plain, but that hadn't happened for centuries.

Bagshot summoned up what courage he had. Mickleham and Fenwick could share the blame for this colossal foul-up, while he, Bagshot, would capture the fugitive soul and save the day. Then maybe they'd let him back on room duty. Even if powered by drugs, a dead soul could not conjure new constructs, so all Bagshot need do was avoid that terrifying driver, or better still, trick it. She'd said something about Walton being ill, which gave him an idea. Bagshot began forming pieces of metal out of the ground, drawing them out and assembling them into a vehicle. This, at least, he knew exactly how to do. When he'd finished, he jumped into the newly created ambulance and drove it off, following the tracks where the minibus had gone.

***

Lysandra led her friends through the crumbling corridors of the dance hall. They staggered through the front door, and turned to see the building collapse in on itself completely, behind them.

"I hope everyone got out," said Janelle.

"I'm not even sure they existed," said Martin.

"Bad place," said Natalia. "It is alive."

The battered yellow minibus was still there, but the surroundings had completely changed. Beyond it, damp pavements and streets stretched in all directions, with dark and grim tower blocks beside them. A man in a kilt wandered by, chewing on what they assumed was a haggis, and carrying a can of lager in his other hand. Someone was playing bagpipes, badly, in the distance. Further down the road, a group of men were having a fight for no apparent reason.

"What's going on here, Natalia?" asked Lucy.

"Why you ask me?" said Natalia.

"You seem to understand it better than anyone else," said Lucy simply.

"I no understand. But we are not in normal place. This place is thinking. Fighting, sometimes."

"It's like, it knows what we expect," said Martin.

"Wotder fook ahh yee Eenglysh shytes deein' hoor?" said a ruddy-faced man clad in leather and tartan, who'd just walked up to them.

"I no understand," said Natalia, earnestly. The man repeated what he'd said, more loudly. "A'm Saucy Jock," he added. "Welcome tae Glasgae!"

"Has anyone here ever been to Glasgow?" asked Martin.

The girls all shook their heads.

"But how did you imagine it would be?" he asked. "Outside of the dance venue, I mean?"

"Wet."

"Dark."

"Lots of drunks."

"Fighting."

"And bagpipes?" asked Martin. At least three pipers were now audible, from different directions, completely out of tune with each other.

"And bagpipes," admitted Janelle.

A group of grizzled policemen were cordoning off a murder scene further up the road. "And I'm guessing at least someone here's watched *Taggart*," pondered Martin.

"You're saying this place forms into what we expect of it?" asked Lucy

"Torkin' ootter shyte, mon" said Saucy Jock.

"How can this be happening?" asked Janelle, clutching her cross.

"It's like a shared dream," said Lysandra.

"More like a nightmare," shivered Janelle.

"If so it's a shared nightmare," said Martin. "It seemed to build what we expected to see, then turned it all against us. I'm worried it might be doing the same to the others."

"Maybe secret police take them," said Natalia. "You have in Scotland secret police?"

"I think we may have been kidnapped by aliens," said Martin knowledgeably. "We're actually all asleep, like they've put drugs into us, exploring our subconscious." Seeing the horrified expressions on the girls, he made an ill-judged attempt to lighten the mood: "probably they'll be probing our bottoms next."

Lucy's face fell. The guy didn't have a clue after all. Time to take charge. "Everyone in the minibus," she ordered. "We may not know what's going on, but something here tried to kill us, and we need to warn our hiking friends, if we're not already too late." They all piled into the bus.

Natalia had to drive carefully, dodging the plethora of drunks, random fights and chalk-outlined corpses scattered along the road. "We should grab some food," suggested Martin. "Judging from that rain, they might need it."

"What do you suggest, chips, chips or chips?" asked Lucy, looking at the range available along the road.

"Whichever serves fastest," said Martin.

"Double chips wi' haggis fuh me!" said Saucy Jock, who'd somehow got into the bus with them.

Behind them, something shuddered in the pile of rubble that had briefly been a dance hall. A red pointed tail burst through, then began picking up and throwing aside chunks of slate and concrete. In time the full figure emerged: a bright red old woman in a shredded dress. She snarled. Young people should never have been allowed to participate in dance festivals. Now, as a result, her lovely dance hall was destroyed. Someone was going to pay. Hissing with fury, she began walking along the street, tossing aside drunks, combatants and murder squad detectives as she went. After a while she got bored walking, and stole a police car.

*****

The Broker was calmly sipping his drink, stroking his dead stuffed cat, and enjoying the shocked silence around the table. Then he broke into a smile. "Oh the cat?" he enquired meekly. "I tried it with a live one, damn thing clawed my hand. But you're much nicer to me after our visit to mister Taxy-Dermy, now, aren't we?"

Theo saw the man opposite him mouth the words "stark, raving mad," but he could also see that the man was sweating.

"Is this some sort of joke?" said a man in his sixties who Theo thought he recognised.

"Well let's see," said the Broker happily. "We have Mister O'Flaherty here, ex-IRA. We have a Scottish gentleman who's asked that I don't give his name. And plenty of Englishmen. I suppose three of you *could* walk into a bar. But the first one who tried to leave this room would drop dead."

"I mean that ridiculous stuffed cat! And the theatrical threat!!"

"Ohh, don't listen to the nasty man, Snuggles. It's not a threat, by the way, it's a prediction. Are you going to test it?"

"Not just yet," said the man.

"What about you, Mr McGregor? Are you going to apply some of that famous blind conviction you demand from your editors, to this situation? Is this yet another case of all the experts being wrong, while you alone know the truth?"

"I don't recognise you as an expert in anything," sneered McGregor.

The short man raised the stuffed cat to his ear, briefly. "Yes, Snuggles, he is being rude to me. May I remind you, McGregor, of all the exclusives you've had thanks to tip-offs from me? The rural affairs minister who thought he'd got a sheep pregnant? The senior royal trapped in a loo for forty minutes because there wasn't any paper? The senior minister who made his fortune from slave labour in the Philippines?"

"YOU did that??" roared a tall man, standing up.

"Calm down, Sir Antony. *The Guardian* were on to you for weeks beforehand. I just tipped Duncan off so he could scoop them."

"And I haven't forgotten the gross exaggerations he printed," said Sir Antony, glaring at McGregor.

"If you can't do the time, don't do the crime," retorted McGregor.

"He did (cough!) stick it to the (cough-cough) *Guardian* though," croaked Sir Herbert, sending another glob of mucus flying across the table. It landed on a piece of clingfilm that the short man had earlier placed on Mr Leather Jacket's shoulder.

"So you see, I'm an expert on everything," said the Broker. "And it matters not at all what I think. The Devils calculate your sentence."

"Sentence?" asked Sir Antony.

"Oh yes, the tallying of deeds does not simply determine our destination," said the Broker. "It determines the length of time we will spend there, until the slate is wiped clean. The average sentence for all of us in this room is well over ten thousand years. Admittedly, I do bump up the average a bit."

"What if we (*cough! cough! guuuaaarrrgghhh*) repent?" croaked Sir Herbert, while the men opposite him made ready to dodge.

"You misunderstand the rules. There is no reward, no pardon for repentance; the Christians made that bit up. Only actions are considered. You could give away your fortune and if you do it cleverly, you might cut your sentence. Unfortunately, saving lives is a lot harder than remotely destroying them. Trust me, I've experimented extensively with both. I'm afraid all the money in this room, even if we spent it well, would do little more than halve your sentence, Sir Herbert."

"The point is," said the Broker, "the Devils' computers take into account every word and action, and every outcome stretching forward hundreds of years."

"Computers?" scoffed McGregor. "What Rubbish. They don't have computers in Hell."

"Oh they do," said the short man. "Very different from ours, of course. They have technicians who imagine what they need, then call it into existence. In fact, I have appropriated one very special such machine for myself."

"Show me," said McGregor.

"No, I'm not going to do that," said the Broker. "You can trust me, or you can not."

McGregor shifted awkwardly in his seat. Then a solitary pair of hands began to clap. "Brilliant!" said their owner, a smart looking man in his forties who hadn't spoken yet. "'Follow me,' he says. 'Believe in me, or burn in Hell.' Yet when physical proof is demanded, he declines. We are witnessing a new religion, born right in front of us. How long have you spent setting this up?"

"Twenty-three years, give or take," answered the Broker.

"So you are the Broker, and we must follow you or be Damned?"

"That's about the size of it, Nigel."

"And if we choose not to?"

"I've already told you. You'll die fairly soon, and go to Hell for a very long time. Of course if you try to leave now, you'll be dead within minutes."

"How can you possibly fall for this," Nigel said, addressing the room. "I mean, look at you! You're leaders of men! People fear you! And yet here you all sit like idiot sheep!"

"If you think he's wrong, prove it," said Theo.

"What?" said Nigel.

"If you're sure he's wrong, walk out the door."

"More parlour tricks. A booby-trap, probably. Hell, he's probably rigged a trap door with crocodiles."

"I tried, but Health and Safety wouldn't allow it," said the Broker. "Said I could have hamsters instead. I passed. There are no obstacles, I promise. I guarantee that I will do nothing to harm you, if you attempt to leave. But what I said before stands."

"There'll be some kind of trap," repeated Nigel. "I know how men like you operate."

"Let me settle this," said Theo, rising suddenly to his feet. His legs, unprepared for this sudden act of folly, almost gave out under him. He managed to steady himself, though his chair clattered onto its back. "Look," he continued, skipping clumsily over to the door. "No traps." He danced from one foot to the other like a mad thing, hoping like Hell he'd remembered the Broker's exact words correctly. *First man who attempts to leave.* He wasn't attempting to leave. He wondered, suddenly, how long it was since he'd last danced, and whether he'd ever get to do it again. For a finale, he pulled the door open and shut a couple of times; nothing happened. Then he bowed, self-consciously, and returned to his seat. The Broker favoured him with a smile.

Nigel turned suddenly and strode straight for the door. He'd almost reached it when he stopped, bent double, and began clutching at his chest.

"You feeling alright, old chap?" asked the Broker.

"What ... did ... you ... do?" gasped Nigel. "Said ... you ... wouldn't ... hurt me."

"Would someone please pull him over a seat? I fear he won't get back to the table, and it's so undignified to simply fall over." The nearest man obliged. "I kept my word, when I said I wouldn't hurt you. I don't need to, because I already had. I knew you'd betray me, knew which glass you'd take, too. So I poisoned it. Setting the dose for the perfect timing, now that was quite tricky. Nothing personal, you understand, it's just you're more use to me dead than alive, if you don't believe in me."

Seated now, the dying man let out a few last moans.

"He'll be dead in about ninety seconds. When that happens, he'll experience judgement. It'll only last a few seconds, but will feel much longer for him. Then he'll forget it's happened, and think he's alive again. That he escaped this room like he planned to. He'll make for the lift. They'll probably take him there."

"Who will?"

"Devils. It'll be two of them, given the events of yesterday. They're spooked. And then, well, wait and see."

*****

The warden was feeling confused. He lived by a simple code: those who broke minor rules lost privileges, and those who broke bigger rules weren't let in at all. Any resultant distress, disease, hypothermia or death was not his concern. People should obey the rules or stay somewhere else. The desperate banging on both the drying room door and the side entrance were of no concern to him, and had both stopped a while ago anyway.

This wasn't what troubled him. It was the sudden, strange urge to stick futuristic electronic probes up his guests' bottoms. He'd first noticed it about twenty minutes ago, and it had been getting steadily stronger. It unsettled him so much so that he'd read the hostel regulations through twice over, looking for a mention of it. He couldn't understand this at all: he was getting an urge to do something not in the rules.

He also wanted to throw all five of them into the dungeon. He hadn't known until now that his building had had a dungeon, having never needed to visit the cellar before, but he'd gone down there five minutes ago and discovered not one dungeon, but two: one was a dark medieval style torture chamber, the other a modern one stocked with kinky outfits and modern killing devices. There were two further rooms down there, too: one contained a brightly lit table with a huge piece of rectal probing equipment above it; the other a police interrogation chamber with a brutal looking Russian man in it, who saluted when he looked in. The Warden had grabbed the Russian by the scruff of his thick fur jacket and propelled him out of the front door, because however strange things might be getting, he wasn't having anyone in the building who hadn't paid their ten percent in advance.

The warden felt tormented; he couldn't decide which one of those rooms he should use for his guests. He'd had yet another idea pop into his head, that he should force the five of them to sit through a two hour "hiking club of the year" award ceremony, at the end of which he'd award them the Worst Organised Club of All Time" award, receipt of which carried a mandatory death sentence. Thinking he must have missed it last time, he reached again for the solace of the regulations book.

Meanwhile in the drying room, the lake of sweat was rising steadily. Dylan gulped and gasped desperately, but the air was now so wet he could barely breathe. He made one last effort to prop up his unconscious colleagues against each other, their heads as far above the water as he could, before himself losing consciousness. The sweat lake began licking at their chins.

Ten miles away, the yellow minibus was struggling up the bumpy, ill-maintained road to the hostel through the sheeting rain. Mist, huge puddles and cracks in the road were slowing them down. Inside, each of the five humans had been imagining their own idea of what horrors the Wacky Walkers club were being subjected to. They were trying not to, but they couldn't help it.

*****

In the coal shed, Helen knew she was nearing the end. Ice was forming on all the wet lumps of coal around her, as the temperature outside continued to plummet. Even the warmth from Mycroft's body wasn't enough. He had all four limbs wrapped around her almost naked body, and hadn't even raised the ghost of an erection. In her delirious state, she couldn't work out if she was relieved or offended. Probably both. She knew he was OK, because he'd been calmly reciting to her the text of a lengthy first aid manual, in the mistaken belief that this would help her stay awake. The windows of the hostel. They'd all been barred. Why was that? To keep people out, or to keep them in? This was strange, she thought. A strange place in which to die.

Chapter Ten

In the drying room, the water now lapped at Dylan, Denny and Bernie's mouths, and was starting to trickle into their lungs. In a few moments, it'd be over. Then, quite suddenly, the drying room door clicked open, and the water surged out into the hallway, and down the stairs to the basement. One by one, the boys were dragged down there, too.

*****

Peter Bellman was shaking. It was ten days since he'd gone to the cops, and he'd been starting to think that he'd got away with it, but then had come the earth tremors. His wife had joked that they were a pair of Godzillas escaped from some film studio. The telly news had no idea what they were. But for Peter, it felt like an omen, signalling his personal doom.

He wanted to run, but he couldn't. His wife didn't know what he'd done, what he'd been. Drawn into the Redmonds' world by greed and stupidity, until the only way out had been to use the police. He'd thought he could keep it a secret, that no-one would know it was him. He'd refused protective custody because that of course would mean telling his wife. No, as long as they didn't know who had told, he was fine. But they did know. Since the tremors, he'd felt strangely sure. And they were coming. If he took his wife with him, he'd have to tell her; if he didn't, they might shoot her instead. So he waited downstairs with the lights off and a baseball bat in his hand, while she slept above. If they came, he would at least make a fight of it.

He heard something, a sort of whining noise. The kitchen! He crept through the hall to its door. There were three silhouettes behind the back door, drilling through the lock. He wondered about going out the front door and running around to behind them, but too much with that could go wrong. No, he should hide behind the living room door, here, let them go past, clobber the last one, then play it by ear.

His heart beat so fast he felt sure it would give him away. Something fell onto the floor in the kitchen, and the back door swung open. A torchlight played across the floor of the hall. Three of them stalked past quietly. Then a gap. *Now or never.* He stepped out behind the third one, and brought the bat down hard on his head. The man fell forward onto the second one, while the first shouted something and wheeled round. On instinct Peter dropped down too, hoping they'd miss him in the dark, among the heap. The first man fired two shots into the corridor. "Come out and take your medicine, grass," he yelled.

"Where is he?" yelled the second man, getting up.

"Living room, must be!" said the first.

The second man moved forward and Peter, with the strength of the desperate, picked him up and threw him onto the first. Peter then grabbed the bat and lunged forward, bringing it down on one of the heads as he lost his balance and pitched forward. There were three more shots. Peter felt a dull thud in his shoulder, and realised he'd been hit. Then came his wife's voice from upstairs, "Peter? What's happening?"

"Get in the bedroom and lock the door! Call the police, phone's on the table!" As he spoke he half staggered, half stumbled backwards, unsure where the gun was but desperate to avoid being an easy target. It fired twice more, and he heard something shatter. He'd lost the bat, couldn't wield it now anyway. He staggered into the living room.

The man appeared at the door, and clicked the light on. Peter recognised him as Sharkboy, Redmond's lead enforcer. "Now Peter," said Sharkboy. "I'll admit, that was impressive. But that's enough, now. You're behind the sofa, aren't you? Come out and give me a clear shot, and I'll leave your wife alone. Make me come round and get you, and I'll do her afterwards. You got five seconds to choose." He started counting, but Peter emerged on four, hands up and eyes closed. "Good boy."

A gun fired twice. Peter clutched his chest, and found it intact; he opened his eyes. Sharkboy staggered backwards, blood spurting from his body. Then the right side of his face exploded. He pitched forward. Peter saw that there was now a third man in the room, horribly burnt and disfigured, yet pointing the gun he'd just fired at Sharkboy's body. Then the burnt man spoke. "Y-you're a good man aren't you, Peter? Underneath it all, I mean? A good man? B-because I think I've staked my soul on it."

"I'm trying to be," said Peter, starting to shake. "I'm trying to be."

"Keep trying," said Barry. "You never know when you'll stop getting the chance." Then he turned, and shouted, "Fenwick, it's time!"

"Who's Fenwick?" said Peter. "Who are you? You've burnt your face!"

Behind Peter, Sharkboy's soul was rising to its feet. Barry was looking around desperately for signs of a portal.

"It's alright," said Peter, as the dead soul headed for the kitchen. "I think we got them all!"

"Fenwick!! He's heading for the garden!" yelled Barry. He followed Sharkboy through the kitchen and overtook him at the door. "Fenwick, quickly!"

"We need to get away," said Sharkboy, as if in a daze. "There's a getaway car coming!"

"Yes, a red one, I imagine," said Barry. He could hear an unearthly rumbling and screeching, getting closer.

"FENWICK!" He glanced around wildly.

A red car with a burning bonnet crashed through the hedge. "Get in!" yelled the driver.

Sharkboy ran towards it. "FENWICK!" yelled Barry again. "Where the fuck are you?!?!" He looked at the car's driver, and knew something had gone badly wrong.

A second man in black stumbled out of the house, with a baseball bat shaped dent in his head. Peter, it seemed, could really hit. He too climbed into the car.

The driver, whose seat also seemed to be on fire, now turned his gaze towards Barry. "You. Dead guy. Come."

Barry had no choice but to walk toward the car. "FENWICK!" he screamed, as loud as he could. "For God's sake get over here quick!" But he didn't. Barry sat down in the back with the man he'd killed, and his mate. The doors slammed shut. The driver turned round to them, and his face glowed fiery red as he bared his shark's teeth.

"Going *down*," he declared, and cackled with delight. The two men in black wailed in terror as the car tipped forwards and a burning tunnel opened up in the grass. The car plunged into it, and their screams faded out of the mortal world. Peter watched, blinking, from the kitchen door. Had he dreamt the red car? He stumbled back into the house. Only one of his attackers was stirring, the one by the front door. Peter picked up a gun from the living room. "I suggest staying put until the cops arrive," Peter told him.

By now, the white van was several blocks away, with its unconscious captive inside. It was pursued by a flock of nine yellow birds, tweeting angrily.

*****

Nigel Milligan's eyes snapped open. Through hazy vision he looked at the room around him. "Seems you survived my little trap," said the Broker. "Ho-hum."

"You'll be hearing from my solicitor," growled Milligan, stumbling to his feet.

"I really don't think we will," replied the Broker. Around the table, the others looked confused, as if they couldn't see who the Broker was talking to.

"Go to Hell," said Milligan.

"That's the plan!"

Milligan stumbled through the door, wondering what they'd put in his drink. Perhaps if he could find a bathroom, get water. No, the lift was a better idea. Get out of here as quick as he could. As he walked towards it, one of the side doors opened and two men walked out. One was African, in his attire as well as his colour; the other looked Indian. They followed him to the lift. Its doors pinged open as he reached them, and a wave of terrible heat hit him. He staggered back but two red grinning creatures emerged from the doors, beckoning him forward. He knew he had to go to them, though he didn't know why. Then two strong arms grabbed him and threw him backwards. After that, he heard howling.

The African man was spraying liquid nitrogen into the lift. Milligan watched the two figures stumble out of the lift, each clutching their eyes with one hand, and searching for their assailants with the other. Then the Indian man struck first one, then the other, on the head with a huge hammer, and they crumpled to the ground. Milligan noticed the reek of sulphur as two large, bright red figures were dragged past him, each with a limp tail slithering along behind them. "Broker," he shouted. "You can stop with the student pranks now!"

An answer came, instead, from the Indian man. "Milligan," he said.

"Yes?"

"Tell them we've got their mates."

Then he and the African man grabbed an arm each and propelled Milligan into the burning hot elevator. The doors slammed shut and he let out a scream as it plunged downwards.

*****

The sound of the doorbell came as a surprise to Suzy. She opened the door to find a figure covered head to toe in protective white hospital overalls, so she couldn't see his face.

"Good evening, err... " the figure paused, crouched down and took a good look up Suzy's minimal skirt, "... madam. I am here to collect a man named Barry Walton. He has the plague."

"No Barrys here," she replied. "Try another house."

"He *is* here," countered Bagshot. "I can hear him moaning!"

"Mmmmgghh!!" came Michael's desperate voice from a room upstairs.

"He's not Barry, and you're not having him!" Suzy's eyes hardened.

Bagshot produced a gun from his overall, pointing it at Suzy. "I must insist!"

Suzy thought for a moment, then led him into another room. As she passed through the door she plucked a whip from the wall, spun round and with one swift crack, yanked the gun from Bagshot's hand. With a second expert swish, she caught both his legs, and yanked him off his feet, leaving it wrapped round his ankles. Then she grabbed a barbed whip from the wall and repeatedly flayed his bottom, shredding the back of his white suit as she did so. Bagshot wailed in pain, but that only made her whip him even harder.

Five minutes later he was begging for mercy. "Cuff your hands behind your back," purred Suzy, tossing him some handcuffs, "and I'll stop."

Bagshot, given a moment to think, remembered that he'd planned for things going wrong. "Emergency detonate!" he shouted. The gun he'd built, lying in the hallway, exploded. He'd designed the explosive to dispel any inanimate constructs caught in the blast (not sentient ones, of course, that would have been suicide). The walls and ceilings around it were obliterated in seconds, along with his suit.

"Mmmmmmmmmmmgg!" THUMP!

A bed landed between them, with a half-naked young man tied to it. A wardrobe fell onto Suzy, smashing her to the ground. "Gotcha," said Bagshot in delight as he staggered forward to the bound man, closely followed by "Ouch! Ow! Aaarrgghh!" as a large quantity of stinging nettles came down on top of him. "Walton, you're (ow!) coming with me!" he growled, and he dragged the bed out and into the ambulance with the man still tied to it. It seemed the simplest way to stop anything else going wrong. The cottage collapsed entirely just as he got out.

Bagshot paused briefly to create a doughnut-shaped inflatable cushion for his painful hindquarters, then started the engine and headed for the Gates of Hell.

*****

72

Theo watched in open-mouthed astonishment as the first of the two Devils was dragged into the room, accompanied by the stink of sulphur. The two men hoisted the devil onto the table, then went back to get the second.

"A shame Mr Milligan couldn't wait to see this final proof, but then someone had to die to make it happen," said the Broker. "These are real genuine Devils of Hell. Pretty junior ones, I'd guess."

"I don't mean to be skeptical," said Sir Antony, "but really? Red skin and sulphur, horns and tail? You almost had me convinced, but this? It's comical."

The Broker strode round the table, pulled out a gun and fired three shots, shattering the Devil's head. "What do you expect them to look like? This is the image we've had for centuries. Maybe a few decades of Tim Burton films, and they'll all turn skinny and black. But right now they are red." He paused, noticing that Theo was wiping devil brain off his face with a tissue. "Oh, don't do that," said the Broker.

"What?" said Theo. "You splattered him all over me. What else should I do?"

"Wait."

They waited. The blood on Theo's face and clothes turned to something like jelly, and fell off. Lumps of jelly started flowing back towards the Devil's head, which was slowly rebuilding itself. "Still a skeptic, Sir Antony?" asked the Broker. "Oh, Yassar, open the window, would you?"

The African man did as asked, and a flock of yellow birds flew in, making for the two stricken devils. The one with an intact head was now bound with thick steel wire, which the Indian man had just finished soldering together. The birds made short work of pecking him awake, before settling onto the back of the second Devil, waiting for his head to reform itself so they could peck it. However, the blood Theo had wiped off seemed unable to extricate itself from the tissue, with the result that the tissue became stuck into the rebuilding head, sticking out from the side of its nose.

"Take that one," said the Broker, indicating the tissue-nosed devil. "You know what to do." The two servants dragged the Devil out, with the birds starting to peck its head as they went. "Does anyone still doubt my word?" asked the Broker. "Devils are real. Hell is real. We are all going to go there. The only question is, on whose terms?"

*****

From the ruins of a cottage, there came a series of bangs, then a small pile of rubble and roofing slates was lifted upwards on the door of a wardrobe and thrown aside. The creature that knew itself as Suzy McCabe emerged and rubbed her head curiously, expecting a dent, finding none. A couple of fetching horns, though, that hadn't been there before. She swished her long red tail. Interesting. She could do some fun things to men with that.

It was disappointing to find that her cottage was gone. Still, with her victim stolen, there wasn't much point in keeping it, she supposed. She'd need to find some other man. Yes, that was her purpose: find a man, seduce him, and then torment him. She was good at that. Suzy was a very clever girl. Somewhere very deep in her mind was the idea that she was halfway through a psychology degree, on the way to an easy First. A father and mother who argued a lot, when they weren't shagging other people. Both of them thought she didn't know! How dumb.

She shook off the momentary confusion. She needed to find a man. Briefly she considered pursuing that red creep who'd stolen her original victim, but in truth she was pretty much done with Michael. The red man could keep him.

A rumble of thunder shook the air. In the distance a single, rugged looking mountain was clothed in the blackest clouds she'd ever seen. The only clouds she'd ever seen. Under the rain, she sensed the presence of sexually inexperienced young men. Best kind. She sauntered over to the taxi, still standing where she'd parked it, wiggling her bum as she went. The red skin might put them off, though. With an effort, she turned it pink. The horns on her head sunk back in, and the tail disappeared up her skirt like a retractable cord on a vacuum cleaner. She checked herself out in the wing mirror, and nodded approvingly, before sliding herself into the driver's seat and smoothing down what little there was of her skirt. She gunned the engine and sped off towards the wet mountain.

*****

Sergeant Sergei Sergeyevitch Sergeyev of the Russian secret police was confused. He'd assumed himself to be in a police cell in Chechnya, where it would be his job to find charges for five terrorist suspects that would result in their swift execution. Instead, apparently, he was in a country that was wetter than Khabarovsk and colder than Siberia. And he'd just been thrown out into the sheeting rain. He looked at the door that had slammed behind him, drew out his gun and fired three times into the lock. The lock disintegrated. Sergei shoved at the door, but the wooden bolt on the other side held it shut.

"Y-y-you arrived late too, did you?"

Sergei turned to see a young man wearing only underpants and glasses.

"No, I was expelled from the building for reasons unclear," said Sergei, whose mouth then hung open in surprise at his sudden command of English.

"I have a female companion who will shortly expire from hypothermia," said Mycroft. "Do you think I could borrow your jacket in a probably futile but morally inevitable attempt to save her life?"

"In return, you will immediately assist me in gaining entry to this building and extracting a confession from the traitor who expelled me from it," said Sergei, removing his coat. Mycroft nodded, took it, and rapidly clambered back through the gap in the pile of coal, to Helen's unconscious form. He wrapped the dry fur jacket around her. It wouldn't be enough. If he left her, she'd freeze.

"Come out, Englishman," said Sergei. "You must help me immediately, and if you do not, then you have lied to Russian police and must be interrogated then shot."

"I will render assistance in two minutes' time," said Mycroft, thinking fast. When those minutes were over, a strange humpbacked creature emerged from the coalshed, wearing Sergei's coat. It had extra legs, the back two hanging limply. Each sleeve had two hands at its end, and at the top an extra female head lolled insensibly behind the male one. "In order to prolong her life, my body heat was necessary," explained the creature. "Yet in order to preserve mine, I am committed to assist you. Therefore I am wearing her on my back, and your coat over both of us. It is fortunate that you are a large man, and that in consequence your coat is big enough."

"Is there another door?" asked Sergei.

"Ninety degrees anti-clockwise around the house," replied Mycroft. So they walked around, but the door was still locked. Sergei fired four rounds at the lock, but this made no difference, for this door too was bolted from within.

"Is there any other door?" asked Sergei.

"No," said Mycroft. "And the windows are all barred."

"Then you must climb to the roof and go in that way."

"There's no way up. The walls are smooth, and no drainpipes."

"Then you have failed me, and are no use. I must interrogate and shoot you."

"Need some help?"

They wheeled around to see the four dancers and Martin emerging into the courtyard from the forest. All were already thoroughly soaked, except parts of Natalia, who was squeezed into a raincoat several sizes too small for her.

"What happened here?" asked Lucy. Then her eyes widened. "Mycroft, what the fuck are you doing to Helen?"

"Keeping her warm," said Mycroft.

"And who's your friend?" asked Lysandra.

"This is a representative of the Russian secret police, whose presence here I cannot at this time explain. He will shortly be interrogating and then shooting me, unless we can find a way to gain access to the hostel."

"Russian secret police?" said Lucy. "Fuck me, Martin was right. This place responds to what we think. Tash, you got a poor opinion of your countrymen."

"I no think Russian police be here" replied Natalia. "I believe what Martin say about aliens, because he was right before."

"So who imagined the Russian ... ah, never mind," said Lucy, seeing Martin's sheepish expression.

Sergei turned to Natalia. "You are from mother Russia. It will be you I interrogate and shoot."

"Start by asking who taught her to drive," muttered Janelle. Martin immediately placed himself between Natalia and the gun.

"Are the other three in there?" asked Lucy.

"We think so," said Mycroft.

"Aaahh!" said Natalia, suddenly. "I can feel them!"

"What?" said Lucy. "What can you feel?"

"Pain and great fear," said Natalia. "And soon, death!"

Chapter Eleven

"FOR WHAT CAUSE HAVE YOU SUMMONED ME HERE, YOU STEAMING TURDS ?" roared Satan Beelzebub III, as flames danced all over his body. The thick hairs on his torso stuck outwards, which on top of his already massive bulk almost filled his end of the room.

"W-well it's an extraordinary Cabal meeting," said Bracknell, a small nervous Devil with buck teeth and crossed eyes. "D-didn't you get the memo, Sir?"

"Of course he got the memo, you dimwit," growled Woking, beside him. "That's his traditional greeting."

"Well I don't know, I've never been to one of these before," said Bracknell.

"And who is this confounded imbecile who disgraces my domain with his stupidity?" bellowed Satan, his long curling horns glowing with displeasure as he indicated Bracknell.

"And I guess that's how he greets new people, is it?" asked Bracknell to Woking, with a nervous grin.

"No, he said that especially for you," replied Woking.

"This is Bracknell, my Lord," said Camberley. "He was the designer of the device from Room X10101."

"I see," boomed Satan. "Describe this device."

"Well it..." began Camberley.

"You," added Satan, pointing to Bracknell.

"It's an-an-an innovative concept in torment, your Lordship," said Bracknell. "It's based on the same predictive technology we use to evaluate newly dead souls. It makes him experience the consequences of his actions."

"Some dead souls would like that," said Byfleet. He was fidgeting constantly, Woking noted with some pleasure, due no doubt to the absence of cigarettes in his mouth.

"Y-you misunderstand," said Bracknell. "I mean, it makes him LIVE it. OK, example. He brokered a deal to sell land mines to a dictator. So it makes him live through the experience of every man, woman and child who was harmed by that choice. First, the one who was blown up. And then, in turn, every mother, spouse, child or friend who suffered grief and loss because of it. Then onto the next one."

"I recall this idea," boomed Satan.

"Well, it won awards, my Lordship" said Bracknell coyly. "For innovation. We were going to make more."

"Going to?" enquired Satan, softly. "It would be a terrible waste of such a brilliant idea to *not* make more, I should think. Assuming of course," his voice darkened, "it worked properly?"

"Ah," said Bracknell. "It was experimental technology, you understand."

"Expand please," said Satan.

"The soul in the room, a very clever human called Brian Coker, found a way to control it,' said Bracknell.

"WHAT?" roared Satan. "Camberley! Explain!"

"The device reached into his mind to pick out decisions from which to extrapolate consequences and for quite a few years it worked very well but then the soul worked out what it was doing and after that he started to be able to tell which decisions it responded to I'm sorry sir and then the soul learned how to invent false decisions that he'd never actually made but tricked the machine into believing he'd made so it played him the consequences of decisions he'd invented like paying high class prostitutes to seek out desperate virgin males and ..."

"He was using it for PLEASURE!?!" roared Satan.

"We caught it very quickly sir it was only a year or two sir please don't dispel me" blurted Camberley.

"So you destroyed the machine and found an alternative torment, with interest?" demanded Satan.

"Err, no," admitted Camberley. "The paperwork would have been horrible. You'd've had to sign several forms yourself, sir, if we were to reassign..."

"Yes, yes. What DID you do?" growled Satan.

"Well, once we knew what the problem was, we could add in psychic locks to the machine," said Bracknell. "Hold it to its assigned purpose. Strapped to his chair, the soul could not remove them."

"And this worked?"

"We checked over several years, it appeared to," said Camberley.

"So remind me," said Satan, "where is the predictor device, now?" He turned his gaze to Woking.

Woking's skin sizzled as sweat broke through. "It isn't there, my Lord. It was taken from the machine!"

"By the soul from Room X10101?"

"We have to assume he has it, my Lord. We still haven't found him."

Satan rose to his feet. "Tell me, which one of you should I dispel over this colossal incompetence!? I've heard enough. Woking, I'm going to ask you to return to this room in a few minutes, and bring with you the two Devils who you feel bear most responsibility for this failure."

Woking looked stunned. This was a massive departure from protocol. "I select Camberley –"

"What?" said Camberley? "How can you pin this on me? Bracknell made the device!"

"...and Aldershot," said Woking.

"Me?" shouted Aldershot. "I had nothing to do with any of this!"

"You were in overall charge of Fenwick! You could have checked, at any time, to find where he was, and you never did! If you had done, all this would have been cleared up two decades ago! You total, utter cassock! Worse than Fenwick!! Hating the man is no excuse, this is Hell!! Everyone hates everyone, it's the rules!"

Aldershot fell silent. Satan grinned a hideous grin. "Very well. I'll see you back here in the boardroom in a minute. At least one of you will be dispelled tonight."

The assembled Devils looked at him in shock. A very small Devil wearing glasses, who'd been diligently taking minutes beside Satan, gingerly raised his hand.

"Yes, Mytchett?" said Satan.

"Great Leader, should we not complete this meeting before you begin summary punishments?"

Satan glared at him for a moment with a face full of fury. Then he broke out into gales of thunderous laughter. "Just my little joke, gentlemen! Got it from a TV show, '*The Appendix*' I think it's called. An angry man pulls people into his office and fires one of them each week. I love it! But isn't it useful, to find out who everyone blames for this little problem?"

Woking, Camberley and Aldershot exchanged venomous glances, each trying to hide their relief, while everyone nervously applauded Satan for his deception.

"Please summarise recent events, Woking," said Satan.

"Fenwick was found in Room Zero, which was emptied of souls. The soul from X10101 had cut through the wall into Room Zero with a Devil knife, somehow rendered Fenwick unconscious, and bound him with strips of wall. We must assume he took the device with him. He then cut through into a third room, the Disco Room. From here, we don't know how, but he got out of the rooms altogether. He may have cut through a further wall, then somehow re-formed it. This happened twenty-three years ago. The likelihood is, he escaped back into the Mortal World at some point subsequently. Byfleet's failsafe would not have stopped him."

"It should not have been possible!" roared Satan.

"There may have been a way – Sir!" said Aldershot. "Contrary to my colleague's dishonest accusations, I do keep a close eye on Fenwick – Sir!"

"No you don't!" countered Woking.

"Get to the point!" boomed Satan.

"Fenwick is recorded as having journeyed to the surface some time after his last visit to room Zero – Sir!" said Aldershot. "He went to the surface and never came back. We thought he had got lost or gone native – Sir! He did it once before, remember?"

"He was punished," said Woking. "And restrictions were made on his abilities."

"I know that," snapped Aldershot. "But the point is, we searched for him at the surface!"

"You think the soul escaped to the surface disguised as Fenwick?" said Woking. "That doesn't say much for you as Fenwick's handler!"

"I don't know *how* he did it!" insisted Aldershot. "But it's the only thing that makes sense – Sir!"

"Ah," said Bracknell brightly. "I believe I can explain. If he disabled the psychic locks on my machine, he could have used it to test out in his mind every possible means of escape, and whether it would work or not. So in time he'd have found one that did."

The rest of the table fixed him with exasperated and furious expressions.

"… which is obviously really unfortunate," Bracknell concluded.

"Is it really that bad?" said Byfleet. "No, bear with me, please. Before the War, there was a time when we regularly intervened in the mortal world, tempting the weak, giving powers to those who were evil, knowing that we'd make them pay for their deeds later on. This escape, well, it's the same thing, isn't it? An extremely bad man is among the living, with a device that makes him powerful. That lets him know the outcome of his every choice. He can cause untold suffering all over the world. He can become unimaginably rich with that predictor, while everyone else gets poorer. Inequality breeds conflict. This is a massive win for us! And of course, up in the mortal realm, he'll start ageing again. We'll get him back soon enough."

"Your point is a good one, though it does not excuse your incompetence," said Satan. "Nor any of you. Your punishments will be severe, but they can wait. Now tell me something more. I have felt tremors within Hell over the last few hours. I cannot feel their source, yet I sense something is amiss, and I do not believe in coincidence. What else has gone wrong?"

Woking looked meaningfully at Aldershot.

Aldershot quivered for a moment, then with an effort straightened his back and shouted: "Following your orders, Fenwick was sent to the surface – Sir! He was fully briefed and reminded of every protocol – Sir! But that was hours ago and he has not returned – Sir!"

"AGAIN?" roared Satan. "Can you not keep him on a lead?"

"I shall do that in future – Sir!" barked Aldershot. "However, the fact is that Fenwick gets lost, stuck or delayed all the time – Sir! I would not want to trouble you with every such incident, or you would be sick of the sight of me – Sir!"

"I already am," declared Satan.

"It is not significant – Sir! Fenwick will be blundering around the Mortal Plane, seeking a route back to Hell – Sir! When he gets here you can decide his punishment – Sir!"

"*I* will decide what is significant!!" boomed Satan. "Fenwick disappears once, and a condemned soul escapes! He disappears again, and suddenly we have unexplained tremors! I sense a connection! I demand answers!!! Find this escaped soul, find out what he's doing. What he's using our device for! And why the ground is shaking! Go!" roared Satan.

The Cabal Room doors burst open. A junior Devil ran in. "Ten billion apologies, my Lord and Master, but we have been attacked! Ashtead and Frimley, taken prisoner by the living!"

Gasps of Horror swept the room, and various senior Angels were named in vain. Finally Satan spoke again, his voice deceptively calm. "Byfleet, tell me again your theory of how Coker can only do good things for us?"

*****

79

Frimley's awareness returned slowly. He could smell stale gasoline, and his head hurt like crazy. He'd been sent to collect a human called Milligan, then something had been sprayed in his face, and after that, nothing. He noticed a tissue sticking out of the side of his nose. What had happened to him?

A horn blared at him. He saw a blurred image of a large vehicle beside him, and a red figure leaning down. "Get up here quick! We need to get out of here!"

"Use the emergency recall!"

"I can't! It's not working! We need to get onto open road and run someone down."

"What happened?" asked Frimley. He was standing now, but his head felt like the inside of a thundercloud, and his vision remained infuriatingly blurred.

"They took us down to the basement, put us in some kind of sealed container with a bomb. Said they were going to blow us into pieces so small they'd flush us down the drain. Somehow you got on top of the bomb, took the blast, left me intact. I fought them off, carried you here in a bucket ... most of you. But there's pieces of both of us missing. We have to get away, and come back with an army!"

Frimley climbed into the vehicle. A truck. He found himself in the driver's seat. "You should drive," he told the other – Ashtead, wasn't it? "I can't see clearly, think part of my eyes must be missing."

"I can't drive either," said the other. "One hand! I'll watch the road for you. Now go!"

Frimley wondered what could have made a Devil of Hell so fearful that he'd run off and leave an arm behind. But with his own body so weak, and his vision so poor, he felt that running away was perhaps the right idea. This time. He started the engine and the truck surged out of the car park, bumping two cars and demolishing a barrier as it went.

"You keep driving, I'll scan for a human with appropriate background. We need a really bad one – get us there faster!"

"But we can't kill them – you know how Heaven will react – "

"Emergency protocol! If it's the only way to return to Hell we're allowed to take a life."

Frimley's head hurt so much that he didn't even try to argue. Normal protocol was to go to hospitals, wasn't it? You'd soon find a suitable person dying there without breaking the rules. But this had been a direct attack, and he agreed that the bosses needed to know.

"There!"

Frimley followed the pointing hand. All he could see was a blurred figure. "Who is he?"

"Small time drug dealer. Certainly ours. Look, I'm not sure if you can hit him, so let's stick him in the front with us and then kill him. Then we can drive straight to Hell and we'll be there in no time!"

"Great plan!" agreed Frimley, glad Ashtead was taking charge. They hopped out of the cab and approached the figure.

"Wot's wiv the fancy dress, you poofs?"

"Manners!" yelled Frimley, and broke the man's nose. They bundled him into the passenger seat, and got in either side of him. Frimley wrapped his tail round the man's throat and told him to remain still. The truck rumbled on, narrowly avoiding collisions as they jumped red lights and mounted pavements, before emerging onto a road between fields.

"Here?" said Frimley.

"Here."

Frimley snapped the drug dealer's neck as if it were a biscuit. Held suddenly in time, Frimley watched the man's life replay, albeit in blurred form: a schoolyard bully who was picked on by larger kids and took it out on smaller ones. Parents who'd thought him a nuisance from the moment he was born, and never changed their minds. The gradual descent from sniffing glue to dealing class A drugs, and all that came with it. The blue bar had barely got started when Frimley had snuffed out his life.

Then the man woke up. "Get your fucking tail off my neck, you poof," he told Frimley.

"You're the boss," said Frimley happily. There was a turning to the left that hadn't been there before, with flames by the roadside, and they took it. The road to hell had appeared, but no Devil had been summoned because Frimley was there. His presence, coupled with the recent damage to the mortal veil that had been caused by Natalia's driving, prevented the vehicle from separating into real and spectral forms, as would normally have happened. So the truck thundered on down towards Hell with its cargo, leaving no trace behind it.

In time, Frimley's truck emerged onto the Abysmal plain. "Where the fuck is this place?" said the dead man. "Looks like fucking Mars."

"Haven't you worked it out yet?" asked Frimley with a grin. It felt good to be back on safe ground.

"What, you're one of those Jeremy fucking Beadle shows?"

"Does this look like fancy dress to you?" asked Frimley, baring his triangular teeth.

"OK, so yours is good, but your mate's is shite. The paint's running on his face, and that fucking tail is stuffed."

"What?" said Frimley. He squinted at his companion, whose red colour did indeed appear to be now streaked with pink. He grabbed for the tail, and it came away in his hand. "Imposter!" gasped Frimley.

"Guilty as charged," said the other, and pressed a button on something in his hand.

Frimley's head exploded. The truck careered wildly to a stop.

"They can rebuild themselves, but if something gets stuck inside them, they can't get rid of it," said the fancy dress man. "They don't even know it's there! So we stuck cataracts into his eyes and a nice little bomb in his head."

"Wot the fuck is going on?" said the drug dealer.

"What's your name?"

"Preston White."

"Now I've got bad news and good news, Preston White. The bad news is, you're dead, our friend with the exploded head killed you about ten minutes ago. The good news is, the afterlife's getting a makeover, and it just so happens I've got a vacancy for a man with your talents. So you can stick with me, or you can go to Hell."

"Lemme think," said Preston.

"I would, but this isn't a place for miracles."

"I don't fucking trust you."

"You can wait for his head to regrow, if you prefer." Already bits of blood and brain were crawling around the cab towards Frimley's neck. Preston recoiled in horror.

"Okay I'm with ya!"

"Then help me get him out. All of him!" They yanked Frimley's inert form out of the cab, and in due course it was followed by a variety of brain-splattered cloths and tissues, some of which they held onto and scattered along the next mile of the road, to slow down Frimley's reassembly. Kane Winkle drove on down the road, with the shocked Preston beside him.

*****

Fenwick awoke, hands and feet tied together behind his back with steel cables, with an iron ballgag forced into his mouth and a bag over his aching head. He'd been all set to return to Hell, but then something had hit him from behind, knocked him out. He was in a vehicle, moving. There was nothing he could do. After a while, the vehicle began to judder – they had left the road. The van stopped and he was roughly dragged out.

"I have a message for you," said a harsh sounding voice.

"Muhhhghh?" said Fenwick.

"It reads, 'Goodbye forever, you useless cassock!'" Then firm hands picked him up, and swung him forward several feet through the air. He expected to land, but didn't. He fell instead, maybe thirty feet, before hitting hard concrete. He was aware of a churning noise, then the wet slap of concrete pouring over him. It wrapped all around him, pressing harder and harder. After a while he could feel nothing but relentless pressure, and the gradual change as the concrete solidified. In his mind he could see his captors driving away, probably laughing. Hell was in danger, terrible danger, and there was nothing he could do.

*****

"So wot's in the back?" asked Preston.

"Housing enforcement officers," replied the red-painted man, who'd introduced himself as Kane Winkle.

"They some kind of death robots?"

"Close. They're anally retentive council workers."

"You mean they can't take a shite like normal people?"

Kane sighed. "You know the kind of people that make everyone else follow really stupid rules?"

"Wot, teachers?"

"These people make your teachers look reasonable. They go into your house, tell you how things should be. Even if you own the house."

"Bastards," said Preston.

"Well, we've got fifty of 'em in the back," said Kane.

"All tied up? Drugged? Or just locked in?"

Kane felt that he understood Preston a little better for this. "No, they're just sitting waiting for us to arrive. You see, the back end of this vehicle is basically a coach. Only the front cabin looks like a truck. We couldn't have Frimley thinking we had passengers. You and I have just smuggled fifty-one living souls into Hell."

"Won't that piss off the Devil and his men?"

Kane turned to him and smiled. "Hell, yeah."

Chapter Twelve

Denny woke suddenly, and gasped with relief that he could breathe dry air again. The relief was short-lived. He was strapped face-down to a white table, with some sort of electronic device inserted up his bottom. The walls were covered with unfamiliar glowing symbols, and pictures of strange grey humanoids. The electric charge from the device began to grow stronger. Denny screamed.

Dylan found himself in some sort of torture cage, swinging from side to side inside a medieval looking dungeon. There was no room to stand up; his legs were bent and his knees already hurt like hell, pressed as they had been against the bars. Directly below him was a large, boiling vat. Then a figure in the doorway pressed a button. He heard the grinding of some mechanism, and the chain from which he was hanging began to move, ever so slowly lowering him towards the vat. "Please!" he yelled, but the tall figure in the doorway simply grinned. It had hideous, triangular teeth. "Heeeellllllllllpppp!"

Bernie awoke. He tried to move but couldn't. He felt exquisite pain all over his body. Then he noticed the mirror, helpfully provided opposite him, and saw with a shock what had been done to him. He was strapped to a cross at the wrists, ankles and neck. On his torso he wore nothing but tight leather pants, with sharp studs that pointed inwards. "If Miss Pinter could see me now, there'd be stern words", he would have said, had the gimp mask on his head not been zipped shut at the mouth. Miss Pinter was his former Religious Education teacher, who had loathed him so utterly for what he had been. Her persecution had changed him, encouraged his reinvention from shy nervous kid into screaming queen. Now he imagined her standing in the room, ranting furiously at him, spitting abuse, "*get off that cross, now! How dare you defile our Lord and Saviour in this way!?*" It was better than thinking about the rotating mechanical spear that was very slowly but inexorably moving towards the side of his bare chest.

The warden looked in on Bernie, as he had on Denny and Dylan. This felt right. From now on, any breach of the rules, however small, would be punishable by slow, painful and humiliating death.

*****

"Okay," said the Broker. "Apologies for the hassle, but you understand the wisdom of switching buildings, I hope. We've declared war on Satan himself, so we don't want to make it easy for them to find us!" They were seated in a long boardroom, not unlike the one they'd been in before. "I have confirmed to you that Hell exists, and that they will come for us when we die." He indicated the bound Devil in the middle of the table. "You have also seen the lengths I will go to, am

84

going to, to fight back. You can imagine, I think, the sort of penalties they will apply to me for attacking two of their own. So I hope none of you will doubt my utter commitment to this cause. Basically, you have a simple choice: accept millennia of torment, or help me."

"Do you seriously expect to overcome the whole of Hell?" asked Sir Antony.

"Why not?" said the Broker. "My people just bashed two of them without really trying too hard. Yet even so, they'll treat it as some sort of small-scale scheme. A bunch of Satanists who got lucky, or more likely that we want these prisoners for some Earthly purpose. The idea that we'd try to take over down there? They couldn't possibly imagine it, they're not equipped to."

"You sound like you've been down there," said Theo.

"Well, I have it on extremely good authority," smiled the Broker.

"So what now?" said Sir Antony. "You've got one of them tied up. You blew up another one's head. What now?"

"I've done far more than that," said the Broker. "I've smuggled fifty-one living souls onto the Abysmal Plain, and given them very precise instructions. The Devils won't notice until it's too late, because they'll think it's the effects of the first incursion."

"First incursion?"

"Oh, there was an accident last night. Bus full of students accidentally drove into Hell … or rather, to the Plain. Well, I say an accident, it took ten years of fine-tuning events to get exactly the right people into exactly the right places at exactly the right time, but to everyone else it'll look like an accident. You see, in the early days, travelling to the Plain was easy, but later on, Hell's Devils erected what they thought were fool-proof defences against living incursions. They had to, when they realised their little design flaw. However, I found the one human on Earth with the power to break through. In doing so she weakened those barriers, allowing my own team to get through."

"And what are your team doing?" asked Sir Antony.

"Oh, they're building an alternative to Hell," said the Broker casually.

"They're *what*?" said a ruddy-faced Scottish man in a crumpled suit.

"You've heard the phrase, 'suburban hell'? Well, I'm building one."

"And this started when?" said sir Antony.

"Oh, probably about ten minutes from now, give or take."

"But you can't possibly expect to finish by – "

"You forget how the Abysmal plain works. It builds things from human thought. My new town will soon be growing by at least two hundred houses per hour."

"We'll start by offering it as an alternative," said the Broker. "See if they'll listen to reason. A home for the middle men – minor miscreants, fraudsters, and gentlemen who can't keep it in their trousers. Plus of course men like us, who'll be running it. I'll offer the Devils a back-to-basics approach: they get to keep the real criminals, the vicious thugs, murderers and rapists, like they did in the good old days, and not bother themselves with so-called white collar crime. Everybody wins!"

"Won't Heaven object?" asked Theo.

"They won't like it," said the Broker. "But a deal was struck aeons ago: Heaven concerns itself only with rewards, Hell only with sins. Heaven won't interfere as long as we take no-one there who doesn't belong."

"And you think Hell will accede to this?" said Sir Antony.

"Probably not, which is why my New Town is also a central part of my alternative strategy."

"And that is?"

"Regime change."

*****

From inside his concrete tomb, Fenwick wondered how long it would take them to find him this time. Once again he was helpless and immobile, with no-one who might help him having a clue where he was. It could be hundreds of years. He wondered why this sort of thing kept happening to him. Was he really *that* inept? He knew that he'd never really fitted in; he sometimes felt that even his name was out of place, somehow. They hadn't cared about his absence last time. Why would they now?

This time was different, though, because he knew that disaster could be coming. Impossible as it seemed, he got the feeling that Hell might not be there by the time he was dug out, or at least not as he knew it. And yet what could he do? In those long years of being sat on by humans, he had eventually found a way to get back at them. All he'd needed to do was force himself unconscious. It seemed unlikely that this would help him now, but it was better than doing nothing.

*****

"This'll do," said Kane, pulling over. "Come with me, into the coach section."

Preston followed him out of the cab, noting first the utterly featureless land in all directions, and then the strange vehicle he'd been in: the cab of a lorry, with the disguised body of a coach behind it. They entered the coach section via a door at the front. Inside the vehicle, the fifty housing officers had each been watching a video describing the layout and appearance of the New Town, via specially mounted screens on the seats in front.

"So now you know exactly what we're up against," Kane told them. "These rulebreakers cannot be allowed to win. I want every single house slapped with a fail notice for improper something, and I want it done by tomorrow night. Are you with me?"

No-one spoke.

"I'm sorry. Hands up who's with me!?"

Fifty hands went up. "Brilliant!" said Kane. "So split them up between you. I suggest you each take a house, mark the door when you've given it a fail notice, then find another that is not yet marked. Return here when there are no more houses to find. I remind you, you'll none of you do a job more important than this, ever again. And remember, time is precious, so move on to the next house as soon as you find a significant fault."

They nodded, silently, and began to file out in a ridiculously orderly fashion. Preston was standing behind Kane with his mouth hanging open, thinking again that it had to be a big joke. There was no town outside, only grass; was the idea that these useless suits would all pile out of the coach carrying hard-ons for the work they were going to do, only to find bare grass? Would Kane drive off and leave them stranded? It'd be funny, sure, but not *that* funny. Then the passengers started filing past him, and stepping out onto the ... pavement. Preston gawped. There hadn't been pavement before. Unable to resist it, Preston pushed into the line and walked out with them. They were in an open town square, surrounded by curving lanes with small white houses packed tight along both sides. Each house had a small clipped lawn in front with a dull hedge. The housing officers divided up soundlessly, each aiming for a particular front door, and going in.

When the last had dispersed, Kane tapped Preston on the shoulder and pointed. "You see the town governor's mansion, at the end of the street," he said, indicating a huge red building the size of a small palace. "That's where we're going to live." The video on the coach had described this building, in some detail, to the housing officers, whose minds had duly called it into existence.

"Any fit birds in there?"

"There might be," said Kane. "The East Wing is yours; if you meet any women, you bring them in there. Clear?"

"Brilliant!"

Kane was beginning to understand why the Broker had carefully directed him to collect this particular man. Preston had no idea what was going on, and therefore couldn't interfere with it. Otherwise, he was just cannon fodder. Kane shivered a little, for he knew some of what was coming next.

∗∗∗∗∗

"So you plan to overthrow Satan?" said Sir Antony.

"Only if he won't negotiate," smiled the Broker.

"And you think it can be done," said another.

"I'm certain of it," said the Broker. "I'll confess there's an element of risk. I call it the Participation Paradox: the more directly I involve myself in events, the less certain the predictions become, because my actions affect the predictions, and vice versa, creating a feedback loop." He looked, seeing that he'd lost half the audience. "Even so, our current predictions give us an 81% chance of success."

"Success meaning?" asked Sir Antony.

"The permanent replacement of Satan and his cabal with myself and all of you."

"I'll give yee this, yee think big," said the nameless Scotsman.

"Knowing what I know, there was no other possible course of action."

"What do you want from us?" asked Theo.

The Broker favoured him with a smile. "Good question. If it does come to battle, I will not expect any of you to fight, though you may if you choose. What I will certainly need, in return for your place at my table, is two things. First, fighters and mercenaries – the best you can recruit at short notice. No-one with anything approaching a conscience, though. And second, a diversion. Just before the crucial moment, I need to have as many as possible of Hell's forces dispersed and away from the field of combat." He stopped, waiting.

"How will we achieve that?" asked Leather Jacket.

"Ah come on, I think we can guess the answer to that," said O'Flaherty, the Irish man.

"Deaths," said the Scotsman, quietly.

"Yes," said the Broker. "When a man of sufficient sinfulness dies, a Devil is compelled to come. It is one of their primary functions."

"So we just drop some bombs on a few extremist camps, job done," said Sir Antony.

"There's a complication to that," said the Broker. "You see, Hell is modular; federal, if you prefer. There's only one Satan, but each country has its own Hell, all occupying the same space but separated by a fourth dimension. Sometimes, several Hells per country, if different cultures and religions exist. Easier to manage that way, you see. Hence killing a load of fanatics in the Middle East isn't going to help us. We need to empty the Hell of England, clearing our line of attack that way.

"Are yee saying that Scotland has its own, *independent* Hell?" said the Scotsman, suddenly becoming animated.

"Oh yes," smiled the Broker. "And it's entirely ruled by public school Tories from southern England, as you'd expect."

Everyone else erupted with laughter, while the Scotsman scowled. "They think of everything down there, you see," said the Broker. "Everything except hostile takeovers, that is. So speed is essential. We need to punch through English Hell before they work out what we're doing, and before the other branches can organise themselves and send help. They have a finite number of staff. Not expecting an attack, why would they be? So I kill Satan, automatically take his place, and that's it. Game over, we win. All of Hell would follow my orders from that point."

"You really believe you can do it, don't you?" said Sir Antony.

"Of course," said the Broker politely.

"Can Devils be killed?" asked Leather Jacket.

"Not killed, no," said the Broker. "Only incapacitated, as you're seen. Unless you have a very special weapon, of course."

"Which you have?" asked Theo.

"I might do," said the Broker.

"But only one?" said Leather Jacket. "That's hardly enough to win a war."

"That rather depends on how clever you are," said the Broker. "Hell has two very big weak spots. The first is the structure itself. It's finite in size – they built it when they had only a few hundred souls to contain. Now it's approaching half a billion. So they simply added two extra dimensions – one to fit in all the thousands of large rooms that contain all the souls, and the other to stack all the variant national Hells on top of one another. They're amazing technicians, actually. Hell is five-dimensional! Now if someone had a way of pulling away those two extra dimensions, then a whole load of matter and souls would suddenly all be trying to occupy the same space. Hell would go up like a thousand Hiroshimas!"

"And you've got a way to do that, too?" asked Sir Antony.

"Oh yes. It's how I intend to force their surrender."

"How?" said Leather Jacket. "And what's the other weak spot?"

The Broker tapped his nose. "All in good time," he replied

There followed a short, thoughtful silence, then Sir Antony spoke again. "Then tell me instead, how you know all this stuff. If you want me to follow you to Hell!"

"A fair question," said the Broker. "Well, I believe we have time. Let me tell you a story. It starts with a man condemned to damnation for as close to eternity as makes no difference. Strapped to a chair in a room on his own with a very subtle and effective form of torment being applied to him. But then he had a visitor..."

**

"I see them!" said Natalia. "In automatic killing machines. In basement. In ten minutes, they are dead!"

"There is absolutely no empirical evidence for extra-sensory perception," declared Mycroft.

"Then you ain't seen the shit we seen!" snapped Lucy. "Believe her! We gotta break down that door! Now!!"

"A gun was insufficient, and we have nothing stronger," said Mycroft.

"Use the minibus!" said Martin.

"Of course," said Natalia! "I go get it!"

"I'll help!" said Martin, and sprinted after her.

"Is the path wide enough?" said Lysandra.

"Don't think so, but we gotta try!" shouted Lucy "Everyone quick, check the path for rocks and big holes, anything that might slow her down! Move 'em and fill 'em!"

"We must also ensure that she takes the correct route," said Mycroft.

"She just seemed to know the way," said Janelle.

It took Natalia and Martin just five minutes to run through the woods to the car park. But they stopped just before reaching the gate.

"Who's she?" said Martin, incredulously. Beside the minibus, a very sexy girl in a white dress that barely concealed her knickers was sitting on the bonnet of a taxi, looking bored. For some reason, no rain seemed to be falling on her.

"Minibus too wide for path. I take her car," said Natalia. "You must distract her."

"Distract her how?" said Martin.

"Look at her. She want sex. You are man. You must offer it."

"But I don't want her, I want you. I love you."

"I know. Maybe I love you too. But you must do this for me and for your friends. Look at me."

Martin did. He saw a smile that he'd die a thousand times for. Then she wrapped her arms round him and kissed him. The earth shook like crazy. The clouds above rumbled in sympathy, and then broke apart. Moments later the sun blasted through, its rays sizzling the wetness from their clothes. The Abysmal Plain had never seen sunshine like it, and might never do again. Martin didn't even feel it. But everyone else did, as the clouds ripped back across the sky, and the sun burst onto the path and the courtyard. Janelle stared upwards in wonder, and whispered a prayer. Mycroft felt his freezing cold limbs suddenly start to warm up. Lucy and Lysandra marvelled as pleasantly warm steam rose from their clothes, drying them out in seconds flat. Helen's eyes snapped open. "Mycroft, what the fuck am I doing strapped to your back?" Mycroft toppled backwards as Helen tried to wrench herself free, and they writhed on the ground for a few moments, before Helen came up wearing the coat. Mycroft didn't object; it was warm enough for him to wear nothing but pants, now.

Natalia pulled away from Martin gently, a strange sadness in her eyes. "You are a good man, Martin, best I ever know. Now do what I need you to do."

Martin smiled back, nodded, strode up to the gate and vaulted it one-handed. It was not something a man should attempt with a massive erection inside tight hiking trousers. He somehow kept the pain from his face as Suzy turned towards him.

"Well hello," she said, admiring the bulge in his trousers.

"Hello beautiful," he said.

"Are you looking for something?"

"You," he said.

"Is there a place we can go?" she murmured.

"The hostel is locked. But there's plenty of room on the back seats of the minibus."

She grinned. He unlocked the passenger door and they climbed in, before struggling their way over the seats towards the back, something Suzy appeared to be turned on by. Martin easily kept her attention, concealing the fact that Natalia had jumped into Suzy's cab and found the key in the ignition.

"Ooh, seat belts," said Suzy. "You ever been tied up by a girl, Martin?"

"Does being trussed up with skipping ropes and stuffed into a locker in the year 3 girls' changing rooms count?" said Martin.

"Oh, I think it can be improved upon," said Suzy, straddling him and pulling a leather strap from behind her dress." Martin whimpered.

"Ga-wan sonny! Gi'e her yin fer mee!" said Saucy Jock, spilling chips as he appeared from behind their seat.

"Sorry!" said a mortified Martin. "I'd completely forgotten he was there!"

"It's fine," she said. "I like an audience."

Then they heard the sound of the taxi engine starting. "My car! Hey!" said Suzy.

The taxi backed away from the gate thirty metres, then Natalia slammed her foot down and smashed through it, hurling the gate into the trees ahead of her.

Horrible scenes flashed through her mind: Dylan, Bernie and Denny. All would be dead within one minute, maybe two. She didn't see how they could possibly reach them in time, but she had to try. She gunned the car along the path as fast as she dared, for if the car got stuck, the last chance was gone. Keep the speed, she thought. If there's a hole, bounce through it. Driving on narrow potholed tracks was something she knew. She rounded a corner and saw some of the others, running back onto the courtyard. The boys in the cellar had half a minute to live – or less. *Right*, thought Natalia. There was the door. She slammed her foot down and hurtled towards it.

Chapter Thirteen

Natalia's car hit the hostel doors with such force that they went flying into the corridor beyond, and the sides of the door frame also crashed inwards, shattering the corridor walls. Above the door, huge granite blocks came crashing down onto the taxi.

Mycroft came skipping over the wreck of the car, ignoring it entirely. Instead he searched what remained of the hostel corridors for what he wanted. Behind him, female voices were screaming Natalia's name. He ignored them, found a white box and pulled it open.

Martin came sprinting out of the forest, Suzy behind him.

"Nataliaaaaaaaaa!!"

"My carrrrrr!!"

Martin's cry of anguish when he reached the car would have brought torment to the very damnedest souls of Hell. Perhaps it did. It seemed to go on forever. He clutched the blood-soaked hand hanging out of the wreckage. Already it was getting cold. Above them, thunder boomed anew, and the clouds rolled back up, even darker than before, swallowing the sun. The rain sheeted down again, harder than ever.

"We'll mourn her later," yelled Helen. "Get to the cellar!" Followed by Sergei, Janelle and Lysandra, she scrambled over the rubble-strewn car, and into the corridor. But before they could move further, the cellar door swung open.

The warden stepped into the corridor. His skin was bright red, and they could almost see flames flicker across it. He had a kitchen knife in each hand, three more in his belt, and a sixth clutched in his tail, which was swishing through the air above his head in a meaningful fashion. He opened his mouth and exhaled through his hideous teeth. The reek of sulphur hit them almost immediately.

"Creature of Satan!" screamed Janelle, brandishing her cross. "I cast you back. *I cast you back!!!!*"

The warden paused, looking confused. Sergei brought up his gun and fired repeatedly at his chest. Holes appeared, and blood spewed forth; otherwise nothing happened.

"Regulation forty seven point three," grinned the warden. "No guest may discharge firearms at the hostel staff. Penalty: death." He raised a knife ready to throw.

"Don't worry," said Mycroft to Sergei. "The knives in youth hostels are always ridiculously blunt."

A knife thudded hard into Sergei's heart.

"Of course," Mycroft added, "the penetrative power of a knife is also a function of the force with which it is thrown."

Sergei hit the floor with a thud. Then he dissolved into nothing. As did his coat. "Oh bugger," said Helen, who was now facing a knife wielding maniac, wearing nothing but her underwear.

"Duck!" someone yelled. Helen and Mycroft obeyed. A jet of foam sailed over their heads towards the warden. He snarled and ran forward, throwing a knife. It clanked off the fire extinguisher in Janelle's hand. Riding her luck, she lunged forward and slammed the thing into the warden's face. "The Lord's my fucking shepherd, and you're going down!" she screamed manically. He toppled backwards, and Janelle threw the extinguisher down onto his head for good measure.

"Get to the cellar!" yelled Lysandra, and Helen and Mycroft jumped over the warden, landed in the foam, slipped over and came down hard on their backsides. Their momentum carried them forward into the cellar staircase, further propelled by a stream of foam from the still active extinguisher. They bumped and slid down the stairs, landing in a foam-soaked jumble of bare limbs at the bottom.

From his cross, Bernie looked up. Two half-naked, foam-clad figures appeared to be wrestling in the corridor just outside his room. Shame one of them was female. Still, it was a sign things were looking up for him at last. Then the two figures got up, hearing wailing cries for help.

"Dylan!" said Helen with delight, running into the dark torture room. "I thought we might be too late!"

"Get me out of here," he wailed. He was in a cage hanging just millimetres above a vat of steaming water. "It was lowering me in!! B-but then there was a crash, and just after that it stopped. But it could start again any ..."

Mycroft offered a rare smile, and produced a handful of fuses. "From the late Miss Vokzalnova's description, I deduced a high probability of an electronic component to the killing contraptions for all three of you. Ergo I sought out the..."

"Yes well done," said Helen. "Now get them out, quick, before the warden recovers!"

In fact, there was no need for urgency. The killing machines in all three rooms had shut down, and Martin was repeatedly bashing the warden's head with a granite block. The others left him to it, and set about cutting their friends free. It took a long time, because the hostel knives were, indeed, exceedingly blunt.

*****

"YOU ODIOUS, INSIGNIFICANT WRETCHES! WHY HAVE YOU SUMMONED ME AGAIN?" bellowed Satan Beelzebub III.

"To watch the record from the final minutes of the life of Nigel Milligan, in order to understand our enemy, your Lordship" said Bracknell, wondering why he had to explain it twice. He clicked on the projection equipment, and the video ran. They had managed to extract from the damned Milligan his memories of what had happened immediately after his death, as well, so they witnessed for themselves the attack upon Frimley and Ashtead.

"Planned," whispered Woking. "This was carefully planned."

"This will not stand," bellowed Satan. "All who have indulged in this saintly atrocity must die!!!"

"Taking the lives of mortals is..."

"Permissible in extreme circumstances!" roared Satan. "Our own have been attacked! Should word of this spread ... we'd be ridiculed! All involved must die painfully, then suffer eternal torment – and bless the consequences!"

"I believe that under the circumstances, the Others might forgive our actions," agreed Camberley.

"Forgive? FORGIVE???" roared Satan in abject fury.

"He simply meant that your actions are just, my Lord" said Woking, quickly.

"No more discussion," boomed Satan. "An assault force of twenty Devils, to locate and destroy all the culprits, and drag Brian Coker screaming to Hell!"

"There could be a risk, your Lordship" said Bracknell.

"Risk? What risk? They surprised us before, but now they'll feel our wrath!" thundered Satan.

"I know but ... the predictor. Coker has it. They'll know we are coming. It means they will flee, or worse, design a perfect trap or defence against us."

"I'm sorry, my Lord, but I fear he may be right," said Woking. "The predictor allowed him to surprise our two people. He'll also know when, where and exactly how we plan to retaliate."

"Do you say we should do nothing?" roared Satan.

"There is one way," said Bracknell, cautiously.

"Tell us," said Woking.

"You recall that I've been involved in research into the Sensitive problem?"

"No," said Woking.

"What relevance has this?" boomed Satan.

"M-my point is, human Sensitives are born maybe once every decade or two. There are hence thankfully only about five alive at any given time. Yet they cause terrible trouble for two reasons. First, they can see us. And the other lot. We are as visible to them as would be another human. Nobody knows why – of course as soon as they die they lose most of their powers, so there's never been any way to research it."

"It causes particular problems if one is nearby for a soul harvest," said Camberley. "Although that has helped maintain our place in popular culture. Bracknell designed the sensitive-check device on the soul-screens used by harvesting Devils – it alerts them when a sensitive is near the fatality."

"Assuming the user remembers to turn it on," observed Aldershot.

"The fact is, Bracknell's work has been essential to keeping us out of sight in the past few centuries," concluded Camberley."

"None of which helps us now,' said Satan. "Will you please GET TO THE POINT!"

"Ah, yes," said Bracknell. "The second confounding trait of the Sensitive is his or her resistance to our mind-scanning devices. The mind somehow senses the device, and confuses it. We cannot for example perform automatic accounting of their lifetime behaviour, when they die. We generally just pack them off to Heaven and forget about them, unless we have old-fashioned evidence of deeds we can get them for."

"I am becoming impatient, here," thundered Satan.

"Don't you see?" said Bracknell. "If our devices can't scan their minds, then neither can the one that was stolen! Predictive devices do not solely take information from the mind of the one being scanned. They pull it from every mind they predict to be affected, until the desired consequence can be accurately calculated. So all we need to do is involve a Sensitive in the decision-making process, and it will render our quarry unable to predict our actions!"

For a moment, all was silent. The Satan boomed, "You are saying we should let a Human decide our actions?"

Not our actions, great Lord," said Bracknell, obsequiously. "You must do that. You have done it already – we attack and destroy. But the method, the strategy, must be chosen by a Sensitive. It is the only way to surprise them, to prevent them designing the perfect defence, or escape."

"As Bracknell's superior, may I assume that you are taking responsibility for this plan?" Satan asked Camberley.

Camberley grinned weakly. "Um, yes."

"We have a list of living sensitives, your Lordship," said Bracknell. He placed a stone tablet onto the table and pressed a series of crystals on it. A list of six names, ages and power grades appeared on the stone in red hot letters:

> *Hu Zengyuan (6)* **
> *Natalia Vokzalnova (21)* ***
> *Yassar Obenkie (32)* *
> *Arjun Singh (45)* *
> *Vivienne Brewster (66)* **
> *Harold Black (80)* *

"You track the locations of these?" said Satan.

"Yes we should be able to … oh," said Bracknell. "Extraordinary."

"What," growled Satan.

"According to our records … this is strange. Vokzalnova, the most powerful one, is in Heaven, but there's no record of her dying. And two of the others, Obenkie and Singh are … gone."

"GONE?" roared Satan. "You mean you've lost them?"

"No-no," said "Bracknell. "We just don't know where they are."

"Oh I see,' said Satan. "Well that's alright then."

"Good," said Bracknell.

"NO IT ISN'T, YOU INCOMPETENT CASSOCK! How is it possible that two such important souls have vanished completely from our records?!"

"I-I can't explain" cowered Bracknell.

"My Lord, I suggest we investigate these matters when the more urgent one is completed," said Woking. "Bracknell, please tell me that the two oldest Sensitives are still where they should be?"

"Y-yes. At least, so it says here."

"Lord, I suggest a reverse séance," said Woking. "Send one of us up to each of them, make them agree to be projected. We're not allowed to kill them, but they don't know that. Put the fear of Hell in them, they'll comply."

"Do it," said Satan. "You, Woking, and you, Byfleet. I grant you emergency transport ability."

Woking and Byfleet nodded, and vanished.

**

In the boardroom, Theo worked furiously on the laptop he'd been provided with. Around the table, everyone else had a computer, too. Each had been given clear instructions – to summon up mercenaries, fighting men, and just generally as many gangsters, thugs and assorted bastards as they could. These were to be given a lump sum of money immediately, then told to gather at specified locations up and down the country, where they'd be given far more in hard cash.

To his surprise, Theo was enjoying himself. He'd built up huge sums of money over the years, and perhaps what had upset him most about the news of his impending death was the fact that he'd never get the chance to properly enjoy it. Now it felt cathartic, squandering it in just minutes. Even better was picking out every bastard who'd ever cheated him or screwed him over, and dangling the carrot in front of them. The Broker had been very candid about the prospects for anyone they recruited: they were cannon fodder, and most or all would suffer a hideous death. Theo, like most of the men in the room, knew many more evil men that he hated, than ones that he liked. Some of them would be suspicious, of course. But Theo knew how they'd struggle to resist having money thrown at them. And so the responses had come, slowly at first, but now they were coming more quickly. Word was spreading to contacts of contacts, who Theo was all too happy to add to the party.

The Broker was not in the room, though. Theo guessed he was a busy man. On the middle of the long table, the bound and gagged Ashtead continued to struggle.

**

Harold Black lived in a battered old homestead in Texas. The weather was so hot these days, he'd set up chairs on three sides of the house so he could always find one that was shaded. It was better than being inside, where dust, memories and unwashed things were ever-present. He looked up as a bright red figure appeared on the parched grass in his yard. Then another.

"I thought you were doing the woman," said Woking.

"You should have said so," said Byfleet, and vanished.

Woking walked forward. "Your presence is required in Hell," he declared.

"Caught the sun, have yer?" said Harold.

"You must come to Hell," repeated Woking, "or I will burn you."

"Tell 'em I ain't givin' up my guns for no man," replied Harold.

"I'm not here for your guns, I'm here for – "

"I ain't givin' up nothin', get away from my house! Judgement day is a-comin', I see it every night! The dead will rise up and the sea will run red with the blood of the livin'! Well a man's got a right ta defend hisself!!"

Ten minutes later, a furious Woking rematerialised in the Cabal room, without Harold, but with several smoking bullet-holes in his chest that were slowly healing. He saw with a mixture of relief and seething envy that Byfleet had beside him a spectral Vivienne Brewster, who was engaged in the important business of knitting a jumper. It had been her condition for coming that this task was not interrupted, he later learned. Byfleet offered Woking a triumphant smirk, and conjured a cigarette to his mouth.

"Those things will kill you, you know," said Vivienne. "Well, perhaps not." Satan clicked his fingers and the cigarette disintegrated; Byfleet tried not to look annoyed. Bracknell was showing the others a tracking device that would point the Devils towards any demonic technology that existed within the mortal world.

"We'll discuss your failure later, Woking," said Satan. "Byfleet, have you explained our dilemma?"

"I was able to show the video from Milligan on her television," he said, "though she knitted all the way through it."

"I paid perfect attention, I will have you know," said Vivienne, clacking her needles as she spoke. "I gather you need my advice on how to fight back."

"Any ideas we have, they will predict," said Camberley.

"Mmm," she nodded, without looking up. "Are you all invulnerable?"

"We can be rendered unconscious and incapacitated," said Camberley.

"You know their exact location, I presume?" The needles kept on clacking furiously in her hands.

"No, we only get that information when they die. But we have a tracking device that will lead us to a piece of demonic equipment in their possession."

"Can you teleport yourselves at will?" (clack, clack).

"Not within the mortal world, no."

"If you locate them, could you then arrange for more of you to be summoned to the spot where they are? (Darn it, I've dropped a stitch!)"

"Not if it was above ground level," said Camberley. "We can appear anywhere, like Byfleet did to you, but doing so limits our powers, and scope. To make a full physical incursion, we would have to erupt from the ground."

"Not very good, are you?" she observed, one critical eye rising up from her important work.

"Camberley's talking a lot of Holy water – Sir!" barked Aldershot. "We only need kill one of them, and a devil will be summoned right among them – Sir! We can briefly alter the summoning rules, have a squad of twenty called to the spot and slaughter them – Sir!"

"Won't work," countered Camberley. "One of us would have to do the killing, and his presence would negate the summoning of any others."

"It's good that you all know the rules so well," said Vivienne, who'd just about picked up her earlier dropped stitch.

"Camberley, can you define 'present' in this case?"

For a moment Camberley reddened with fury, before he realised what Bracknell had meant. "Are you suggesting we kill one remotely?"

"Indeed," said Bracknell. "Use a pitchfork as a long range sniping device, and shoot one from the next building."

"Goodness me," said Vivienne.

"You have a problem with this?" said Camberley.

"Yes, you're all idiots. You've forgotten that they've got one of you tied up in the room with them, or at least very close by. So it won't work. They've obviously thought of this."

"May I remind you to whom you are speaking?" roared Satan.

"I mean no disrespect to you, Lord Horn-ed Beast, Sir," said Vivienne meekly. "I merely question the intelligence of your underlings."

"As do I, puny human, as do I," agreed Satan.

"Perhaps it is no wonder that someone is attempting a hostile takeover of Hell," she observed, again not looking up from her knitting.

"What???" the entire room chorused.

"Seriously?" she asked, raising one critical eye. "It hadn't occurred to any of you to ask what they were doing?"

"Takeover of Hell is impossible!" boomed Satan.

"Oh that's good then," she said. "So you don't need to worry. None of my business anyway." What she didn't mention was the cold, petrifying fear she'd felt when she'd watched Byfleet's video on her telly. The destructive ambition she'd sensed from the smug little man who'd been in charge, and the shocked realisation that she'd seen that same face, or one very like it, in a series of recent nightmares she'd had. There'd been apocalyptic explosions, fearsome battles with fantastical creatures, and armies of furious ghosts spewing forth to destroy the world, yet none of it had scared her as much as that one, smiling face that had always been there, on the sidelines, controlling it all. Even here, face to face with the Lord of Hell, she found that even He terrified her far less than the name that went with that face: *Coker*.

Chapter Fourteen

"So Myra, did the Earth move for you?"

"Har har." Myra Tiwari rolled her eyes at the camera, then reassembled her prefabricated smile. "I guess it's as good a theory as anyone else has come up with, Johnny! Now, the earth tremors are not the only thing to have scientists scratching their heads this morning. A completely new kind of bird may have been discovered, and it's right here in Britain! We go over live to Harry Daniels at Fellingham freightyard."

The screen cut to Harry, who was braving the wind in a thick padded jacket, standing outside a construction site. "Thank you, Myra. Yes, there's a flock of nine birds, and they haven't moved from the spot where they were first sighted around one a.m. last night. Bright yellow, about the size of robins. I'm no expert, but they're like nothing I've ever seen in this country."

"Could they have escaped from an aviary, Harry?"

"Well there are two experts here from the University of Bristol, and a growing army of twitchers turning up for a look, and nobody has the slightest clue what these things are. Other than birds, of course."

The camera panned around. The construction site was surrounded on all sides by fences or walls, and through the fences at least forty men and (very occasionally) women with telescopes and binoculars were peering in.

"And I gather the birds are behaving in an unusual way as well, Harry? Can we get a shot of that?"

"Yes, Myra. The birds are all rising up and then diving at high speed into what seems to be recently set concrete. I can't believe they're not injuring themselves, but each time they hit the ground they bounce off, right themselves and fly up again. With me is Professor Eustace McTavish from the University of Bristol. Professor, you've never seen anything like this, have you?"

The camera swung round to a serious looking older man with a bowtie and neat beard. "This type of behaviour is completely without precedent in ..."

"Thank you, Professor!" said Harry, and the camera swung back to him. "Now we can speak to Gordon Perotha, one of the two men who made the discovery. "Gordon, how does it feel to discover a completely new type of bird?"

The camera swung to Harry's other side, to reveal an excessively bulky man with flat black hair, who seemed to be wearing at least three jackets, none of which fitted properly.

"I don't know what it is, yet," the man said, in a deep, slow and monotone voice. "I thought maybe it was sparrows painted yellow and my mum thought so too when I said it."

"I think we can rule that out," said the professor, off camera.

"How did you make this moonlit discovery, Gordon?" said Harry.

"There wasn't a moon last night, it was cloudy."

"My mistake, Gordon. So how?"

"Solomon Blakey was standing on the path there looking at engines. Sometimes you get engines coming here at night that didn't come through the stations, and if you've got a strong enough torch you can get their numbers. They don't like him being there but it's a public right of way so they can't stop him. He saw the birds and he phoned me. I don't know how he got my number, I didn't give it to him because he's boring. But he did. I think he called Keith and Keith gave it to him. So Solomon called and said I should come because there were birds, but my mum answered and said no I shouldn't come because it was one in the morning. But I got up and got the phone and said what kind of birds and he said yellow ones that glowed a bit in the dark. And I said no, birds don't glow in the dark but he said these ones did, so I came even though mum said it was night and I shouldn't go out."

"Get him off!" said a voice from Harry's earpiece.

"No no, keep him, he's brilliant," said another, who sounded like the producer. So Harry let him talk.

"So Solomon said I had to bring tea but mum wouldn't make it and I had to go without. He got really cross and said he wouldn't tell me next time there were birds but I said it wasn't my fault and I'd bring tea next time."

"What did you think, when you first saw the birds?"

"I thought they were sparrows with paint on them. At first I thought Solomon had done it but then I thought no because he's too boring to think of anything like that. So I called my uncle George because he likes birds more than I do and he came as well and he said they weren't any British bird at all. And he called more friends and then more and more people started coming. Nobody knows what they are, though."

"Professor McTavish, I understand you've been denied permission to enter the site and examine the birds at close quarters?" asked Myra, from the studio.

The professor blinked in surprise as the camera swung back to him. "Our office has struggled to identify who owns this site. We are talking to the police about being escorted onto the site instead."

"What about the glow, professor?" said Johnny, leaning into shot beside Myra on the sofa, his eyes wide with excitement. "Do you think these birds might be radioactive, and a danger to public health?"

"Young man, radioactive objects do not glow," said McTavish snootily. "Please do not propagate idiot misconceptions on national television."

This time Myra's smile was entirely genuine. "Thanks for the correction, professor, but can you explain the glow?"

"I have not seen proof that they glow. It is not visible in the daylight."

Harry cut in. "One of the twitchers took some phone footage. I promise you, Prof, it's true!"

"Bioluminescence is common in marine creatures and occasional in arthropods, but it is unknown in birds. I would not like to speculate until we have a specimen to examine at close quarters. I will say this though, I have never seen a bird strike a solid surface even half as hard as that, without incurring serious or fatal injuries."

"Okay, we'll come back to Harry and the birds later in the program if there are any developments," said Myra. "Our main stories again ..."

*****

The Broker clicked off the TV screen. He hated wild cards, and cursed himself for not taking a more permanent approach to Fenwick's disposal, but then he only had so many of his special bullets. The predictor had stubbornly refused to see past this point with Fenwick, and at the time he'd assumed it was because there was nothing to see. Now, he was having doubts; those blasted birds were creating too much commotion, and it could lead to someone digging Fenwick up. He couldn't allow it. He glanced at his watch anxiously, and then made a phone call.

Instructions delivered, the Broker sat down, alone in a small office. For the first time in decades, he felt a strong wave of physical fear, as he thought about what was coming. He wondered yet again how the Devils had done it, how they'd concealed from his machine their plan of attack. It was strangely exciting, not knowing exactly what would happen! He went through his defences again, and the special escape route. He wondered for a moment if he was doing the right thing, but he pushed the thought away. Yes, it was right. He had no other options, really. He looked again at the screen, showing the assembled cabal working away in the absence of their leader. Whatever happened next, this plan had been a towering achievement. Some losses, he knew, were inevitable and acceptable. Perhaps, though, there was time for just one last conversation, and this time he wouldn't talk tactics.

In a nearby room, another man wept openly, for what he was fairly sure would be the very last time. Then his watery eyes looked up in surprise when he heard the knock on the door.

*****

Vivienne Brewster had spent most of her life repressing her strange visions, and hiding them from everyone else. She'd feared that doing otherwise would lead into a life of crystals, cats and ridicule. Yet now, she realised, the increasingly apocalyptic visions had all had a purpose, to prepare her for this very moment. For here she was, sitting in a cave full of Devils, with Satan himself asking for her help. Because of the visions, she didn't fear them, but she did fear their failure.

Vivienne had always been smarter than the men in her family. She'd lost count of the times she'd had to extricate one of them from some complex mess they'd created. This was no different; it just needed a little creative thinking. So, having extracted a promise that she'd be returned safely home once she was done, she laid out to the Devils, step by step, a plan of attack that she thought might just work.

*****

Suzy understood men. They were selfish, overproud, arrogant, shallow creatures who thought about nothing but sex. Her job was to break them, humiliate and torment them, and show them that they were worthless. It had worked so easily with Michael and ... the times before. There had been lots of times before, she was sure, but when she tried to remember any of them, she found the details impossible to retrieve. So she turned her mind back to the current one. He was proving unusually difficult. At first everything had gone fine, he'd walked straight into her arms just like Michael had done, and had seemed willing to let her tie him to the minibus seat. Then they'd heard the taxi engine start and he'd pushed her off and scrambled out, before she could follow.

Now he was sitting on a ruined wall, crying and holding the cold hand of a woman who most certainly wouldn't be having sex with him, or indeed anyone, ever again. What could be going through his head?

"She's dead, you know," Suzy said, sitting down beside Martin. She watched, curiously, as he continued to stroke Natalia's bloodstained hand.

Martin nodded.

"She can't have sex with you anymore."

He nodded again.

"The solution is to find a woman who is still alive, and therefore capable of sex acts."

He nodded. Then the words slowly registered. "What?"

"I am explaining that your desire for sex cannot be satisfied by a woman who has been crushed to death in a car."

"That's what I thought you said," agreed Martin.

"And therefore you should seek an alternative mate, one who is still in possession of fully functioning reproductive apparatus."

"That's good advice, I suppose," said Martin, numbly.

"By coincidence, I too am in search of sex. You have already seduced me. You rendered me positively ravenous when you ran out on me before. I must have you. Look, my skirt is so short, you can almost see my knickers."

"Well, that's nice then," said Martin.

"You do not appear to have developed an erection," she observed, feeling puzzled.

A tear leaked from Martin's eye. "I think I had one earlier," he said quietly.

"Put your hand on my leg, maybe that'll help," she said. When Martin didn't respond, she gently but firmly took his free hand, placed it on her knee, and then drew it all the way up her thigh. There was no visible response inside his trousers. Intrigued and frustrated, she unzipped them to take a look. Nothing.

She paused, unsure what to do next. A banging noise was coming from the cellar door. "What's happening down there?" she asked.

"They're nailing the warden to a cross and putting a gimp mask on him."

"Well, I expect they're enjoying that," she said.

"I think there are stern words being said to him, too."

"Oh, good." His hand had slipped from the top of her leg, but she'd kept hold of it. Instinctively she gave it a squeeze. He surprised her by squeezing it back.

Their attention was diverted by footsteps from the cellar. Helen emerged, wearing a tight leather dominatrix bodice and fishnet tights. "Just popped up to check on you, Martin." She saw Suzy. "Hey, who are you?"

"Name's Suzy. Nice outfit, sister. Got any more?"

"There's a whole rack of them downstairs. Only dry clothes in the whole bloody place!"

Martin sniffed.

Helen looked at him, with empathetic eyes completely at odds with her outfit. "Mind, you should see what Mycroft's wearing."

Martin sniffed again. And again. Then he burst into a stop-start fit of laughter, which rapidly transformed into heaving sobs. Arms wrapped around him and he found himself sobbing into Suzy's barely contained bosom.

Helen walked forward, carefully because the floor was still covered in foam. "Not that I don't appreciate you helping him, but who are you exactly?"

Suzy looked at her in puzzlement. She felt oddly unsure how to talk to a person she wasn't trying to draw into sexual entrapment, and in fact could not ever remember having talked to a woman before, at all. "Suzy McCabe. I'm Michael Price's girlfriend." Reading something in Helen's eyes, which were firmly fixed on the current location of Martin's head, she added: "Ex-girlfriend, now."

"But how on Earth did you get here? Do you even know where we are?"

"No idea," said Suzy. "One minute I was at home, then I was picking up Michael, then he ran out on me. I got in the taxi and looked for him. Ended up here."

"Is Michael in danger?" asked Helen.

"Some red guy with horns took him," said Suzy.

"Oh no," said Helen.

"I'm sure he'll be fine," said Suzy. "It was an ambulance. He was a bit poorly."

"Why didn't you go with him?" asked Helen crossly.

"I was under a wardrobe," said Suzy, truthfully.

"OK," said Helen. "We have to find him. He's in terrible danger. This place .... I'm not sure, but I'm starting to think that it's Hell. And it sounds like you met a Devil, too."

"Hmm," said Suzy, fingering the spots on her head where the horns had been.

"Look, you're the only lead we've got. Can you take us to where you last saw him, and show us which way the ambulance went?"

"I could, if someone hadn't smashed my taxi."

Martin wailed aloud.

"Can you drive a minibus?" asked Helen.

"Does it have a really big gear stick?" asked Suzy.

"Yes."

"Then I can."

"Then we'll all go together and you can drive – and keep the wretched bus if you get us all home. They're nearly done downstairs I think, so we'll need to get going soon." Helen made for the stairs but Suzy got up and caught up with her.

"You're a girl," Suzy whispered. Helen nodded quizzically. "I'm trying to get that man to have sex with me but he won't. He can't be gay because he fancied the dead girl in the car. Still does, for some reason. So what's going on?"

Helen bit back a furious reply. Suzy's confusion seemed totally genuine, almost childlike. She told herself to think practically: they needed Suzy, and they also needed Martin to be snapped out of his misery, however understandable it might be. "He didn't just fancy her, he loved her" Helen said.

"How long did he know her?"

"About nine hours," said Helen. "I've lost track of time a bit."

"And that's long enough, is it?"

"For him, it seems to be."

"So what should I do?" asked Suzy. Again, that openly questioning face. Yes, just like a child, Helen thought.

"Comfort him. Talk to him. Help him to deal with the pain, and the loss."

"That's what I was doing!"

"Then you were doing it wrong," Helen snapped, her patience failing. She turned towards the cellar, but saw that the others were now coming up. Lysandra was talking quietly but insistently to Janelle, who looked like she'd been crying. Behind them came Bernie, Dylan and Denny, carrying a huge object that revealed itself as an eight-foot long and three feet wide hollow half-cylinder with small spikes in it.

"It's half an Iron Maiden, duckies," said Bernie, who was walking very stiffly because of the very tight leather trousers he was wearing. His leather top flopped around a bit where his breasts weren't. "We can use it as an umbrella to get to the bus."

"Given that dry clothing has proved extremely challenging to obtain, we concluded that this makeshift portable roof was the most efficient solution," added Mycroft, behind him. He was wearing a black French maid's outfit with short frilly skirt, while each leg was clad in five layers of stockings.

"He thinks he's allergic to leather," whispered Helen to Martin, eliciting a weak smile.

The others came up, bringing the other half of the iron maiden. All had paid respects to Natalia already, but they filed past the car one by one, some touching her hand as they went. Only Bernie spoke aloud: "Goodbye sweet rescuing angel. May you find your reward up above."

Bernie, Mycroft, Janelle, Denny and Lucy went under the first Iron maiden, tottering into the rain like a drunken woodlouse that swore from time to time. Dylan and Lysandra waited under the second, but Martin didn't move. "How can I leave her? Like this? Let me stay! I'll stay with her!"

"You can't," Helen pleaded. "Sooner or later the warden will get free and he'll kill you!"

"I don't care!"

"Then you should!" she shouted. "Natalia died saving our friends! She wouldn't want anyone to die for nothing, especially not you!"

Martin didn't answer, he just convulsed, sobbing and clutching Natalia's hand.

Suzy spoke. "We are in Hell, Martin. Your woman is not. She died and is not here. She did a good thing and that means ..." she paused, scratching her head.

"She'll have gone to Heaven," Helen whispered, feeling a massive weight lift from her own shoulders as she said it. "She's in heaven, Martin, like Bernie said!"

"H-heaven?" said Martin, looking up. "She went to Heaven?"

"Yes," said Helen and Suzy in unison.

"Then I should go too. Where's the warden?" He stood, suddenly and made for the cellar.

"No!" screamed Suzy.

"You can't," said Helen. "If you kill yourself, you'll stay in Hell, everyone knows that! You can't get to her that way!"

Martin stopped. He'd read it somewhere, that suicide was a sin. He sagged.

"She'll wait for you," said Helen. "If you truly love her, she'll wait for you. It's eternal, remember."

He nodded, tears flooding from his eyes.

"And we need you. She'd want you to be strong, now," said Helen.

Martin walked slowly from the corridor. "Goodbye my love. I'll see you soon," he said, stroking Natalia's hand for the final time as he passed her. At last they were under the iron maiden, shuffling along the path trying not to spike their hands as they made their way back to the minibus.

"I'm starving," said Helen.

"That's okay," said Lysandra. "We've got chips in the bus!"

"Uhhh, I'm not sure we do anymore, said Martin."

"You said there was food!" said Dylan, as his group got into the bus. "You said you had ten bags of chips!"

"We did!" said Lucy

"Burrrrrrpp!" said Saucy Jock, from the back.

Suzy slipped into the driving seat of the minibus. Martin was seated beside her – she'd insisted. She rubbed her bare knee against the steering wheel, and caressed the gear stick with her hands.

"So which way?" asked Helen, taking the third seat at the front.

"We need to drive through Glasgow," said Suzy.

"Brilliant!" said Bernie happily. "I *love* Glasgow! You know, it really is the most *wonderful* city. So beautiful, so vibrant. The night-life – oooh!! And the people, so joyous and friendly. Do anything for you. Funny, that's never how anyone imagines the place, though."

Lucy, Lysandra, Martin and Janelle said nothing.

Chapter Fifteen

Manor Road was a popular shopping street. Half of the cars on the road were looking forlornly for a parking space. Diana Morgan watched with eagle eyes through the windows of currently parked cars, looking for anyone who might be about to vacate a space. If she saw one, she'd stop and wait till they drove away, and to Hell with the traffic behind her. There was no way she was driving to the multi-storey a few blocks away. She was sure young men peed in it every weekend. Then she let out a scream as her car hit something that hadn't been there an instant before. A man. Horrified, she hit the brakes.

A bright red man with a pitchfork was shaking his first at her from beyond the bonnet of her car. Several others stood up and joined him. Instinctively she reversed, banging into a car behind her. Its horn blared furiously. Wobbling with shock, she got out.

There was a huge hole in the road just ahead of her car, and chunks of tarmac were scattered around it, as if something had burst out through it. In fact, things were still bursting from it: man after man, all red, all with pitchforks, tails and horns, were climbing out and assembling on the road. One, however, was lying deathly still right in front of her car, with yellow birds pecking at his head.

"What the bloody hell are you doing you bloody woman driver you ... oh" said the fat man who'd been in the car behind her.

"B-bloody Hell," she said. "Yes."

The last of the Devils emerged. For a moment, they all glared furiously at Diana. Two of them grabbed their broken colleague and tipped him unceremoniously back into the hole. A gathering crowd of shoppers stared at the scene, open mouthed and horrified. Several of them made the sign of the cross on their chests.

Then suddenly, the Devils' expressions all switched into comical grins.

"GOT-CHAAA!" they all chorused.

"Wh-what?"

Then a Devil in a suit popped up on top of a car, with a megaphone. "My name is Max Esher from the Devil's Prank Show, and you've just been Hellpranked!" he declared.

"Wh-what? Who? How? Wh-where?" Diana stammered.

"Smile, you're on national TV!" said the suit. Several more suited Devils had now appeared, pointing cameras at her and the Horde of Hell.

"B-but you dented my car!"

"And she dented mine!" said the fat man.

"I think you'll find the appearance fees will cover all the repairs," said 'Max Esher' happily. "Go to Devilsprankshow-dot-com, all one word, and enter your details. Okay folks, that's a wrap!"

The assembled Devils all waved at the assembled crowd, who broke into spontaneous (albeit nervous) applause. *En masse* they walked off down the road, some of them bowing in response to occasional cheers from the crowd.

"Well that was fun," said Byfleet. "I could get used to a reception like that."

"We're not *supposed* to be welcome," Woking reminded him.

"I can't believe that worked," said Camberley. "Nineteen of us enter the mortal world, and no-one bats an eyelid."

"Ms Brewster is a genius," said Bracknell. "We should employ her full time."

"Damned irresponsible, blowing a hole in the road, just for a telly prank," said a tweed suited man in the road behind them. "Oy! You with the cameras! Are you going to do something about this hole?"

He and several others looked around. 'Max Esher' and the men with the cameras had vanished.

"The hole's only a few feet deep," said someone. "How the Devil did they all fit in there?"

*****

"The Broker's back," said the man beside Theo. Theo watched his boss sit down, noting the change in his manner. He looked nervous. Theo didn't like that at all – he'd bought into the whole thing as much for the Broker's utter self-assurance as anything else. You only met people like that very rarely: people so totally sure they were right that you had to believe them, at least if you were Theo.

A message pinged across the screen of Theo's computer. *The Devils have found us. Don't worry, I planned for it. Please open your drawer and take from it the weapon inside. It fires hollowed out bullets filled with Holy Water. Please no-one speak, the Devils can scan for our voices. I have put up a series of measures in place to stop them getting in, we shall see if they work. The fire sprinklers are full of Holy water and will trigger automatically if the room is breached. Should they fail, shoot them with the guns provided. Aim for the eyes. They are several times stronger than us but as you have seen, not invulnerable. If we survive the next hour, then victory is all but assured.*

Theo's heart pounded. He'd handled guns before, many times, even fired a few, but only ever to check the quality of shipments he was sending to a client. He cursed the fact that he was sitting closest to the door.

*****

"They've switched buildings, I'm certain," said Camberley.

"You're sure that's where the attack happened?" asked Woking, pointing up at the office block.

"Stag do," said Byfleet, casually, to an open-mouthed passer-by.

"I managed to hack into the human 'internet' thing," said Bracknell. "One of the floors on that building is registered to "B. Coker Associates.""

"That confirms it," said Woking.

"As if there'd been any doubt," said Aldershot.

"But judging from the direction indicated by my detector," said Bracknell, pointing upwards at a distant building, "they're on about the seventh floor of that office block over there."

"Walking all that way will attract attention," said Woking. "Bless it, I thought they'd be closer."

Byfleet scratched his massive chin. He'd studied human behaviour in his spare time. "See those people standing by that concrete pole with a sign at the top?"

"Yes?" said Woking.

"I believe it is called a 'Bus Stop'."

"Stag do," said Camberley happily to the shocked line of people, as nineteen Devils joined them.

*****

Theo had never liked the saying that war was all about waiting. For him, it was all about making sure that someone was making money, and that the someone in question was him. People would fight each other anyway, so they might as well do it with up-to-date modern equipment. Yet now he was forced to concede that waiting was indeed the worst part of battle. Half an hour he'd been seated here, alternately staring at the screen and glancing nervously at the door. He willed another email to arrive, just for the distraction. He thought about starting an online game of some sort, anything to pass the time.

The door burst open. Three Devils charged through, screaming battle cries and wielding pitchforks. The floor beneath them gave way immediately and they plunged from view, followed by a 'splatch' sort of sound. A fourth Devil behind them tried to stop, but found the floor by the door extremely slippery, and so he skidded on into the hole as well. Two more stopped in the doorway, but then a huge hammer swung down from the ceiling behind them and knocked them in, too. Now Theo knew why the Broker had led them all into this room via the fire escape.

Two of the men in the room ran for the fire escape now, but its door flew open before they got there. Two Devils stepped through, firing steel arrows from the prongs of their pitchforks into the two running men, who both fell down dead. Then a huge cube of concrete slammed down onto the Devils from above, smashing them into the floor and blocking the way to the fire exit. Theo looked up at the sprinklers in the roof, which were doing nothing. Then, suddenly terrified, he got up and ran to the corner of the room, beside the pit blocking the way to the main door, hoping in desperation to stay out of the way. In the pit, six Devils were struggling in some sort of cement, while liquid poured in from six holes in the pit's side. The cement was rapidly setting as the liquid mixed in.

The ceiling in the centre of the room disintegrated. Through it fell eleven Devils, most of them landing on the table. The exceptions were Bracknell and Camberley, who landed on top of the hogtied Ashtead, and toppled over backwards onto the floor. Gomshall, with a flourish, unrolled a bundle in his hand, releasing a magnificent gold-plated wasp, the size of a cat, into the air. It circled the room firing poisoned barbs at the humans, while the other devils swung their pitchforks, blasting fire and steel arrows into the men round the table.

"Yaaaaaarrrrrgggghhhhhh!!!" chorused Woking and the others, enjoying the moment. A few of the men fired back, and one even grappled with a devil, sending a jet of fire into the wasp, which exploded. The air filled with unearthly wailing, as one by one the humans died in agony. Within minutes, the floor was littered with corpses.

"Did we miss it?" said Camberley, getting to his feet. The room was now milling with confused, newly deceased souls.

"It was brilliant!" exulted a junior Devil. "Was it like this in Surrey?"

"We don't talk about Surrey," said Woking darkly.

"Would someone stop that celestial racket!" yelled Aldershot.

"Gomshall! Hush!!" growled Woking. The unearthly wailing ceased, and Gomshall now continued in silence with the business of pounding his fists into the hapless devil who'd accidentally incinerated his wasp.

"Dead humans, atten-shun!" barked Aldershot. "Stand up straight! No talking! Proceed in orderly fashion to that corner there, where you will await your fate in silence! Move!" The souls of the slaughtered cabal obeyed.

"Where's Coker?" roared Woking.

"There's a tunnel here, looks like an escape route," said a Devil at the end of the table.

Woking and Aldershot ran over. The huge armchair that the Broker had sat in now had a hole instead of a cushion. The hole ran straight down into darkness. "Bracknell! Detector!" yelled Woking.

Bracknell waved his detector. It pointed straight down. "Below us," he said.

"Bracknell, Camberley, Aldershot, follow! Byfleet, take charge here!" yelled Woking. Then he jumped into the hole. The other three jumped in after, as instructed.

Woking broke Aldershot's fall. The two of them broke Bracknell and Camberley's falls. Woking himself was severely broken: he'd landed on sharp metal spikes.

"Some sort of airbag, here, deflating," said Bracknell, impressed. "Must have broken Coker's fall!"

"There's a doorway right above us," said Camberley. "I'm guessing he went through there."

Yellow birds swooped from the hole above, and started pecking at Woking's head. "Shoo!" said Aldershot, as they pulled Woking off the spikes.

"We'd better leave him," said Camberley.

"No, he'd dispel us all!" said Aldershot.

"We'll never get him up to the door, he's too heavy! That ridiculous fat belly!! And he'll slow us down!" said Bracknell.

Aldershot looked down at Woking's broken body. The spikes had almost cut his body in two. Almost…

Bracknell went up first, after which the others passed him Woking's top half, and then his bottom half, before climbing up themselves. Soon they were running down the tunnel: Bracknell leading with the detector, Aldershot carrying Woking's crotch and legs, and Camberley his voluminous upper half. The tweeting birds flew along after them.

Ten minutes later they came to a locked door. Bracknell melted it with his pitchfork. They stumbled out onto a tube station. A train was on the platform. The detector pointed to it. The Devils ran forward but the train was pulling away. Bracknell aimed his pitchfork and fired: the three-pronged end thudded into the receding end of the train, trailing a cord behind it. "Hold on to me!" he yelled.

Camberley and Aldershot grabbed him, just in time. The line tensed and the three of them shot across the floor in an accelerating bundle of limbs, tails and pitchforks, bowling over terrified passengers as they went. "The legs!" yelled Camberley, seeing Woking's lower half lying on the platform behind them. In desperation he aimed and fired his own pitchfork, catching the legs in one shin. A lot more passengers were flung to the floor as the legs skidded across the platform after them.

Now they were on the track. Aldershot, on the bottom, had his back on a rail and used his legs to keep it there, ignoring the agony of friction and the weight on his back as they screamed along. Woking's legs bounced again and again behind them, but Camberley drew in the cord and tucked the legs under his arm. "Pull us nearer the train," he gasped, but Bracknell's pitchfork wasn't strong enough. At last the train stopped; ahead was the light of a platform. They stumbled to their feet and tried to run forward, but Camberley stood on the wrong rail and got electrocuted. He toppled over, and a new set of birds started pecking him. The train started moving. Aldershot fired his own pitchfork at it.

"You take Woking, I'll take Camberley," he called. Bracknell just had time to put Woking's legs underneath him, and he rode on them down the rail, clutching Woking's torso. Aldershot did a similar thing on Camberley's body. This time, with less weight on each cord, they could draw themselves in, closer and closer until they were touching the train. They waited for it to stop, then melted their way in, pulling Camberley and both halves of Woking in after them. They were now in a driver's cabin empty of humans. Camberley stirred under the relentless pecking of the birds.

"Check if he's still on the train," said Aldershot.

Bracknell waved his detector. "He's straight ahead and close, so yes!"

"Let's try and stick Woking back together," said Aldershot. Other than the crotch, which was mangled, black and smoking from friction on the rail, the two halves of Woking had now healed themselves. Bracknell held the legs while Aldershot manoeuvred the torso onto the top. They felt the train start moving again. The separated parts of Woking started knitting themselves back together, and the birds pecked his head with renewed vigour.

They waited. Bracknell said, "of course it's possible Coker abandoned his device and got off the train. We're tracking it, not him."

"It's central to his strategy," said Aldershot. "I doubt he'll give it up. He'll outrun us or die trying."

"AAAaaaarrrgghhhhh!!" screamed Woking, his hands flying to his crotch and knocking Aldershot flying. "What in Sainted Heaven did that Blessed Human do to me?"

"I'm sure Bracknell will tell you later," said Aldershot. "Right now we're in an underground train, and Coker's on board too. Let's get him!"

Bracknell pointed his pitchfork at the door into the carriage. "Wait, try the handle first," said Aldershot. "Minimum visible impact, remember?"

Bracknell nodded, pulled the handle, and the door opened. The four of them walked through, eliciting gasps from the surprised passengers.

"Stag do," said Aldershot.

"Oy-oy!" said one of a group of young men standing by the side doors. "'Ee the groom, eh?" he pointed to Woking's crotch. "Whaddid yer do to 'im?"

"Don't think the bride'll be very pleased, know wot I mean?" said another.

Nodding and smiling awkwardly, the four Devils filed past, with a waddling Woking bringing up the rear. More young men slapped his backside as he went past, merrily shouting words of encouragement.

They passed through three more carriages, repeating their 'Stag Do' mantra as they went.

"Who thought old Dickie would ever tie the knot?" said Aldershot at one point, when a pair of old ladies' expressions showed skepticism.

"Umm, yes, well, if anyone was going to tame him, it was old Dickette," added Camberley.

"Indeed. I imagine old Dickie is looking forward to having intercourse with old Dickette on a regular basis once they are married," concluded Bracknell.

"He's seen us!" said Woking, looking through into the next carriage. "Come on!"

"Who's seen you," said one of the old ladies with a fierce face. She blocked their way with a walking stick. "Who are you chasing?"

"Old Dickie, of course," said Bracknell, thinking fast. "We're going to drag his willy along the rails as a stag do prank!"

Woking looked down at his crotch and scowled, putting two and two together.

"I shall call the police," said the lady. Aldershot pushed her stick down with his pitchfork and ran past, followed by the others.

They chased their quarry into the next carriage and the one after, shouting "stag do, stag do," as they went, but the spell had been broken, passengers were screaming now. "To Heaven with subtlety," roared Woking, and Bracknell happily raised his pitchfork as they ran, and melted the doors between carriages to save time. They ran through into another carriage, then another, gaining on him now. Then a screeching of brakes, and they all tumbled forward into a heap. Some sort of alarm sounded. Ahead they saw someone force open the side doors and jump onto the track. Bracknell melted the nearest doors on the same side and they all bundled out after him.

"Give up, Coker, you can't escape now," yelled Aldershot.

"We'll consider shaving a million years off your sentence," shouted Woking.

Still the figure ran on. Bracknell and Aldershot fired a few times, but it was hard to aim in near-darkness. The figure reached an alcove, and disappeared into it.

110

The Devils caught up to find a locked metal door. Two pitchforks made short work of it. They saw a man scrabbling with another door's lock.

"Cease!" called Woking.

The man stopped, turned around. "It is him?" asked Woking.

"Yes," said Camberley.

"That's him," agreed Bracknell. "The man from room X10101."

"Brian Coker," said Aldershot.

"Please, call me the Broker," said the man, trying to smile.

"You are coming with us," said Aldershot. "First, place the device you stole on the table." He indicated a small and dusty old table next to where Coker was.

The man did as he was told. He stroked the device with his fingers as he drew them away. "Is that the predictor?" asked Aldershot of Bracknell.

"Oh yes," said Bracknell. Then he looked away, not wanting to see what came next.

"Dispel the blessed thing!" roared Woking.

Aldershot raised his pitchfork and fired, but at that exact moment, Coker sprang forward, taking the whole of the blast. "Sentence ... rescinded," he gasped, with a look of triumph. Then he dissolved into nothing.

"Raaaarrrghhh!" yelled Aldershot, firing again and dispelling the predictor device.

"You cassock!" said Woking. "Satan wanted him alive, to suffer. We're all for it, now."

"At least we know it was him," said Bracknell. "You can't dispel living souls."

"The threat to Hell has been nullified," said Aldershot. "I think He'll accept that, once he calms down. Let's get back to the others." They stepped out onto the railway.

"Bracknell," said Woking.

"Yes?"

"Tell me exactly how I came by this groin injury?"

✻✻✻✻✻

The minibus had made it through Glasgow with surprisingly little trouble. Now, they stood by the remains of Suzy's cottage. There was only one road away from it other than the way they'd come, so that had to be where Bagshot's ambulance had gone.

"You were in that when it collapsed?" asked Helen, indicating the rubble.

"Yeah," replied Suzy. "Under a wardrobe."

"We should not remain in any one place for longer than is necessary," said Mycroft. "On both occasions when we were attacked, the threat developed gradually."

"That's right," said Lysandra. "It seems to build them from our deepest fears. I mean, *we* were all terrified of doing a bad dem dance, but no-one else would be."

"Seriously?" said Dylan. "That's what happened to you? We were drowning in sweat and baby poo, and that was the nice bit! After that he put me in a mediaeval torture chamber!"

"There was hanging too," said Lysandra.

"Ah."

"Did something attack Michael?" Helen asked Suzy. "Before the ambulance took him away, I mean?"

"Ummmm...." said Suzy.

"So as long as we keep moving, we'll be safe?" asked Lucy.

"Relatively speaking," replied Mycroft.

"Won't make any difference if we can't get OUT of here," said Janelle.

"That is a valid concern," agreed Mycroft. "Our point of entry is uncertain, hence our point of exit, doubly so."

"Suzy, you said a Devil took Michael," said Helen. "Perhaps he'd know the way out?"

"He did seem to know what he wanted to do," agreed Suzy. "Also he seemed a bit, well, incompetent!"

"He beat you," said Janelle.

"That was luck," Suzy replied.

"Uhhh, guys," said Lysandra. A thicket of giant nettles now surrounded the minibus.

"How did they get there?" asked Helen, stunned.

"They walked," said Dylan, watching several more amble over.

"Don't touch them," said Suzy. "They're probably deadly."

"As I said, staying in one place for too long here is not advisable," said Mycroft.

More nettles were approaching, heading towards the huddled students.

*****

"Excuse me," said Sir Antony for about the sixth time. "I demand to know what will happen to us!"

"We're boond fer Hell, of course, yee Sassenach scunner," said the Scotsman. "Can ye not see wha' they are?"

The dead men were standing in the corner of the room, watched over by a couple of Devils who casually impaled them with pitchforks from time to time. More Devils were using their pitchforks to crumble the huge concrete block. The Devils who seemed to be in charge were calmly asking questions of the dead souls, two at a time. Whenever they were done with a dead soul, he was ordered to jump into a burning hole, and another was beckoned over to replace him.

"This one's still alive!" called a Devil, yanking a man from the pit.

Theo found himself back in the room. He'd dived into the pit when the shooting began, and spent the next minutes fighting for breath among furious, squirming devils as the cement set fast. Now he looked round at the bloody mess they'd made of everyone else, and the grinning Devil faces looming over him.

Chapter Sixteen

"I understand that we can now go back to Fellingham freightyards, where scientists and birdwatchers believe they've discovered an entirely new kind of bird, one that appears to spend all its time pecking at concrete. Harry Daniels is there. Harry, what news?"

"Hi Myra," said Harry. "You wouldn't believe this so I'm just going to show it to you. What these birds are doing!"

The screen cut to another camera, which for a moment showed empty sky, and then four birds somehow lifting a loose chunk of metal between them, into the air. It was bigger than all of them combined. They rose further and further, then all pulled back and released it. The camera swooped down, showing the chunk smashing into the newly set concrete where the birds had been pecking. Five more birds then repeated the exercise with an even larger chunk. "Professor, any idea what they're doing?" asked Harry.

"Clearly they're trying to break the surface," said Professor McTavish. "A working hypothesis would be that they have eggs buried under there. We have asked the police to let us scan the concrete with imaging equipment, to see what it is they are trying to get at. We believe we'll get permission to enter the site within the half-hour."

"Not sure about that, Prof, look!" said Harry. The camera panned round. An unmarked white van had pulled up, and four men wearing what looked like spacesuits got out.

"Who's in charge here?" shouted one.

A policeman went over to talk to the spacesuit, and the camera caught his astonished expression as the spacesuit explained something to him. The policeman then indicated the camera, and the spacesuited man nodded. The spacesuits walked onto the site carrying nets and odd bits of equipment, while the shaken policeman walked up to Harry. Two other news crews were there, and they converged on him.

"These birds have escaped from a secret government laboratory," said the policeman. "They were freed by animal rights activists last night. They are trained to sniff out sources of radioactivity. It is likely this site has a discarded radioactive source. Anyone who has been on the site will need to see a doctor urgently. The birds will be recaptured now and returned to their lab."

The spacesuited men brought down four of the birds – one each – with taser guns. They stuffed the four into a box. The remaining five birds dived at them, swooping and pecking. The spacesuited men fought back with cricket bats, bringing down three more birds. A man stooped to pick them up, and a beak drove hard into his bottom, rapidly followed by a very hard whack from a cricket bat, smashing both man and bird to the ground. "Oops, sorry Bob!" said the bat wielder, as he removed the stunned bird from his colleague's bottom and put it into a box. The other two men bundled the injured Bob back to their van.

"One more," screamed a voice through their earpieces. "There were nine, get them all! Then cut them in pieces and bury the fuckers!"

The lead spacesuit looked around. No sign of the last bird. "We need to catch the last one!" He yelled at the assembled twitchers. "Fifty pounds to the man who helps me catch it."

Among the crowd was one Andrew Travis, nineteen years old and already a seasoned spotter of rare birds. In his pocket was a yellow stuffed toy called Duckalinda, that he'd taken with him just about everywhere since he was five. He fingered it lovingly, now. But he didn't believe that birds should be captive, and nor was he the sort to accept official explanations for anything. He stroked Duckalinda once more, and made his choice. He sprang up onto the fence, hauled himself over, landed on the other side. The spacesuit saw him and ran in his direction. Andrew ignored him, took two careful steps forward, and then dived hands first into a pile of rubble. He came up with his hands clasped around something yellow, his arms jiggling as if it was fighting to get free.

"Box!" he yelled at the space-suit. "Get the box! It's chewing my hand!"

The suit ran forward with a new box, and opened the lid for a moment so that Andrew could shove the yellow bird in. The suit slammed the lid shut, clicked down the clips on all four sides, shoved fifty pounds into Andrew's hand, and said "get off the site quick mate, it's radioactive."

Andrew ran to the fence and climbed over.

"Tell me you got all that," said Harry to the cameraman. Not that he cared, really, but saying it made him feel so much more important than he really was.

The white van with the spacesuits drove off. Unseen by anyone except Andrew, a yellow bird high in the sky watched it go.

*****

Todd Jennings had done some very odd things in his role as "General Assistant" for Coker Associates. He'd bribed voters in a student hiking club election, paid an actress to impersonate some Australian woman on the phone, helped arrange an exchange visit for one Russian student, and once spent several days finding out which house a child's bicycle had been stolen from, just so he could tell them who'd got it. And now he was speeding along a road in a white van, wearing a fake radiation suit, with three colleagues and nine captured birds in the back. His job was to do what he was told. A lack of imagination made him ideally qualified. When his boss had told him that the birds couldn't be killed, only stunned, he'd accepted it.

"It's getting worse," said one of his colleagues behind him. Indeed, he could hear two of the boxes rattling more and more vigorously as the birds struggled to get out. Nothing was coming from the third box, into which he'd put the final bird. Maybe the boy who caught it had somehow stunned it. He wasn't going to check, though. The damned things were clever; it was probably playing dead.

He looked up to see a yellow speck in the sky, dead in front of him. It had something dark grey beneath it. The distant speck was getting bigger, quickly, as it rushed towards him. Suddenly he realised it was going to hit him square on. He swerved to the left, but the yellow thing swerved too. It was another of the damned birds! And it had –

The bird pulled up at the last second, but the steel bolt it had been carrying shot towards him in a dead straight line, right through the windscreen and into his head, killing him instantly. With its driver dead, the van raced off the road, tipped over and smashed into a tree. The engine ran for another few seconds and cut out, leaving the wheels circling slowly to a halt. After that, the only sound coming from within was the clattering of birds trying to get out of their boxes.

When Todd died, he didn't drive on down to Hell. He did not, after all, know who he worked for, or the terrible goal that his actions were working towards. So when all of his good and bad deeds had been tallied, neither bar had grown very large. The red man had looked thoroughly uninterested, and the blue man had appeared to be shouting at him to pay attention. Todd found himself standing by the wreck of the van, watching the yellow bird that had killed him fly into the wreckage, before emerging a minute or so later with eight of its fellows. The young birdwatcher had tricked him, he realised. It didn't matter now. He wondered if his colleagues had survived. Especially Terry. Well, none of them were standing there in spectral form beside him, so maybe they had.

He turned around, and saw a massive white sign, the size and shape of a door, standing beside a table with three enormous leather-bound books on it, each the size of a paving slab. The tiny red man from his flashback sequence flew over and wrote Todd's name in red ink into a gap among the big lettering on the giant road sign. A little lower down, the blue man had flown in and written numbers into two smaller gaps. Todd read the sign in full.

> 'Final judgement upon _Todd Jenkins_. The actions of your life had been examined in detail, and you are judged to be neither very good nor very evil. You therefore have two choices for your afterlife, going forward. The first is dispelment. This means the immediate and permanent cessation of your conscious existence. If you choose this option, press the black button below. The second is to pay an appropriate forfeit for your misdeeds, which in your case is _19_ years in Hell, after which you may claim your entitlement to _47_ years in Heaven based on your good deeds. If you choose this option, you should press the red button. Terms and conditions apply. Please tick the box to confirm that you have read and accepted these before you proceed.'

Most of his years in Heaven were granted because he'd died young. As for the time in Hell, he'd considered the possibility of going to prison a couple of times, when following the Broker's more dodgy assignments. Indeed, it was the fact that he'd gone ahead despite these suspicions that had earned him most of his misdeed points. He would endure his sentence in Hell. How bad could it be? He did not, after all, have a great imagination. Without further consideration, he pressed the red button. The sign went blank for a second, then returned to how it was, except that the words at the bottom of the sign flashed red: the ones about Terms and Conditions.

Todd walked round to the back of the sign to see where the Terms and Conditions might be written, but the back was blank. Then he walked back round to where the table was, and his eyes alighted on the three massive books.

Oh, no.

The cover of the first one carried the words '*TERMS AND CONDITIONS. VOLUME I.*' Below this was a tickbox. Miserably he opened the book to look at the first page. The font was tiny. There had to be several thousand words on that page alone. Every following page had a similar number.

"This isn't fair!!" he yelled, at nobody. After a while, he did what he assumed everyone else must do, and ticked the box without reading anything. After all, it wasn't as if he had any other options, did he? Then he pressed the red button again.

The sign swung inwards, revealing a doorway and a downward staircase that seemed to go on forever. Meekly, Todd stepped through and began his long journey downwards. From the roof of the ruined van, nine yellow birds watched with interest.

Inside the wrecked van, things weren't too good. The man who'd been in the passenger seat had been knocked unconscious, while in the back of the van, the man with the pecked and whacked buttocks lay moaning, for he now had a broken leg. Beside him, the fourth man was dying. The birds could sense it. Internal injuries; he'd be gone in under an hour. This gave the lead bird an idea. One even better than picking up the steel bolt.

"In here! We're in here," wailed the man with broken legs, as he heard the buckled back doors of the van start to move. He watched in horror as something powerful but clearly not human wrenched the doors open. In his fevered state, he expected to see some lumbering beast appear where the doors had been, but instead there were only a group of small yellow birds. The first one flew in and landed on the head of his stricken colleague, before turning round and tweeting at the others. Now eight more birds gripped the prone man in different places, and began flapping their wings hard. "Wh-what are you doing," gasped the broken-legged man, but the lead bird turned to him and silenced him with a long, hard look. Then they lifted up the other man and flew with him out of the van.

Harry Daniels and his crew had packed up and were heading home. The phone rang. "Harry Daniels," he answered. "What is it?"

"Danny, park the car and look up!" It was the deputy producer. "Reports of a flying man, right near the freight yards where you were. Twitter's going mad with it! I don't think it's a hoax, too many people have seen it!"

"Yes! There!" said the sound man in the back seat. "On the left!!" The driver pulled the car over and they all got out. They saw several other parked cars and pedestrians, all pointing their mobile phones upwards.

"Get the camera out! Fast!" yelled Harry to the TV van that had just stopped behind them. Above them a puffy, silvery figure, its arms and legs stretched out, was slowly progressing through the sky. Harry whipped out his own mobile phone, and tried to zoom in on the object with its camera. Its clothing was silvery, very like the radiation suits worn by those men who'd caught the birds. The helmetless head was lolling downwards. There were yellow things sticking out from it, two on each arm and leg, and one holding the man's hair with its feet. The longer he watched, the more they looked like the exact same yellow birds he'd been filming earlier. The birds and the man were slowly gaining height.

"Tell me you got that," Harry said to the cameraman for the second time today.

The camera man nodded. "It's those birds again, I'd swear it," he said. "They're carrying him. And he looks ... dead!"

"They could be heading back to the spot where we found them," said Harry. "Let's get back there, beat them to it!"

Harry decided, to Hell with police, secret services and alleged radioactivity. This was a story of a lifetime and he was going in. So he climbed into the fenced off area where the birds had been, and walked over to examine the spot where they'd been pecking and bombing the ground. For all their efforts, the concrete was barely dented. And yet they'd kept going, good for them. Something else caught his attention, though. The concrete here was of a different kind to the rest. As if, yes, someone had dumped a dead body and hidden it by pouring concrete on top of it, like they did in gangster films. So why the birds? Could it have been a crime lord with his own secret aviary of strangely loyal birds? One way or another, Harry Daniels was going to find out.

High above him, the yellow birds had picked their spot, high in the air. Some instinct told them exactly where to aim for. The leader cheeped once, and they all let go. The body smashed into the concrete four metres from Harry. Nine birds fluttered down after it, feeling pleased with themselves. "Did you get that?" mouthed Harry. The cameraman nodded. Harry grabbed his microphone. It wouldn't go out live, but that didn't matter. "This is Harry Daniels, at Fellingham freightyards, where earlier today a flock of nine birds were seen pecking the freshly laid concrete. I say freshly laid, only one patch here is fresh, the rest much older, as if someone had drilled a hole and dropped a dead body into it. Whether or not that's true, we've certainly got a dead body here now..."

Terry Jenkins had watched Harry deliver this news report with little interest. He'd just seen his life flash before him, and found out that, much like his brother Todd, he'd done little of anything that could be classed as really good or properly evil. Standing on the spot where he'd died, the big white sign obscured the annoying newsman from his view. Its contents depressed him a little: twelve years in Hell, then forty-two in Heaven. Not much of an afterlife, really. Still it was better than nothing. He pressed the red button. The text at the end flashed red. He glanced down at the three mighty volumes on the table, and then ticked the box on the books without even opening them, before pressing the red button again. The white sign opened like a door, calling into existence a staircase descending downwards out of sight.

"Muuuggghhhhhh!!!!"

THUMP!

The sudden disappearance of the concrete around him had woken Fenwick immediately from his self-imposed sleep. For an instant he'd hung, still hogtied and gagged, in the air in the tunnel of a stairway to Hell. Then he'd dropped down onto the steps.

Terry watched and listened in astonishment as a series of thumps and bumps and muffled yelps of pain receded into the distance down the subterranean stairway, as Fenwick finally tumbled his way back to Hell.

Above him, the nine birds cheeped triumphantly, and joined their wings to perform a brief can-can in the air. Moments later, they vanished.

Confused, Terry hesitated. The rest had made some sort of sense, but he couldn't work out how the tumbling man fitted in. Eventually he shrugged and began his descent.

Harry Daniels had been continuing his monologue, standing over the mashed remains of Terry and speculating as to who'd ordered his end. Bare moments after Terry had stepped onto the stairway, Harry had walked back towards the fresh set concrete by the direct route, stepping straight through the doorway that he couldn't see. He found himself on the stairway. That shouldn't have happened; on a normal day he'd have stepped clean through as if it hadn't been there. But this wasn't a normal day. Sixty one living souls were at this moment loose in the world of the dead, and the mortal veil had been doubly weakened. Harry didn't know this, of course. "Ooh, secret underground bunker," he whispered. "I'm going in to investigate!" he yelled at his crew. "Are you getting this?" But they weren't, not any more.

****

Suzy started the minibus and pulled it onto the road. "Nice work with the whip," said Helen.

"You're welcome," said Suzy, casually wiping the nettle juice off her whip as she drove. "But I might want payment later," she added, looking meaningfully at Martin.

"Do you think we'll catch that Devil? Do you know where he's going?"

Suzy paused, reaching into her mind and finding answers that she hadn't known were there. "Hell. This is only the outside of it. We might be lucky. Sometimes there are queues."

"We're driving TO Hell?!?" said Dylan.

"Anyone has any better ideas, I'm ready to hear them," said Helen.

They drove on in silence.

"Do you believe that?" Dylan asked Lysandra, next to him. "That we're somewhere outside of Hell?"

"I'm not sure what I believe," she replied, cautiously. "But that Suzy girl seems to live here. I don't pretend to understand it. But we have met Devils, and seen

118

things that should be impossible. So we are outside of the physical world as we know it. We could be in some sort of limbo, between Heaven and Hell."

"But there is no between!" said Janelle.

"If we accept that our concepts of Heaven and Hell are merely religious archetypes, at best heavily distorted by the self-serving agendas of various religions, then we must conclude that the Afterlife may indeed have aspects to it that fall outside the teachings of Christianity," said Mycroft.

"Not helping," hissed Lysandra.

"Perhaps this is a place that everyone normally passes through, really quickly, on the way to Heaven or Hell?" suggested Dylan. "So it just never gets a mention? But for us, something went wrong, and we got stuck?" Lysandra gave his hand a quick squeeze.

"You think?" said Janelle.

"Then how did we get stuck here?" asked Bernie.

"On the motorway," said Lysandra. "Everything went weird after that. Something happened on the motorway."

"You think we're dead?" said Dylan.

"No," said Lysandra thoughtfully. She dropped her voice. "I mean, we all saw Natalia ... die. Really die. I don't see how a person can die twice. So we're alive, but we're somewhere I don't think living people are meant to be. And it's ... of course!! It's making antibodies! Like we're invading microbes in a human body, and it's trying to get rid of us! That's why it's trying to kill us!"

"I do not believe that your observations will offer comfort to your fellows," observed Mycroft.

"But it *does* explain things," she persisted. "The place is behaving like a living organism."

"Not right ... " said Janelle. "That's not right!"

"But what do we *do*?" said Dylan.

"Following the Devil has three possible beneficial outcomes," explained Mycroft. "Two have already been noted: rescuing Michael, and gaining information from the Devil who took him. I would like to postulate a third: perhaps the goal of the Devil is to expel him back into the mortal world, in which case he could lead us to the exit. If indeed we are treated as foreign objects as if in a body, would that not be a possible scenario?"

"Yes," said Lysandra. "A body would either destroy or expel a foreign object, whichever was easier."

"Devils don't do that," said Janelle. "They torture, and lie, and ..."

"It just looked like a Devil," said Lysandra. "Like the dance lady, and the warden. I think these are quite separate from the Satan of the Bible. He's somewhere else, if He exists."

"He exists," said Janelle firmly.

*****

Bagshot was singing as his ambulance trundled along. He'd just begun to convince himself that he might make it to the Gates without anything else going wrong. Then Mickleham's face appeared, from nowhere, glaring through his windscreen. Bagshot screeched to a halt. "What are you doing?" he yelled, surprised by his own courage.

"Taking no chances," answered Mickleham. He had a windscreen wiper embedded in his neck, from the yellow minibus. It caused a whistling sound whenever he spoke.

"Look, I've got Walton, he's tied down, and I'm taking him in. You are not needed."

"I'm your superior! I'm taking your captive, and you're taking the blame!" Mickleham yanked Bagshot out of the bus.

"No I won't let you! "

"I wasn't asking." Mickleham struck Bagshot hard on the head with a rock, then caught his crumpling body and tossed it as far away as he could. Yellow tweeting birds flew after it.

"Bye bye Baggie," said Mickleham, walking around to the back of the ambulance and pulling it open. He looked with satisfaction at the quivering human. Its wobbling bottom attracted him most. Mickleham yanked the bed from the ambulance. "Hello puny human," he said. "Now I wonder, are you a dead soul or a construct?" In his hand grew a nine-stringed whip made of viciously thorned creepers. He waved it in front of Michael's eyes so he could see it. "This will flay off your skin, and the pain will be exquisite. If you're a dead soul, then the wounds will keep healing, even as I make more! But if you're a construct, they won't heal, and you'll soon die and evaporate. Let's find out, shall we?" Mickleham' yanked down Michael's jeans and underpants. "Ready?"

"Mmmm," said Michael, and unclenched.

A Plinian eruption of jet-propelled excrement caught Mickleham full in the face, carrying him several feet into the air, flipping him over and bringing him down hard on his head. Dazed, the dung-splattered Devil staggered briefly to his feet, then pitched forward again to reveal Bagshot, standing behind him holding a crowbar. "If anyone asks, he just hit his head twice on the ground, OK, Barry?" he said.

"Mmmm," agreed Michael.

"Let's get going before he wakes up," said Bagshot, and he pulled Michael's bed back into the ambulance and drove off.

A flock of yellow birds appeared around Mickleham, took one sniff, and then flew away.

Bagshot drove on down the road, singing louder this time, inventing lyrics about Mickleham as he went along. He could see the Gates now, in the distance.

Within Hell itself, an ancient warning system sensed his approach, or rather, that of the living soul he was carrying. Alarms went off in Woking's and Byfleet's offices, but neither was there to hear them.

Chapter Seventeen

Frimley awoke, his head sore. He didn't understand at all what had happened. He put his hands to his face, and yelped in horror. It felt like a giant mop: masses of rags and tissues all over his face and scalp. The birds had been tugging at these to wake him. At least his vision had cleared. What had happened? He staggered to his feet and looked around. A straight road ran past him, but in every other direction, there was featureless, flat ground. "This is the Abysmal Plain," he muttered to himself. "But that's not possible ... I was on the surface with Ashtead and then ..."

He spread his arms and lifted himself gingerly into the sky. It confirmed his idea, because Devils could not fly in the mortal world. He needed to get back and report. They'd been attacked. He lifted himself higher, and followed the road with his eyes.

"What??"

The road ended some miles further on, but not at the familiar Gates of Hell. It disappeared into a mass of identical white human houses. There had to be hundreds of them, a sizeable human town. But it couldn't be here! The Abysmal Plain contained only Hell, there'd been nothing else there since they blocked all the ways in for living souls. Only the passing deceased, following routes into Hell maintained by the Devils. Nothing else could exist here unless ...

Frimley remembered the truck they'd been driving. Ashtead hadn't said what was in it, Frimley had assumed he'd checked ... but there'd been something very off about Ashtead. Frimley recalled running makeup and a detaching tail ... an imposter! He'd been tricked! If he'd brought living humans down here ... it didn't bear thinking about!! Out here on the Plain they'd cause trouble, but if one of them tried to get into Hell ... it would destroy everything. This was no time to investigate. He had to alert his superiors, fast, but Devils could fly no faster than humans could run. Desperately he followed the road backwards away from the town. Ahead loomed the familiar thirteen-lane motorway that took damned souls towards Hell. One of the dead souls was on a motorbike, and Frimley swooped down beside him, kicked the soul off onto the road, dropped himself onto the bike and put his foot down hard. His bike accelerated past two hundred miles per hour as he shot towards the gates of hell, smashing through several walls as he failed to stop fast enough. "Remain still!," he yelled at the souls spilling out of the ruptured rooms, as he sought the emergency summons button.

****

In the Broker's former room, all of the Devils felt the summons instantly. All except Ashtead, who was still venting his fury on Theo's behind with a whip. "We have to get back!" said Woking, who'd just arrived.

"We can't leave these corpses like this," said Camberley. "They have supernatural injuries! If someone connects it with sightings of us, religious belief will skyrocket! And we're barely coping with the daily influx of souls into Hell as it is!"

"Suggestion! Sir!!" barked Aldershot.

"Yes?" said Woking.

"Make this one do it!" he said, indicating Theo.

Woking raised an eyebrow, then nodded.

"You," said Aldershot, bringing his face close to Theo's. "Attention to orders! You will dispose of these bodies! You will conceal all the evidence that it was Devils that killed them. Failure to comply will mean punishment! Do you understand?"

"Aaaargh!!" said Theo.

"Ashtead, desist!!" growled Aldershot. The whip was petulantly withdrawn. "If you comply, we will halve your sentence! Fail, and we will torture you to death, and then double your sentence! Are we clear?"

Theo whimpered his assent. Aldershot turned round to Woking, who nodded. Then all the Devils vanished. Hauling himself to his feet, shaking, Theo wondered how on earth he'd complete this grisly task. He quickly worked out what he'd need: a very big bomb.

***

Those 'grey' souls like Todd and Terry Jenkins, who descended via staircase, emerged within a mile of the Side Gate of Hell, to which they were required to continue on foot. There was, however, a bit of a backlog. When Todd emerged, he encountered a queue stretching back far out of sight, whose occupants all mutedly pointed him towards its far end. When finally he got one to talk, he was told that they'd been waiting for more than four years, there being (they reckoned) about a quarter of a million souls in the queue. Worse, those four years, or five by the time you reached the front, were not included in your time served in Hell. Apparently one exceedingly patient soul had actually read that in the Terms and Conditions. The start of the queue was about fifty miles away, Todd was told, so he started his long walk past the sullen, silent souls.

The size of the processing backlog at the Side Gate of Hell caused some headaches for the Devils, though the misery on the faces of new arrivals like Todd was some consolation for them.

Normally, souls arrived in silence. The approaching sound of "Muuuughhhhh"-Thud-Thud-Thud! was therefore the only interesting thing that the souls in the front part of the queue had heard in over four years. The entire queue section that heard it turned to their right, mouths open in astonishment, as the sound drew closer and closer, then out of a stairway tumbled a hog-tied Devil, coming to rest right by the queue. They waited for something else to happen but nothing did, other than the emergence of Terry Jenkins, who knew no more about where the hapless devil had come from than did anyone else. The queuing souls watched Fenwick struggling and failing to get free. After a while, a few of them took advantage of his presence and sat down for a rest. Fenwick didn't even mind too much. He was used to it, now.

Elsewhere on the Plain, Mickleham was awake. He looked down at his excrement-covered body in disgust, and attempted to clean off the muck. He couldn't. Mickleham didn't understand it; if the stuff had come out of a dead soul, then a Devil could control it, just as he could the soul itself. Yet this faecal matter felt horribly real. Mickleham gazed at the large lump of it in his hand. It *was* real. He could sense the living bacteria swimming around in it. Yet if the excrement was real, then the soul it had come out of would have to be ... alive.

Oh, no!

*****

"WHY HAVE YOU DESECRATED MY CHAMBER ONCE MORE, YOU FESTERING SKIDMARKS?" roared Satan.

"You summoned us, great Lordship" said Bracknell. Camberley clopped him on the head with his tail. Another traditional greeting, he thought.

"Are our enemies destroyed?" bellowed Satan.

"Dead or dispelled, my Lord" said Woking.

"We have a new problem," said Mytchett. He was a short, neat Devil with small eyes and a fidgety manner; he wore glasses, and no-one in Hell knew why. "We have identified the source of the tremors." He indicated a figure at the far end of the room.

"AaaAAaahhhh!" said Bracknell. "What the Heaven is that?"

"It's me you idiot! Frimley," said the mass of dirty rags.

"What happened?" said Camberley.

"I was attacked by the humans. Then blown up. We seemed to escape, then somehow I was blown up again. Worse this time. On the Abysmal Plain. I think I was tricked into delivering living souls there!"

"How many?" said Woking, his face pink with fear.

"I don't know!" pleaded Frimley.

"I have analysed the tremors," said Mytchett. "Based on my readings, and making some reasonable assumptions, I calculate around eight humans last night, then thirty to fifty more a few hours ago."

"FIFTY?" roared Satan. "FIFTY??"

"Would not the Plain have destroyed the invaders?" enquired Woking.

"A single live soul would stand no chance," said Mytchett, who seemed utterly unfazed by Satan's wrath. "It would be dead, or helpless, within about two hours. But four or more together ... well we have no precise data, because it's never happened, but research has suggested that if each human feared different things, then the constructs from so many could interfere with one another. Furthermore the humans would tend to protect one another … and moreover the longer they last, the less often the Plain would attack them."

"So they could wander around indefinitely?" roared Satan. "Unacceptable!!"

"We do however have evidence of a beam-up to Heaven last night. Indicating that at least one of them was extirpated," said Mytchett.

"That is hardly a comfort," bellowed Satan. "Fifty!! That is more than all previous incursions through history combined! How did this happen?"

"The first one would appear to have involved Fenwick," said Mytchett. Most of the assembled Devils nodded as if no further explanation was needed.

"Fenwick, Fenwick, always the immaculate Fenwick!" bellowed Satan. "Why was he not dispelled?!

Aldershot, Woking and Camberley shared meaningful glances, but none wished to remind Satan of his own earlier instruction.

"I will be glad to arrange it – Sir!" barked Aldershot.

"Then bring him hither!" roared Satan.

"At this time we have not yet located him – Sir!" said Aldershot.

"STILL?"

"My Lord, discipline can wait," said Woking desperately. "We must erect defences!"

"If they still work," said Camberley.

Satan turned round to him slowly, with venomously narrow eyes. Camberley spoke very fast: "There has not been an incursion from Mortal World for over a thousand years because we built such good defences against living souls crossing the veil that it totally stopped happening and with no living incursions for hundreds of years people not me but other people started to say it was a waste of resources to maintain them so mostly we stopped and they haven't been checked since the sixteenth century please don't dispel me!"

"In addition, Lord, our defences date back from before the invention of motor vehicles, therefore most of them would be ineffective in this instance, assuming the invaders are driving," said Mytchett.

"There used to be a proximity alarm that would be activated if live souls got too close, didn't there?" enquired Byfleet.

"Have you checked it?" asked Aldershot.

"Ummm … ah. It's flashing!" said Camberley.

"That means they're two miles away?" asked Woking.

"Or closer!" said Byfleet.

"There's still the moat – Sir!" said Aldershot.

"It's got bridges over it, idiot!" roared Satan.

"Do you think they are all in vehicles?" said Woking.

"The second incursion of thirty to fifty souls was almost instantaneous, implicating a vehicle," said Mytchett, fiddling importantly with his glasses. "The same applies to the first grouping as well. Furthermore, know Fenwick was attending a *routine* road death." He glanced accusingly at Aldershot. "We must assume that the wrong vehicle came down the road to Hell, driven by one of the psychic sensitives who've disappeared from the records. As a corporeal vehicle has not yet arrived at our gates, so we must assume it is roaming the plain."

"I must also add that Bagshot and Mickleham are missing from greet duty, my Lord" said Woking.

"Halleh-blessing-lulya!" roared Satan. Everyone winced at the double profanity. "Words cannot describe the incompetence!!!"

"We must put aside all other concerns," said Woking desperately. "I don't need to remind anyone what would happen should a living soul penetrate into Hell itself, do I?!"

There was an awkward pause, and one nervous hand went up at the back.

"Seriously?" said Woking. "Seriously?? Hell is a breathtakingly complex structure, a triumph of five-dimensional engineering built by geniuses like Camberley and Bracknell."

Camberley beamed.

"… who somehow managed to forget the most basic principles of security! You all built an edifice so complex that no mortal mind could even begin to conceptualise it! They're not equipped!! So if one passed into Hell, they'd instantly imagine the fourth and fifth dimensions *out* of existence, and suddenly all the rooms of every variant Hell would be squeezed into an impossibly small space, meaning…"

"Boom," said Camberley, who at least had the decency to look embarrassed.

***

Not too far away, Bagshot had never felt so good. He'd shown Mickleham who was boss. He'd recaptured the runaway soul, who was still tied to the bed in the back. He'd built himself a lovely ambulance, which he was going to keep after he'd delivered his captive. He was now on the fast lane of the thirteen-lane motorway. Just half a mile ahead of him, the Gates of Hell loomed. *Home*, he thought.

***

"They could be heading straight for Hell right now!" wailed Camberley. "We don't check the cars coming in, never did! There's not been incursions since cars were invented! We don't have a single device to even slow them down! The car park reception is INSIDE of Hell! If there's living souls coming, we're doomed!"

"Close the Gates of Hell!" boomed Satan. "Close every entrance!"

"The Gates haven't closed since 1834!" said a frantic Camberley. "People not me of course but people kept saying it was too much work to repair them and anyway the mechanism on the old gates was buggered and we'd have to replace them and people not me but people said no we can't replace them they're iconic and I said OK get some extra gates just for defence and they said no it would spoil the effect so I'm sorry we can't close the gates please don't dispel me!"

"Blow up the bridge!" roared Satan.

"I-i-it's nearly indestructible," wailed Camberley.

"Send Devils to the Bridge," ordered Woking. "Whoever's closest! Any driver who isn't a Devil, shoot them to make sure they're dead!"

"There's one more thing we can try," said Byfleet quickly. "Mytchett, Bracknell, I need a transmitting radio and I need one NOW!"

"If I modify this tablet," said Bracknell.

"I shall assist you," said Mytchett.

"All frequencies," said Byfleet. "And it needs to transmit whether the receiving radio's on or not!"

"What are you planning?" said Woking.

"Room six-seven-two," replied Byfleet.

"Good thinking!" said Woking.

"Explain!" bellowed Satan.

"It's genius!" said Woking, then flinched. Compliments weren't allowed in Hell. He quickly went, on hoping no-one would notice. "It uses the power of the Plain! It'll stop living souls in their tracks but it won't affect dead ones, or us!"

"It's ready," said Bracknell.

*****

Martin yelped as the minibus radio came on, out of the blue.

"We interrupt this program to bring you an urgent travel news flash. All roads in this area are subject to major roadworks. Traffic has slowed to a standstill. You are strongly advised to abandon your journey. Now back to your program."

The radio went dead again. Suzy, Martin and Helen exchanged confused glances. Behind, Mycroft said "those devices that interrupt music with traffic reports can save on average five percent of journey time. However sixty percent of drivers don't know how to turn them on, or off."

"Mycroft, we weren't playing a CD," said Helen. "The radio's been broken since we got the bus!"

"They weren't lying though," said Suzy. Ahead was a line of stationery backlights, stretching as far ahead as the eye could see.

The housing enforcement officers all heard it. It played through the radio in every house they had visited. Each was surprised by the speed with which traffic cones, road holes and temporary traffic lights had appeared in the cul-de-sacs they were investigating.

Mickleham didn't hear it. He was flying as fast as he could, praying to Lucifer that he could catch up with Bagshot before he passed through the gates. *Please let me be in time, please let me be in time!*

Bagshot in his ambulance heard it. It had no effect on his mind, of course, for he was a Devil, nor on Michael, who didn't hear it. Bagshot passed two anxious Devils, who waved him on through, then fired spikes at the driver behind him. He drove onto the bridge of Hell, passing over the moat, with the open Gates right in front of him. Just a few moments now, and his job would be done, and done well.

In the back, on the bed, Michael felt strangely relaxed. It was all some strange prank, he was telling himself. No more harm would come to him now.

The sound of a million fingernails scraping down blackboards screamed out across Hell. "The proximity alarm!" cried Camberley, over the noise. "It's the proximity alarm! A live soul is crossing the bridge!"

"All Devils to the bridge! Stop all traffic!" yelled Woking. "Stop everything!"

Mickleham saw Devils swooping from all sides towards the Ambulance. One raised a pitchfork to fire, but too late. Then came an explosion so massive that they heard it in Heaven.

End of Part One

Part Two

Chapter Eighteen

The sky was a perfect crystal blue. Fluffy white clouds drifted past, but never impeded the rays of the sun. The sunshine gave that perfect warmth that one only feels on days when it's just a little too cold whenever the sun isn't out. By her feet, flowers of every colour and kind grew out from the grass. Butterflies patterned like stained glass windows fluttered from flower to flower, while further away animals that should be trying to eat one another gambolled and played together instead.

Natalia walked on. So far, the people she'd met had been no use at all. A man with a net was running around catching butterflies shouting "new species! new species" and she hadn't even bothered talking to him. She needed to find whoever was in charge.

In the distance, a winged figure moved through the sky. "Angel! Oi, Angel! Come here please! Come here!" The figure turned, and headed straight for her, alighting a few feet away. Its skin had a gentle blue colour, and it wore nothing but a short, fluffy white skirt with feathers on it. At first it looked strangely androgynous, but it looked at her and changed as she watched: bulging biceps, bulging triceps, and bulging groin area. It flexed its expanded muscles, and moved its now chiselled jaw and chin from side to side. Then it approached her.

"Am I in Heaven?" she asked.

"Yes. Would you like to have sex? We find it helps new arrivals to remove any inhibitions that – "

Natalia pursed her lips in surprise. Her mother and granny were due for one big shock when they got here, she thought. "No right now," she said. "I want to know how I get here."

"You died," said the Angel, simply. "You were judged virtuous, and a celestial stairway descended to invite you Home."

"This no happen," she said. "I drive car into wall to save friends. Then next thing, I am here."

"Then you are suffering memory loss. Sex is a good cure for memory loss."

"It no matter if I forget thing. My friends are in danger. I know where they are now, they are in Hell!"

"If they did bad things and then died, they will have gone to Hell. It is sad for them but deserved. I know a way I can help you stop thinking about it."

"You no understand! I go there with them! We were still alive! They ARE still alive!"

"You cannot be alive and also in Hell," said the Angel.

"You are no sure. I see in your eyes."

"There are rules. There are barriers. Once, it could happen. Now it is impossible. You have become unbalanced and irrational. The cure is – "

"Sex, yes," she completed for him to save time.

"Good!" said the Angel, and moved to pull off his white feathery skirt.

"No!" said Natalia. "I never want sex with blue sex maniac man who before look a bit like a girl. Stop asking, okay?"

"Okay," said the Angel. "What about a game of Buckaroo, or Twister? These have also been shown to release stress and create enjoyment. Or Tiddly-Winks?"

"Stop it! Give me what I want. Send me to Hell. I want to go help my friends."

"You cannot. You have been sent to Heaven."

"So send me to Hell."

"I cannot. How about Scrabble? Maybe snakes and ladders?"

"Then send one of you to help them! Send Angel!"

"We cannot interfere in Hell."

"Then take me to someone who is in charge!"

"No angel commands. All here are equal."

"Like communists?" said Natalia. Maybe her gran would like the place after all. "It no work, soon you have McDonalds come."

The Angel just nodded.

"Then take me to God," she said, arms folded.

"I cannot," he replied.

"I demand it!"

"God isn't here."

"He no exist?" she said, eyes widening.

"We are not really sure," he admitted.

"But you are Angel!" she said.

"I help to run Heaven, as do we all. But the presence of God is not physical. He exists in our hearts."

"But that just the same as in world!" she exclaimed.

"Souls are not here for ever," said the Angel. "We think they go to Him when their time here ends."

"You THINK?"

The Angel scratched its head. It wasn't supposed to answer these questions truthfully. It never had done before. "You are not a normal soul," it said.

"I am very angry soul," she replied. "And I want to go to Hell."

"It is impossible," he said again.

"Why?" she asked.

"It is not determined by choice. It is determined by the quality of your deeds."

"Really?" she asked, and kneed him hard in the groin. "How many bad points I get for hurting an Angel?"

"Only when you are alive," the angel gasped.

"That is shame," she said, and kneed his groin harder.

"You're dead," croaked the angel. "Your deeds here change nothing."

She kicked his groin, this time. "Are you sure?"

"Yes," he rasped.

"You use this a lot, I think?" she said, crunching her knee into his crotch once again.

The angel's face screwed up in pain. "But when I do this you no punish?" (Crunch!)

Then the ground shook, and they heard a deep distant rumble.

"What was that?" asked Natalia.

"I don't know," croaked the Angel. "It sounded like an explosion in Hell. A big one!"

Natalia's eyes widened in horror. "My friends are in danger! Send me there now!"

"I can't!"

"My friends need my help!" (Knee!) "So I do this again till you help!" (Kick!) "Send me to Hell or I no stop!" (Crunch!)

*****

Satan's chamber shook violently, rocks fell from the ceiling, and the assembled Devils staggered from side to side a bit.

"Is that it?" roared Satan, concealing his fear. "Are we rent asunder?"

"It sounded more like a bomb, my Lord" said Woking.

"It cannot have been a live soul, for the dimensions of Hell remain intact," said Bracknell. "We would all have been annihilated instantly, had it been a live soul!"

"Indeed," said Camberley, almost crying with relief. "The last line of defence was a ring of explosive devices placed under the Gate and the Side Gate of Hell, which would go off if a living soul crossed them. "I didn't think they could still work, but it seems they've grown stronger with time!"

"Some kinds of explosive do that," said Mytchett.

"It would appear that this bomb just prevented disaster," said Woking. "One or more living souls tried to cross the threshold. All our other efforts came too late."

"Inspect the damage," boomed Satan. "Check every entrance! No-one in or out till I'm satisfied."

The gates of Hell were gone. Initially, the Devils thought them annihilated entirely, but they were later found sticking out of the ground at odd angles, about six miles away on the plain. Where they had stood, there was now a huge crater, a mile across and hundreds of metres deep, interrupting the Walls and Moat of Hell either side of it, and the thirteen-lane motorway into Hell, too. A colossal dust cloud rose above it, shooting occasional lightning bolts down for good measure. Slowly the contents of the moat, which was boiling hydrofluoric acid, began flowing into the crater.

*****

Over the next few hours, a strange kind of calm began to descend. The boundaries of Hell were secure, arguably more so than they had ever been, as the main highway terminated in the newly formed Lake of Hell, filled with bubbling acid. Of course, vehicles were still driving towards Hell on the motorway, and the Devils simply allowed them to drive straight into the lake, upon which they promptly dissolved. From these, there came a procession of screaming souls scrambling back up to the shore, covered in blistering skin, and amazed that they had not died again.

After an hour of discussion, Satan and his Cabal agreed to begin admitting dead souls once again – the last thing they needed was another backlog. So a detail of Devils was chosen to fly souls one by one across the lake into Hell, after they'd checked they were really dead, of course. A burning spike through the heart was a good way to do that. The queue at the Side Gate of Hell started moving again, although the new burning spike test slowed things down a bit there, as well.

Further back down the queue, the souls lucky enough to be close to Fenwick took it in turns to rest their legs by sitting on him. Fenwick ignored them, thinking about his birds. It couldn't have been a coincidence, that tunnel opening in exactly the right place. He'd expected them to try to free him, but his only real hope had been that they might attract the attention of humans who might dig him up. For them to devise such a clever solution … it went far beyond the simple pecking they normally did. Perhaps being above the surface might have changed them, he pondered. Like most Devils, he was very familiar with the speeches of a rather smug human called Richard Dawkins, about something called "Evolution" that happened up there. Dawkins' lectures were played on a continuous loop to far right 'Christian' souls in Hell, of which there were rather a lot. Had Fenwick's own birds managed to change, to evolve, over time? If so, well, maybe it was time to call on them again. He clamped his jaw tightly on the ballgag, the pressure on the roof of his mouth rising and rising, until eventually he passed out.

The two old ladies and one man sitting on him had to dive out of the way as a flock of nine birds swooped in to peck at Fenwick's head. Yet they stopped after a moment. The lead one waddled over to his mouth, still clamped tight about the iron ballgag. It pondered for a moment, then flew off, cheeping at its fellows to follow.

A few minutes later, the birds arrived at the walls of Hell, with their moat of hydrofluoric acid. Nearby, a line of very nervous, very weary souls stood on a narrow, rickety bridge, waiting to finally be admitted through the Side Gate by a bored Devil clerk with a burning spike. The birds dived straight into the acid, drank as much as they could, and then emerged unscathed onto the surface. They swam to the shore, shook themselves down (causing serious burns on the shins of the five souls unlucky enough to be standing nearby), and then flew off back to Fenwick. Upon reaching him, each bird would take its turn to stand on his top lip and squirt from its rear end a mix of acid and guano onto the ballgag in his mouth. Slowly the gag began to fizz and dissolve. Its acid delivered, each bird would then fly off for another load. Those souls sitting on Fenwick were careful to stay away from his head.

The charred remains of a Devil were found, a mile or so from the crater, accompanied by a hideous stench of burnt excrement. On Aldershot's orders he was carried to the edge of the Lake of Hell, where he reassembled himself.

"Bagshot!" cried Mickleham as he eyes suddenly opened. "He's got a live soul! We've got to stop him! He's heading for Hell!"

"You knew this!?" enquired Aldershot, with a cruel smile "And you let it happen?"

"Well I ... he ... yes ... no ... Bagshot went crazy, sir!"

"Bagshot is generally agreed to be the weakest, most pathetic cassock in Hell!" shouted Aldershot. "And you, you worthless excuse for a Devil, you let him beat you!? Is that what you're saying?"

"Well, there was man tied to a bed as well," replied Mickleham. "And he ..."

"Oh I *see*," interrupted Aldershot. "Clearly you faced unimaginable odds."

Mickleham hung his head.

"I could have you dispelled! I should!" roared Aldershot. "But Satan himself could not abide your stench long enough to do it! So from this moment forwards, you are barred from entering Hell! You will remain by the lake and greet the arriving souls as they crawl out of it."

"As you command, sir," said Mickleham.

"So go and join them, you utter failure!" yelled Aldershot, and he threw Mickleham into the lake. Mickleham floundered and wailed as his skin burnt, but unknown to him, he had company. The atoms of Bagshot were currently floating free in the lake, gradually trying to find one another.

*****

Another Devil for whom execution for incompetence looked likely was Frimley, his face still a mass of tissues. For now, he'd been kept alive to guide a squadron of Devils to the strange new town he'd reported. When they reached it, it had more than doubled in size from what he'd seen before. As they hung in the air and watched, they saw new streets being added at its edges, one by one. The streets were undriveable, full as they were of traffic cones and fenced off holes.

The Housing Enforcement Officers had received revised instructions a couple of hours into their jobs. Now, instead of checking every house, they were to check the first two in each street. If they could find the same rule violation in both houses, they could assume the same fault in every house on that street, and issue fail notices to all of them. They always did – they were good at their jobs. It got each of them on to the next street much quicker. Beyond each street, they imagined another, of much the same kind, and that was what they found. Hence the continual growth of the town. Their fears were not like those of normal people; on bad nights they dreamt of dangerous wiring that they'd missed, or an imperfect fire door they'd let pass for some ridiculous reason like it not being in any way necessary in that location. As a result of these fears, a wide range of faults were called into being in houses that they'd inspected, and one or two even burnt down. This only urged them on.

In the Governor's Mansion, Kane Winkle's palmtop computer bleeped. For a moment he thought that it was a text message, even though the Broker had told him that would be impossible where he was. Instead, the message was a time-delayed one from the Broker himself.

If I have not joined you by now, I'll be dead. Do not concern yourself with this, it's unfortunate but cannot be helped. My goal now is revenge. You are from this moment the leader. Your army is forming. If my timing is right, the enemy knows about your little town by now. Go to the window and look up.

Kane did. A flock of seven Devils was hanging there, high in the sky. Kane felt a wave of fear. He was stuck here now, following the plans of a dead man, whose only stated goal was revenge. The Devils would come; they could not fail to find him in this huge, red mansion. His only help, Preston, was still searching the house for young women. Kane saw the Devils wheel around and fly off into the distance. He returned his attention to the palmtop, and read the rest of the message, amazed by the instructions he now received.

****

What felt like many hours after the explosion, the Wacky Walkers' minibus had progressed thirty yards. Bernie passed the time with some sing-songs, which the Folksoc girls occasionally joined in with. He was currently singing about how the wheels of the bus didn't go round and round when caught in British roadworks.

Suzy told Martin that it would help him to grieve if he described to her in detail the things he'd have liked to do with the lovely Natalia.

"I'd have loved to take her for a walk through one of the Peak District valleys," he said.

"And after that?"

"Well, we'd probably have to get the bus home, because I don't drive and I don't think she had a car."

"I was thinking more about what you'd like to do in the evening," she murmured.

"Ah. Well, I hope she might have let me cook her a meal. I can do a fairly good bolognaise sauce now."

"And so, after the meal had been a success, the lights are down low, and she's looking at you admiringly, what then?"

"Well perhaps, if I was lucky, really lucky, then maybe I could persuade her to watch some *Blakes-7* with me. It's a really underrated show."

"Is it a romantic show?"

"Oh, no, it's about these six fugitives who gain control of an incredible alien ship, and there's this totally evil Federation that they …"

"And when you finished watching the telly?"

None of them saw the Devil high above, who had spotted the traffic jam and correctly deduced that there were live humans caught somewhere within it.

*****

"We have found the interlopers, my Lord! They are trapped in a traffic jam, inside a battered old van. Just say the word and they shall be slaughtered like the irritating scum that they are!!"

Satan cocked a disdainful eye at the breathless Devil who'd delivered the news. "You seem very pleased with yourself, Merton!"

The young Devil flinched with horror. "N-no, my Lord! M-merely proud to have been able to serve at a time of ... erm ..."

"Proud, Merton? Are you saying you're better than us? And a time of *what*, exactly? A time when junior underlings know better than the Lord of Hell what action should be taken?"

Merton began to gnaw his knuckles in misery.

"I shall decide how to deal with you when this ... 'time' you speak of is over," bellowed Satan. "BEGONE!!"

Merton rushed from the room, trying not to cry.

"Admirable cruelty, my Lord," observed Woking. "But he is merely young and enthusiastic."

"I *HATE* young and enthusiastic," harrumphed Satan.

"So what of the students?" enquired Woking. "They caused great trouble, but it was not exactly their fault."

Satan thought for a moment. "Send a squadron!! They shall be slaughtered like the irritating scum that they are!!"

Chapter Nineteen

Up in Heaven, Natalia kicked the Angel in the groin for the two hundred and thirteenth time.

"I think … " he croaked.

"Yes?" she enquired.

"I think I might ask for a second opinion."

*****

"FOR WHAT REASON AM I FORCED TO ENDURE YOUR INSUFFERABLE PRESENCE, YOU PATHETIC INSECT?

Camberley recoiled in shock. "W-well you asked me to … hang on … Woking? What's with the Satan impression?"

"Good, was it?" said Woking.

"If He knew you were doing it…" said Camberley

"And you'd tell him, would you?" asked Woking, sweetly.

"No, no, not I, sir," said Camberley meekly.

"As it happens, there is a rumour that Beelzebub III might abdicate after this fiasco. I thought I might go for the top job!"

In fact there was no such rumour, but there would be now. Yet there would be some substance behind it. Woking had been updating Satan every hour about the situation around the Lake of Hell, and on the Abysmal Plain. He'd relayed the news about the rapidly growing New Town, and sightings of a strange, dystopian version of Glasgow beyond it. He'd casually recommended the latter as a holiday destination for Devils. This has drawn an unexpected response from his Master.

"I am tired, Woking. So very tired and bored. Convention does not allow me to leave the inner core of Hell, do you know that? Yet at the same time, we seldom admit human souls so deep. I spend my days signing memos, Woking! I have not inflicted torment on a Human soul for six hundred years! Six hundred! Seeing that soul in my room, even just a projection, brought home to me all that I miss!"

"Your leadership is vital to the torment of millions!" Woking had replied.

"Where is the joy in that, when I see none of it? In my free time, I find nothing more to relieve the tedium than watching *The Appendage* or *I'm a Celeriac get me out of here!*"

"Oh we all watch *I'm a Celeriac*," Woking had replied, careful not to correct the mistake. "Great source of ideas."

"I hear there's a room where souls are stuck for eternity in the company of Peter André and Katie Price, yes," agreed Satan, with a weak smile.

"It's a series of rooms, actually" said Woking. "Each one gets a Peter and Katie to themselves."

"It's good work," said Satan.

"Yes," said Woking.

An awkward silence had followed.

"If there's nothing else?" Woking had said.

"Has there ever been anything else?" Satan had replied. "I miss the old days, sometimes."

"You didn't much like your old job, either, I thought." Many centuries earlier, Beezlebub III had been plain old Dorking, who'd risen from the celestial liaison to become leader of English Hell. But when Beelzebub II had started going off the rails, Dorking had challenged him for the Satanship, and won.

"In some of the other Hells, the Devils just fight each other all the time," observed Satan. "It's chaos. Threatening to dispel them doesn't help, because they all do it. I've seen dead souls laughing at them. Laughing! Oh, I deal with it when I see it, but I can't be everywhere."

Would help if you learned some of the languages, Woking thought, but he said nothing.

Now, Camberley was eyeing Woking curiously. "A Satan cannot abdicate, you know that," he said. "Satanship can only pass from one to another through mortal combat."

"I believe that the last few such combats have each been a farce," said Woking. "A tired, old Satan so fed up that he preferred his destruction to continuing in the job. So he groomed a challenger and allowed him to win."

"And you think that will be you?" sneered Camberley.

"If Satan requests it, I will not deny him," replied Woking.

"Your sense of duty shames us all," said Camberley.

Woking bristled at the sarcasm. "What have you come to report?"

Camberley's smile weakened. "Well, you ordered that all rooms be checked for absences and missing devices."

"And??" growled Woking.

"Another device has gone missing."

"Raziel's halo!!" yelled Woking, as a bolt of fear spiked through his anger. "What device??"

"It was from Room 22-E."

"Room 22-E?" replied Woking, puzzled. "Room 22s don't need devices, they're old school. Take two fanatical hardliners with opposite views and leave them to fight it out. It's simple and it works! And now you're going to tell me you fiddled with that formula, aren't you?"

"Well, there was research," said Camberley, cautiously.

"What research?" thundered Woking. He'd never had much time for research.

"Not by us!" added Camberley quickly. "Israeli Hell. They'd been happily pairing their rightwing hardliners up with Islamic extremists for decades, but when somebody actually studied them, it turned out they got too much pleasure from beating the heaven out of each other, and they were enjoying it! Some even thought they were in Heaven! The Israeli Devils were pretty embarrassed, as you'd imagine."

"Hmmm," said Woking.

"So they invented the consciousness swap. Come to 22-E and I'll show you!"

The scene that greeted Woking as he entered the room was quite unlike the 22-E he remembered. On one side of the room, shaven-headed thugs with Nazi tattoos either cried or smashed their heads against mirrors. On the other side, bearded religious fanatics did likewise.

"It works so much better!" said Camberley. "We bring them in two at a time, swap over their minds between bodies. They each spend their sentence being the thing they despise most!"

"Except when it all goes wrong," said Woking, pointing at two figures viciously punching each other on the ground."

"They came in about two hours ago," and the swap failed to work," said Camberley. "The key component has been removed."

"So it was recent," said Woking. "It can't have been Coker."

"No."

"It means we've got a traitor in Hell!"

"That can't be," said Camberley. "It must be another dead soul, who's escaped. You can't accuse one of us!"

"Can't I?" said Woking. "Coker is dispelled, yet so much has happened, we have none of us asked, how did he get the Devil knife, when first he escaped? This answers it for us, Camberley! Someone in Hell is working against us! I believe that a Devil has conspired with humans for our overthrow!"

"But we smashed the conspiracy."

"I repeat, someone gave Coker the knife. It has to have been a Devil. Coker was used, then sacrificed when the time came! The threat is not over, Camberley! With this device, there is surely some trickery planned! Tell me exactly, what can it do?" demanded Woking.

"It can swap the conscious minds across between any two dead souls."

"Only dead souls?" asked Woking.

"Oh no, in theory it can work on anyone. I made Bracknell and Mytchett try it out for ten minutes. It really was quite funny…"

"'In theory'?" queried Woking.

"It can only be operated by a Devil, we made quite sure of that. We couldn't have dead souls taking one of us over, could we?"

"But a Devil works against us!" declared Woking "So that isn't much comfort!"

"And moreover," added Camberley, "it could not be used on a Devil without his consent."

"The thief must have known that, yet still he took it. Think, you fool! What could he be planning? To smuggle a live soul into Hell without destroying it? To infiltrate Heaven? What?"

"I'm no good at conspiracies!" pleaded Camberley.

Like Heaven you're not, thought Woking. "Have the rooms checked again. Repeatedly!! The traitor might steal something else. Conscript extra Devils if you need to! And interrogate the souls in this room! Don't let them give you that 'all look the same' crap. Show them mugshots if you have to! We must know who the traitor is!" Woking strode off down the corridor.

The theft was concerning, of course, yet Woking felt oddly elated. For the consciousness swap device, if retrieved, might just give him a means of advancement that didn't involve slaughtering his superior. One that Beelzebub might be inclined to agree to. Then he stopped, suddenly. Perhaps, he considered, the traitor had thought the same thing.

*****

Kane had summoned the Housing Enforcement Operatives for an emergency briefing. They had gathered unhappily in the courtyard of Kane's mansion, eager to get back to the business of violating other peoples' homes.

"I regret to inform you that complaints have been received about your conduct," said Kane.

The Operatives looked at one another in shock and confusion. "From how many people," asked one.

"Oh, all of them," said Kane. "I did warn you, I think, that these houses were all occupied by angry old ladies, often several per house, who might resent your inspections."

"Everyone resents our inspections" said an Operative.

"Well, these seem to have been particularly enraged," said Kane. "Many are threatening violence."

"They seemed quite compliant when we went in, all of them," said an officer, to general nods from the rest.

"That was before they received your Fail notices. Each is required to pay thousands of pounds to correct defects that they weren't told about when they bought their houses. Of course they'd be cross. Furious."

"We're only doing our jobs," said an Operative defiantly. "As instructed by you," she added.

"And indeed you've done them very well," declared Kane in avuncular fashion, extending his arms and beaming. "With exemplary efficiency! Not a single house so far passed as satisfactory, I could not be more proud. Please do not mistake my intent here, I merely share this for your safety. Word is beginning to spread to the houses not yet inspected. You may expect increasingly hostile receptions."

"They're old ladies, I think we can handle them," said an Operative.

"Good," said Kane. "Oh, one more thing, I need a volunteer. Anyone here ever flown in a jet plane?"

Fifty Housing Operatives shook their heads.

"Anyone want to?"

Fifty Housing Operatives shook their heads.

"I've got four state of the art vertical take-off fighter jets out behind the mansion, with trained pilots, but I need someone to ride in one for me and deliver a message.

"Have you got appropriate permission to house military aircraft in a residential area?" asked one Operative near the front.

"Why don't you come with me and take a look?" said Kane happily.

Realising he'd trapped himself, the Operative looked from left to right at his colleagues, none of whom met his eye. Reluctantly he stepped forward to join Kane.

"The rest of you, back to work, make me proud!" declared Kane. The Operatives dispersed. In the houses they walked past, old ladies stared venomously through the windows. Some of the old ladies scratched at two bumps that were starting to grow on the tops of their heads. Others wondered what was erupting from the base of their backs, or why their pasty skin tone was beginning to redden.

*****

By the time Kane had led the Operative through the many corridors of his mansion, the imaginations of his 49 colleagues had done what was intended, and four bright new fighter planes did indeed stand in the courtyard behind the mansion. "It's a Fail, I'm afraid," said the officer, whose name was Wiley. "Seventeen regulations broken. I shall have to recommend demolition."

"If that is the rules, then of course I must accede," replied Kane. "However, you are currently under contract to me, so before you do that you'll deliver this message for me." He handed Wiley a letter, with a seal that looked oddly like blood. Wiley noticed the plaster on Kane's thumb, but took the letter as instructed. "Pick a plane," said Kane.

Wiley simply got into the nearest one. The helmeted Pilot turned to him. "Where to, guv?"

Kane called up from below. "Fly that sort of direction," he said, indicating the way the Devils had flown, earlier. "Keep going till you see a massive motorway that ends in a lake with a city beyond. Don't go too near the city, they'll shoot you down. Land by the end of the motorway. You can contact me by radio if anything goes amiss. Wiley, there'll be a man there painted red from head to tail – I mean, toe. You're to deliver this message to him and no other. Tell him it's for his boss, from Brian Coker."

Wiley was by now starting to suspect that something was greatly amiss, but it was too late. The engines roared, the plane shook, and he had no choice but to strap himself in. The ground fell away from beneath him. He gazed lovingly down at the sprawling mass of houses below, so many of which he had not yet inspected. The sound of the engines changed, and he felt himself pushed back into his seat as the plane started going forwards. As it flew over the houses, he at last got a sense of the size of this New Town, it had to be four miles across at least. Yet what lay beyond surprised him – mile after mile of empty grassland. Why hadn't anyone developed it? It was a totally wasted opportunity for someone to build houses wrongly and create even more paperwork.

The journey took just fifteen minutes. As they began circling to land, Wiley was astonished to see the thirteen lane motorway, not least because all thirteen lanes were going the same way. Equally strangely, quite a few of the vehicles on it were ambulances. He looked on in horror when he saw what happened at its end: vehicles simply drove straight on into a giant lake, where they seemed to fizz and dissolve.

"Oh my ..." said Wiley, picking up the radio mike. "This is ... this is ..."

Kane, sitting with his feet up on the sofa, waited a moment before responding "Yes, Wiley?"

"This is ... oh my God ..." stuttered Wiley.

"Yes?" repeated Kane, savouring the moment. "Where are you, Wiley?"

"This is ..." spluttered Wiley "... this is the worst violation of traffic safety regulations I've ever seen!"

"Just land the sodding plane and give the red guy the letter," said Kane.

**

In the world of the living, throughout that morning a motley assemblage of thugs, mercenaries, gang members and shady characters had been turning up at various disused airfields or derelict sites now owned by Coker Associates. Each was met by a bored young woman who explained that the instructions she'd been expecting had not come, and that therefore the plan had been put on hold, whatever it had been. Every visitor was given a thousand pounds in cash, and promised a transfer of ten thousand more into an account of their choice, or one set up specially for them. Lastly, they each received a very old looking, unregistered mobile phone, with instructions to keep it close and answer if immediately if it rang, for the money on offer would be immense if the plan were resumed. Most went away feeling content at having earned such easy money, while others stuck around to buy and sell weapons, or in a few cases, kill one another.

The British lunchtime news was bursting with strange stories. Unexplained tremors, mysterious birds, a reporter who'd vanished into thin air, a missing bus full of students and, most recently, a massive gas explosion demolishing a floor of an office block owned by a company no-one had heard of. Numerous casualties, all burnt beyond recognition. An extraordinary series of pranks involving men in devil costumes rounded out the half hour on a light-hearted note.

Others, however, were making connections the TV news had carefully avoided. The Earth tremors, coupled with rumours (and pictures) of Devils in London, and the gas explosion close by. Within hours, many were convinced that the Day of Judgement had arrived. In America, Fox News reported that large parts of London were now under the control of Satan and his Demonic Hordes, and were therefore no-go areas for Christians.

It was enough to rattle the British Prime Minister. Some hours earlier, he'd ordered his operatives to track down the TV crew that supposedly staged the first stunt, to provide hard evidence that it was indeed a hoax; now he was becoming worried by their failure to do so. At the suggestion of a colleague, he arranged for some actors to dress up in none-too-convincing devil suits and create a few similar scenes, to be shown on the six o'clock news. This, he thought, ought to dampen the rumour, if not his own fear. His much-publicised conversion to Christianity, soon after taking office, had had nothing to do with political expediency (as had been widely suspected), and everything to do with top secret papers he'd been given, detailing evidence scattered through the centuries that Hell was, most certainly, real. Was he to be the last PM ever? The secret report he'd been given, identifying one of the gas victims as Sir Antony Mellstrom, would normally have been a cause for celebration. Instead, it made him think that this was very, very serious indeed.

*****

Theo had never, he thought, felt so tired. He thanked the Lord that he'd found that gas pipe within the building. He hadn't been sure he'd get out in time, but he had. He was surprised at how little this mattered to him. The blood from his buttocks was caked onto his underpants as he staggered down the road. He didn't know which way he was going, though he supposed he ought to go home. But what was the point? Was it not better to die and get on with serving his long sentence? He wondered if the Devil had been telling the truth about halving his sentence. Then he felt a tap on the shoulder and turned round, his mouth falling open. "You??"

Chapter Twenty

For those damned souls who crawled screaming from the Lake of Hell, a different kind of torment waited on the shore. "I demand to know what that hideous smell is!" said Sir Antony Mellstrom, as Mickleham moved along the lakeside queue towards them.

"Yer not foolin' me," said the Scotsman behind him. "It's yee kakkin' yer kecks at the sight o' the De'il!"

"I'll have you know that my y-fronts are pristine," said Sir Antony. Then he smiled a crooked smile. "And I'll tell you something more: it looks like you Scots don't get an independent Hell after all. Stuck in the queue with us Sassenachs, you are, and quite right too! What do you say to that, eh?"

"AAArrrrgghhhh!" said the Scotsman.

"Yep, definitely dead," said Mickleham, withdrawing his burning stake from the man's heart. Sir Antony gave a similar scream as it plunged into his.

"Och, this place is shite," said the Scotsman, as the hole in his chest began to shrink.

"It does appear quite unpleasant, yes," agreed Sir Antony. "It seems that we ..." the rest of his words were drowned out by the roar of jet engines, as the plane carrying Wiley descended to the ground.

They watched a man get out. When Mickleham walked over to him, the man tried to give him the letter he was carrying. Mickleham pointed to the queue.

"I MUST give you this letter," said Wiley, reeling from the smell. "It is for your boss, from Brian Coker!"

"Join the queue," said Mickleham. "I command it!"

"But you just stabbed everyone in it!" said Wiley.

"Yes, that's how we check you're all dead!" said Mickleham. Casually he whipped out his burning stake and plunged it into Wiley's heart. Wiley was dead before the scream left his mouth. Mickleham looked in puzzlement at the limp corpse now hanging off his stake. "Just as well I checked," he said, pulling it back. Wiley's body slumped to the ground, leaving a dead Wiley standing in his place.

"Well, that wasn't a nice thing to do," said the dead Wiley. "All I wanted to do was give you this letter. Now I shall have to report you for a fatal assault on a council Operative."

Below them the ground rumbled. The Abysmal Plain really didn't know what to do when a living soul died there, especially so close to Hell. Wiley looked around to see a side road curving in a circle before rejoining the motorway just as it plunged into the lake. Beside him stood a spanking new motorbike, with the words 'Council Housing Operative of The Year' emblazoned across it.

"Care to try out your new wheels?" grinned Mickleham.

"Regrettably, there is not a road here that meets legal standards for driveability," replied Wiley.

"Oh go on," said Mickleham, picking up Wiley and depositing him on the seat. The engine started up immediately.

"I wish to record that I'm using this road under duress!" wailed Wiley, as the bike steered itself round the circling road. "Aaaarrrrggghhhh," he added, as he and the bike plunged into the lake. Mickleham smiled. He liked things to be done properly. Wiley managed not to scream as he crawled from the searing Lake. "I-I-I f-fear I must report you for multiple v-violations of water quality edicts, a-as well," he stuttered.

"Back of the queue and shut up," said Mickleham. Looking around, he noticed the letter on the ground. "I think this should go in as well, don't you?" he said picking it up. Then he saw the words on it, words that hadn't been there before, but which appeared as he touched it. *To His Lordship, Satan Beelzebub III*. Before he could ponder this further, he heard a thud behind him, as the plane's pilot crashed to the ground.

"Are yee sure yee can fly this thing?" said a voice from the cockpit.

The plane's engines started, drowning out the response. Mickleham ran towards it, but it was too late: the plane left the ground, turning as it did so. Then the back engines roared, and it sped into the distance, far faster than Mickleham could fly. He turned to see that Sir Antony and the Scotsman were missing from the queue. Cursing, he looked at the letter. Well, it might prove a distraction from the two escaped souls, he thought hopefully.

*****

Fenwick awoke to find his ballgag dissolved, though his mouth was now full of disgusting acidic bird-guano. "Euurrrrhggghh!!" he said.

"Tweet." A yellow bird was hanging in the air, looking crossly at him.

"How can you still be there when I'm awake?" asked Fenwick. *Evolution*, he thought, answering his own question. Then he realised that he could talk again. "Now hear this!" he bellowed. "You are all compelled to obey my commands! So I order you all to uhhhhmmmmff!!"

A human had just stuffed a shoe in his mouth. "Thanks for the warning," she told him.

The bird considered this for a moment, then flew off towards the moat.

*****

"YOU SELF-RIGHTEOUS OBSCENITY!" Boomed Satan. "FOR WHAT REASON HAVE YOU VI-"

"Shut up, this is important, said Gabriel. "I want to know why nineteen Devils invaded the mortal world this morning and slaughtered sixteen humans."

Satan regarded the Angel with narrowed eyes and unconcealed hatred. "'*I* want to know?' I thought Heaven was a collective of equals."

"WE want to know the reason for this incursion, in blatant violation of the terms of your *surrender*," said Gabriel, emphasising the last word.

In truth, Satan wondered why it had taken them so long to come. Still, an uninvited Angel in his cave was a great insult. "We were attacked!" Satan declared. "Two of our number – maybe three, assaulted and taken prisoner! We were obliged to respond!"

"You should have consulted us!" said Gabriel.

"We handled the matter," said Satan. "Interference from you Wimples would have made everything worse, as it always does!"

"NINETEEN Devils outside in broad daylight! Were you TRYING to provoke us? Are you so weak that so many were needed to deal with mere MORTALS?"

"There were ... complications," said Satan carefully. At all costs, he thought, they must not learn of the theft, or that one of their souls had escaped. If he mentioned their use of psychic sensitives, Gabriel would want to know how the Broker had found them.

"How terribly weak you've become," observed Gabriel. "Devils attacked, and they need an army to respond?" He smiled, sweetly. "What complications?"

Satan chose his words carefully. "There was an accidental incursion last night. We believe a bus driven by a psychic sensitive unintentionally drove down the Road to Hell."

"This would explain the reported earth tremors," agreed Gabriel. "But how does it explain why two of your number were attacked so soon after?"

"The incursion will have weakened the Veil of Mortality," said Satan. "Making it easier for them to see and interact with us. Surely your people have noticed it too?"

"Indeed there have been several cases of live humans seeing our stairways when they appeared," agreed Gabriel. "A woman with a lot of fake jewellery even tried to purchase one," he added. "I've no idea why. But let me just get your story straight: you're saying that these humans happened to see a pair of you harvesting a soul, and on impulse attacked them and somehow overcame *two* Devils, or was it three?"

Satan shifted uncomfortably. Evading difficult questions was hardly his area of expertise.

"Because, if you've all got so weak that an unplanned attack could nail TWO of you, or even three, then I don't see how we could continue to allow you to operate independently at all."

"Okay it was planned!!" blurted Satan furiously. "They had foreknowledge!" He paused, thinking quickly. "They knew that killing the right man would bring Devils to collect him, so they waited and attacked!"

Gabriel nodded, thoughtfully. "That implies an intimate knowledge of how we all operate."

"It does, yes," said Satan non-committally.

"No doubt you've interrogated the humans you killed to find out how they obtained this knowledge."

"It's underway," said Satan.

"By now you'll have at least some preliminary answers you could share with me?" said Gabriel.

"Not yet," said Satan. "We've been a bit busy."

"You have, haven't you. You know, I did intend to go through formal channels for my visit, and knock at the gates of Hell. But they don't appear to be there anymore."

"Yes, there was an accident," said Satan.

"Connected to one of the incursions you mentioned? The first or the second one?"

"We think it's the first inc ... hang on, I didn't say there were two!"

"You have now," said Gabriel. "One incursion could be an accident, albeit an extremely improbable one. But two, it is planned. All of it is planned. You are failing to defend your borders. What good are you, if you cannot do that?"

"Our enemy is cunning and extremely resourceful," said Satan. "So now you understand why we struck back with force!"

"Yet still their influence grows across the Plain! You're a failure, Beelzebub Three! I could destroy you right now! The terms of your *surrender* permit this, in the event of such failure to defend the underworld."

"Go ahead!" roared Satan. He pulled a knife from a pouch fused to his hip. "Take it! You know what this is, don't you? Some of your colleagues certainly did, back in the day. So use it – I won't stop you!"

"MONSTER!" screamed Gabriel. "You would dare try to make me an architect of destruction? You think I have forgotten that killing you would undo all of Hell? That the evil contained here would spill out and consume all of Creation?" He shook with anger.

"Well, maybe just slice off the odd finger, if it would make you feel better?"

"You dare to tempt *ME*, Lord of Evil?"

"I'm just making helpful suggestions."

"I know of these knives. If I cut any part of your body, you would die, taking all of Hell with you, releasing countless dead souls to devour the living!" He shivered with horror. "Judgement Day."

Satan cackled. "Only if you throw it."

A look of realisation spread over Gabriel's face. "Ah. Of course. If I'm touching the knife at the time, I would become Lord of Hell myself."

"That would be worth dying for!" boomed Satan. "You, trapped in my job, hating every second of it, until you begged them to put you down!"

Gabriel paused, annoyed that he'd been drawn off the point. "We want a full report. Give us one of the dead souls you killed, for our own interrogation."

"They were evil!" declared Satan. "They do not belong in Heaven!"

"I could send a team to interrogate them here, if you prefer?" said Gabriel.

"I will see if we can make an exception," said Satan.

"See that you do."

"However," said Satan, slyly.

"Yes?"

"There's one thing we've both missed, I think."

"What is that?" asked Gabriel.

"We know they've invaded Hell, but only the outermost part. Yet of Hell and Heaven, which would a human prefer to be king of?"

Gabriel blinked.

"They've got into Hell," said Satan. "Is it not possible that they've invaded Heaven, too? Maybe you've been so busy watching us that you haven't noticed?"

"We've checked our territories very carefully," said Gabriel.

Satan grinned broadly. "They never taught you Angels to lie properly, did they?"

"I'll be back," snarled Gabriel. "Soon!" He vanished.

The Lord of Hell sat back down on His throne. All he'd done was buy time, he knew, but at least that smug smile had been wiped out, for the moment.

**

Sir Antony and the Scotsman were flying alongside the wall of Hell. "Fook me, it's massive!" said the Scotsman. He'd not volunteered his name, and Sir Antony hadn't asked. "What are yee looking for? Why not just fly awa'?"

"I'm hoping to find the Broker," said Sir Antony. "He wasn't in the queue with us, I'm sure of that."

"Tha' smug-faced shite was the one who goat us intae this mess!"

"True," said Sir Antony. "But he implied that he escaped from Hell once, and I believe him. I don't think that simply flying away across this featureless land would help us very much. We have no idea how to get out."

"There's a line o' folks doon thar," said the Scotsman.

Sir Antony saw the queue, stretching back out of sight. Mostly it was just one person wide, but in one place it bulged just a little, as if there was something of interest at that spot. They had no better lead, so he set the plane down close by, and got out.

"What's happening here?" said Sir Antony, in a commanding voice that normally served him well.

"Our furniture keeps swearing at us," said an old man who was sitting down, wearing one shoe.

"Uhhghhfffmmm!" said the furniture, which had a shoe sticking out of its mouth. Then it closed its eyes, as a bird landed on its head, and squirted guano at the shoe. The shoe fizzed and went floppy. The head spat it out. "I order you all to – uhmmmmffff!!" said the head, as the old man calmly inserted his other shoe into its mouth. There were two others sitting down too, a man and a woman. Both had no shoes. Nor, indeed, did the five people forward of them in the queue.

"Is that a Devil you're sitting on?" said Sir Antony.

"Certainly swears like one," said the newly shoeless old man.

"Would you mind awfully if we borrowed him?"

"I suppose we are running out of shoes," said the man. "But what would we get in return?"

"We could take one of you with us," said Sir Antony. "We hope to get back to the world of the living." The shoeless man looked ecstatic for a moment, then his expression changed, and he looked at the young lady beside him. Four years, they'd been queuing together. He knew she'd died young, from her face, but he realised with a shock that he knew almost nothing else. He'd never been an especially generous man. If he had, would he be standing here, now? "Take her," he said quickly. "Take the young lady!"

"Me?" The woman stood up, looking nervous. "You mean I can leave the queue?" she said.

"They're offering the chance to try, I think," said the old man. "I suggest you take it. You deserve another chance at life."

"How do you know?" she said. "You never asked about my life. All these years!"

"Did you ask about mine?" he said gently.

"No," she admitted.

"I didn't know if you would want me to," said the old man. "Because if you didn't, you'd be stuck behind this prying old man for five years or more."

A tear formed in her eye. "My name is Yelena O'Connor, and I –"

"HELLLLPPP! For Satan's sake, heeeeeeeellllpppp! Ge – uuhmmfff."

Now Fenwick had socks in his mouth. "And I really liked those shoes," said the barefoot old man, looking down at their half-dissolved carcasses, then up at the woman. "Go with my blessing, Yelena."

She nodded, mouthed "thank you", and ran to the plane. Sir Antony, the old man and the Scotsman carried Fenwick to the plane between them. "Better hurry," said the old man. "One of those infernal birds comes back every minute or so, with its caustic diarrhoea. They keep trying to free him! Don't let one get into the plane!"

"Thank you," said Sir Antony. In fact the plane only had two seats, but they stuffed Fenwick behind them.

"Looks like yee'll have tae sit on mah lap, hen," said the Scotsman. Yelena did so, just about preferring him to a swearing Devil. The plane lifted off, and headed away from Hell. A stream of yellow birds followed behind.

Chapter Twenty-One

"WHY HAVE YOU BROUGHT THIS PUNY HUMAN EXCRESCENCE INTO MY PRESENCE?" boomed Satan.

"Well I thought you might wish to interrogate him personally, my Lord," said Woking. Beside him, the terrified human in a leather jacket quailed.

"Are the rest of you not up to the task?" enquired Satan.

"We are more than capable," replied Woking, carefully. "But following our earlier conversation ..."

"Did you bring him here simply to please me?" asked Satan, sweetly.

Woking's mouth moved, but no sounds came out.

"Because," went on Satan, "that would be toadying, and I would have to dispel you."

"Oh, no, my Lord. I merely responded to your earlier implication that a lack of contact with human souls might impair your efficiency at delivering your role."

"Ah," said Satan.

"He's one of the Coker gang. Also, far be it for me to say, but I wondered if you might like new furniture?"

"I had been considering a sideboard," agreed Satan.

"Then you could interrogate him at length," went on Woking.

"I could."

"He's responsible for twenty-two deaths, five of them first-hand," said Woking.

"Good tally," approved Satan.

"And the Angels would not be able to remove him. I'm sorry, Lord, but I heard the last few words you said to that smug Holy Wimple."

Satan glared at him for a moment, decided he couldn't be bothered being angry, and turned his eye to the wall of his cave. "Sideboard it is, then." He muttered a few mystic words, and the human felt himself lifted into the air, before being pulled sideways against the rock wall. He felt bones growing out from his shoulder and his hip, and fusing with the wall. A few books appeared on his back, the weight starting to hurt.

"What have you learned from him and the others?" asked Satan.

"They know very little," said Woking. "They were asked to begin the process of gathering an army of the living, of evil men who can fight, but that was just before we wiped them out. Those recruits perhaps number a few hundred, but they are scattered across the country and, as far as we know, leaderless. Only one of the Broker's recruits is still alive, the one Aldershot left to clear up."

"With your approval," added Satan.

"Yes," admitted Woking. "But he was genuinely terrified; I don't believe he's a threat. My Lord, there is another matter that requires your attention." He handed Satan the letter. Satan opened it, and they both read.

To Satan Beelzebub III, Lord of Hell,

First let me apologise for any upset I have caused with the kidnap of your employees. It was an unfortunate necessity, but I fully regret any slight on your greatness. Please take solace in the fact that every boss has a few useless staff members, and we must bear it as well as we can. Furthermore, if you are reading this letter, then I am dispelled and gone, and you have exacted quite ample revenge. However, there are others to whom I owe a debt, and for this reason I have asked for this letter to be passed to you in the event of my dispellation. I, or rather my successor, is offering you a deal of mutual benefit.

Control of Coker Associates and all its ongoing business has passed to Kane Winkle, who at present resides in the New Town that is growing outside of Hell. He is waiting there now for your visit, or that of your chosen representative. You may choose to kill him, of course, but please hear him out first.

You see, the full purpose of my plan was to build a new domain for the afterlife. Not Heaven, not Hell, but something in between. For the countless millions of souls who are not very good, but not really evil, just boring. Are you not fed up with punishing tiddling sins like not paying taxes, or failing to pick up their dog-dirt? Was that what the great empire of Hell was conceived for? Do you not desire a return to the good old days, when Hell was for murderers and rapists, the thugs and the thieves? It could be again. Relieved of this unwanted burden, a personal touch could return to the way that you do things. I know, I have seen it, remember?

If this does not tempt you at all, you may burn this letter, as is your right. But a chance like this will never come to you again. Also, we ask very little in return: a short list of souls, to be pardoned and set free, or just given a room free from torment. Heaven need not know.

Mr Winkle awaits your response.

Yours from beyond the veil,

Brian "the Broker" Coker.

"Well clearly we can't consider such an offer," said Woking.

"It would be dereliction of duty," said Satan.

"The administration of the 'grey' souls is an important and vital part of our work," said Woking.

"Something we'd never outsource," agreed Satan.

"Even if the price was very low," nodded Woking.

"And especially not to a human," concurred Satan.

"Furthermore Heaven would never allow it," added Woking.

"Indeed they'd be enraged if we even considered it."

They looked at each other with raised eyebrows.

"But it could be a trap," pondered Woking.

"Though that's not really relevant as we are not considering the offer," said Satan.

"Good point. Although ..."

"Yes?"

"We do need to find out the full extent of the Broker's plan, and round up every human involved," said Woking.

"We do."

"And a good way to do that would be to agree to a meeting, and see what they all have to say, before killing and interrogating them."

"That is indeed a good plan," said Satan.

"So shall I take a party and go to the New Town to talk and then kill?" said Woking.

"Yes," said Satan. "Take control of the place, however you can."

Woking nodded.

"And Woking?" added Satan.

"Yes?"

"If you make a mistake now, the consequences for you will be dire."

"My Lord, if any of us make a mistake now, the consequences for all will be dire."

"That is true," agreed Satan. Woking bowed, and took his leave. He hadn't told Satan his suspicions of a traitor in Hell. He needed hard evidence, and moreover, a name. Otherwise Satan might just dispel everyone. They could not hope to handle problems if they all mistrusted each other. More than they usually did.

Satan turned to face his new sideboard. "Now, where were those Terms and Conditions books that I needed some storage space for?"

*****

Council Housing Operative Ben Short was having the most productive day of his life. Twenty-six houses visited, and every one adjudged a fail. Better still, he'd failed around seventy more thanks to Kane's innovative 'fail two, then fail the whole street' policy. Kane had been right with his warning though, the old ladies in the houses were becoming more and more hostile. Sometimes, they jabbered on the phone as he looked at a house, fixing him with venomous eyes. He'd taken to saying nothing about his verdict except that they'd hear from him in due course. Then he'd closed the door and slipped the Fail note through the letterbox, before legging it back down the path.

On his way to the next house, Ben was accosted. "What's this," asked the angry old lady, waving scrunched up paper.

"It's a fail notice," said Ben. "Your house isn't a safe place to live in."

"How do you know? You haven't been in it!"

"Houses in your street are all built to the same specifications," explained Ben. "A fault that's present in one will be present in all."

"What am I s'posed to do with it?"

"You have to correct the defects within ninety days."

"And who's going to pay for that?"

"You need to contact the developers."

"I want to appeal."

"That is your right. The process takes six to nine months. After it fails, you'll have missed the ninety day deadline and will be liable for a hefty fine."

The lady glared at him. Her pink skin appeared to be reddening. Then she drew back her lips. Her false teeth were awfully sharp, thought Ben.

"I think I'll appeal," she concluded.

Two minutes later a battered and bruised Ben was wedged upside down inside a wheelie bin full of rotting TV dinners, with his trousers removed and the Fail notice inserted somewhere that wasn't a letterbox.

Over the hours that followed, there were more casualties among his colleagues. One was locked up in a cellar with haphazard wiring, and no way to report it. Worse still, water began leaking in from a damaged pipe, and he spent the next three hours in a doomed attempt to avoid getting electrocuted. Another became trapped in a tiny loo, whose door had no handle on the inside, and where the caustic stench of bleach slowly ate into his lungs. One more had his arm sliced off by a fire door that he'd just failed for closing improperly, after which he bled to death while his host drank tea. The much-lauded Gareth Rawle was inspecting inadequate loft insulation, but froze to death when an exceptionally cold draught gusted in through a crack. Ben Short's wheelie bin became a tomb as the fermenting TV dinners rose up and drowned him. And so Kane's council army began to dwindle in size.

*****

"Wake up," shouted Helen. "Everyone, wake up!"

Martin had been dribbling on the smooth, white pillow. He turned his head to see legs sticking out of it. "Ooh, you've made a wet patch," observed Suzy. Martin levered himself up from her lap, and blushed when he saw where the wet patch was.

Helen was sitting in the driver's seat. The bus had progressed at a quarter-mile per hour while the others had slept, and she'd coped well enough despite being only a learner driver. "We've got trouble," she said, pointing ahead. "Don't suppose anyone brought any binoculars?"

Denny wordlessly produced a pair from his bag, and someone passed them forward. Helen looked through them, then passed them to Martin. "Devils," she said. "Checking the cars one by one. Think they're looking for us?"

"Knowing our luck, yes" said Bernie, his head poking through from behind them.

"They're carrying pitchforks," said Martin.

"If those pitchforks are weapons..." said Lucy.

"I don't think they're here for stern words," observed Bernie.

"I count nine at least," said Martin. "They'll be here in minutes!"

"I won't let them hurt you," said Suzy, suddenly. Martin looked with amazement at the fearsome determination in her eyes. "No-one's going to stop me having you." She got out.

"Suzy, come back!" yelled Martin.

"She can look after herself," said Helen. "Tougher than she looks, I'm sure of it! But I think we may have to fight them off, guys." They'd already tried turning the bus round, but the road was too narrow. Helen thought for a moment. "Devils like fire and the heat," she said. "And I'm getting an idea of how this place works. Wacky Walkers, get your boots on! We're going for a hike!"

"What??" chorused Dylan and Bernie.

"I am not clad in suitable attire," stated Mycroft. Quite truthfully.

"Do it!" Helen snapped.

A rumble of thunder cracked overhead. The first raindrops started hitting the windscreen. "A nice ten mile round trip, I think! Don't bother with waterproofs!" said Helen. The rain came down faster and faster. Soon they could barely see in front, even with the wipers on full power. When Dylan made ready to climb over the seats, Helen stopped him with a gesture. "We'll go when the rain eases, eh?"

A movement caught Helen's eye, and she turned to her driver's side window. A red, grinning face was staring in at her. Then a red arm smashed through the window and grabbed her throat. She whacked it repeatedly with Denny's binoculars, but still it pressed harder, and harder. "I've found them!" the red face yelled.

*****

Bernie added his admittedly limited strength to Helen's efforts, releasing the pressure on her throat just a little. But if eight more were coming ...

A small car pulled up by the half-open passenger door suddenly. "Martin! Get in!" yelled Suzy.

"We can't fit everyone in that!" he yelled back.

"I'm just saving you," she called out.

Martin jumped from the bus to stand by Suzy's open car window. "I won't leave my friends!"

"But you can't hope to save them!"

"Then I will die trying!"

"But *I* want to save *you*!"

"Help me to save them and I'll do what you want me to! Deal, or no deal?" shouted Martin.

She smiled at him. "Deal!" Then she hit the reverse gear hard, and flattened a Devil she'd spotted in the rear view mirror.

Martin heard the thuds as two more Devils landed on the minibus roof. "Die, puny Human," laughed one, pointing his pitchfork directly at Martin. But the pitchfork fizzed in the rain, and its Devil user shook it furiously. Next moment, he flashed white as he took the full brunt of a bolt of lightning. Then, smoking, immobile and black, he pitched over sideways off the roof. The other Devil quickly jumped off the roof before the same could happen to him. Martin ran forward and jumped into Suzy's new car. "There's another one!" she cried, as a Devil landed by the bus passenger door. She slammed the car forwards and knocked him to the ground. Then a pitchfork came flying out of nowhere, smashed through the windscreen and hard into her chest. Blood poured out from all three puncture holes. "Sorry," she mouthed, then went still. Martin saw a Devil hanging in the air, celebrating its kill, and he filled with a terrible rage. He plucked the pitchfork out of Suzy's chest and jumped out into the rain. He saw a line of buttons along its shaft and aimed, pressing the red one. Flames squirted forth, catching the Devil full in the chest. The flames fell away, and the barely harmed Devil snarled back at Martin, baring his sharp fangs. The Devil dived towards Martin, and instantly dissolved into dust. Martin looked briefly at the black button he'd just pressed; it had the word 'dispel' etched below it. Then he wheeled around, firing with that button again and again at the red figures arriving from the sky. One turned to dust, then another, before a jet of fire scorched from the sky, searing the pitchfork from Martin's hand. On instinct he dived to the side just as a second jet ignited the spot he'd been standing on.

Dylan kicked harder and harder at the back minibus door, until finally it burst open. He leapt onto the road with an ice-axe in his hand. "Looks like I'll get to use this baby after all," he yelled with the thrill of adrenaline. He ran round the side and slammed the axe point into the head of the Devil grasping Helen. It staggered and fell, snapping its pitchfork as it did so.

"Look out, there's more of the bastards!" cried Lucy, as four Devils appeared above Dylan, raising their pitchforks to fire.

"The Lord's my shehh-perrrd I'll not want. He lee-eeads me down, to liiiiie!" All four Devils stopped moving. Janelle sang on in her pitchy voice, with Lysandra trying to join in. *"In pa-a-stures green, he lee-ee-deth me, the qui-i-et waaters by."*

"Uhh guys," said Lucy, as the other two sang on, "the fuckers seem to be dancing to it."

"Yeah, but they're not trying to kill us!" said Helen.

The Devils above them were grinning, swaying, lolling their heads or moving their arms in tune with the hymn. Then one of them erupted into raucous laughter. "Do you think hymns can harm us? There are rooms in Hell where the damned have to sing them for all eternity, in a church they never wanted to go to!" The other three laughed as well.

Janelle felt a chill down her spine.

"You don't mean it, either, do you," taunted another. "Well do you?" They cackled in unison. Janelle felt a terrible rage building inside her, but then an idea struck her, and she ran with it.

"Chrissssstmas time! Mistletoe and wine! Chilllllldren sinnnnging Christian rhymes. With logs on the fire and gifts on the tree ..."

"Aaaarrrghhh!!!" chorused the Devils, their faces contorted with pain. All four shot fire from their pitchforks in random directions, before managing to train them all at the roof of the minibus. Dylan, who'd fled to some distance away, looked on in horror. In seconds the heat from the roof became searing, the metal beginning to melt.

"Everyone out!" screamed Helen, but the front door was jammed as the roof above warped. Denny flipped over the back row of seats, and jumped out to the road. Three steel bolts hit his chest, and he fell down, dead. A Devil above cackled. Everyone in the bus started screaming. Then they saw something rocket into the sky among shattering glass. The white and red object flew into the foursome of fire-spewing Devils so fast that they couldn't react; it hit one head-on, sliced an arm off another, and disarmed a third with its foot. The first Devil dropped out of sight, while the second glanced down at his missing arm and was hit hard on the nose, sending him falling headfirst into the roof of the minibus, where he stuck fast in the cooling metal. The third Devil dived down after his pitchfork, but Martin saw it falling. They caught it together, but Martin had the shaft end. The Devil's grin turned to horror, as Martin found the black button. The Devil dissolved.

Above him, the white and red object was grappling for control of a pitchfork with the fourth Devil. Martin looked up in astonishment: it was Suzy. The three bloody holes in the front of her dress were still there, but the wounds were almost healed. Her skin, though, was bright red. A fifth Devil flew towards them, but Suzy wrenched the pitchfork around and shot fire at him. The Devil erupted in flame, but kept coming. "Black button!" yelled Martin, and Suzy obliged before either Devil could react. The burning Devil was dispelled.

"Well," said Suzy to the shocked Devil still sharing control of the pitchfork with her. "Not doing very well, are you?" Her eyes blazed with a fiery passion to match Satan himself. The Devil twisted suddenly, snapping the pitchfork, then flew off fast out of sight. As he went, he made a curious whistling sound, and the yellow birds furiously pecking at the four unconscious Devils changed their strategy. They began to lift the prone figures: one charred black Devil, one with a misshapen head, and one with an ice-axe in his skull. The students watched them head off out of sight.

There was one Devil left, though, the one who'd fallen into the half-melted roof. It had quickly solidified around him thanks to the cold rain, and the birds couldn't shift him. Even so, the birds were strong. Helen could feel the bus getting lighter. "It's birds," shouted Dylan. "Birds trying to lift us!"

Helen had a brainwave. "Everyone out!" she yelled. "Quick, before they give up!" The shocked students stumbled out of the back doors. Helen scrambled over to the passenger door, also jammed, and squeezed out through the window. "This is our chance to get clear of this jam!" she yelled. "Help the birds lift up the bus, and turn it around!"

Between birds and students, the bus was raised up into the air. "Now turn it to the right," commanded Helen. "No, the other right," when someone pushed against her. Still this didn't help.

"Clockwise," said Mycroft. "As seen from above." That did it. Quite quickly the bus was swung round, and into the clear carriageway going back the way they came.

"But where will we go?" asked Lucy. "If the only way out of here's blocked?"

"I'm not sure," said Helen. "But I know they'll come back, and this time with more of them. We've no hope of rescuing Michael ... but we can get the guy in the roof to talk!" Everyone got back inside, bringing with them Denny's body. They were joined by Denny's ghost, who'd been looking at a sign with some big books beside it. Then they tried and failed to shut the back doors.

Helen started the engine. At first the bus wouldn't move, with the birds pulling it upwards and backwards; its wheels wouldn't grip the road.

"Wake up the Devil," said Denny's ghost.

The head and shoulders of the Devil who'd fallen were sticking through the buckled roof at a funny angle. Sulphurous dribble was trickling from its mouth. A hand stuck through nearby. Bernie gave the face a hard slap. "Wakey-wake-eeeee!!"

The Devil's eyes opened. They felt the bus bump as the birds above disappeared. Helen started the engine, and they were off down the road, leaving the traffic jam behind them.

"*Puny humans,*" crackled the radio, suddenly. "*Savour your escape while you can!*"

"It wasn't an escape, it was a victory," said Suzy.

"They can't bring themselves to admit that," agreed Helen.

"*A new army will soon be on its way to you. You are doomed, I tell you! Doomed! But we offer you a choice. Surrender now for immediate slaughter, and we will have mercy on your souls. Choose to fight, and you'll each spend a million years in damnation for your defiance!*"

"Are they allowed to do that?" said Helen.

"I don't think they are. There are rules," said Suzy.

"And you'd know that, how, exactly?" asked Helen.

The radio crackled again. "*Oh, and this time we'll turn the dispel function off on our pitchforks. So there!*"

"You're one of them, aren't you?" Helen said to Suzy, quietly.

"She saved us!" Martin retorted.

"I know that," said Helen. "Somehow she's switched sides, if only to get in your pants."

"I don't know where I came from," said Suzy. "First thing I remember was driving my taxi. And an urge to torment Michael sexually. There was nothing else. I was human, or thought I was. Then after that Devil turned up to take Michael, I started to have these ... well, powers!"

"So what are you?" said Helen. "I mean I'm grateful, truly I am, but I don't understand."

"Nor do I," said Suzy. "But I'd die to protect Martin, even though I hardly know him."

"We may all die, very soon," replied Helen, staring at the radio.

Chapter Twenty-Two

"Blithering imbeciles!" roared Woking, throwing down the radio. "Of all the seraphimous ineptitude!"

"Something amiss, Sir?" said Camberley. They were standing with a horde of sixty-six junior Devils, readying themselves to travel to New Town.

Woking seethed. "We sent a squadron of ten Devils armed with state-of-the-art pitchforks to eradicate a group of about ten unarmed, lost humans. Tell me, who would you expect to win such a confrontation?"

"Us, of course."

"And who do you think actually did?"

"I'm guessing, not us?"

"It was a beatific disaster! Have we forgotten how to fight?"

"Well, there's not been a battle in Hell for millennia, and before that there was only ever one, which we lost. So yes, I think probably we have."

"The question was rhetorical!" shouted Woking.

"Nonetheless, sir, lack of practice is a factor we must consider. Humans fight all the time, while we've lost the habit. It renders us ..."

"Beatable, yes," said Woking. "Bless it to Heaven!"

"How bad was it?" asked Camberley. "The defeat, I mean?"

"Five Devils dispelled! By humans, who somehow disarmed them!"

"It'll save Satan a job, I suppose," observed Camberley.

"Oh, he'd love to dispel the survivors. If I didn't dispel them first, and believe me I would do! But we're understaffed, you know that! We're barely coping with the workload as it is! I've had to pull all these off maintenance and greet duties," he said, indicating the assembled horde. "And I've just called up forty more to finish off the job on the minibus humans! Forty! We've had to stop processing souls completely! We're so stretched, I've even had to bring along Mickleham!"

"I wondered what the smell was," said Camberley, noting how all the Devils were giving one a wide berth.

"In fact," said Woking, "He could be useful. The stench is bad enough for us, it'll be even worse for a living human. It might put him off balance. Now listen to me, all of you. "I'm going to play along with this ... human called Kane. I will give the appearance of willingness to consider or even accept his offer. You are none of you to contradict me, understand? Instead, I want all who are close enough to watch his face as he answers. Watch every reaction. We need to know what he knows, what he expects, and what he intends. Whenever I speak, watch his face for surprise. Understood?"

The horde all nodded. Then one raised a hand. "Why not just shoot him? Once he's dead he'll have to answer truthfully!"

"That's true, but only up to a point. They only have to supply information that is directly demanded from them. A live soul can volunteer information that we didn't know we needed, if you ask the right questions."

The horde looked uncertain.

"Plus we can shoot him afterwards, then interrogate him again," added Woking. Now the horde grinned.

"Do we really need all of us for one human?" asked one.

"It isn't just one. There are fifty living souls in that Town," said Woking.

"Actually, sir, our instruments indicate that about half the humans in the city have died in the past two hours," said Camberley. "I'm guessing the plain is reacting to them. If we wait, sir, the odds could become even better."

"We've done too much waiting," said Woking. "While we wait, the enemy builds and plans. Is the New Town still expanding?"

"No sir, it's almost stopped."

"That's something, I suppose. But perhaps that means it is ready, whatever its purpose. Come, it is time!" He stretched out his arms, and raised himself up into the air. Camberley and the horde of Hell followed. They streamed through the air towards Kane and his New Town.

In the governor's mansion, Kane waited, and smiled.

*****

Staz Houghton wasn't going to school today. This would be a massive source of relief to all Staz's classmates. It wouldn't be fair to call Staz a bully, because bullies are cowards and Staz wasn't that. He picked on the kids who thought they were tough, and showed them that they weren't. Then he'd pick on the rest of them too, just to remind them who was top dog. He might be the shortest boy in his year, but even the older kids feared him for his unrestrained viciousness: Staz could hit hard and repeatedly, and did not seem to notice when you hit him back.

Yesterday, a man had given him two fifty-pound notes, and told Staz he could earn lots more cash if he met him this morning. Staz had agreed. The man was there now: tall, black suit and sunglasses, and a cool set of wheels. "There's a guy that needs teaching a lesson," said the man. "A thousand pounds in it for you. You in?"

Staz was in. He jumped into the car, and they were off. An hour later they reached an abandoned airfield. "Here we are," he said, walking with Staz to a metal door on a brick hut. Staz was as dim as he was violent, yet even he felt a brief tang of concern at this point. Still, he reasoned, if the man was a perv, then he'd just beat the crap out of him and that would be that.

"There'll be six of you on this job," said the man. "Time to meet the team." Staz immediately imagined some ex-army tough guys, a computer geek and a beautiful woman in a slick red dress. Then he walked into a room with five other grumpy kids, all as small as he was. They exchanged glances warily.

"As soon as the boss arrives, we'll get started," said the man. "Meanwhile, how about a drink? I've got beer, or fizzy pop."

The six of them eyed each other warily. "Beer," they all said. The man left the room briefly and came back with six full half pint glasses full of dark ale. He then tried not to laugh as the six kids each did their best to pretend that they were enjoying the drink, while ruthlessly eyeing their fellows for a sign that they weren't. Five minutes later the drinks were all gone, and one of them belched. Another followed. The atmosphere in the room began to lighten as it quickly became a contest.

Ten minutes later, Staz's vision was blurring. The last of the other five toppled over, asleep. "Can't take your drink, you poofs?" he said, before the world started spinning and he too collapsed.

Another five minutes and the suited man came back. He clicked on his phone. "They're all out, let's get them ready," he said.

*****

"Legions of Hell, welcome," declared Kane. He stood by a desk in a massive round room, plushly set out with silk draperies, antique chests, Ming vases and gold statues. On the wall hung huge paintings. One showed Kane, in the same gold and black finery he was wearing now. Another showed the Broker, wearing sunglasses, standing behind a drab desk. A third depicted Preston in a track suit, with huge-breasted, scantily clad women on either side. Preston stood at Kane's side, now.

"I understand you wish to make us an offer," said Woking. He stood at the front of a group of twenty Devils. The rest waited outside, alert.

"Well, I'll start by offering use of my bathroom, I think one of you needs it," said Kane. Mickleham's pitchfork twitched.

"Oh, don't mind our Mickleham, he's trying out a new aftershave," said Woking. "What do you think?"

"Needs work," said Kane.

"Smells like shite," agreed Preston.

"I'm inclined to agree," said Woking genially. "Now, to your offer?"

"Well, as the letter explained, I'm offering this place to you as a permanent annexe to Hell. It contains, I believe, over five thousand houses now, and if you wish we'll set its expansion to continue for you."

"Yes, how did you achieve that?" said Camberley.

"I'll tell you if you accept our deal," said Kane.

"Tell 'em what we called it, Kaney," said Preston.

"Ah, yes," said Kane. "Well, I thought it should be called ''Nevaeh', which is Heaven written backwards. But my associate here, Preston, thought it should be 'Hell B'. Because you guys are 'Hell A', of course."

"We are simply Hell," said Woking darkly.

"Indeed. So we compromised, and are calling it 'Bleh'!"

"Bleh?" said Woking in astonishment.

"Bleh," confirmed Kane. "'Hell B' written backwards. But we dropped one of the 'L's, to make it more catchy."

"Bleh," repeated Woking.

"Yeah, I wasn't sold on it at first, but in fact it encapsulates all that we're trying to achieve here!"

"Really."

"We're here for the rubbish ones, you see. 'So you had a boring life, you weren't very good, but you didn't do anything impressively bad, either? Bleh. So you stole a few shirts from a shop once, ran out of a café without paying? Bleh. So you cheated on your wife once when you were pissed, or stuck your old mum in a crap nursing home? Bleh. Didn't do your recycling? Bleh. You want one word summing up the life that you've led? Bleh.

"It's a name that tells all of them, in one short sweet syllable, how utterly unremarkable they have been, and now always will be. They've been sent to Bleh. Their lives have been judged, and found to be, Bleh."

"Good, innit?" said Preston.

"Bleh," repeated Woking, but with a little less condescension.

"Of course, if you agree to our deal, you can rename it if you really want to," said Kane.

"So in return, you're asking for pardons for certain souls, I understand?" said Woking.

"Yes," said Kane. Some living at present, some dead. All are to be given freedom from the torments of Hell. The simplest way would be for them to live in this mansion, for the duration of their period of damnation."

"I thought you were ceding this 'Bleh' place to us," said Woking.

"We are. If you agree. But they won't accept those souls in Heaven, will they? They have to go somewhere. There's plenty of space in this mansion for your people to take governing duties, while the freed souls can live in the recreational wing."

"Which souls do you speak of?" asked Woking.

"Myself and Preston, of course. Some relatives of the Broker – Brian Coker, as you knew him. Here's the full list." He handed Woking a piece of paper with thirteen names on it.

"What about all the humans you brought with you?"

"Do with them as you will. They're quite useful, you'll find, and they follow orders. Or kill them. If you take the deal, you get to choose."

"I will take your offer to Lord Satan," said Woking. "Would you like to accompany me?"

"I fear I cannot," said Kane.

"I can promise your safe return," said Woking.

"Now, now, you are lying," said Kane. "We both know that's impossible."

"Do you?" said Woking, eyebrows raised.

Kane paused, realising that he'd given away how much he and the Broker knew. "Living souls can't enter Hell, we both know that. Something to do with dimensional stacking and our limited imaginations, isn't it? Hell would explode, tearing a hole in creation! So why did you lie to me?"

"It is our nature to lie," said Woking, enjoying himself, and hoping he'd just proved his earlier point to the horde.

"Does it not scare you?" said Kane. "Just one living soul – just one, is enough to tear your whole edifice down? To end all you have worked for? To bring about Judgement Day? If even one of my many employees were to, say, sneak over or under your walls, then boom! Game over for Hell."

"There are defences," scowled Woking.

"Yes, I heard the explosion!" said Kane. "Yet I can't help but think, if they're willing to blow up their own gates and God knows what else just to stop a live soul getting in, then I'm guessing that had to be a last resort. Meaning you don't have many other defences. That little army standing behind you, the bigger one waiting outside. And what else? Very little, as far as I see. You just never planned for this, did you? Well we're here now, and offering a deal. A good deal. Given what you stand to lose, I'd strongly advise that you take it."

Kane could see fury welling within Woking, as he laid bare Hell's vulnerability. Yet Woking in turn watched the sweat forming on Kane's forehead as he'd spoken. For some moments, each one stood quiet.

"You'll forgive me if I remain cautious," said Woking. "We have clear evidence that your predecessor intended far more than this deal. He intended a takeover! His minions have admitted as much!"

"How could he do that, if a living soul can't enter Hell?" enquired Kane.

"He was already dead – you must have known this?" replied Woking

Kane shrugged. "He never described to me the rest of his plan. It died with him. This place, and this deal, were his back-up plan."

"I do not believe you," said Woking.

"I cannot help that," answered Kane.

"Coker was seeking to become Satan of Hell, was he not?"

"He didn't go into specifics with me," replied Winkle. "He was secretive with his plans." Yet Woking noted his lack of surprise at the suggestion.

"But the idea I'm sure must appeal to you as well? Kane Winkle, Lord Satan of Hell?"

"Haven't really thought about it."

"You lie!" hissed Woking.

"Maybe a little," said Kane. "But only in passing."

"There is no need to be coy," said Woking. "Every Devil in Hell desires to overthrow Satan and take the top job. Treacherous creatures, we are." Woking's eyes bored into Winkle. "A Devil – or Angel, theoretically – may fight Satan to the death in a ritual duel. If the challenger kills Satan, then Satanship passes to him, with all attendant powers. Your boss will have told you this?"

"He did not," replied Winkle.

Woking went on. "Yet Satanship cannot pass into a mortal soul, living or dead. It's impossible. Were such a soul to kill Satan, even if that were possible, Satan would end. Perhaps that is your plan, then? Kill Satan and rule as yourself?"

Kane shook his head.

"Not even a little tempted?" asked Woking.

"You sound like you'd like me to try," replied Kane.

"You would exist in luxury, with domain over billions," said Woking.

"Just this little mansion is enough,' replied Kane.

"You know, don't you, what would happen?" probed Woking. "If a mortal killed Satan?"

"Why don't you tell me?" smiled Kane.

"There is no need to tell you, because someone else already has," replied Woking. "I see it in your eyes. But the question is, who told *him*? Because it is something that only a Devil could know."

"A traitor?" gasped a Devil from behind him.

Woking ignored this. "A Devil could kill Satan and take his place, with no trouble."

"Of course," agreed Kane, nervous now. "You said."

"Or even a human could, having first swapped his consciousness with that of a collaborating Devil, by mutual consent. We know you have a device that permits it."

"I don't!" protested Kane, and to Woking it sounded like the truth.

"Although it is hard to believe that a Devil could be working against Hell, we are created as creatures of misdeed," went on Woking. "I think you have already made a deal, and that this deal has not been with us. How am I doing?"

"I really don't know!"

"Someone has offered you riches, and power, and eternal life, in turn for assisting his becoming Satan."

"Not me! He told nothing to me!!"

"Give me the name," said Woking. "The name of this Devil. I don't care if you knew of his purpose or not. Who was the one who helped Coker escape? Who is the one he's been working with?"

"Please believe me, I don't know!"

"Just a name. Maybe a name that you heard? A face that you saw?"

"Nothing! I promise!"

"Then let me jog your memory."

Woking raised his pitchfork and fired steel bolts through Kane's heart. Kane was dead before he hit the ground, although not before several other Devils had shot him too, for good measure. Some of them shot Preston too, not wanting to be left out. "Now everyone watch," said Woking.

Kane's life played out before them. A life of failed ambitions and random acts of nastiness, borne of frustration. Then the Broker appeared, always wearing sunglasses, drawing Kane under his wing. Yet through all of their meetings, not once did the Broker give anything away. Not a name, not a hint that he had help below. Woking twitched in frustration. Yet there was something about the Broker that wasn't quite right. He couldn't work out what, though. Then something else hit him. Maybe he didn't need to know *who* the traitor was, he just needed to know *why*. And he was sure there could only be one reason. He would have to speak to Satan, in person. It was not a conversation that could end well, but he knew now that there was no choice.

The video ended, and Kane found himself standing over his own body. "That wasn't a nice thing to do," he said.

"Nor was invading our territory and building a massive city without our permission. Tell us the name of the Devil traitor."

"I don't know," said Kane automatically. And then, "the offer still stands."

"You didn't know about the consciousness swap device, before I told you, did you?" asked Woking.

"No."

"But you were told by the Broker that killing Satan would destroy all of the Devils, and disintegrate the walls of Hell, thus unleashing an army of the undead, yes?"

"Yes, and yes," answered Kane.

"What were your instructions, should we refuse the deal you laid out?"

"Wait."

"No I will not wait. Tell me now!"

"I was told to wait," said Kane.

"For what?"

Above them a window smashed, and the leg of a Devil landed on the floor with a thump. Moments later a Devil ran into the room, with one missing arm, and three thin white shafts that might have been arrows sticking out of his head.

"What is it?" said Woking, looking round.

"We've got trouble outside. Big trouble!" gasped the Devil.

"For that," answered Kane.

Chapter Twenty-Three

"I got three years in Hell. I deserve it." Denny was talking far more now than he ever had when he was alive. "I stole some rare bird's eggs from a nest when I was thirteen. I was stupid, I didn't understand, well maybe I did but chose not to. This man I'd met in a hide, we'd got talking, well he'd got talking, asking me how good I was at tracking down rare birds. I said very good. And he kept leading me and leading me, all the while making me feel like the best that there was. So I ended up stealing … it doesn't matter. Point is, I sold the eggs to him to pay for a birdwatching trip abroad. Didn't go in the end, too guilty. I'm glad, now. Glad I'll get the chance to pay properly for it. I only came on this trip because I thought I might see a golden eagle. Funny how things turned out."

"Hell is forever!" said Janelle.

"Uh-uh," said Suzy. "Most people do time in Hell then go on to Heaven."

"No!" said Janelle.

"Keep your knickers on, honey," said Suzy. "Just telling what I know."

"And you know it, HOW exactly?" challenged Janelle.

"It's what the sign said," insisted Denny. "Three years in Hell, then Sixty-one in Heaven. Maybe because I gave all that cash to the RSPB instead."

"Then this isn't the afterlife," said Janelle. "It's some sort of elaborate trick and SHE's part of it!

"On second thoughts, maybe your problem is, you keep them on too much," retorted Suzy happily.

"You're a monster! A thing!" shouted Janelle. "I saw you in the car, saw the pitchfork hit you and – "

"Enough!!" shouted Helen. "This isn't helping anyone!! Next person I hear arguing, I'll have Mycroft read them the constitution. Twice!! I need you all focused. We need some suggestions. We barely fought off ten of them, and even then we were extremely lucky. Well, not you Denny, sorry."

"No problem," said the ghost.

"Somehow, we've got to find some weapons, or a way to escape."

"Surrender!" said the upside down one-armed Devil trapped in the roof. "You cannot possibly defeat the hordes of Hell!"

"The fact that you are currently immobilised, missing a limb and encased in the roof of a minibus driven by humans who can torment you at will would appear to contradict that assertion," said Mycroft.

Thus far, the Devil had been subjected to every one of Cliff Richard's Christmas singles, Bernie's rendition of "My Favourite Things", and a detailed account of the biology of newborn babies from Lysandra. All of these had caused much screaming, mostly but not only from the Devil, but he had so far refused to tell them anything useful.

"Right, you," said Lucy to the Devil. "You're going to tell us how to get out of here and back to the mortal world."

"Like Heaven I will! You're all doomed! Torment awaits you!"

"Yeah?" said Lucy. "Well, torment begins for you right now, you fucker. Anytime you want to tell us what we want, just say. Janelle, how about the entire Cliff Richard *oeuvre*, from start to finish?"

Janelle began with Summer Holiday, accompanied by more demonic screaming. Mycroft produced a digital camera from his bag and filmed the whole thing.

"Mycroft, what the fuck?" said Lucy.

"In the unlikely event that we escape from here, this will strengthen our case with the hire company, when the time comes to account for the condition of this minibus," Mycroft explained. "Furthermore, 250 pounds from *You've Been Framed* will allay the somewhat parlous condition of club funds."

"Hang on," said Dylan, his mind casting back to when he'd hired the bus. "What if we could get a SatNav?"

"Yeah, because Hell is just brimming with useful electronic equipment shops," muttered Lucy.

"But if we could, then maybe it would show us the way out. This place is so fucking weird, who knows what'd work."

"A great big fuck-off missile launcher would be more use," said Lucy.

"You can buy them both in Glasgow," said Bernie brightly.

"You said they had nothing but chips," said Helen. "Bernie, you really think we can get a satnav in … our Glasgow?"

"I know the shops there very well, darls. If we can get in and out before the shopkeepers turn on us, then there's a chance. There's also a guy, works out of a nightclub called Hot Spot, sells all sorts of stolen gear, including every kind of weapon short of nuclear, but we'd best steer clear. He's dangerous enough when he's real!"

"How do you know about him?" asked Helen, incredulously.

"Pillow talk, darlings. Anyway, forget him, we need to look for shops."

"Okay," said Helen. "I'll get us there fast as I can."

Behind her, the Devil still wasn't cracking. "I think we might need to something even stronger, darls," said Bernie.

The Devil's eyes darted from side to side, apprehensively.

"Disney?" said Lucy.

"Disney," said Bernie

Lucy produced four soundtracks from her bag. "Shame the fucking stereo's buggered," she grunted.

"I know them all, darling," said Bernie. "Do you?"

"'Course I fucking do," said Lucy, affronted.

"I feel some duets coming on," said Bernie.

"Please, Satan, no!" said the Devil.

"You gonna tell us the way out!"

"Please! They'll dispel me if I tell you!"

"Let's start with *A Whole New World*" said Bernie.

Suzy cringed. "Martin, I need a distraction, and I need one now! It is time for you to honour our agreement."

"What is it you want me to do?" he asked tentatively.

She ran her hands down the sides of her body. "I think you know," she said. Martin looked at the three bloody red patches around the breasts of her dress. Its high hemline was ripped in a few places. She'd been ready to die for him, had died for him, but somehow she'd healed herself. Once it would have terrified him. Yet now, after Natalia, a girlfriend who couldn't die seemed a good option.

"Okay," he said, nervously. "But we're in a bit of a hurry, and I don't see any good places to stop."

"That's okay, the back three seats of the minibus are free!" said Suzy.

"There's a dead body on them, just now," said a voice from behind them.

"Then, of course, we can't," said Martin.

"It's okay, it's mine," said the same voice. "Actually, would you mind getting rid of it? Giving me the creeps a bit. Just toss it out the back doors, no need for sentiment. I'm here, you see?"

"We can't just … dump it," said Janelle in horror.

"*A whole new wo-o-o-o-rllld, don't you dare close your eyes*" chorused Lucy and Bernie.

"It would also be a serious violation of road safety laws," observed Mycroft. "It would impede following traffic."

"That sounds good to me," said Helen. Suzy, Lysandra and Dylan lifted Denny's body and pitched it out through the open back doors. It landed in a sad little heap, and quickly receded into darkness. Beside them, Denny's ghost sadly waved it goodbye. The others watched in surprise as the ghost now became more and more solid, until they could touch him.

"No excuse now," said Suzy.

"B-b-but it's not very private!"

"*With new horizons to pursue …*"

"Oh, the ladies won't look, they're refined," purred Suzy. "And as for the boys, well, I'm sure they won't mind watching."

"I'd mind!" said Martin.

"You don't need to worry," said Helen. "One's gay, one's a ghost, one's Mycroft, one's a Devil, and Dylan … can sit in the front."

"Do I have to?" said Dylan.

"Yes," said various voices.

"Tell you what, I'll come to the front too, keep you company," said Lysandra.

"There IS more to relationships than sex, you know," said Janelle, frostily.

"Is there?" said Suzy, her eyes registering genuine surprise at the idea. She found herself remembering an earlier conversation with Martin. "Do you … err … want to do *Blake's Seven* instead? That's something boys do with girls, is it?"

"I … ummm … we haven't got a video player," replied Martin.

"So it's settled then," said Suzy happily. She stood up on the seat and climbed over it, making sure Martin had a full view of her barely concealed rear quarters.

"I don't know," said Martin. "Natalia ..."

"Would want you to be happy!" said Helen, who'd worked out that keeping Suzy happy might be key to their survival. "Suzy's right, we may not be alive very much longer, you should seize this chance. And actually, you've known Suzy for as long as you knew Natalia, have you thought of that?"

Martin straightened his shoulders. "I'm going to the back of the minibus," he declared. "I may be some time."

*****

"Try to order us to do anything, and we'll gag you," said Sir Antony to Fenwick. The Scotsman had removed one of his shoes, to emphasise the point. "Now, how do we get out of here?" asked Sir Antony.

"Out of Hell?" asked Fenwick.

"Yes."

Fenwick considered for a moment. "Why should I tell you?"

"Because it seems to me that you can't untie yourself," said Sir Antony. "And that this featureless plain goes on for ever. We could just fly for a few hours, find a nice spot, and bury you deep. You'd be there for eternity."

"We'll get you in the end," said Fenwick. "We always do."

"Maybe," said Sir Antony. "Or maybe not. The Broker came quite close to beating you, didn't he?"

"But this time we'll be ready," said Fenwick. "In fact, I want to be there, to see them take you down. So, I'll tell you. Getting out of here is simple: first fly to the motorway that leads to the Gates of Hell."

"Yon Gates are nae there nae more," said the Scotsman.

Fenwick ignored this. "Then follow the middle lane back, till it splits from the others. That'll give you the best chance. You're waiting for a portal to open in the sky. You can't miss it, it'll be sky blue, like a bright day on Earth. Fly through it, and you'll get back home."

Sir Antony turned the plane. Fenwick allowed himself a smile. What he'd said was true, up to a point. He hadn't told them, of course, that air deaths over Britain were exceedingly rare, so it could be a very long wait. That suited him fine – more than enough time for the birds to work out how to rescue him. He also wondered about the failsafe – would three souls be enough to trigger it? He couldn't remember, but it might be fun finding out.

*****

Theo's plane roared through the air. "Just keep on in a straight line," said the voice on the radio, from the plane behind him. He had no idea why he'd been told to make this flight. When he'd asked, he'd simply been told it was part of the plan.

"The plan's null and void," he'd protested. "We got slaughtered by the Legion of Hell, or didn't you notice?"

"Oh I noticed," had been the response. "And it couldn't have gone better if I'd planned it! Now, I believe you own a small private jet? I shall be needing your services."

Theo had seen what was behind him. A small passenger plane, with perhaps a hundred seats on it. He did not dare wonder who was on board. Now a third plane was approaching from the side, a war plane. "Fighter jet approaching!" he called into the radio. "I repeat, fighter jet – "

"Don't worry, it's ours," said the radio. In the big plane, Arjun sweated at the controls. He did not understand why he and Yassar had been plucked from their home countries and offered massive amounts of money, to learn English and train as pilots. Both had been told that the world faced an invasion by Devils from Hell, and they'd been involved in the capture of three of them. Yet he'd been told today that this flight was his most important mission yet, and that when it was done he could go home.

The man sitting beside him smiled. "Okay, it's time. Just keep the plane steady, Arjun, and if you see a black cloud, aim for its centre." Then he punched a few keys on his mobile phone, and Theo's plane exploded.

Theo blinked. He couldn't see the burning fragments of his plane hurtling towards the ground; only the spectral plane he was now flying. He felt as if something important had had happened, but he could not think what it was. From nowhere a huge black storm cloud had appeared in front of him. *Keep flying straight on*, his instructions had been. There was a red speck in front of the cloud. Drawing closer, he saw it was one of those Devil things, beckoning him forward.

"Right," said Theo with a growl, and he aimed his nosecone right at the Devil's groin.

*****

"There!" said Yelena. "On the left!!"

Fenwick looked up in disbelief.

"I see it," said Sir Antony. He turned the plane towards the expanding patch of blue. As they approached it, a small plane shot out of it, with something red and screaming impaled on its nosecone. It was followed in rapid succession by a much larger plane, and a fighter jet.

"How long do the portals last?" said Sir Antony.

"A minute or two," said Fenwick.

"We should just make it then," said Sir Antony.

"Scoatland! Ah'm coming home!" said the Scotsman. Yelena closed her eyes and clutched her chest in hope. Then something hit the windscreen. It looked like a patch of bird poo. Moments later the screen where it had hit dissolved and flew inwards, striking Sir Antony's face. He screamed with pain. Two yellow birds flew in through the hole and pecked at his eyes. He screamed again, fending them off with his hands, and the plane started to dip.

"Pull up!" yelled the Scotsman.

"Or we'll miss the blue window!" cried Yelena.

"Har har!" cackled Fenwick

"Yon beasties are yours?" asked the Scotsman.

"Heaven, yeah," said Fenwick. "They've been evolving!"

Sir Antony slumped off his chair. The plane dipped down further.

"Aw naw," said the Scotsman, as the blue patch began to pass above them.

"Eject!" screamed Yelena. She grabbed a red lever.

There was a series of bangs as the roof flew off, and their seat rocketed up, carrying them out of the plane and into the blue haze, where they vanished from sight. Seven more birds swooped into the plane, through the now open roof, and plucked the bound Fenwick into the air. As the birds flapped away, the plane with Sir Antony still in it spiralled down to the ground, and exploded.

"Take me to Hell, fast!" said Fenwick to the birds.

The lead bird flew in front of his face and chirped at him angrily.

"What?" said Fenwick.

"Tweet-tweet-TWEET!"

"Oh, I do beg your pardon. Take me to Hell, *please*."

The birds started flying.

Out of a dark cloud on Earth, a parachute fell, beneath which two figures clung on for their lives.

*****

"Martin, you're falling asleep! Stop it!"

Martin felt like a deflated sex doll, albeit a happy one. "Need a rest," he mumbled.

"Uh-uh, no resting." With astonishing strength she hoisted him up and put him down over her knees, with his bare bottom sticking in the air. "I'll spank you awake!" she declared.

Martin managed to look up at her. "Stop doing that!" he said.

"Doing what? I haven't started!"

"The horns and the red and the pointy teeth!"

"Oh," said Suzy. She lowered her hand. "I didn't realize I was." The sexual fervour drained from her eyes, and her skin turned pink again. "I'm sorry. I can't fully control it."

"Why does it happen?" asked Martin. "Will you turn into one of them?"

Suzy looked at her hands. They turned red, then back to flesh coloured. "I'm not sure I understand it myself. I was made by this place – the Abysmal Plain. It's been making beings like me ever since the first living human came here."

"How do you know this?" asked Martin.

"I don't know, I just do. It's like it's someone else's memories."

"Whose?" asked Martin, cautiously.

Suzy seemed not to hear him. "Before ... before me, constructs almost always turned evil. No, not evil, just destructive. Our purpose is to rid the Plain of living souls."

"Why?" he asked. "Why is that necessary? Why can't it just let us leave? Spit us back out where we belong?"

"Well it's like an immune system, isn't it?" said Lysandra from the front. "It'll do whatever's easier."

"Of course the place is trying to kill us," said Janelle. "It's part of Hell."

"Actually, no," said Suzy. "Hell is a part of the Plain. The Plain was here long before Hell."

"That's nonsense!" protested Janelle.

"No, it's true. For as long as there have been people, the dead would arrive here, look around a bit, realise there was fuck-all to do, and fade away over decades of boredom. Or maybe some of them found *something* to do," she added with a wink. "Then later, somehow, living souls found a way to come visiting. Not sure why, just nosy, I guess. Anyway, the plain made constructs which killed the visitors, and then the constructs faded away. Always.

"Then, thousands of years later, these two old guys had this stupid argument about what happened to the dead. The old goats couldn't agree, so in the end they both took funky drugs and got themselves here – it was a lot easier back then. The first guy, well, he expected this terrible being who punished the sinful and devoured all their souls. What kind of idiot would think that, then come here just to find out? Anyway, he did, and the great Lord Lucifer was called into being, *to begin his dreadful reign! The foolish mortal was cast down into the newly forged pits of Hell, there to face the most horrible of torments!! And then when he could take no more, his sinful soul was devoured!*"

"Suzy!" cried Martin in alarm!

Suzy blinked. "What?"

"You were going all demonic. Your voice … it went all deep and … dark."

"Did you like it?"

"No I didn't!!"

Suzy cocked her head sideways, and took in the various alarmed to concerned expressions from the others in the bus. "I'm a part of this place," she said simply. "You know this. Recalling these shared memories brings out the Devil in me! But don't worry, I can keep him in check. Look, if it's creeping you out, I can stop. Find some other way to pass my time …"

"No, go on," said Helen. "We need to know this stuff, anything that might help us find a way out of this."

"If you insist! OK, so the second guy, he thought the souls of the good were carried up to paradise by Angels. And because of that, he lost his soul too, because the Angel he'd called into being was compelled to do precisely that – rip his soul from him and carry it away. Paradise didn't exist at that point, so Heaven was called into existence for the soul to be taken to. But stealing an unwilling soul gave the Angel a massive guilt complex, too, and they've never lost it. 'Wimples.' Ha haa! We call them Wimples!"

"We?" said Janelle.

"Constructs like me," said Suzy

"That's rubbish!" said Janelle loudly. "The Angels were created by the Lord God, not some idiot wandering witch-doctor!"

"Believe that if you want to," replied Suzy. "Makes no difference to me. But it's funny how you mortals are all so convinced that the creator spends all his time lounging about with the Angels."

"That's what Heaven *IS*," said Janelle.

"Heaven is a load of Angels being sickeningly nice to everyone, and trying to avoid being asked if God is real."

"What kind of a monster are you?" hissed Janelle.

"Please," said Lysandra. "Let's hear her story, it could be useful. We can talk about it later, whether it's true or not."

"Thank you," said Suzy. "Anyway, absorbing a living soul changed both Lucifer and the Angel, forever. They became more than conscious; they became eternal. The constructive and destructive power of this place, harnessed and controlled by a powerful mind. But their minds, in turn, were compelled to do as they'd been imagined to – punishing the naughty, and rewarding the WAKE UP MARTIN!"

Martin yelped as Suzy's flat palm came down hard on his buttocks. Then she spanked him again, harder. "And that's for falling asleep in the first place!!"

Undeterred, Suzy continued. "Now, there were too many souls for either to judge on their own. The Angel went to the mortal world, seeking pious twits who'd give up their souls willingly, and from each one who did would be born a new Angel. So in Heaven, all Angels are equal; they built Heaven as a collective and have run it that way ever since.

"Lucifer was cleverer – he tricked the wicked and greedy into visiting his domain, promising untold riches, obedient servants and beautiful, sex-obsessed girls."

"Like you?" said Martin, anxious to show he was still awake.

"Like me," she agreed, stroking his thigh. "In return, they had to agree that when they came at last to the world of the dead, they would surrender to the Devils and have their soul consumed by Satan."

"And of course, they didn't realise that Lucifer's domain WAS the world of the dead," offered Martin.

"Yep. The poor fools had just a few minutes to enjoy their slaves and concubines, before they were marched off to feed Lucifer. Unlike the Angels, Lucifer consumed for himself every living soul he entrapped, concentrating power inside his own being. In time, his influence grew such that every new construct created, unless it was angelic in form, or disappeared quickly, would transform over time into a new Devil to swell the ranks of Hell, all working under Him. It backfired in the end, though, when one of them killed Him and gained all his power. There've been at least four Satans, I think. The rest of us are just aspects, extensions of Him."

"Have I ..." said Martin nervously ... "have I just fucked Satan?"

"Only a little bit," she replied.

"Really?" came Bernie's voice. "It didn't sound like a little bit to me – "

"No, I mean his influence on me is quite weak so far," said Suzy. "And yet, I know what I am, now. I was a construct, brought into being by Michael Price's sexual fantasies, but I lived long enough to absorb Satan's essence and become, well, me! Without him, no Devil could exist, and I'd have faded away when Michael died."

"Michael's dead??" asked Helen, Dylan and Bernie, in unison.

"Yes, and I'm sorry. I felt it happen. He was in that explosion we heard, just after we hit the traffic jam."

Martin's head span with all of this, but the gently probing fingers between his thighs brought his focus back to the more immediate. "But will you become a full Devil?" he asked. "Will you start trying to kill us, like the Warden?"

"I'm fairly sure I won't, as long as something's distracting me," she said, as her probing hand found life returning to Martin's lower parts.

*****

"Oooooogggghhhh!" said Gabriel.

"I am asking again, can you send me to Hell?" asked Natalia.

"Like my colleague said," gasped Gabriel, we can grant you any desire within Heaven, but not send you outside it!"

The knee hit his groin again, harder. Gabriel staggered back, and transformed into female form. "It can't be done, I tell you," she said.

"I desire you to be man again," snapped Natalia. Gabriel obeyed automatically, for they existed to serve. No sooner had his balls returned than a knee once again flattened them.

"Lord Gabriel," said another Angel. "There may be a way."

"Please let you be right," gasped Gabriel.

"You said there was trouble in Hell. Is it bad?"

"I'm not sure," said Gabriel. "It could be very bad indeed."

"Yet we cannot intervene?"

"Unless we are asked for, we cannot assist. We can remove their people for malpractice, but an actual attack by the mortals, if true … we never imagined it."

"But if a particular Angel were asked for, could he-stroke-she go there?"

"That is within the rules, yes. You are suggesting we … "

"Make her an Angel, yes."

"But someone would have to ask for her help, and they haven't yet," said Gabriel.

"Still it is our best chance, and hers," said the other Angel.

"Are you willing to become an Angel?" asked Gabriel of Natalia.

"I no wear your fluffy white skirts," said Natalia. "But if only way, I agree."

Chapter Twenty-Four

"This is NOT about my mother!!"

"Jan, I never said it was," protested Lysandra.

"Yes you bloody did! You said, 'I know this is personal for you'! I know *exactly* what you meant!"

"Religion is personal! Belief is personal! That's all I ... Janelle, I'm just worried about you, is all..."

"About ME? You're worried about me?? Lyssie, you need a serious priority-check! The legions of Hell are out there trying to kill us – I mean literally trying to kill us – and you're worried about MY EMOTIONAL FEELINGS??!!!???"

"Might I observe that you are currently screaming your head off despite a temporary absence of any external threats, which tends to imply that ..."

"Shut up Mycroft!!!" chorused Janelle and Lysandra.

"Janelle, I'm sorry, OK? Sorry I upset you, sorry if I implied something I shouldn't have. But look, whatever problem you've got with Suzy, you need to put it aside. We need her. I don't care what she is, or where she's from. All I want is for us to survive this: you, me, everyone. And that means not antagonising one another!"

"Indeed, our situation is basically a war for survival, and as such divides beings very simply into those trying to kill us, and those trying to keep up alive."

"Mycroft, shu – oh, no, actually, no, that's a very good point," said Lysandra. "Yes. Suzy is on our side, and right now I couldn't care why. Anything else can wait. I need you to stop having a go at her, Jan. I think you're blaming her for things not being how you think ... I mean, how you were taught that they should be. But I'm going to suggest something – and please think about it before you get angry. Does it actually matter?"

"Yes of course!" said Janelle, somewhat thrown by the question.

"Look," said Lysandra. "I thought about this a lot in that bloody traffic jam. We've learned one thing for certain on this trip, and that is that our universe is not just matter and energy. It's consciousness too, as a powerful constructive force. Don't you see? That changes the whole way that we look at it all. The sterile Big Bang theory doesn't work, on its own. It doesn't explain where we are right now. There has to be some source of this conscious existence, just as there was for matter and energy. As I see it, God *has* to exist!"

"But not your big man with a beard," said Bernie.

"Or woman," said Lysandra.

"Or your big woman with a beard," agreed Bernie.

"The things that we've seen prove a God," said Lysandra, "I'm sure of it, even if they didn't come about quite how we were taught. But then, that's true of the physical world too, isn't it? Evolution, not Adam and Eve, but faith survived that. What Suzy said fits what we've seen. God is a bit further removed from our lives than we thought, but He's there. But why would such a being, who built countless trillions of stars, choose to while away eternity hanging out with dead humans? Even nice ones? It doesn't make sense. It's never made sense. We've just all chosen to believe it, and there's never been evidence against, until now. The afterlife's real, Jan, and I think so is God. They're just not in the same place."

"It's like the Queen," said Bernie happily. "Most of us will never meet her, but we're happy to know that she's there."

"Quite," said Lysandra, unsure if this helped.

"Maybe you're right," conceded Janelle, though it didn't seem to make her any happier.

*****

For some in the minibus, this was their first proper look at this strange, dystopian version of Glasgow. The presence of Bernie – the only one who actually knew the real city – had changed it somewhat, but his was one mind against many. So the things he recalled and loved most had popped up amidst the unrelenting grimness. Lights from a modern Art gallery shone out onto the fighters and drinkers and murder investigators, none of whom paid it any attention at all. Clothes shops and nightclubs were nestled among chip shops. Less appealing but equally true to the real city, a motorway now thundered through its centre on a big flyover, though they couldn't work out how to get onto it. However, they hadn't seen a single shop that sold anything electronic; not even a petrol station.

Martin was snoring as Suzy's head popped up over the seat back. "Hello Bernie," she said brightly. "I'm in need of a new man, I seem to have worn this one out."

"I bat for the other team, darling," replied Bernie cheerfully.

"You're an Angel? Where are the wings?"

"That's not what he means," said Lysandra. "It means he's not interested in you."

"Oh," said Suzy. She felt an odd flush of relief. "I'm not sure I want a different man actually. I think I quite like the one I've got."

"Good for you," said Lysandra.

"I think we've arrived," said Helen.

"You sure about this?" said Lucy.

"We'll run out of time if we keep looking for shops," replied Helen.

Outside the bus, a red neon sign bore the words 'Hot Spot.'

*****

"We're under attack" yelled Woking, addressing the Devils in the room with him. "You lot get out there, whatever it is, deal with it! Not you, Camberley!"

The Devils charged out, happily chanting war cries. Woking turned to glare at Kane. "Who's attacking us?"

"Some angry old ladies," said Kane, with a smile.

Behind him, one more of the huge windows shattered, and something big and red thudded to the ground. Another Devil, bound loosely with thin coloured rope. Woking ran to him. No, it wasn't rope, it was wool. Five knitting needles were sticking from his chest, and a set of false teeth were embedded in his neck.

"O-old women ..." said the stricken Devil. "Th-thousands of them!"

"Thousands?" said Woking. "Uriel's feathers!"

"Oooh, you're in trouble now," said Kane.

"Did you do this?" growled Woking.

"Well, the Broker planned it, but I did the legwork," said Kane.

Another window smashed, and three brawling figures tumbled through: one Devil, and two screaming old ladies, tearing at him.

"You see," said Kane happily, "we told our human staff that all the houses contained old ladies, so they did. We then told them to deliver these notes to every house, based on building faults they'd found." He handed Woking a leaflet.

```
Dear Homeowner(s)
    I write to appraise you of the results of our recent Home
Safety inspection.  I regret¹ to inform you that your home has
been adjudged a Fail, and therefore not suitable as a living
abode, based on the following categories:
```

- ☐ Inadequate wiring somewhere
- ☐ Loft insulation below specifications
- ☐ Fire doors that close too hard
- ☐ Fire doors that don't close hard enough
- ☐ Inadequate wiring somewhere else
- ☐ Nasty smell in toilet
- ☐ Lingering odour of stale pot-pourri
- ☐ Wet rot
- ☐ Dry rot
- ☐ Sort of slightly damp rot
- ☐ Hot and cold taps that are hard to tell apart
- ☐ A regulation too complex to describe to you here
- ☐ Other:

```
    You are required by council rules to move out of the house
immediately.  You must also contact the party that sold you this
house, and arrange for them to correct all these faults within
ninety days. You'll find the house seller's Terms and Conditions
in the third drawer down in your bedroom. If they fail to conduct
these repairs, the house will be deemed permanently unsafe for
habitation, and you will be held liable for council demolition
expenses upon it.
    Have a nice day,
        Your council.

                                    1. Figure of speech
```

"So you made them angry," said Woking. "But why are they attacking us, not you?"

Kane showed him a copy of the Terms and Conditions. "I showed these to my employees, had them all read through it before they started. Called the things into existence. The old ladies of course went to read it as soon as the Fail note came through."

The front cover had two grinning red Devils on it. It bore the name 'Red Demon Homes, Ltd.' Inside, Woking found pictures of bright red Devils on every page. The text congratulated the new owner on her purchase, and explained how the company had a policy of only employing men born with a rare genetic condition, that caused them to have red skin, horns and a tail.

"The last page is key," said Kane happily.

"*By the way,*" Woking read, "*There are probably quite a few things wrong with your house. Tough! You should have read the small print. The council in this area are terrible sticklers, so they'll probably knock your house down. We don't care, we've already got your money. Har, har, har, loser.*"

"So," concluded Kane. "You've got an army of constructs out there that outnumbers you, what, thirty to one? And who hate the sight of you. Wishing you did the deal with me now?"

Woking punched him to the ground. He reached for the stone on his wrist. "This is Woking, at the New Town. We're under attack from a construct army! Repeat, under attack, massive numbers! Yeeeaaaargghhh!!"

Woking yanked the knitting needle from his eye, just as more thudded into his chest. Three cackling old ladies were there by the broken windows. Another threw a ball of wool, which opened into a net and trapped Camberley. Woking aimed his pitchfork at them, and pressed the black button, but nothing happened. More needles thudded into his face and chest. Howling with rage, he tried the red button, and a thick jet of flame shot at the old ladies, who tumbled from sight. Then he turned it for a moment onto Camberley, who was still struggling in the wool. Camberley yelped as the wool all burnt off. Next, Woking fired his pitchfork's prongs into one of the brawling old ladies on the floor, before retracting the cord, pulling her off the Devil she was on, and towards him. Woking span on the spot, sliced her head off with his tail, and kicked it out through the window. The Devil on the floor gained the upper hand now, and Woking beheaded his remaining assailant too. But moments later, the door to the room flew open, and more old ladies started charging in. Woking and a smoking Camberley drove them back with jets of flame, but there were other ways into the room. "Barricade those doors!" Woking ordered. "And Camberley, my blessed dispel function doesn't work!"

"You ordered them disabled, sir!"

"Holy communion wafers!" yelled Woking. "Turn them back on again, fast!"

"Well I can certainly do it to the ones in this room," replied Camberley, pressing buttons on a stone and pointing at Woking's pitchfork, then his own and that of the Devil who'd staggered in earlier. Woking tested his dispel function on Preston, who'd been standing in the corner mutely the whole time. He dissolved into nothing. Woking looked around for Kane, but saw a side door quickly shutting. Frustrated, he dispelled the two headless old ladies.

Outside, the battle was clearly going against them. No more whole Devils had come in through the window, instead it was pieces of Devils, arms and legs mainly, and a few heads. "We have to get out there," said Woking. "Re-enable dispel on as many as you can, Camberley, that's your priority." Woking watched a dozen old ladies charge into the room, all of which he dispelled. Then he and his colleagues flew out of the windows into a three-dimensional melee.

***

"Are you sure you want to deal with this guy?" asked Lysandra. "After what Bernie said. It's not like we've got much to offer him, either."

"We'll play that by ear," said Helen. "I'm hoping we might trick him into fighting the Devils for us, tell him they're a rival gang, or something." She managed to find a place to park the bus where it didn't cover any chalk outlines of bodies, and they all got out, warily. All except Martin, who asked if he could stay in the bus and rest a bit, because he wasn't quite sure if he'd be able to walk. From under the back seats a head popped up. Saucy Jock yawned, asked if he'd missed anything, and then staggered off towards the nearest chip shop. Suzy, still sprightly and full of energy (and, Helen noticed, a certain glow) wanted to stand guard of the minibus and Martin. Helen thought for a moment and asked Suzy to go with the others. "They may need your strength," she said. "I'll watch the bus."

Nondescript dance music played as they passed through the corridor. "The Dark Laird's Dungeon is next door, boys!" said the man taking coats, noting Bernie's attire.

"Oh this?" he replied. "I just put it on to stay dry."

"And I suppose he did too?" he said, indicating Mycroft's French Maid outfit.

"That is indeed factually correct," Mycroft replied. "We were subjected to a prolonged period of highly localised rainfall, and ..."

"Never mind him, Duckie," said Bernie, leaning forward to address the man. "We're here to see Mad Harry."

"Seriously?" replied the man.

"Seriously," said Bernie.

"Even him?" the man pointed at Mycroft.

"Yes, even him."

"Well, it'll be interesting. Can I keep your clothes after he kills you?"

"Ooh, you tease," replied Bernie.

"Guy with a scar, corner with the blue light," said the man.

Bernie thanked him and led the others through. The dance music got louder as they entered a large room, dimly lit in red. In the near part, there were tables with thin seats, and rings of fixed seats with cushions around thick pillars. Absurdly attractive and scantily clad dancers of both sexes were gyrating for the pleasure of those around them on lit raised platforms. Further back, a large crowd were making use of the dance floor.

They spotted a wall with a bluish light falling on it and made their way towards it. Dylan however stopped, transfixed by a dancer. Lucy tried to move him, but he wouldn't budge. "Oh leave him," said Bernie. "We'll pick him up on our way out. Lizzie will watch him, won't you?"

Lysandra looked unimpressed, but nodded. Denny decided to stay with them too. He was a bird watcher, after all. The rest progressed over to the corner, where they quickly spotted a man with a thick diagonal scar across his face, and two huge henchmen beside him.

"Just our luck that he's real, when there aren't any shops," grumbled Lucy.

"Not luck at all," observed Mycroft. "Bernard deliberately described him as a figure of fear, causing the Plain to make him manifest. It only worked because we were consciously wanting the shops to be real, which of course meant that they weren't, while not wanting him to be real, which made him become so."

"Guilty as charged, darling," replied Bernie, while the others tried to catch up with Mycroft's reasoning.

Bernie continued. "I suggest Suzy and I handle this. Janny, you look a bit too virtuous, and Mycroft, well you look like an unsuccessful Eurovision entrant. Lucy, keep your eye out for threats. If it's anything like the other places we've been..." She nodded. Bernie and Suzy went up to the scarred man. "Follow my lead," he said.

"That's easy, its hanging round your neck."

"Are you Mad Harry?" Bernie asked the man.

"Who's asking?"

"I'm offended!" said Bernie. "Surely you remember? OK, my attire may have been a bit more conventional last time I was here."

"But only a bit," said Suzy.

"It would have involved some pink, or maybe bright green."

Mad Harry's eyes glazed over briefly. "That's as maybe, but I cannae help you."

"We're here to offer a deal," said Bernie. "We need a satnav, and the best missile launchers you've got."

Mad Harry pulled a face. His henchmen sniggered. "And how much are you paying?"

"Something money can't buy." Said Bernie.

"Heard that before."

"Suggest you come and see, it's outside."

"Why would I bother?"

"I promise, it'll change your world."

Mad Harry thought for a moment. "Gunter, go with him. Find out what he's on about. The girl stays with me. Siddown, sweetheart. Rough hands pushed Suzy onto the sofa beside him, while Bernie, holding his nerve, followed the thug called Gunter outside.

The minibus had attracted a large crowd of drunks. Helen was shouting that she'd start the engine and run them down if they didn't disperse, but it only seemed to encourage them. "There," said Bernie. "On top, look."

"So it's some upside down bloke with sunburn, so what?" said the thug.

"Look at the tail!"

"On a string," said the thug.

"Go up and look closer," said Bernie.

The henchman climbed up, and tried to finger the Devil's tail. It whipped from left to right, then caught his neck and snapped it. The henchman dissolved.

"Ah," said Bernie. "Not as planned. Lucky he's got a spare!"

"What's the idea?" said Helen?

"To show him a real Devil," said Bernie. "Then he'll either fight them or run, either way helps us!"

"Okay. I'm not sure how long I can hold off this crowd," she said.

"I think they just want entertainment," he said, running back in.

Bernie met Lucy inside. "He took Suzy through that door," she said, indicating a firmly shut door in the blue-lit corner, beside which a lone henchman sat, staring blankly at the wall. As they watched, the door opened, and the henchman's head exploded. Suzy lowered the gun in her hand, as the henchman dissolved.

"Where's Mad Harry?" asked Bernie.

"Having a lie down," said Suzy. "He very reasonably agreed to trade this for a pair of scissors," she added, handing him a satnav. "But I didn't say I'd put them where he could reach them, though."

"That's brilliant," said Lucy. "What about the other weapons?"

"Nothing else." They looked at the screen on the device. It showed a huge area called 'nowhere', with a small dot marked 'you' in the middle.

"Well that's fuck all use," declared Lucy.

"I wouldn't be so sure," replied Bernie, noticing a very large number of red dots appearing at the side of the screen, moving inwards. Each had the little word "Devil" beside it. They were perhaps ten minutes from reaching the 'you'.

"We gotta run," said Lucy. "Get the others!"

"There's a problem!" said Janelle. "Look at them! They've all gone rigid, and they're staring at the …"

She didn't finish the sentence. Dylan, Lysandra and even Denny were all standing stock still, with their wide eyes fixed on the dancer. Now Janelle herself took on a similar pose. Bernie looked up at the dancing girl before he could stop himself. If it was a girl. One side was female, slim waisted and lithe, with big breasts. But she turned to reveal a male body at her back, with perfect muscle tone and a thick waist and arms that could not possibly be the same person. Bernie knew which side he liked better. Indeed there was suddenly no thought in his mind but that perfect male side to the body.

"Oh fuck," said Lucy. "It's got Suzy too!" She slapped Suzy hard, but Suzy's gaze stayed fixed on the dancer.

"Its hair's moving!" said Mycroft.

"Like snakes?" said Lucy, her eyes now screwed shut.

"More like worms, but they're getting thicker!"

"Oh my God, it's a Medusa!" said Lucy. "It'll turn them to stone!" Terror coursed through her as she placed her trembling fingers onto Lysandra's arm, which already felt hard and brittle.

Chapter Twenty-Five

The dancing monster wore two hideous grins as the snakes on its head writhed and hissed in triumph. All of Dylan, Bernie, Janelle, Lysandra, the ghostly Denny and the demonic Suzy were fixed to the spot by its gaze, their skins slowly turning to stone. Lucy tried to wrench the gun from Suzy's hand, but the gun crumbled like clay.

"We need a mirror!" said Lucy. "We have to get a mirror! Nothing else can stop a Medusa!"

"I wish people would get their mythology right," said Mycroft. "Medusa was an individual. Gorgons are the species. Clearly this individual is not Medusa. I would say, taxonomically speaking, that it is a hermaphrodite species related to the Gorgon, which hypnotises its victims via the power of sexual attraction, prior to consuming their life force in some no doubt gruesome fashion. It is therefore highly fortunate that I exist on an intellectual plane that is free from trivial sexual desires." He picked up one of the thin metal-legged chairs. "Furthermore, in this instance I postulate that the hypnotic effect is dependent upon the rhythm of the dance moves." He inserted two chair legs between the dancer's legs, and twisted the chair.

"Wo-ahhhhh!" said the dancer in two different voices, as it tumbled from its platform.

"Which means it can be broken by the precise application of basic slapstick," concluded Mycroft. The transfixed students started moving again.

"Run!" shouted Lucy.

Everyone ran but in different directions, colliding with pillars and tumbling over chairs. "They're still under!" said Mycroft.

"Wake up!" shouted Lucy. The others all stopped or got up, confused and disorientated. "Follow me quick!" shouted Lucy, and they ran out to the bus. It was now completely surrounded by drunks. They were gyrating and bumbling from side to side in perfect lack of time.

"*With your hands on your hips (jump-jump-jump),*

… you bring you knees in ti-i-ight" sang Helen from the roof, doing the actions with her fishnet-clad legs. The upside down Devil legs sticking from the roof were attempting to join in, too.

"Free drinks in the bar!" shouted Lucy. The drunks all stopped dancing and tottered towards the nightclub door.

"*But it's the pelvic thru-u-sts, that really drive you in-say-yay-*eh?" sang Helen. "Oh. Hello. Bernie said I should keep them entertained."

"Probably a good idea, yes," said Lucy.

"You can come down, now," said Janelle.

"I can't be-*lieeeve* I missed that!" said Bernie.

"Did it work?" asked Helen.

"Total fuck-up," said Lucy. "We've got nothing!"

"And they're coming," said Suzy.

*****

"Go up!" shouted Woking, soaring up through the blizzard of flying needles, purple wigs, flames, false teeth, zimmer frames and Devil body parts. Somehow he and Camberley managed to reach the top of the flying battle and look down. As Kane had said, the Devils were hopelessly outnumbered by furious eldsters.

"It's like a scene out of Heaven, sir," said Camberley, directing his control stone randomly into the melee in the hope it would hit some pitchforks. "It's hard to tell what's going on!"

Indeed, the old biddies were now as red as their opponents, and flying just as well. The Devils could be picked out though, either by where jets of flame were coming from, or because something had to be at the centre of the tight clusters of jeering old ladies, all stabbing and ripping.

"We're losing, that's what! We have to get back to Hell and get help!" shouted Woking. He made a decision, fired the dispel ray at one of the swarming old lady masses. Eleven old ladies and one hapless Devil disintegrated.

"You've already called for back-up," said Camberley.

"It won't be enough! Look how many there are! We need outside help!"

"So tell them to call for it!"

"No-one else will do it, has to come from me in person! Even though it'll end me!"

Camberley caught his eye for a moment. Devil careers only ended one way, and it wasn't resignation or demotion. Then the moment was broken. "They've seen us," shouted Camberley, as a phalanx of marauding old dears swooped towards them. Both devils fired dispel rays, and one by one the attackers disintegrated. Then a Zimmer frame crashed onto Woking's head, so hard that he lost the grip on his pitchfork. It tumbled out of sight. "They're coming from all sides" shouted Camberley. "We'll never make it back with this lot attacking us!"

"Young rascal," screeched the voice from behind Woking, and he turned just in time to be caught on the head by the Zimmer frame again, in a sideways swipe. He was knocked to the side, but lashed out with his tail, detaching her arm. "Have you no respect?" she screeched, as the arm too fell from view. Her own tail pierced Woking's eye.

"It's not," yelled Woking, while grabbing her tail, "in the job description!" He began to whirl on the spot, faster and faster, spinning the wailing one-armed spinster around him. There was a series of satisfying cracks as she connected with one after another of the looming attackers. Then Camberley noticed a new noise: a roaring of engines.

"A jet!" shouted Camberley. "Kane is escaping!"

"Mickleham mentioned a jet plane too," shouted Woking. "They might just have more! Be a lot faster than flying ourselves!" The tail in his hands jerked and went limp. There was nothing left on the end of it.

"Dive!" shouted Woking, and they plunged through the massed combatants. Bits and pieces of Devils were flying around, trying to reassemble, and not always getting it right. They spotted one Devil with a leg in the place of his head, which was kicking out at its opponents, while a head on its buttocks urged it on. "Back into the mansion," said Woking, and they swooped in through the smashed windows.

They re-entered the large room, to find several old ladies vandalising the room, cackling in angry delight as they spoke.

"Broken chest of drawers. Fail!"

"Desk is on fire. Fail!"

"Dismembered Devil on floor. Fail!"

"Fake glasses and moustache drawn on painting. Fail!"

"Evidence of defecation on carpet. Fail!"

"Wiring being ripped out of light switch. Fai-aieeeeegghhhhh!"

"Charred remains of electrocuted woman by light switch. Fail!"

Woking grabbed Camberley's pitchfork and dispelled them all. They ran through the building, dispelling old ladies as they went. "Which way?" shouted Camberley.

"We've seen the front of the house and one side, and they're not there," said Woking. "Best guess is, the back!" After several wrong turns, they burst out into the back courtyard. Two small jet planes stood there, but some of the old ladies had found them.

"Wool in the left engine. Fail!"

"Zimmer frame shaped dents in the wing. Fail!"

"Someone did a wee in the cockpit. Fail!"

"False teeth in the fuel tank! Fail!"

Woking dispelled them. Judging which plane was less damaged, he flew to its cockpit, with Camberley in tow. A mass of old ladies swooped down from the sky, too many to fight. Woking hit the engines, the plane lifted clear of the back wall, then he gunned it forwards. It tore through the air, and a series of red bodies bounced off the windscreen, some clad in purple, some not. He felt something rattle, and the right engine caught fire, but still they held speed. Now they emerged from the warzone, too fast for the ladies to follow. The burning engine spluttered. Woking angled the plane upwards. The burning engine exploded. "Camberley, push upwards and forwards on the right side!"

Camberley obeyed, pressing himself to the side of the cockpit and adding his flight power to that of the plane's remaining engines. Woking used his power the same way, as best as he could while still holding the controls. But it wasn't enough. The plane started to dip, albeit slowly. "I can see the Walls of Hell," shouted Camberley. But we're too low! We're heading for the lake! Bail out!"

"We'll lose too much time," countered Woking. "Move to the other side! Push the left side forwards instead!"

"But we'll spin!"

"Yes, I know!" The view from the front started whipping past them from right to left, faster and faster. Woking retracted the wheels. The spinning plane shot towards the lake at high speed, over the heads of the damned, then it hit the Lake surface, and bounced back into the air. Three hundred more metres, and it bounced again, but less high this time. A third bounce, a fourth, then the assembled figures on the far side saw them coming, skimming towards them with frightening speed. Forty dead souls and the one Devil who'd been left in charge had no time to get out of the way. The spinning plane sliced its way through them as it bounced the last time off the lake. Dented and smoking, with the acid corroding its belly, it skidded to a stop. Camberley staggered out, tottered round in a circle, collapsed in a heap and threw up. Woking blundered out after him, his red face decidedly greenish.

"I can't believe that worked," croaked Camberley.

"Once saw humans do it with stones," replied Woking, unsteadily. "Help the Devil here reassemble himself. Find out how many we've still got here, in case there's another attack. We will need everybody. I've got to get to Satan." He stumbled off, leaving Camberley to search for red parts among all the pink and brown ones.

*****

On the satnav in Lucy's hands, about forty red dots were getting steadily closer.

"*Yea, though I walk through the valley in the shadow of death, I shall fear no evil,*" uttered Janelle, shaking.

"Fear!" shouted Dylan. "Hypnosis! Hypnosis can stop people's fears, can't it?"

"That is often claimed to be so," agreed Mycroft. "However the evidence is…"

"Could it create a fear too? One that could help us?"

"It might," agreed Helen. "But are you a hypnotist?"

"We've already met one! That dancer!" said Lucy.

"But it'll never help us," said Lysandra.

"There may be a method," said Mycroft, "let me get my camera! I shall need about two minutes!"

"Not sure if we've got that long," said Lysandra, as Mycroft grabbed his camera.

"I'll delay them," said Suzy.

"That's suicide," said Helen.

"I'm touched that you care," replied Suzy. "You look after Martin, or else!" Then she took off, as Mycroft ran back into the nightclub.

"Suzy?" said Martin, crawling dazed from the minibus.

*****

In the sky above the city that thought it was Glasgow, Byfleet was leading the Devil horde. He'd switched his cigarettes for cigars, which he felt gave him the look of a general. With him was Bracknell, whom Woking had transferred to his command. "Look! Flying car!" shouted Bracknell, and all of them swooped.

"Gi'e us oor wheels back!" shouted a grizzled murder detective, as his car flew away with a straining Suzy beneath it, now in full Devil form. "Awww noo," he added, as umpteen jets of fire erupted from above, melting the top of the car. Suzy veered left, and crashed the car into a chip shop. The Devil horde split, half after the car, the other half following a scout who'd seen the minibus. Suzy ripped off her dress, then shot out of the back of the chip shop, and swooped into the middle of the second Devil pack. Before they could work out that she didn't belong, she snatched a pitchfork from one and shot fire in a circle at as many as she could. Surprised, half the Devils fired back.

The students looked on as that group of Devils erupted in an inferno of friendly fire. A dozen charred figures fell out of the centre, none more burnt than Suzy. The others glanced round in confusion, seeking the unseen attacker, while the Devils from the chip shop flew back to assist. Mycroft ran out of the nightclub and joined the students in the minibus. Helen gunned the engine and they screeched down the road. Twenty-eight angry Devils flew after them, gaining with every second.

Everyone but Denny and Helen was squashed together in the middle of the bus, watching the screen on the back of Mycroft's camera. It showed the bisexual dancer, and quickly the film had its effect. Then the camera angle swung round to show a moving selfie of Mycroft. "You are now under my hypnotic power," the Mycroft on the screen told them. You now have only one fear, and that is that great powerful creatures could exist, that will fight off Devils and defend this minibus and everyone in it. This fear consumes your every waking moment, and you will think about nothing else until I snap my fingers."

Mycroft's hand went limp, dropping the camera to the floor. "Mycroft?" said Denny, alarmed. "Mycroft wake up! Helen, he's gone under too! But the dancing thing didn't affect him!"

"Yeah, but he loves the sound of his own voice," said Helen. "It must have been that!"

"I don't think it matters," said Denny, in a wavering voice. "We're out of time!"

A squadron of Devils were swooping down towards them, raising their pitchforks to fire.

**

Denny leapt out of the passenger door, drawing ten jets of flame, and he screamed with the pain. "Incinerate the vehicle," ordered Byfleet. "Oof!", he added, as a car crashed into him from the side, scattering the Devil horde. This car really was flying, and Natalia was driving it. Confused Devils took aim, but the car moved fast, and now a second car arrived, and a third, each smashing into as many Devils as it could. Natalia was somehow driving all of them. The Devil horde scattered, distracted from the minibus, and began firing at flying cars instead. One of the cars erupted into flame, and Natalia jumped out. A jet of fire caught her arm and the flesh burnt off, revealing the metallic innards of an android. Flying on jets from her limbs, she looked round for a moment, and then started kneeing Devils in the groin.

Once, Martin might have called forth from his mind Daleks, Jedi Knights, the Liberator, or Klingon Birds of Prey, when asked to select a fearsome ally. Yet now there was only one being that he could imagine. His call to Natalia had echoed across the Abysmal Plain, and was heard up in Heaven, too.

Twenty-eight Devils against ten flying cars is not an even contest, and one by one the cars were shot down, though out of each came a Natalia android. Those Devils not defending their crotches aimed their pitchforks at the minibus, once more. Then a series of unearthly screeches erupted from above. Harpies dived in, each with the face of the organiser from the dance hall, the scariest thing Lucy could think of. The screeching disorientated the nearest Devils, forcing them to cover their ears while huge claws tore at their bodies or ripped off the odd limb. Yet it only took one true shot with a pitchfork to bring down each harpy.

Those Devils who were burnt or broken did not stay down for long. Three of them staggered to their feet, looked up at the battle above and launched into the air, whereupon they were blasted into pieces once more by a hail of bullets. Past them swooped bizarre creatures that were half eagle, half fighter jet. These bullet-hawks were fast, but with fifteen jets of fire now aimed at them, one of the bullet-hawks was hit squarely by two jets of flame and exploded. The Devils all lined up their pitchforks to fire as the remaining hawks turned to come again, then the top of a building smashed into the horde.

Thirty-foot, muscle-bound giants in tight leopardskin speedos were approaching from all four directions, roaring their defiance, and ripping off chunks of buildings to use as missiles. They were careful to avoid damaging the art galleries, though. Sometimes they threw the chunks whole, other times they crushed them and hurled a blizzard of bricks and pieces, which the Devils could not hope to avoid. More Devils fell to the ground, stunned, while a few were pinned under large pieces. The giants avoided the minibus carefully with their missiles. But forty Devils is a lot, even when many are stunned at any given moment, and multiple jets of flame started driving the giants back.

Next to arrive were technicolour dragons, belching forth fire and smoke. One settled on the minibus, shielding it from flame, and firing back at any Devil that took aim at the bus. Soon after came a large flock of swooping Pterosaurs.

Janelle's eyes snapped open. She was standing some way off from the minibus, watching the battle. She blinked a few times, trying to work out how she'd got there.

"Exciting, isn't it?" said a deep voice from beside her.

"Uhh, yes," she said, without taking her eyes off the melee above. "I think I should be helping."

"Beautiful dragons. I never made any of those, you know."

"Yes, Lysandra's always … oh." Janelle looked round, into the eyes of the stranger. "My Lord," she said reverentially.

"At your service. You were saying?"

"Oh. Errr. Yes. Lysandra, she's always had a thing for dragons. She's a quarter Chinese. But then you knew that. Of course. Errr. I can't figure out those half metal giant birds though."

"Aha, there I can help. Dylan used to play Dungeons and Dragons, that's a role-playing game. He invented those on the one and only occasion they let him be dungeon master. They slaughtered everyone else's characters within minutes, you see. It didn't go down well. He calls them bullet-hawks."

"Oh. Thank you." It seemed a supremely useless piece of information for the Almighty to have given her. Except that ... she observed the other combatants. The robot Natalias were a no-brainer, and the giants in loincloths could not be more Bernie. "But who did the Pterodactyls?"

"Those are *Geosternbergia sternbergii*, Pterosaurs from the early Campanian epoch of the Cretaceous period. Not much good in a fight, to be honest, but they are paleontologically accurate. See how the crest on the head points upwards instead of backwards? Most people get that wrong."

"Mycroft," deduced Janelle. "Hang on, Cretaceous? You're saying Genesis didn't happen?"

"Let's not get into that," said God cheerfully. "I'm sure you have more pressing questions."

"Yes," admit Janelle. "Why isn't there anything from me?"

"Each of you summoned the most powerful ally or allies that your subconscious mind could conjure."

"Then what did I ... oh." She regarded the huge glowing figure before her. "My Lord, I humbly beseech you to smite these demons and return us to the world of the living."

"Ah," said God. "There we might have hit a wee problem."

The dystopian Glasgow was soon ablaze all around them, with so many flame jets now missing their marks. Thick smoke barrelled up towards two figures who watched the whole thing from above. "Lucifer's Horns!" cried Byfleet, exultantly. "I luuurve the smell of burnt flesh in the evening!" He conjured another cigar.

"It should have been over by now!" said Bracknell. "I can't understand how they've done this!"

"Not wanting to get stuck in yourself?" queried Byfleet.

"Well I've never really been the hand-to-hand type," quivered Bracknell.

"That's OK," smiled Byfleet. "You're needed right where you are. The humans are somehow using the powers of the Abysmal plain against us, so we shall use human weapons against them. Build me a hovering missile platform. Each missile big enough to annihilate that bus and everyone in it."

Bracknell grinned toothily. This he could do. He began forming the platform from the matter in the smoke, and the rain from the thundercloud.

Chapter Twenty-Six

Theo's plane emerged from the cloud. The sky was now a uniform grey all around him. He knew which way to go now, there could only be one way. Indeed, the Devil impaled on the nosecone, his face a rictus of pain, was also trying to point him in that same direction. The big plane was still behind him, but the warplane that had followed it was now dropping back. As he flew on, Theo became aware of a series of one-lane roads beneath him, converging one by one into a colossal motorway. Little cars could be seen moving along it, all in the same direction. From time to time, burning lifts plunged down from the sky, each one landing neatly on one of the trucks parked in the sidings. As soon as this happened, the truck in question would start along the motorway. The odd thing was, although this kept happening, the number of trucks in the sidings did not seem to diminish.

The motorway ended abruptly in a massive, oddly coloured lake. The vehicles all seemed to be just driving on into it. Theo could see figures milling around, watching this happen. He noticed a landing strip, parallel to the road right by the lake's edge, and felt a compulsion to land there. He felt the wheels hit the ground and applied the brakes. They kicked in, but not very hard. The end of the strip was approaching, and the plane wasn't going to stop in time! Theo got up, opened the side door, made a quick choice, and jumped.

The plane skidded off the edge of the strip into the Lake. Theo bounced and scraped along beside it, and just about stopped himself going in after it. He watched his beloved plane start to sink, then fizz furiously as the acid began to dissolve it. The acrid stench caught in his throat. He looked up. Massive walls rose either side of the lake. Beyond them were towering black buildings, around which flames played casually. Theo suddenly knew where he was. A roar of engines that had been building in his ear grew stronger, and he turned to see the large plane landing behind him. It, unlike any of the other vehicles, had somehow managed to stop before the strip ran out.

As the plane's engines cut out and the noise receded, he became aware of a series of splashes from his right, where the road ended. As he'd seen from above, none of the vehicles on the roads seemed to slow down at all, they just plunged right off into the lake. In fact, the crowds of people by the road's end were gesturing frantically at them to stop, but it had no effect. He watched the expression of one of the drivers: clearly the man knew the lake was there, and was repeatedly slamming his foot on the brakes. But it had no effect and the car just went in all the same. Yet there was a steady stream of screaming people pulling themselves out of the lake, as well. Theo realised that if you were already dead, you couldn't die again, but you could hurt. It was not a happy thought. He started to wonder if he, too, might be dead.

A door opened on the side of the big plane, and a ladder came out. A short figure in sunglasses appeared at the door, and strolled down it, carrying a suitcase. Theo saw how some of the crowd by the road began walking towards this man, some with awe in their eyes. Theo looked from him to them. There was a difference, he realised. He couldn't see it as much as feel it. The man from the plane was alive.

"Hey," said a voice from behind Theo.

"Yes?" he turned round.

"This is for sticking your cone through my special bits!" A knee struck his groin, belonging to the wet, somewhat blistered Devil that had been impaled by his plane. "Now go over there and wait with everyone else!" As Theo bent double, the Devil walked past him, or rather moseyed, for there was still a gaping hole in his crotch. Drips of acid fell from him as he did so. Theo noticed with horror that the knee had left a wet patch on his trousers. The wet material fizzed and fell apart, leaving the front of his boxers exposed.

Theo followed the Devil, in a similar painful mosey, towards the man from the plane.

"Miserable human!" said the Devil, in a menacing voice. "You cannot leave the plane on the runway. I order you to drive it into the lake for destruction!"

"Well I order you to sing the Birdie Song and do all the actions," said the man.

"What?" said the Devil. "I don't take orders."

"Neither do I," said the man, and blasted the Devil in both knees with a pistol. The Devil screamed with pain and collapsed to the ground.

"You will pay for this!" yelled the Devil, as he tried to sit up.

"No I won't," said the man. "I've done far worse, and I will do again. Speaking of which, it's lucky you're here. I need to check that something works." He drew out another gun, only this one had a home-made look about it. It was larger, with a wide barrel. "I was given a Devil-Knife, you see, by, well, that's not your concern. Nice as it was, it could only kill you at close quarters. So I cut off some little shards. Had them made into the tips of some bullets. Paid five thousand pounds for each one, just to be sure. In theory, it should kill and destroy any living thing – or any dead thing, for that matter – that it pierces. Which is all very well, but really what I need to be sure about – absolutely sure – is that it can kill one of you."

"No, wait!" said the Devil! "I've got something to tell you, something important about …" he thought, desperately, "… what they know about your plan. You're him, aren't you? You're Coker … but you can't be! And they said they'd dispelled you, but you're alive …"

"My name," said the man, smiling, "is the Broker." He fired. A red wound appeared in the Devil's chest. Blood spurted from his mouth. He pitched over backwards, and crumbled into red dust.

"He's dead," said Theo, in nervous wonder.

"Deader than you," agreed the Broker, with a smile.

"You really meant it all, didn't you? You said you had a way to kill them."

"Every word," said the Broker. "Devil knives are an ancient weapon, last used for combat in the War Against Heaven. Unless you count duels. Now they're mostly used for emergency repairs, apparently. Oh, and Pitchforks can dispel almost anything, unless you've turned that function off, of course."

"Almost?" said Theo.

"Anything without a living soul," said the Broker. "Which means all Devils except, unfortunately, Satan, within whom hundreds of ancient souls reside. I possess the only projectile weapon that has ever existed, that can kill Him."

"You're really going to fight him?" asked Theo.

"Yes and no," said the Broker.

"But you can't take on all of Hell! Where's your army?"

"I'm doing pretty well without one, wouldn't you say? See that great big hole ahead of us?"

"The lake?"

"It was gates, until a few hours ago."

"You blew it up?"

"Caused it to be blown up. Amazing, the damage you can cause with a bunch of lost students. You wouldn't believe how hard it was to get them here, but my God they've been brilliant! Weakened the mortal veil enough to get a coachload of idiots through, caused a massive diversion, and now they're fighting off forty Devils who we'd otherwise have had to deal with! Still, I really don't think they can last much longer. I don't need them anymore, now that I've got my legion of grannies!"

"Legion of ... grannies?"

"Oh yes, I never told you that bit, did I? That's my bigger diversion, so I could get my plane down, unhindered. Anyway," said the Broker. "I'm glad you're here, Theo. I've rather used up all my underlings."

"I'm here because you got me killed," said Theo.

"True," said the Broker. "Better than a slow death from cancer, wasn't it?"

"Depends what happens next," said Theo.

"Too true," said the Broker. He glanced at his watch. "Need to wait a few more seconds, this has to be timed perfectly. Three ... two ... one, here we go." He whipped out a megaphone.

"Souls of the condemned!" he shouted. The crowd that was already forming paid attention. "I am here to offer you a second chance. I escaped from Hell once and now I shall free you as well. You saw me slay that Devil, with ease. Some of you perhaps also wonder why no others are flying in to fight me? Why there's a lake there, and not gates? Because of me. I have them on the ropes. It now suits my purposes to free all of you – or as many as can be conveyed on my plane (health and safety, you know). This plane will be leaving for the mortal coil just as soon as every seat is filled. Form an orderly queue, please!"

They didn't, of course. They fought, punched, stabbed, and bludgeoned their way to the front. After five minutes of scrumming, the stepway to the plane was covered in blood, but somehow everyone had got on. "Looks like there's enough seats for everyone," said Theo.

"Oh yes," said the Broker.

"And you knew that?" asked Theo.

"Yes I did," said the Broker. "But I do love a good ruck, don't you? Plus it stopped anyone hesitating. Do you want to go with them?"

"I don't think so, no," said Theo. He wasn't sure why.

The plane taxied around in a tight circle, and took off.

Theo looked at the road. The rate of cars' arrival had dropped quite a lot. "Not so many coming now," he said.

"Ah yes," said the Broker. "I needed a planeful, so I arranged quite a few accidents."

"So they're all dead because of you," said Theo.

"Mostly, yes. Now, can you assist me? We need to prepare for the final act."

*****

"What do you mean, you can't intervene?" shouted Janelle. "Meaning no disrespect," she added hurriedly.

God shrugged apologetically, unconcerned by her tone. Perhaps millennia of having one's name taken in vain could do that to a deity, she supposed. "Unfortunately the circumstances surrounding my manifestation here prevent me from taking physical action of any kind," He explained. "Sorry."

Janelle sank to her knees as a wave of despair hit her. "Oh no … not this. My friends need me. They need our help! Please, not this again."

God cocked an eyebrow. "Again?"

She shot him a fearsome look. "Yes, again!"

"Good," said God. "Now we may be getting somewhere."

*****

Woking crashed into the left side of the corridor, then the right, as he hurtled along it. At the far end a red lift waited. Woking smashed through the doors without bothering to open them, and hit the lowermost button. The lift plunged and screamed down to the depths. Woking stumbled out through its smashed doors, along the short tunnel and flung open the doors without knocking.

"WHY HAVE YOU – "

"We've got a traitor!"

"Not possible!"

"It's the only way Coker could have escaped!"

"You are covering up for your failure!"

"I am not," pleaded Woking. "I know I'll be dust when this all ends, but first, hear me out. I am asking for help from the other Hells!"

"YOU CALLED FOR HELP WITHOUT MY SAY-SO?" roared Satan.

"There was no time to wait! An army of thousands is overwhelming our forces! And I tell you, this could not have been achieved without inside help! Maybe someone tampered with Bracknell's machine, maybe not, but I tell you one thing, he was given a Devil knife! Coker was given a Devil knife! And object that can kill even you! I tell you, we've been betrayed!"

"Why did you not tell me sooner?"

"I thought I could bring you the name of the traitor! Unmask him and drag him to you, here, in chains! But he's covered his tracks far too well. Yet one thing he can't mask is the motive. It has to be thwarted ambition! What else can there be? So you must tell me truly, and I know it's supposed to be private, on pain of dispelment and so on, but for all of Hell, tell me: has anyone ever challenged you – for a fight to the death for the Satanship – and been rejected? Has anyone ever been barred from such a contest?"

"You are right, it is strictly and absolutely confidential. If I told you, I could not then suffer you to live!"

"You could give me twenty-four hours," pleaded Woking. "To finish this battle, may we win or lose. A great army faces us, yet even that, I believe, is a deliberate distraction. The traitor has not yet made his play!"

"Willing self-sacrifice?" pondered Satan. "An interesting concept. One I think they favour up there," he said, twisting his nose in disgust. "Yet the threat is real and I feel that you – POURQUOI AS TU INFLICTÉ TON PRÉSENCE TRÉS MALODORANT SUR MOI???"

A French Devil had just appeared in the room. He replied to Satan in French.

"What did he say?" said Satan.

The French Devil spoke again, more crossly.

"He says it's about time you learned more French than just your insulting greetings," said Woking.

"No, before that!"

"He said, why does the English Devil have knitting needles sticking out of his head," said Woking, pulling one out absent-mindedly, "and that it sounds like we English need some – "

"HYAAAAAARR KWAAAAA SHAAAAA … hang on …" Satan lunged towards one of the books on Leather Jacket's back.

"It is okay, we all speak the very good English," said the Chinese Devil who'd manifested next to the French one. "I am come to ask what happen in English Hell and if Chinese Devil army is need to bring order."

Satan turned to Woking. "How many different Hells did you HEY YOU STINKY BASTARD! WHAT THE FUCK ARE YOU DOING IN MY CAVE, YOU DRONGO?!"

· "G'day," said a cheerful Devil in yellow budgie smugglers. "I hear that you Poms are up shit creek again? In need of some Aussie grit?"

"Three," said Woking.

"Well, Woking?" said Satan. "Asking for help is the ultimate disgrace. Go ahead. I will give you your 24 hours before execution."

Woking cleared his throat. "In the name of the Great British Hell, I formally request your assistance in mounting our defence!"

"You got it, mate!"

"Our great army will come."

"Nous venons pour aider les pauvres Anglais."

"Assemble your armies!" boomed Satan. "I will open the portal between Hells!" The three visitors vanished.

"So will you tell me?" said Woking. "Has ever a challenge to you been rejected?"

"Only from one," said Satan.

"For what reason?" said Woking.

"His views and his plans broke the rules. He could not be allowed to be Satan. I refused to fight him on those grounds. On three occasions!"

"Who was it?" said Woking.

Satan told him.

*****

"Aldershot, thank Lucifer I've found you," said Mytchett. "Where is everyone?"

"There's some kind of battle going on. Woking's with Satan now, I think."

"Then you need to tell them this! A plane just took off from by the Lake of Hell. I've been designing a new scanner, a kind of radar that works down – "

"Get to the point!"

"A plane is speeding away from the Lake of Hell now. There are almost no souls waiting there, despite lots of arrivals over the past hour. I think they're all on that plane!"

"Well that's not a problem, is it?!" yelled Aldershot. "If that many souls tried to pass through a portal, the failsafe would … " his voice trailed off.

"… activate, sealing the portals between our Hell and all other domains, mortal or otherwise!"

"And denying us any help from outside! Someone's planned this," said Aldershot.

"What do we do?"

"Deactivate the failsafe!"

"Only Woking, Byfleet or Satan have the authority!"

"Keep tracking the plane!" said Aldershot. "I'll try to reach Satan in time!" He ran off down the corridor."

Mytchett watched the screen on his home-made device. They might be alright, because the plane couldn't try to leave unless a portal was opened by somebody dying in the sky over England…

*****

A devil's head bounced into the space between God and Janelle. "Oops, sorry to intrude," said the head. "Oh my Badness! It's You! We all thought you were made up. Hang on, where's my bod - uhhh."

God look down at the now inert Devil head. He clutched his hands together at head height, turned sideways, and jiggled His legs while looking thoughtfully at the roof of a distant building. Then He booted the Devil's head high over a huge pair of rugby goalposts, that had momentarily been called into existence for the purpose. Janelle watched the battle for some moments, transfixed. Devils were being ripped apart … but on the ground, the pieces of them we re-assembling. She saw a pair of heads arguing over ownership of a limb. Their opponents, however magnificent, were not reassembling once destroyed. Slowly, but inexorably, the Devils were gaining the upper hand. Only she could turn the battle around.

"Please," she said to God. "Please, I beseech you, please do something. My friends will die!"

"You think of them before yourself," said God. "I admire that."

"Don't change the subject!" she snapped. Then she cringed. "I meant no offence, Lord, please forgive me."

"Forgiven, my child."

"I don't understand it. I don't understand why you won't help! Are you really Him? Or just some useless facsimile I've dreamed up? N-no offence!"

"You called me into being here. That's not to say I don't exist elsewhere. Suzy McCabe does."

"Don't talk about *her*! So are you God, or aren't you?"

"You really don't like Suzy, do you?" He replied.

"She's one of them!"

"Technically, yes. But you are familiar with the parable of the Good Samaritan, are you not?"

"That was about people! No race is all good or all evil – you know that! But she ... it's her inner nature. It can't be changed!"

"Can't it? She has died for you all, twice now. OK, the first time it was just for Martin, but still. She'll reassemble, of course, but do not under-estimate how painful the process is."

"I know," said Janelle. "I appreciate what's she's doing for us, I do."

"So why all the hatred?"

"Does it matter?"

"Yes. It matters rather a lot."

"She's part of this place! A place that shouldn't even exist! It isn't what we learned!! It isn't what we were told to believe!"

"That makes you angry, doesn't it?"

"Damned right it d – oops, forgive me, Lord. I mean, yes it does, Sir."

"It is a lot to take in, I agree."

"We're getting off the point! Please, I need to you do something. Save my friends. I don't think they can hold out forever. I'll do anything!"

"The last is not in doubt, but I cannot. I am as you imagined me."

"I imagined you helping!"

"You imagined the same God that you asked for help before. You did ask before, didn't you?"

"You know I did," she said bitterly.

"Remind me," He said.

"My mother. She was dying, and I prayed to you, and you did nothing. Every hour of every day for a month. You did NOTHING! I loved you, and she died. I was devoted to you, and you didn't help! I sat in church all day, that last day, praying to you! I was ready to give my whole life to you. My whole life. And I asked that one thing ... one thing ... " she began to sob.

"How old were you?"

"Sixteen. No age to lose your mother, is it? Why? Why did you let it happen?"

*****

The Devils were increasingly trying to focus on destroying the minibus, and whenever they snatched the chance, fired in its direction. The defending dragon shot back, but it took many hits and got more and more ragged. Aiding the defence were a recovered Suzy, and a very charred Denny.

"It's ready," said Bracknell. "Eight missiles, voice activated. Just tell it how many to fire. Once fired, each barrel will form a new missile in about two minutes. Just one of these beauties will be enough to blow the bus and the whole lot of them to smithereens."

"Oh good," said Byfleet, chewing his cigars. "Target on minibus. Fire eight!"

Chapter Twenty-Seven

The missiles from Bracknell's platform soared down through the air. Four of them struck flying creatures, exploding in rapid succession on a bullet-hawk, a *Geosternbergia sternbergii* and the last two robotic Natalias, who'd thrown themselves into the missiles' paths. The four balls of flame merged into one, lighting the whole battle, as the other four missiles plunged on through. The dragon on the bus saw them coming and roared into the air, firing a narrow jet of flame at one until it too blew up. The dragon met another a few moments later, and both exploded in flames.

Suzy followed the dragon up. There were two more missiles, and no way she could stop both. One was just slightly ahead of the other. She kicked the first one sideways and ploughed into the other. Denny watched in horror as it blew her to pieces. The missile she'd kicked plunged on unchallenged, but slightly diverted. Denny saw that it would strike the ground just metres from the bus. He jumped from the roof to between impact point and minibus, and caught the full blast.

The bus windows shattered as it lifted into the air, flying and tumbling sideways. Helen screamed in terror as the world span around her. A burning giant saw it all, and some instinct told him, catch the bus. So he dived, reaching forward, and clutched it in his fingertips as he crashed to the ground, piercing his torso with street lamps. He groaned, then lay still. His hands went limp, and the bus rolled out of them, landing by chance on its smoking wheels. But the vehicle had now had enough: the ceiling cracked around the Devil still imprisoned within, and the pieces fell away to the ground, along with the doors and the sides. Finally freed, the Devil looked around him with glee. Only the human in the driving seat was conscious, and she only just. A swift slash of the tail to the neck would see to her.

Then a knee thudded into his groin. "You no hurt my friends!"

"Natalia," murmured Martin, her presence almost breaking the hypnosis. "Are you ... real?" He saw before him a glowing vision of beauty, dressed almost as she had been before, except that the garments were all now sky blue, and she had gossamer wings out behind her. He watched her knee slam into the Devil's groin again. Then she grabbed a chunk of jagged metal and sliced its head off, before chucking it away as far as she could.

"Natalia, you came back," said Lucy suddenly. She was sitting up, alert. Lucy wondered why Natalia's face fell.

"Oh Lucy, I'm sorry," said Natalia. Lucy turned her head slowly to see the body in her seat, with a piece of shrapnel embedded in its head.

"Well that sucks," said Lucy. She began to glow blue.

"No!" yelled Natalia. "We needing her here! Take her up later!"

The blue glow faded. "Is OK," said Natalia. "Is real Heaven and you go there. Just not yet, OK?"

"No problem, got serious Devil butt to kick," growled Lucy. "Are the others OK?"

"Think so ..." gasped Helen. "Made 'em all wear ... seatbelts ..."

"Those missiles," said Lucy. "Have they got more?"

"Yes," said Natalia. "There were eight, and soon they'll have reloaded. They blew up half our defenders. Suzy and the dragon."

"Can you stop them?" asked Lucy.

"Not all," said Natalia.

"Then we're fucked."

Far above them, the missile platform had almost reloaded. "We'll get them this time," declared Byfleet.

*****

"Lucy ..." wept Janelle. "They killed Lucy. And you did nothing! Again!!"

"I am sorry. Truly," said God. "But as I said, the circumstances of my presence here do not permit..."

"Oh no," said Janelle. "Oh no, don't say that. Don't say it's because of me."

God looked at her sadly, his lips firmly closed.

"That's why you're not helping, isn't it? Because, stupid me, I made you the same God that failed to save my mum! The God who never does anything!!"

"Well, yes, but there's a bit more to it than that," He replied.

"Really? There's more? More than you doing fuck all to help anyone? I'd love to hear it!"

"There's something else you're hiding from. About me, and your feelings."

"What? No. There's nothing. NOTHING!"

"Oh, very convincing. A six year-old would see through that lie. Do you expect it to fool me?"

"That isn't fair!" she spat, through tears.

"Fair? What about your friends who've died already? And the others who'll join them, when the next set of missiles strike in, oooh, about sixty seconds?"

"Because YOU won't help!"

"Because you imagined me that way!"

"Aaaaarrgggh!!!" She screamed in fury, fixing Him with blazing eyes, as she pummelled His chest with her fists. "Alright! You wanna know? You really wanna fucking know! Alright!" Despair and rage now blotted out everything around her, and thoughts she'd battled for years to keep separate finally slammed together, and came bursting out.

"So you didn't save my mum. I sat there in church praying, and achieved fuck all. She died and I wasn't even there!! So what did I do? I should have jacked you in there and then, but no, I went straight back. Every single day. Services, prayer meetings, Faithsoc, I made you my life! So I was never there for Dad and Sis after that – they needed me! They'd lost Mum and they needed me and I was never there! Dad once said it was like they'd lost me too! But I couldn't look at them. I couldn't because they were there with Mum and I wasn't. At the end. And – and I had to prove that I hadn't been wrong, that being in church that day was still the right thing to have done. I had to prove it! So I kept on going!! And then when I realised I was letting my family down, well I did it all the more, because then I had to prove that I was *still* making the right choice! That it all had meaning! And then I come here and find out that some of the stuff in the Bible isn't even true!! So you see, everything I'd done for you in the last five years has been built on a lie! My whole life is a total mess and it's your fault! Your fault ..."

Above her, a gleeful, cigar-chomping Byfleet declared "fire eight!", and Bracknell obeyed.

Janelle's rage had left her now, and she'd collapsed into helpless sobs. God stepped forward and took her in His arms, and she wept into his glowing cloak. "Hush, my child," he whispered. I only need one more thing from you, then I can help your friends."

"Huh?"

"There were two things holding me back. The first was how you imagined me, and the second was what you truly needed from me. You said you wanted help, but deep inside, your tormented heart craved absolution, for your perceived failure to support your family. This I give, unconditionally. I forgive you, and demand that you forgive yourself."

"I ... I'll try."

"That'll do for now."

"Does that mean ... there'll be smiting?"

God clicked his fingers, and the eight missiles streaking down towards the minibus all exploded in mid-air. He unwrapped his arms from Janelle, and stepped back. "Of a kind. Thunderbolts wouldn't stop them for very long; as you've seen, they'll simply re-form. You need warriors who can counter the Devils. Angelic Hordes, come forth!!" He boomed.

A patch of sky ripped open, and from it emerged thirty Angels. They swooped down, saluting to God and Janelle, before joining the fray.

"Thank you," she gasped. "Are they real? True Angels from Heaven?"

"Alas no," smiled God. "Heaven is forbidden from intervention down here unless Devils request it.

"But you're here!"

"I do seem to be, don't I?"

"Can you send us home? Back to the world of the living? I mean I'm grateful for the Angels, really I am, but we've still no idea how to get out of here!"

"I'm afraid that wouldn't be a good idea, just now," he replied.

"What? Why not?"

"Oh, you'll see. Oh look, here come some Angels!"

Janelle watched a pair of Angels sail over, and her mouth fell open.

"Vince. They all look like Vincent from Faithsoc."

God smirked "You really should send more time praising him, instead of me. He might respond well to it."

"Janelle blushed. "You're not supposed to ..."

"Set you up? Why not? I know your heart. I *come* from the heart.""

He was starting to fade.

"Wait!" She said. "You're real! Please, tell me you're real, out there, in Heaven and in Earth!"

"Like I said, I come from the heart." And he was gone.

"That's not an answer!" she protested. Yet as she stood there, watching the Angels take on the Devils, she wondered if maybe it was answer enough.

***

On board the big passenger jet, a stewardess walked down the aisle. She was well over sixty but her face looked as if it had been cryogenically frozen at thirty five. "We will be passing through the mortal veil in approximately five minutes," she said to the seated souls. "Be prepared for some turbulence."

***

Steve Bannerman specialised in illegal flying, no questions asked. Even so, he was struggling to work out why he'd been given twenty thousand pounds to fly a small plane from that Wiltshire airfield up to Scotland. He couldn't work out what laws he was breaking, or what cargo, if any, he was carrying. It turned that out the cargo was one very big bomb, right under the cockpit, which exploded somewhere over the Pennines. Moments later, a sky portal to Hell opened in front of him.

***

"There it is" said Arjun, in the pilot's seat of the passenger jet. "A blue patch, exactly where the Broker said it would be. Wait till the plane comes out, then we go through it!"

"This time I see it too," said the co-pilot, who'd been blind to the sudden dark cloud that they'd flown through earlier. Steve Bannerman's plane shot out of the patch, then Arjun and co-pilot steered their plane towards the blue.

***

At the moment that Steve's plane had exploded, Dave Metzler was driving home from a strange but profitable trip to that same place in Wiltshire, when he heard something beeping out the opening bars of *Carmina Burana* from the bag next to him. He reached in and plucked out the odd, chunky mobile phone from among the wads of money. He pressed the answer button and brought it to his ear. A moment later, he felt a sharp prick in his skin by that ear. Thirty seconds later he was dead.

Dave wasn't alone. One hundred and thirty of the nastiest, most sinful souls in Britain had each been given a sack of money and a similar phone by the Broker's employees. All but a handful had answered the phone when it rang. Each one who did had had a poisoned needle fired into the side of their head, and dropped dead half a minute later. Each one was destined for damnation in Hell, and each had to be met by a Devil. It was an unbreakable rule.

Hell had a room set aside for soul harvesting duty. Devils there just waited their turn, watching the last moments of their targets, and vanished automatically when called to attend the death. Since the Broker's apparent defeat, they'd gone back to one Devil per collection. Fifteen Devils on duty would normally be enough, but now nearly 100 unmanned monitors were flashing urgently, each showing an imminent fatality. All fifteen Devils in the room vanished within moments of each other. With that room empty, Devils were automatically called from elsewhere within Hell, starting with those closest by. The few still on duty in or around Hell, watching out for trouble or building new pitchforks, vanished next. Woking saw Mytchett running towards him, one hand holding his glasses in place as he shouted a warning: "sir – you've got to – " but Mytchett vanished before he could finish. Gomshall had almost completed a new, improved killer wasp, but he winked out before he could complete it, and the wasp fell to the ground and exploded. Twenty devils, who'd been told by Woking to fly around the Wall looking for threats, were called up to the surface next, leaving the Walls unguarded. Still not quite all of the deaths of that minute were covered. So Devils from the fight with the grannies were called up as well. A gang of fifteen screeching old ladies found themselves tearing at nothing, while those Devils that remained found themselves even more outnumbered than before. In all, 109 Devils were called to the Mortal World within thirty seconds. Other than the most senior Devils and some of those fighting old ladies, only Fenwick and the fighters in Glasgow, the furthest from Hell on the plain, escaped the effect.

All across England, portals to Hell opened up. Most were on the road, but some were in homes, streets, offices, or in the case of Ged Spencer, the bed of another man's wife. Each portal was accompanied by a Devil, as the rules required. Mytchett found himself listening to a naked woman, who was shouting at a naked Ged Spencer for answering his mobile phone at 'a critical moment' and then falling asleep, unaware that her lover's bewildered ghost was sitting up in the bed staring at his own body in horror. "You are dead, and need to go through this door now," said Mytchett. "Grrr!!" he added, remembering that during surface duty Devils were supposed to be terrifying. He indicated a sinister black burning doorway in the wall. "And can you be quick about it? I am somewhat in the middle of something."

"So was I!" said Ged. "Hang on – am I dead? How??"

"I have no time to explain," said Mytchett, so he picked up the naked man and threw him at the black doorway.

***

Arjun's plane entered the blue haze. Moments later, a brick wall appeared out of nowhere, bang in front of the plane, stretching out of sight in every direction. There was no time to say even one word of prayer. The plane smashed into the wall and crumpled like a stamped-on drinks can, killing Arjun, co-pilot and stewardess, the only three living souls on board. All the dead souls were painfully crushed in the concertinaed metal. For a moment, the plane remained still, as if stuck, like a cartoon cat who'd run into a door. Then it fell like a stone, back to the Abysmal Plain. The wall was completely undented.

*****

In empty offices all over Hell, mournful gongs sounded, warning that the emergency failsafe had been activated.

*****

"OWW" said Ged, as he smashed into the wall that now occupied the black doorway. "Why did you do that?"

"Oh, incense-sticks!" said Mytchett.

"Eeeeeeeekkkk!" said the woman, pointing at Mytchett. Then, gasping for control, "Ged, if you're there, then who's this in bed who just failed to fuck me?"

"This is going to be difficult to explain," said Mytchett.

When Dave Metzler saw the sudden extra turning on the road, he took it immediately, without knowing why. He noticed with a shock that a red man with no arms and one leg was hopping about by the junction shouting "this way, Dave! This way!" So Dave turned off the road and ran smack into a wall that had suddenly appeared. Painfully he pulled himself out of the car, amazed that he wasn't more seriously hurt. The side road and wall had both vanished.

"Where did the road go?" asked the red hopping man.

"I don't know! You saw it too?"

"Of course I did! It was there!" said the red man. He seemed very confused, but then you probably would be if you went hopping around vanishing road junctions with only one limb, and knitting needles sticking out of your eye, reasoned Dave.

"Well it isn't there now," said Dave.

"Which means we're both stuck," said the red man. "Would you mind helping me re-attach some limbs?"

Across Britain, a total of one hundred and nine Devils were stranded, with no way back to Hell until the failsafe could be reset, which would take several hours at least. A side effect was that the dead souls were trapped there as well, and became visible, including anyone else who'd happened to die at the same time. Loved ones at bedsides were joined in their mourning by the one who'd just died, and sometimes also a puzzled looking Angel, or a red bloke who kept walking angrily into the wall and shouting "where's it gone??" or words to that effect. One of the Devils got arrested, having been found at the scene of a suspicious death, and later sat back and laughed while a succession of increasingly nervous policemen tried and failed to remove his make-up and tail.

The pattern was repeated across the world. In Sicily, Carlo Bracconi and his grandmother Eliza both died when their car was forced off a mountain road. One had been a Mafia enforcer, the other a church activist. Those who stopped at the scene heard the following conversation, translated from the Italian.

"Well you've done it this time!"

"It wasn't my fault! Why can you never accept that anything might be yours?"

"Because *I* have God on my side?"

"Yeah? Well where is He?"

"He's got better things to do than – "

"He doesn't exist! He never existed!"

"How dare you! He's real!"

"Then prove it! Go-*od*! Where arrrre you??"

"Do not belittle our Lord!"

"Yeah? What are you going to do about it?"

"Shut your evil mouth!"

"Gonna make me?"

"You've had this coming, you little creep!"

"Come on then!!"

"Take that!"

"Oof!!"

"Aaarrgghh!"

Close by, the stranded spirits of Eliza and Carlo hugged one another as the Devil and Angel beat the Hell – and Heaven – out of each other. "I told you no good could come of you whacking Don Ferroni and his men, Gran," said Carlo.

*****

"Angels!!" shouted Bracknell in horror. "They've got Angels!! How did they get here?" Below, every Devil was now grappling with an Angel, and Byfleet had had to shoot several with his own pitchfork to stop them attacking him.

"Blessed Wimples won't die, either," growled Byfleet. "Focus on the minibus. Duplicate your missile platform – I want sixteen missiles, all fired at once. I'll go tell as many of ours as I can – plan is to distract the Angels, pull as many away as we can – at the moment you fire it. Signal me when you're ready. There's no way they can stop all sixteen!"

*****

In Hell, Woking seemed to be alone. He was one of a small number of Devils of sufficiently high rank to be exempt from surface duty unless he chose it. He looked at Bracknell's tracking device. There was a small blip on it, moving towards a large blob that he took to be Hell. Then he heard the gongs go off, indicating that the failsafe had been triggered. He ran out to the lake, and flew out across it. He would meet what was coming alone, if he had to.

In French Hell, an army of 160 Devils had assembled. All wore berets, striped shirts, and strings of garlic around their necks. This wasn't what they usually wore, of course, they just wanted to rub it in as much as possible to the English that they'd pleaded for French help. They marched in line towards the between-Hell portal, and smack into a wall.

The Chinese had assembled an army of fifty thousand. They did things big in Chinese Hell, and efficiently too. But even so, these were also too late to get through the portal before it closed.

One hundred Australians, armed with cricket bats and chuckable lager cans, turned up at the Australian Hell muster site to find the portal closed. "Looks like the Poms are screwed," said one. "Anyone for a brew?"

*****

Above them in Heaven, Gabriel and some others looked down. They felt the wall form between realities. "Hell is attacked, and we can't help them now, even if they call for it," said Gabriel.

"I feel fear," said an Angel. "I feel as if all things are ending. Is this Judgement Day, Lord Gabriel? Are the dead about to invade the Earth?"

Gabriel hoped to reassure him, but when asked a direct question he could not lie. "If Hell or Satan falls, then yes. But they may yet prevail."

"Can we really do nothing?" said another.

"We have one Angel there already, of a kind," said Gabriel. "It is difficult, but not impossible, for a thought to cross the veil. Maybe one word, or just two?"

"'Save Hell'?" said the worried Angel.

"Save Hell," they all thought, over and over, imagining Natalia's face, or in two cases, her knee.

*****

"We have to move bus before more bombs come down," said Natalia.

"Not a chance, sister!" said Lucy, climbing to the front seat. "It's fucked!"

"Russian truck still go if like this."

"Then this ain't Russian. 'Tal, you stop the next lot of missiles, find out where they come from and scrag 'em!" Lucy saw Mycroft's camera and picked it up, amazed it still worked. "I'll create reinforcements!" She placed the camera on the dashboard in front of the moaning Helen, and clicked the video to play again. "Watch this!" she told Helen, and the dazed girl's eyes flickered open for long enough for the video to entrance her.

Natalia caught a glimpse of something high above. She saw sixteen flashes as the next missiles launched. She looked around for something that could stop them. All buildings were now flattened for half a mile around them, but there was one thing that might be big enough – the dead giant. She flew under its chest and lifted with all her might, shouting "Lord God, help me!", just in case it helped. She was an Angel now, after all.

Almost all of Janelle's Angels were locked in melee with Devils, but they responded immediately to Natalia's call, detaching and flying downwards. Half of them swooped down to pick up the giant and fly it into the path of the missiles, all of which smashed into its chest. There was a colossal explosion, then fragments of giant flesh rained down as a dozen burnt Angels fell to the ground. The minibus seemed undamaged.

"They OK?" asked a blood-splattered Natalia, staggering out of a pile of giant offal some moments later.

"Yes! Go get what's firing the missiles!" said Lucy

"I think my wings are – how you say it? – fucked."

"They'll repair won't they?"

"Not fast enough."

"Yo! Angels! Help her fly!" Two of the angels appeared and took Natalia from either side, then the three of them soared upwards. As they approached the platform, they heard Byfleet's voice.

"Target minibus! Fire sixteen!"

"No!" screamed Natalia, and her two Angels threw her upwards, detached from her and shot thunderbolts down, destroying two missiles. Other angels threw thunderbolts too, destroying six more. The rest plunged on down. "I will rip you apart," cried Natalia to the two Devils, but her wings could barely hold her up in the sky.

"Gottem!" yelled Bracknell, as further explosions were heard down below. Byfleet was too busy fighting off a flying sheep to join in. Then a second sheep appeared, firing pellets from its rear end, propelling it forward to sink its sharp teeth into Byfleet's leg

"Angels! Come to me!" yelled Natalia. White figures began emerging from the smoke below. She was about to command them to destroy the two Devils, when her knee started tingling. Then voices in her head: "*save Hell, save Hell, save Hell…*"

"Fire again, when ready," said Byfleet. "Get off of me, sainted sheep!"

"Please stop," said Natalia. "We not your enemy!"

"Missiles almost ready," said Bracknell. "Let's make sure of 'em, eh?"

"Hell is attacked! Not by us!" said Natalia.

"Nice try," said Byfleet. "Target on – aaarggghh!"

The lightning bolt struck him from behind. Natalia raised her other hand, called down lightning again, and the first missile platform exploded. Byfleet yelled "fire eight" to the second platform, but as he did so, Natalia kicked the edge of the platform hard, causing it to flip over. The missiles roared upwards, carrying a screaming Byfleet with them. Several Devils saw this and began flying towards Natalia for revenge.

"You can't reason with the fuckers," declared Lucy, who'd rode up on the back of an Angel. "The others are safe, though – the missiles hit a load of sheep!" Lucy watched a whole flock of black, dung-propelled sheep swooping past, and wondered about Helen's imagination.

"We must go and save Hell," said Natalia. "If Hell is destroyed, Heaven and Earth is destroyed too!"

"Then we gotta end this battle, and quick," said Lucy.

"There is deep hole in ground where giant fell," said Natalia. "Get all humans in it from minibus. And quick. Take three Angels."

Lucy nodded, and her angel steed swooped, without waiting for more. Natalia had something about her now that didn't need questioning. Lucy and the Angels plunged through thick smoke and caught glimpses of fanatical joy on the faces of Devils, who had not had such fun for centuries. They were mainly now fighting black sheep, with the Angels withdrawn from the conflict.

Natalia, her wings now recovered, led nine more Angels towards a huge thundercloud. They swooped past its side, and began to circle it, faster and faster. "What are they doing?" croaked a dazed Bracknell, who was trying to repair his damaged missile platform. The thunder cloud began to rotate, slowly at first, then faster and faster as the Angels created an airflow around it. Bracknell watched in horror as a conical shape began to poke out from its underside. "Oh, no," he said, and he abandoned his platform and fled. The conical shape grew longer and longer, into the twisting cylinder of a tornado. It hoovered up smoke, Devils, black sheep, stunned Angels, and just about everything else. For long moments it roared across the ruined city like a triumphant beast, and then it seemed to burst, flinging out everything it had swallowed, in every direction. Suddenly, all was quiet.

*****

Staz Burton woke up. He wished that he hadn't. He was stuffed into a dark, cylindrical space, with tape over his mouth. He couldn't work out if they'd taped his arms too, because there was so little space he could not move them anyway. The tube he was trapped in was vibrating and he was deafened by the roar of an engine. One thought ruled now in Staz's small mind: someone was going to get a serious kicking for this.

Camberley saw the warplane approaching Hell and flew up towards it. It had six very large missiles hanging below it, and other smaller weapons at its front. He raised his trident, but the plane fired first, and a hail of exploding bullets ripped Camberley apart.

The Broker pulled an umbrella from his suitcase and opened it, just in time to stop pieces of Camberley falling on top of him. He didn't offer one to Theo, who stood miserably beside him being splattered with pieces of Devil. This was followed by a creeping sensation as the pieces on his skin and clothes began crawling around trying to reassemble themselves. Yellow birds were also flying around Theo, trying to work out what to peck. "Ah, here comes Woking," said the Broker. "He runs English Hell, and answers only to Satan. For now. And he's quite alone."

They watched the lone Devil fly towards them over the lake.

Chapter Twenty-Eight

Fenwick could see the new Lake of Hell, far ahead. He sensed that something was terribly wrong. They'd not seen a single Devil anywhere, during their entire journey. And a human warplane was hanging in the air near the Wall, pointing its missiles at Hell.

"Hell is under attack!" he shouted to the birds! "We have to find a way to help! You have to – "

"Tweet," said the lead bird.

"What?"

"Tweet-tweety-tweet-TWEET-tweet."

"What do you mean, I'm not in charge?"

"Tweety-tweet-TWEETY-tweety-tweet."

"I am NOT incompetent!"

"Tweet-tweeeeeeeety-tweet-tweet-tweet."

"And I didn't LET myself get tied up! Plus you wouldn't be here right now if I hadn't practiced making you appear by knocking myself out!"

"Tweet."

"It is NOT the only useful or sensible thing I've ever done!"

"Tweet-tweet."

"Fine, you're in charge." Fenwick didn't think it would matter. They were too far away, and going too slowly.

*****

"D-did it work?" asked Dylan. Lucy had forcibly clicked Mycroft's fingers, and the students were waking to find themselves in a large hole, below clearing skies.

"For most of us," replied Lucy sadly. She wondered where her own body had ended up. She supposed that it didn't matter.

Natalia landed beside them, with some Angels behind her. Two held a struggling Bracknell.

"Natalia? Are you real?" said Martin.

"I'm an Angel," she replied.

"Well I said it," said Bernie.

"Hell is attacked," said Natalia. "I think they need help."

"They've been trying to kill us!" said Dylan. "Why should we help them?"

"If Hell destroyed, Earth and Heaven die too," said Natalia.

"We're only doing our jobs!" said Bracknell. Then he looked at Natalia. "Is it true? Is Hell really in danger?" He saw the answer in her eyes, and fell silent.

"How fast Devils fly?" asked Natalia.

"Not fast enough," said Lucy. Look at how long it took them to get here between the first and second attacks!"

"She's right," said Bracknell. "We do not fly fast. I could build us a speed plane."

"How long would that take?" said Lucy.

"Too long, maybe," he admitted.

"Devils coming back," said Bernie. Above them a few Devils were starting to find their way back, though they were harried by high speed black sheep.

"Tell them to stand down," said Natalia to Bracknell. "We must work together!" Bracknell nodded, and the two of them rose into the air.

"It might be pertinent to our situation to note that those melanistic giant ovines are achieving impressive speed and acceleration, generated by the rapid ejection of faecal material from their rear ends, and Newton's third law." Mycroft was awake.

"Do you mean, riding the black sheep could get us there faster?" asked Bernie.

"That is, I believe, what I said."

"Someone wake Lysandra!" shouted Lucy suddenly. "It's Helen!"

In all the chaos, no-one had till that moment seen the piece of metal sticking into Helen's side, with far too much blood leaking out around it. "It must have been same time as me," said Lucy, distraught. "Dammit, I should have helped her! All I did was make her a weapon with that stupid camera!"

"If you had not, maybe all would be dead," said Natalia.

Lysandra stumbled to her side. "It's deep. She needs surgery, fast, or she'll ..."

"No," said Lucy. "We will not lose another one. Bernie, there's a hospital in Glasgow isn't there?"

"Well of course there is! I mean, there must be!"

"You made those art galleries appear! Did you imagine a Hospital too? And if so where is it?"

"I'm sorry," said Bernie. "Honestly never once thought about it!"

"The camera!" cried Lucy. "We'll make one that way!" She'd brought it from the bus, and picked it up now. "Dammit, why isn't it working?"

"Battery's dead," said Mycroft, pushing buttons as Lucy despaired.

"Natalia! Can you heal her?"

The Angel shook her head.

"God damn it!" screamed Lucy. "We can't let her die!"

*****

"Now hear this!" boomed the Broker's voice. "In the sky now is a warplane, piloted by a living human. It has six missiles trained upon Hell. Each missile contains a small, living human. If any one missile should penetrate Hell ... boom! Hell will be destroyed. You have no longer the manpower to stop those missiles, should we choose to fire. You are defenceless."

"If anyone tries to approach this plane, it will fire. If any kind of missile or weapon is fired at my plane, it will fire. If anyone approaches, or tries to harm me or my associate, it will fire. Do I have your attention?"

Woking nodded. "Then I call to Satan, Lord of Hell," declared the Broker. Come out here and face me. I give you five minutes, then Hell will be destroyed.

"Destroying Hell will end everything!" Woking said. "Surely you know that!"

"Willing to risk it, are you?" said the Broker.

"Take your sunglasses off," said Woking.

"Why?" said the Broker.

"Let me see your eyes. Then I'll know if you'd really do it. If you don't take them off, I shall call your bluff."

The Broker smiled, and pulled of his sunglasses.

"You're not Brian Coker," said Woking. "You look very like him, but you are not him."

"Brendan Coker, at your service. So come on, look in my eyes, am I bluffing?"

Woking looked. What he saw in them chilled him in a way that he didn't think possible. "You're not," he admitted.

"Four minutes, Satan!" yelled the Broker, through his sound system.

"You're Coker's son, aren't you?" said Woking.

"Yes," said Brendan. Then he affected a stroppy teenage voice: "and you killed my dad!"

"He was already dead," said Woking. "We dispelled him. Which, given the sentence upon him, was an unfortunate mercy."

"You expect me to be *grateful*?" said Brendan.

"I don't really care," said Woking. "Judging by what's happened, you planned it that way anyway."

"We both did," sneered Brendan. "He could not face returning here. Do you blame him? That infernal machine!"

"He was judged," bellowed Woking. "The sentence was deserved!"

"Who decides that?" shouted Brendan. "My dad was a hero! An innovator! He would have changed the world if he'd lived!"

"He caused deaths and suffering," said Woking. "He bore responsibility for poisoning thousands of people!"

"He created jobs for far more! You're all a load of lefties!"

"So you couldn't accept our judgement upon him, and came here for revenge?"

"Oh, far more than revenge," said Brendan. "I was only a child when he died. Imagine the joy when he came back to me, nineteen years later, not a day older than the day that he'd died. Somehow, re-entering the mortal world had given him his body back – how *does* that work? Oh never mind, it hardly matters. Many would have doubted it was him, but not I. I told him I'd lost all his money, but he didn't mind. Said there was nothing to forgive. Said we'd get it back, and more! And we did."

Brendan went on: "He didn't want to go outside, or do anything except help me. When he had to leave the house, he just put on shades, and said he was me. We looked the same age. And a bit at a time, he told me what had happened. And what waited for me when I died.

"I'd been a bad boy, you see. Much worse than my father. It was your fault – you and whoever else decided that he should die when he did. I was angry, so I did bad things. So many very bad things. I enjoyed them all – I deserve to be here, really I do. But if I'd known he'd come back, I wouldn't have … I'd have kept myself pure for him. So he wouldn't have to do what he did. He told me what would happen. He worked out exactly how long I'd have to spend in Hell. Said he wouldn't let it happen. To either of us. For him it was easy, just get himself dispelled. He said it would fool you, make you think that the Broker was gone, and the threat was over. And you did, didn't you? Har har!!

"I feel strangely compelled to explain all this – isn't it interesting? It passes the time while we wait, I suppose. Anyway, where was I? Oh yes. Piercing the mortal veil is so close to impossible that you thought it *was* impossible, but my father and I spent years moving all the pieces into place to put the only person with the power to do it into a position where she would. We couldn't predict her directly, so we manipulated all the people around her, and smuggled eleven living souls to the Abysmal Plain. Your barriers weakened, making it possible for my lesser psychic sensitives to attack your men, and use one of *yours* to smuggle in fifty more live souls, who imagined into being an army who hated you. By this time of course you were onto us, so we gave you a victory, and sacrificed Dad."

"And many others," said Woking.

"Worthless pawns," answered Brendan. "While you congratulated yourselves on a job well done, my granny army grew in size. So you all flew off to fight them, leaving a skeleton staff. Though I'm guessing some others were off fighting the students, yes? I'd worked out, you see, that with the right balance of people, the students could fight off both the Plain and the first Devil attack, stretching your forces still further. And because of that, there were too few of you left here, to stop my passenger plane landing and carrying off eighty souls towards freedom. Then I killed a hundred more humans – bad humans – all moments before my plane hit the exit and triggered your failsafe. A hundred Devils called to Earth and stranded there, plus no way for the other Hells, or Heaven, to intervene. Good, eh? Now you have no-one. '*Hell is empty, and all of the Devils … aren't here!*' No-one to stop my plane from destroying Hell if you don't do exactly what I say."

"PUNY HUMAN! WHY HAVE I BEEN CALLED INTO YOUR MALODOROUS PRESENCE?" boomed Satan, as he erupted from the ground.

The Broker grinned. Now the fun would begin.

****

It was a desperate plan, or rather two plans – one to save Helen, the other to save Hell. Byfleet had denied that Hell could be at risk, and flatly refused to consider any course of action other than killing the students. Following a protracted conversation with Natalia's knee, he had flown off to Hell to get reinforcements. The other Devils had been glad to see the back of him, for they believed what Natalia was saying.

They'd managed to snare four black sheep, each of which had been harnessed with a Devil tail. These now shot off into the distance, each sheep with one Devil and one human rider: Dylan, Janelle, Mycroft, and Martin: a desperate race to reach Hell before disaster befell it. Some of Janelles's angels went with them, but they weren't as quick.

To save Helen, what they needed was batteries for the camera. Bracknell sat with Bernie and Lysandra, slowly creating new batteries from thin air. Lucy cradled the dying Helen, while Natalia stood guard, keeping a wary eye on the other Devils.

****

"State your purpose, here, Human," said Satan to the Broker.

"Oh, I'm waiting for one more to join the party," he replied. "Ah, here he comes."

Aldershot dropped out of the sky, landing between Woking and the Broker. He walked towards the Broker.

"Aldershot!" boomed Satan "Do not attack him, or do anything without my say-so!"

"I told you," said Woking. "Seems those two are old pals."

"The traitor," hissed Satan. "I did not want to believe it."

The Broker handed the microphone to Aldershot, and stepped back.

"Now hear me, all of Hell," rang out Aldershot's voice.

"There's only the three of us here," said Woking.

Aldershot ignored this. "Forty-nine years ago, I called challenge upon our so-called leader, and he refused me. Called my ideas unacceptable."

"They are!" boomed Satan.

"Hell is not fit for purpose. We have too few staff. As has been shown, we are badly defended. And why? We do not use our resources."

"Resources?" asked Woking.

"We have, in our rooms, the very worst humanity ever produced. Foul minds far crueller and more devious than anything we could conjure. And what do we do with them? Stick them in cages. If we made use of them, even one in a thousand, we could greatly lighten our workload. Let them be our torturers, our tormenters. Why waste this resource?

"And moreover, look at the leaders among them. The organisers. The men who make things happen. So they plundered a country, helped start a war, or taught their countrymen how to hate. So what? They would run our operations far better than us. Again, just a small, select few. We can make Hell great again!"

"And what of justice?" boomed Satan.

"Humans call it Community Service," said Aldershot. "But I have not come to debate it, not this time. I have come to fight. Reject my challenge, and Hell will be destroyed."

"Then I accept," bellowed Satan. "I shall enjoy destroying you!"

"Are you sure?" grinned Aldershot. "You are old now, old and slow. Whereas I have been training. I offer an alternative!"

"Oh yes?"

"Consciousness swap. You don't have to die. You can switch to my body, and live on as a normal Devil." He tossed the device to Satan.

Satan boomed with laughter. "I'll take that as a no, shall I?" said Aldershot.

From a leather pouch fused to his hairy hip, Satan drew forth two small knives. He threw one onto the ground, before Aldershot. "The rules are known. Whoever is struck first must yield, for any strike with a Devil Knife will be fatal, and one to the head or chest, instantly so. Should you win, Satanhood will pass through the knife into you. Not that you will." He drew a ring of flame around himself, ten metres across, with his pitchfork, then threw the fork out of the ring. Aldershot picked up the knife and stepped in. Both Devils then placed their knife-hands into the flames, fusing the knives to their palms.

Woking watched helplessly as Aldershot stepped into the ring of flame with Satan, knowing that only one of them could step out again.

Chapter Twenty-Nine

"Wooo-hoooo!" said Dylan as he clung to the back of a Devil, rocketing through the sky on a dung-powered black sheep. He watched Janelle, Martin and Mycroft riding similarly nearby, though none seemed to be enjoying it. Dylan was. He'd never do anything cooler than this, he was sure of it.

For Janelle, the sensation was very different. At first she'd recoiled at having to touch the Devil, but now she felt strangely elated. This creature was, in some way, part of Creation. She understood now that faith and love went far beyond anything she could have dreamed of. For if Angels, Devils and humans could work together for the greater good, then surely anything was possible?

They whipped past Byfleet, flying alone in the sky, and as they did so, all four Devil riders turned their sheep just slightly. Dylan looked round to see jets of sheep poo hitting Byfleet in the face. Dylan joined in with the cackles of the four Devil riders.

"How long till we get there?" called Martin.

"Maybe ten minutes?" said the Devil riding with him.

Bracknell finished the batteries and put them in the camera. They played to Lysandra the first part of the video, but the camera sparked and went blank after 20 seconds. It was enough – she looked ahead, blankly. They had been planning to make Lysandra call forth a hospital, but Helen was now deathly pale and barely breathing. She wouldn't last long enough to get her to the operating theatre. Even if they teleported her there, thought Lucy, they probably couldn't …

"*Star Trek*!!" yelled Lucy. "Lysandra, you're under my power, and you are utterly terrified of *Star Trek*! Especially that stupid doctor who can cure anything just by a waving an unconvincing prop at the patient!"

Natalia looked up to see something white come soaring from the sky. It had small wings, and a logo of an inverted V in a circle. It set down on the ground beside them. Out of the shuttle came three men in tight, brightly coloured uniforms: a doctor, a serious-faced man with jet black hair and pointed ears, and a grinning captain who immediately started hitting on Natalia. The doctor began waving flashing and beeping devices around Helen's wound. Bernie watched in amazement as the twisted metal floated out of the wound, and Helen's colour began to improve. Then Bernie looked at the shuttle, and turned to the serious-looking man. "Could you give me a ride in your shuttle? This planet's in danger!"

The serious man turned to his captain, who said "you go! I'm busy." Then the captain returned his attention to Natalia, who was trying to work out why her face had gone into soft focus. Bernie followed the serious man into the cockpit, and the shuttle shot into the air.

*****

Aldershot and Satan circled warily within the flames, occasionally jabbing their knives towards each other. "Exciting, isn't it?" said the Broker to Woking, from outside the fire ring.

"He has played you, foolish one" hissed Satan. "Can you not see that? He never expected you to win, never wanted you to. What he does next, he will do whether you win, or I do. No-one goes to this much effort for the aid of another."

"I will make him my highest lieutenant!" said Aldershot. "An unheard of honour for a mortal!"

"And if he had offered you the same, would you have taken it?"

Aldershot snarled. "You are just trying to distract me, because you fear my strength!"

"No, I just wish you to know that you are dying for nothing. As a patsy. Said all the right things, did he? As you came into his room to check on the device? Even after the device had been fixed, he'd have already learned all of your hopes, and your fears. He probably even knew you were saddled with the incompetent Fenwick to manage! And he listened, didn't he? When no-one else would? People with stupid ideas are so hopelessly easy to manipulate."

Aldershot lunged, but Satan skipped aside. "I'm going to enjoy killing you," said Aldershot.

"He sacrificed *himself,*" continued Satan. "Let you fire the killing shot, as I heard it, and you made it look unintentional. Tell me, please, how you think that he did that all for you?"

"He did it for his son!" shouted Aldershot. "To spare him from damnation!"

"Placing all of his trust in a Devil? Really? One who, once he was Satan, had no reason to fulfil his promise?"

"But I will!" protested Aldershot. "He is exactly the type of man I had in mind for my new structure of Hell!"

Satan smiled. He'd made no attempt to cut Aldershot, not yet, he was using his knife hand only to keep him at bay. "A human who's infinitely cleverer than you," replied Satan. "Who knows you would soon suspect him of plotting against you. Who knows that you would soon have to dispose of him. Remember, he's looked ahead in time."

"He has given me this chance! The chance that YOU denied me!"

"Of course he has. He knew what you wanted, all along. He knows that you started that ridiculous faux-military shouting soon after I refused your challenge, to cover for your resentment, and thoughts of treason. And he knows how this contest will end, did you ever think of that? Whichever the outcome, he has worked out the next move, to his advantage, not yours!"

"You lie! You are the Lord of Lies!"

"No, I am the Lord of Hell. A Hell which will fall because of your error! You have destroyed Hell through your greed and misjudgement!"

"No! I will rule! I have been promised victory!"

"Do humans not lie?"

"Not to me! He did not lie to me!!"

"Then prove it," said Satan. "Close your eyes, and take your best shot. If you are destined to win, it will be true."

"Nice try," snarled Aldershot. "But he did not predict that I'd be stupid!"

"Predict?" Satan howled with laughter, and the circle of flames grew higher all around them. "That would not be a prediction, it's a statement of fact! You were used, hapless one!"

"I – was – NOT!"

Satan cocked his head gleefully to the side, and played his trump. "So he told you, did he, that he needed Fenwick alive, for his plan to work? He told you that your mentioning the horsefly incident would stop me from dispelling him?"

For one crucial second, Aldershot's mouth hung open. "O-of course he did," he tried, as his opponent laughed still harder. The horrible icy chill of doubt coursed through his body.

"Patsy!" taunted Satan. "Stooge!"

Aldershot's doubt morphed into terrible rage. He would slay the anachronism before him, then torture the Broker through all eternity. "Yaaaaargghhh!" he screamed, lunging wildly. Satan skipped clear, slashing down with his knife as he did so.

Aldershot looked down in horror to see the arm holding his knife lying on the ground, and blood spurting from his shoulder, taking his life-force with it. "Normally I would do this with regret," said Satan, plunging his knife into Aldershot's heart. "But not this time."

****

"Is that Hell?" asked Janelle in fearful wonder, as the walls came into view.

"It is," said the Devil she was riding with. "Don't worry, you cannot go in. Not yet, anyway."

"I can see fire in the distance," said Martin. "By that yellow lake!"

"It is a duel!" said a Devil. "We must hurry!"

"You have already implied that our speed is the maximum possible," said Mycroft.

Bernie could see the whole scene on a screen in the cockpit. A small man in a suit was pointing a gun at a large Devil. A helpful red arrow was hanging over the small man's head on the screen, with the words "Bad Guy" above them. Woking was indicated by a blue arrow and "Good Guy (!)". When Satan emerged from the flames, he was labelled "also Good Guy (!!!)".

"Do we have phasers on this shuttle?" asked Bernie.

"It is a medical shuttle, so no," said his pilot.

"Then ram him!" said Bernie. "Run down the bad guy, before he kills Satan!"

"That seems highly illogical – "

"DO   IT!"

Satan stepped forth from the ring of flame, with Aldershot's head in his hands. THE TREACHEROUS, UNWORTHY CHALLENGER IS NO MORE," he declared.

"Remain still, Lord of Hell," said the Broker. "This gun is loaded with bullets tipped with Devil-Knife. Make one wrong move and I fire. And remember, those missiles are trained on Hell. I have nothing to lose but aeons of damnation."

"You are not a Devil!" declared Satan. "Killing me will not make you Satan!"

"I know that, silly!" said the Broker. "It'll just undo all of Hell and spew forth evil across all creation!"

"You intend the Apocalypse?" gasped Satan. "Why?"

"Hold on, we have unwelcome guests," said the Broker. "They're flying on sheep! I love students!" He pulled the rocket launcher from his back and fired all four rockets. They streaked through the fifty metres between him and the sheep.

"Bail Out!" shouted Dylan, and both humans and Devils jumped off. The missiles slammed into the sheep, exploding in a haze of fried mutton. The Devil riders caught the stunned humans mid-air, and lowered them down to the ground, too far away to help.

Fenwick and his birds looked down from above. He wondered why Woking and Satan weren't attacking the human with the gun. Why they looked scared of him. "The plane," Fenwick said. "You should take out the warplane!"

"Tweet."

"Not an order, a suggestion," Fenwick added.

*****

"Kill Satan?" spluttered Theo, as if woken from a trance. "That's your plan? That's what all of this slaughter was about!"

"Don't you want to escape damnation, Theo?" said the Broker.

"Not at this cost!"

"It's lucky I've got some spare bullets then," and the Broker swung his gun round and shot Theo. "You're surplus to requirements now, anyway." He turned his gun back towards Satan. Theo felt a stab of exquisite pain, but only for a moment, then numbness and oblivion.

"In a moment, I will fire," said the Broker to Satan. "The bullet will enter your body, and kill you in an instant. It will, as you said, bring the apocalypse: reality falls without Satan. You have one way to stop me. Take out the consciousness swap device." Satan did. "Use it. Let my mind into your body, or die and take everything with you."

Satan looked around, gauging his surroundings. He saw a white shuttle hurtling through the sky, aiming directly at the Broker. The Broker's small gun wouldn't stop it.

"Oh, Woking?" said the Broker. "If that shuttle hits me, the missiles will fire, and Hell will be destroyed. Be a good boy and stop it, would you?

Woking felt something he'd never known before: pure, unalloyed, absolute hatred. Yet he knew there was no choice. He waited as long as he dared, then pressed the dispel button on his pitchfork and fired. The shuttle, its pilot and

Bernie's clothes crumbled to nothing from the front backwards, leaving Bernie flying naked through the air. "Look mum, I can fly," he said stretching his arms and closing his eyes for the expected impact, but it didn't come. Instead Woking took off and caught him, the two tumbling to the ground metres from the Broker and Satan.

"Last chance, Satan," said the Broker, his gun aimed at the Lord of Hell's heart. His own heart was pounding – he'd seen everything up to this moment, but no further. "Swap with me now, and thereby appoint me as Satan. Save all creation."

Satan briefly glanced round, confirming that no-one, not even Fenwick's birds, was close enough to help. Then his eyes met the Broker's. "And hand it to you? I choose death and destruction," he declared.

For an instant, the Broker looked crestfallen, like a child whose best toy had been snatched. Moments later, a crooked grin spread over his face. "Then so do I," he said, and fired.

Chapter Thirty

Bernie started running. It should not have been possible to reach Satan in time. The bullet would hit in a fraction of a second. But this was the edge of Hell, a place built on human imagination, where human belief had power, and narrative conventions doubly so. Satan stood frozen as the bullet moved towards him in very slow motion. Somehow, Bernie moved faster.

Bernie did not think of his life, and the fact that it was ending. Nor did he think of the afterlife, which he'd never have. He was a thespian at heart, always would be, and this was his moment to stand centre stage. Satan saw the bullet fly closer, and closer, then at the last instant the naked, green-haired mortal threw himself in front of him, throwing his arms wide as he did so, shouting:

"Get Thee Behind Me, Satan!"

The bullet pierced Bernie's chest, and he crashed to the ground. The Broker took a moment to take in what had happened, then he aimed his gun again. As he did so, something chirped from above him. He looked up to see a yellow bird diving at him; on instinct he raised his gun and fired. The poor bird was ripped apart, but the Broker's face and gun-hand were splattered with acid from inside the bird's stomach. He screamed and dropped the gun.

High above, in the cockpit of the warplane, Yassar had been watching the whole scene below via a video screen, relayed from a camera below the plane, programmed to focus on the Broker. Now, he saw the Broker felled by an unknown attack from above. His instructions were clear: *if I'm attacked, you fire.* His finger stretched for the fire button, but something stopped him. A yellow bird glared at him through the windscreen, shaking its head slowly. Yassar blinked in disbelief. Then as he reached for the button again, he felt a thud, and the plane shook.

Yassar knew what it was, from flight simulations. A bird had flown into one of the engines. Before he could respond, there was a second thud, then a third, and a fourth. All four engines cut out. Yassar screamed, and the plane plummeted.

Bernie gasped as the pain from his wound filled his torso. He could feel his life force ebbing away. Huge hands lifted him up, and he found himself cradled in the arms of the Lord of Misrule, while Janelle, Dylan, Mycroft and Martin were carried to their side by Devils.

"You're all covered in sheep guts," said Bernie.

"Don't try to talk," Dylan said.

"Are you kidding?" he coughed. "It's my death scene, so I'll talk all I want. My big line, did you hear it?"

"I didn't," Dylan said, with a tear in his eye.

"I did," said Satan. "He said, 'Get thee behind me Satan!' It was magnificent." The watching Devils looked at him in astonishment. His face drooped with sorrow, a look that any of his underlings would have been dispelled for.

"Naked in the arms of Satan," whispered Bernie. "If Mumsie saw me now, there'd be stern words … stern words."

Woking turned to see another Devil stagger towards them, having just about reassembled himself. "Ah, Camberley, good to have you back with us!"

The Broker, meanwhile, was thinking about narrative conventions. He'd seen three in quick succession: the villain explaining his plan, the improbable last-minute save, and now the interminable death scene, when logically Bernie should have died instantly. Was there one more that might help him, now? He turned, slowly, to see his gun lying on the ground. No-one noticed. He reached down with his good left hand, and picked it up. The Devils and students acted like he wasn't there. He did a brief jig on the spot. No response. *No-one ever watches the defeated, injured or dying bad guy*, he thought, pointing his gun towards Satan for the third and final time. *And he usually gets off at least one shot.* He paused for a few seconds, savouring the moment (convention, again). Then Fenwick fell onto his head and killed him.

"Would somebody blessing-well untie me?" yelled Fenwick, as he rolled off the corpse of the Broker.

"Oh bollocks," said the Broker, looking at his broken body, the smashed gun, and at Fenwick. At least he had somewhere to sit, he thought.

"Where the Heaven have YOU been?" asked Camberley crossly.

"I just saved Hell! Three times! That's my birds up there, they took out that plane that was threatening Hell! And I told them to use me as a weapon, too!"

You didn't save Hell, you cassock," sneered Camberley. "He did! A human!"

"Satan," whispered Bernie.

"Call me Beelzebub, please."

"Will you do something for me, Beelzebub?"

"Name it, brave one."

"Have a Devil put aside for me?"

"I think I can do better than that," said the Lord of Hell, and he whispered into Bernie's ear.

"That would be … good," said Bernie. His head slumped to the side.

"Oh Bernie," said Dylan.

The slumped head raised up again. "I want to thank you all … I know I'm not supposed to say it, but I love you." And then he was gone.

All around him, students began weeping, while the Devils dipped their heads in respect. Except Fenwick, who was furious that no-one had acknowledged his role. And also Camberley, who was now being angrily pecked by a pair of Fenwick's birds, who'd decided that no-one but them was allowed to ridicule their master.

*****

Satan ordered that Bernie's body should be buried on the spot where it fell, and a giant statue built commemorating his moment of sacrifice. He insisted on hugging each of the humans to thank them (except Janelle, for whom it was just a little too much). Then he declared that he wished for solitude, and vanished back into the ground.

Woking indicated the Broker. "Find him a cell. Encase him in concrete from the neck down. I will see to the rest of his punishment personally," he told a pair of eager Devils. "In his case eternity will mean eternity," he added darkly.

"You have not heard the last of me!" yelled the Broker. "I shall return and wreak deadly rev-ummff!" One of his captors had rammed a large chunk of dead sheep into his mouth.

Byfleet appeared, covered in sheep dung, and Woking sent him to reset the failsafe, and reopen the walls between realities. A few minutes later Natalia returned, with Bracknell and some more Devils carrying Lucy, Lysandra and a fully recovered Helen. These too shed tears over Bernie, of course, and the fact that, unlike Lucy, he'd get no afterlife.

"I am Angel, now," Natalia told Martin. "I must go back to Heaven soon."

"I know," he blubbered.

"You must not wait. You must find other love," she told him.

The others said nothing. Martin nodded. "You made me a man," he whispered. "Maybe you belong in Heaven."

"I do, now." She gave him a kiss which sent tingles throughout his whole body. Angels had kissed mortals many times throughout history, but never like that. As she pulled away, Woking caught her attention.

"You're not like any Angel that I've seen. Nowhere near smug enough. Who are you?"

"Natalia Vokzalnova. Honorary member of the Celestial Host."

"Tell me, are you good at talking to old ladies? We have a little ongoing problem that needs tidying up."

"In return, you get my friends home, yes?"

"Yes."

"Then I help you," she said.

*****

Byfleet returned, with the news that the barrier between worlds would be down in a few minutes; he was then sent away to wash. Bracknell was busily building a new minibus for the students. Helen reflected sadly that her party would now almost fit into a car. Lysandra agreed, suggesting that she could sit on Dylan's lap for the journey. In the event, she did anyway.

Suzy arrived, carrying Denny. Having finally reassembled herself, she'd found him pancaked onto a piece of minibus, and peeled him free. He'd then snapped back to his usual shape. He shook everyone's hands and told them he had no regrets. Suzy gave Martin a kiss on the cheek and told him to find a great girl. Then she sidled over to Woking, wiggling her hips as she did so. She'd learned how to recreate her white dress, but saw no reason to extend its hemline.

"So, you're in charge here, huh?"

"For now," said Woking. "If Satan wishes it so."

"Got any openings for a little girl like me?" she caressed his buttocks with her tail.

"Umm ... we did suffer some losses, it's true."

"I'll do anything you ask me to. Anything at all."

"Uhh, that's good then," said Woking.

"That's settled then. You'll find me extremely co-operative."

"G'day! You Poms still need fightin' Aussies, or what?"

Woking looked round to see a series of drunken Devils in shorts and cork hats stumbling merrily through a portal. "I did send a message to cancel our request," said Camberley crossly.

"It looks like the way home is open," said Woking to Helen's party. "Thank you ... and I'm sorry for your losses. All of Hell sends you its gratitude. Now begone, before I let loose the Hounds of Hell upon you!"

"We have seen no evidence of any canine life-forms during our time here," said Mycroft, as Helen started the engine.

"It's probably a figure of speech," she replied, as the minibus sped up, and then lifted itself into the sky. "Hey, do you think this thing will still be able to fly when we get back to Earth?"

Below, Fenwick's birds, now depleted to eight, had finally freed him using acid from the nearby Lake, as no-one else had seemed bothered by his plight. Fenwick stood up and stretched his limbs.

"Those are smart birds you've got there, Fenwick!" said Woking. "How did you get them to exist while you're awake?"

"They probably can't tell the difference," said Camberley.

"Evolution," said Fenwick. "I don't think our birds have ever spent so long in the mortal world. They started to become conscious. And clever."

"Well the brains had to go somewhere," said Camberley. The birds swooped and pecked at him.

"And it gave me an idea," said Fenwick. "We could all do this, get ourselves a permanent flock of birds each. Then get them to memorise and deliver short messages to one another, by a sort of Morse code. We can call it 'tweeter', or 'twitcher', or something like that!"

"What a thoroughly stupid idea," said Woking.

EPILOGUE

The Broker – Brendan Coker – freely admitted that he'd expected all along that his plan to become Satan would quite possibly fail, and that his secondary aim had always been to destroy the whole of creation. If he couldn't rule Hell, he'd end it rather than suffer there for a millennium or more. Of course, for a man who'd tried to kill everything, eternity really meant eternity. The Broker's punishment is known only to one or two senior Devils, for his cell has been sealed for all time. Some say that every possible torment is visited upon him, so the next time something hurts, upsets or enrages you, it is probably happening to him down there, too.

****

Natalia successfully calmed down the legion of furious old bats. Following Woking's suggestion, she explained to them that the council had tricked them, placing false leaflets from the house-sellers into their drawer, to deflect attention from the real scandal: an attempt by the council to demolish their houses, and sell off the land. They bought that, and the War of New Town reached a truce. Slowly they were trained up and inducted into the staff of Hell. With personnel limited, even the few hours a day they were willing to work proved invaluable. Plus there was a constant stream of self-centred old men coming in who were deserving of round-the-clock henpecking. There was also a steady supply of new jumpers being knitted, which were doled out to those souls who cared more than they should about their appearance.

****

Woking wasn't dispelled after all. Satan seemed remarkably pleased with the outcome. "Hell endures. And so, therefore, will you," he had said.

****

The Lake of Hell, in time, became a feature as iconic as the great Gates that it had replaced. Human artists and writers are sometimes permitted to see views of Hell in their sleep, and gradually the lake entered popular culture above, as well. Paintings of it included its two notable features: a jet black stone bridge, over which the worst of humanity were carried or driven to start their damnation, and a strangely shaped red monster that patrolled the waters below. Some said that it had once been a Devil, who'd been transformed by some hideous accident, others that he had chosen this form because it would grant him an easier life. Whatever the truth, the monster made a point of grabbing Mickleham with a tentacle and dragging him into its acidic domain, whenever he strayed too close. That could be construed as evidence of prior enmity, but maybe the monster just didn't like his smell.

⁎⁎⁎⁎⁎

Michael Price was sentenced to just seven years in Hell, mostly for his general attitude towards women. Some wanted him to get much more, but eventually had to concede that it wasn't his fault that the gates of Hell had been destroyed. The youngest of the new intake of Devils convinced the others that Michael should spend his punishment just as he had spent his last hours, tied to a bed and gagged. For the first few days, Suzy visited him armed with a riding crop, and flayed his buttocks for two hours every day. Yet on the fourth day, she stopped halfway through, and Michael saw her regarding the riding crop with a curious expression. He'd seen it once before when his sister, packing for University, had happened upon what had once been her favourite doll. She'd regarded it with a mixture of affection and regret, before casually tossing it aside and paying it no more attention. Suzy now did the same with her riding crop, discarding it on the bedside table and walking from the room. The next morning, Michael woke to see the walls of his room crammed with bookshelves which contained, Suzy told him, every piece of feminist literature ever written. "Which shall we start with?" she asked him sweetly. As the months crawled by, Suzy would often see him gazing longingly at the riding crop, gathering dust beside him. Occasionally she'd pick it up and pretend she was about to use it, before setting it aside and selecting a book instead. She also made sure to record her daily readings so they could be played on a loop to other misogynist souls.

This was only the first of many ideas Suzy had for how to increase the efficiency of Hell, and she wasn't shy about sharing them. Woking soon gave her Byfleet's old job, just to shut her up. When not reading to Michael, she listed for him all the different ways in which Hell was badly run, and how this was only to be expected given that it had been entirely run by males since its inception. The solution of course was a female Satan. "But not yet," she told him fondly. "We've got all these books to finish first, for a start."

⁎⁎⁎⁎⁎

Heaven gained thirty new Angels as well, for the ones that Janelle had created had now become sentient, and the Devils certainly didn't want them roaming the Plain. Also in Heaven, a being who looked very like God started turning up from time to time, often finding the time to talk to virtuous souls who were troubled by unresolved issues from their mortal lives. Gabriel and the others would often ask this being if he really was God, but He proved annoyingly adept at dodging this question.

⁎⁎⁎⁎⁎

Under Camberley's watchful supervision, Bracknell and Mytchett continued to invent new and innovative devices for torment in a modern world, not all of which went wrong.

*****

With reports of Devils running around everywhere, and ghosts of the recently dead walking the streets and the hospital corridors, many had thought it was Judgement Day. Later, of course, they would find that the world was still there, and the Devils and ghosts disappeared without trace. Many concluded that humanity had been given a final warning. Judgement was coming, and it would be harsh. Others dismissed it as an elaborate hoax. Still, the churches filled up, and pretty much everyone started being nicer to one another, and more virtuous in all that they did. For about six months. After that, everyone went back to living the same way as before. It's what humans do.

For those who had lost someone, of course, it was not possible to forget. For Helen especially, the weight of what to tell the parents of Lucy, Michael, Natalia, Denny and Bernie weighed heavily on her mind. Yet she and her companions were soon accosted by suited men, and taken to a police station, where they were asked questions about their strange disappearance by an old man who reeked of power, and was used to getting answers. He soon found that these young people could not be intimidated. Helen told him, "we've battled the armies of Hell and won, do you think we are scared of you?" The man had then calmly asked how they'd won, and after a while they'd found common ground. A deal was made, and a cover story was agreed upon, after which the students told him the full story.

Bernie had been missing for a week when the two women from MI5 turned up at the door of his family home. His parents knew immediately what the message would be. The son they'd spent so many years struggling to accept was gone for good. Yet their mouths fell open at the story that was relayed to them: a terrorist plot so terrible there'd been a media blackout, which had been foiled by some students, at the cost of their lives. Their son had been a hero, they were told, which of course was true.

And so, they wept openly for him alongside the minibus survivors at the funeral. One of the young ladies told them how Bernie had given a final request that she couldn't explain, or wouldn't. His gravestone therefore bore the words GET THEE BEHIND ME SATAN, by which he would be remembered – by only a bare few on Earth, but by everyone in Hell and Heaven.

*****

Some months later, Martin was walking home from chess club. He'd started winning, recently. A trio of girls were walking the other way, chatting to each other. Martin felt a bolt through his heart as he looked at the blonde one. "Hello," he said, touching her hand.

She stopped walking, surprised. "Hello," she said back, with a curious smile. "Do I know you?"

"I think we met once. My name's Martin."

"I'm Suzy."

"Are you doing anything tonight?"

The other two girls looked at him in puzzlement. He was small and skinny, with absolutely no idea how to dress – the type of man Susy normally stamped all over, when she could be bothered to notice them at all. Yet he had something about him, an aura of absolute confidence.

"What had you in mind?" Suzy asked.

****

Janelle came back transformed. Friends were amazed at how she stopped going to church, instead spending as much time as she could with her family. She now had a remarkable warmth about her, and among the many who were drawn to this new Janelle was Vincent, whom she would eventually marry. After a while, she began to re-engage with religion, promoting the idea that worship was a waste of time, and that Christianity should be all about actions. Through all of her life she'd be driven to improve the lives of as many people as she could, driven sometimes by regret at not having been able to save Lucy, but more often by the calm conviction that comes from having met God. As she rose through the church, those who opposed Janelle's agenda came to fear her, for she had this unnerving ability to convince them that even their tiniest sins would most certainly be finding them out in time.

****

Denny began serving his time in Hell without complaint, hanging from a tree while being repeatedly pecked by angry mother birds. Pecking birds were something they knew about, in Hell. Then after three months, he was suddenly pardoned. For the next two hundred years he would run around Heaven in search of rare birds.

****

Dylan and Lysandra dated for nearly a year, then split up. She said it was because they didn't have enough in common, whereas for him it was because there were simply too many other pretty girls looking at him in a certain way.

****

It's not true that everyone behaves themselves in Heaven. Some don't. It's usually the ones who have spent their whole life being virtuous, only to find after a few years of Heaven that perhaps they'd have liked to misbehave at least once or twice, even if it had cost them a brief spell in Hell. For example, a group of former monks had spent a month running round mooning at women, and the Angels at the time could do nothing to deter them.

But now word began spreading of the Angel Natalia, whose divine knee would bring holy guidance to the balls of those who had strayed from the path of goodness. Errant souls of the female persuasion could expect a good hard kick up the arse.

*****

Lucy could not adjust to life in Heaven. She was a doer by nature, a practical person, and her time in Hell had left her with unusual awareness of the truth about Heaven: nothing she did there really mattered. After a few years, and a conversation with someone who appeared to be God, she confided in Natalia, who then asked Gabriel if anything could be done. Quite persuasively. Gabriel called in a favour from one of the other Heavens, where things were done differently.

Nine months later, a baby called Lucy was born. As she grew up, she began to have vivid dreams of strange adventures and incredible battles. In fleeting moments between sleeping and waking, she almost remembered her other life. That the child had been called Lucy was not a coincidence, and sometimes her mother Janelle would think that she recognised something in her new daughter's eyes.

*****

Staz Burton survived the plane crash, and was eventually dumped back on Earth. He learned precisely nothing from his experience, except that when a suited man offers you money, it's best to just take it and then kick his head in. He never even knew where he'd been.

*****

Ace TV reporter Harry Daniels went 45 steps down the Stairway to Hell, before getting scared and turning round again.

*****

Kane Winkle, knowing that all of Hell's portals would shortly be sealed, had flown off into the plain to hide out until the outcome became clear. He saw to his surprise that another city had grown up on the plain, very different from his own. It seemed a good place to lie low, although it was very dark and damp, and half of it was in ruins, bearing the scars of some titanic battle. He set the plane down and looked around. There seemed to be a lot of drinking and fighting going on, but there was plenty to eat. Provided you liked chips. Most of the buildings were dark and forbidding, but scattered among them were brightly lit art galleries and eclectic cafes.

A hand clapped onto his shoulder. "Hey, yee?"

"Yes?" he said.

"Ah want tae speak to yee aboot a moidah!"

"A murder?"

"Tha's wha' ah said. Where were yee last night, yee English basstad?"

"That's going to be difficult to explain."

"Then yee'd better come doon tae the station and try. We've got fifty unsolved moidahs here, and you're the only man in town who doesnae have a solid alibi."

Kane was marched down to a cold, damp cell for interrogation. He would never leave it again.

*****

Somewhere on the Abysmal plain, an angry dance teacher is still driving around in a stolen police car, wondering when she's going to re-enter the plot.

*****

With a team of old lady Devils efficiently processing incomers, the Queue of Hell finally started to move more quickly. When they'd got the backlog down to six months, they were careful to slow things down again. They felt that the wait did souls good.

When an old man with bare feet reached the front of the queue, there was briefly a moment of confusion. "Hilda, look at this," one Devil had said. "This one's been given credit for a good deed after he was dead. He's been let off! That can't be right!"

"Aggie, we've got hundreds of thousands waiting in line. If it says he's excused, he's excused. Away with you, now! Off to Heaven! And tell them to give you some shoes!"

*****

Johnny O'Connor was trying to clear the never-ending mountain of washing up. He'd got through three plates before he heard a crash and a wail. "Boys!" he yelled. "Not again, for *God's* sake!" The wailing went on. He stumbled over toys, discarded clothes and a few mouldy globs of food, to find his four-year-old clutching his head and pointing at his brother.

For the umpteenth time that day, he picked up the small boy and began singing the magic 'make it better' song. "Roger will you *please* move some of those toys from the kitchen floor?" he pleaded, in between verses. The older boy shook his head and ran upstairs.

The doorbell rang. *Go away*, Johnny thought. It rang again and he stomped over to open the door.

"Hello Johnny."

"Yelena?? But you're ..." (*dead*, he didn't say).

"No I'm not, Johnny, it was all a mistake."

"Jacky, it's your mummy!," said Johnny, giddy with ecstatic confusion.

"Hello my boy!" she said, regarding the child who'd unknowingly killed her, four years ago.

"Mum-my?" said the boy, uncertainly. They engaged in a three-way hug, the two adults kissing like crazy. They stumbled inside.

"Mummy!" said Roger from the stairs.

"So where have you been all this time?" said Johnny.

Yelena opened her mouth but said nothing, recalling a hogtied Devil, a shoeless old man, a plane being attacked by birds, and then clinging to that strange Scottish man, as they'd parachuted together down to England. "Stuck in a queue," replied Yelena.

Johnny blinked, utterly confused. "I told you we should have switched banks," he said.

*****

Coker Associates had been drifting like a rudderless ship. Its CEO and his deputy had both vanished without trace, and no provision seemed to have been made for their absence. It didn't help that one of their main offices had been blown to smithereens. Its employees turned up at the other office, day after day, waiting for someone to tell them what to do. They hadn't been chosen to think for themselves. So when a battered looking Scotsman turned up at the office and calmly announced that he was the new boss, they just accepted it. After a few weeks in charge, he'd announced that Coker Associates would become a humanitarian organisation, fighting poverty, hunger and climate change, worldwide. One of them had asked him why, thinking he didn't look the type.

"Tae save what's left of mah soul," he'd said.

*****

Fenwick strutted around Hell with a new confidence. He reminded his colleagues, whenever he could, that he had saved Hell, not once but three times. When someone retorted that two of these had been his birds, not him, and the other had been by falling while hogtied, Fenwick would just smile and watch while his new best friends dropped a mass of acidic guano onto his critic's head.

*****

Satan decided that someone needed to take the blame for the near-destruction of Hell, and chose Byfleet. There are rooms in Hell where damned souls swim in sewage, and someone has to make the stuff. Byfleet is now that someone.

*****

Ten years after the events described, Helen organised a "Hell bus" reunion weekend. Everyone was told to come in appropriate clothing. Mycroft again wore a French Maid outfit, while Helen herself had a difficult time finding a tight-fitting leather dominatrix bodice that would work on a woman who was five months pregnant. Suzy, now Martin's wife, wore one of the very short white dresses that he often bought for her. He'd told her the full story shortly before he proposed to her, but it would not be till that weekend that she fully believed it. Tales were shared, and absent friends remembered. By the Saturday night, Dylan and Lysandra were back together, for he was now older and wiser, and she'd found that they did have something in common, after all. Then on the Sunday morning, they were shocked to find an unexpected guest in the living room.

*****

The Lord of Hell, too, seemed to have been rejuvenated by the battle to save Hell. He started bringing in bold changes to the rules: from now on, Satan would walk abroad wherever and whenever he chose. Human souls could be pardoned when judged to be truly remorseful about all of their sins. Those who maintained that it wasn't their fault, though, would not be released until they relented, even if their initial sentence had expired. Gabriel questioned him about both decisions, but eventually they came to agreement. Gabriel wondered at Satan's change of attitude. He got the strange feeling that the Lord of Hell had started enjoying his visits. He seemed to contrive subtle rule changes each week, which meant that Gabriel kept having to come and discuss them. Yet Satan refused to address him at all if he turned up in female form. This puzzled Gabriel: Satan might have been evil incarnate, but he'd never been sexist.

In time, the gates of Hell were rebuilt at the edge of the lake, in a fetching pink that Satan said was all the rage. He had statues built of all those who'd been in the minibus, alongside that of Bernie, to remind everyone of how nearly Hell had fallen. Or so he claimed. Woking would see him looking at the statue of Bernie sometimes, with a strange sense of loss in his eye. Most thought he was just thanking the human who'd saved him, but Woking knew otherwise. For one thing, Satan had suddenly learned French.

One day, more than a decade after Hell had been saved, Woking asked him if he still had the consciousness transfer device, and Satan had said yes. "Planning to use it again?" Woking asked.

They'd looked at each other then, and formed an unspoken understanding.

"Maybe," said Satan. "If you keep that fine body of yours in good condition. When I get bored. But I haven't yet."

"We all keep in good condition. Since you insisted we all build up our muscles, and initiated those combat trials and gladiatorial contests."

"In case we're attacked again," said Satan.

"Of course," agreed Woking. "Though I still don't understand why we have to wear loincloths for them."

"Style, darling."

"Or the point of the annual beauty pageant."

"The 'Miss Judgement Day' contests? Hell is half female now. We need to have something for the old dears to take part in."

"I think they would rather enter the gladiatorial contests."

"Yes, but would we want to watch them?"

"Hmm. By the way, there may be a way to permanently transform a Devil body into human form," said Woking. "It's never been done before, but these seem to be times of change. For example, I've never known a Satan to attend a mortals' reunion party before."

Satan raised an eyebrow. "Is that a criticism?"

226

Woking flinched. "Not from me, my Lord … it just surprised a few of the others, that's all."

"Surprised as in…?"

"They weren't sure it was a good idea."

"Send those critics to me," roared Satan, his body erupting in flame. "I will not brook dissent!"

"Right away, my Lord," said Woking.

"There will be stern words," boomed Satan. "Stern words!"

THE END

Acknowledgements.

Sincere thanks are due to Elena Brebner, my lovely wife Nenya, and a few others for carefully reading this story, picking up errors and suggesting improvements. Thanks are also due to a certain council employee, whose behaviour when he came to my house one day inspired a major plot element in this book.

By the same author …

If you enjoy reading about evil cabals hungry for absolute power, and incompetent devils who make a mess of everything they touch, then you might enjoy **Bojo's Woe Show!** *These books contain a series of full colour cartoons featuring characters who are sadly not fictitious: Boris Johnson and his lackeys.*

Available on Kindle, Print-on-Demand and Kindle Unlimited. Search for "Bojo's Woe Show". Books 1 and 2 are out now; 3 and 4 are coming soon.

Sample pages follow.

From Bojo's Woe Show book 1:

BoJo's Woe Show

Edition 1

Crapping on Britain since August 2019

Catastrophus Copulatus

8th November 2019

Election called for December 12th	**Grenfell victims "lacked common sense" says Jacob Rees Mogg**

Phwoffle. Phwiffle phwaffle >burp<!

Prime Minister …

Are you eating a baby?

Ah. Well. Umm. That is … *eughh!!* should have taken the nappy off first. Phwahhh!!

Blame for this unfortunate incident rests entirely with the baby, I'm afraid.

Infans culpam.

It showed no common sense in approaching the PM when he was hungry.

Scuffle!!

Stick him in the cupboard with Mark Francois, Liz Truss and all the other liabilities. I don't want to see any of them again till Xmas!

Now I need to speak to Mr Neil…

A senior Downing Street source has just told me that it was not Boris Johnson eating that baby; it was in fact Jeremy Corbyn in a cunning disguise. What a monster!!

Good thing we cleared that up. I'd hate to be spreading fake news!

From Bojo's Woe Show book 2:

Printed in Great Britain
by Amazon